SLEEPER AGENT

NOVELS BY IB MELCHIOR

SLEEPER AGENT

ORDER OF BATTLE

To Rosemary —
with best wishes —

[signature]

SLEEPER AGENT

BY

IB MELCHIOR

HARPER & ROW, PUBLISHERS

New York, Evanston,

San Francisco, London

FIRST EDITION

Designed by Janice Stern

Library of Congress Cataloging in Publication Data
Melchior, Ib.
  Sleeper agent.

  Bibliography: p.
  I. Title.
PZ4.M51457Sl3   [PS3563.E435]   813'.5'4   74–15882
ISBN 0–06–012942–5

---

75 76 77 78 79 10 9 8 7 6 5 4 3 2 1

TO CLEO — AGAIN

CONTENTS

PART 1

18 APRIL 1945   1

PART 2

21—29 APRIL 1945   37

PART 3

30 APRIL—5 MAY 1945   151

POSTSCRIPT   294

ESCAPE ROUTES   295

BIBLIOGRAPHY   297

AUTHOR'S NOTE

A "sleeper agent" is a highly trained, totally dedicated secret agent placed in a country by a foreign power well in advance of any contemplated action. His cover will be impenetrable. He will assimilate completely, becoming a citizen of the target country. He will marry, work—and wait for the day his native land may call upon him to carry out at any risk any task demanded, be his wait as a sleeper years or decades.

Although the novel *Sleeper Agent* is fiction, the existence of such agents is fact, and many of the elements and incidents of the story are based on actual events and upon the author's personal experiences.

NAZI WAR CRIMINAL HUNT PRESSED IN U.S.

U.S. officials have begun a new investigation of immigrants and naturalized American citizens suspected of being Nazi war criminals, according to Sol Marks, district director of the U.S. Immigration and Naturalization Service. A list of 38, including 25 naturalized U.S. citizens, was compiled from a larger list submitted by Jewish organizations, Marks told the *New York Times*.

Los Angeles *Times*
December 31, 1973

I swear to you, Adolf Hitler, as Führer and Reichschancellor, loyalty and valor. I vow to you, and to those you have named to command me, obedience unto death, so help me God.

SS LOYALTY OATH

PART 1

18 APRIL 1945

PROLOGUE

SOMEWHERE IN BAVARIA

Twenty-two hours and seventeen minutes ago it had begun.

He knew it exactly. To the minute. The big clock with its lighted face hung on the bare wall before him like a mocking moon. It was the first thing he'd seen when he entered the room twenty-two hours and seventeen minutes ago. They had made certain the ordeal of time oozing on would be inescapable.

He stood at attention. His legs trembled painfully. He had long since given up trying to hide the fact. His mouth was dry, his lips parched. They'd given him nothing to drink, nothing to eat since he took up his position facing the glowing clock. It was perhaps just as well, he thought. His gut ached with the dull, leaden pressure of his swollen bladder. That was another thing the bastards had forced him to endure. Damn them to hell!

His eyes burned with fatigue. He blinked and stared at the two men sitting behind the solid table before him. Their pale faces swam in the murkiness like bloated balloons. One of them was glaring back at him. The man had a look on his naked round face as if he enjoyed himself immensely. He had come to loathe that look with a growing hatred during the last several hours. He was careful not to show it. The other man was poring through a thick file, frowning in displeased concentration.

The room was quite large, the walls bare concrete. *The room.* When he thought of it, it took on a menacing personality, a presence as of a thing alive, holding him inexorably in a massive stone fist. It was dark, except for the pool of glaring white light in which he stood before his interrogators.

There was the sudden noise of a door opening behind him. The two men at the table looked up.

He almost turned. With the chilling surge of adrenalin shock shooting through his aching body, he caught himself in time. He stood stock still. He knew what would happen to him if he moved without permission. But his heart beat faster. Was it over? Had he reached the end? Could he— could he at last—rest?

The two men got up from the table. The one with the file folder closed it with a thud of finality. The other one yawned and stretched. He glanced at his watch, and back at the clock on the wall behind him.

Twenty-two hours and nineteen minutes ago . . .

Without a word the two men walked away from the table. Two others took their places. Like all the rest they wore black SS officers' uniforms. Carefully, as if performing a sacred ceremony, they placed their caps on the table before them. The silver death's-head emblems gleamed malevolently.

With cold curiosity the two officers stared at the young man standing leadenly before them.

He felt despair blanket him. And at the same time rage swelled in him. Another team! Another goddamned tricky-mouthed team. He couldn't take it. No more! His mind shrieked for relief. His body trembled with exhaustion. He couldn't face it all over again. Twenty-two hours and twenty minutes they'd hammered at him, taunted him, tormented him. And now . . .

Two more!

Two more well-rested, fresh Gestapo bastards eager to batter him down. He suddenly felt hot tears sting his burning eyes. No, dammit! They weren't going to get him down. They weren't going to break him. Not yet. Not . . . ever.

He blinked his eyes back into focus. He glared at the two new men settling down behind the table. Had they been there before? He found it hard to think. Hard to remember. He didn't know if they were new tormentors or simply old ones returned to torture him after a good rest.

Suddenly he didn't care.

One of the men portentously opened the big file. That damned all-knowing file.

The other glanced to the side and almost imperceptibly nodded his head. He'd forgotten. The other two men. They were still there. They were sitting in the shadows of the dim room where he stood in the pool of light. They'd been there when he came in. He'd been able to make them out but not to recognize them. He'd been aware of them occasionally, quietly leaving—and returning within a short time. At least he supposed they were the same two men. They had been a felt yet unfelt presence all through his ordeal. And they had said not a word. They were only . . . there.

The man with the open file folder looked up at him. He wore steel-rimmed glasses and his hair was close-cropped, shaved high above the ears. "Name?" he rasped. His voice was unpleasantly high. He spoke in English. The characteristic guttural German accent made him sound at once both harsh and shrill.

The young man before him shuddered. Oh, God, not again! *Not—all —over—again!* With a conscious effort he drew himself erect. "Robert Kane," he said. "First lieutenant, 0324569." He tried defiantly to make his voice firm. But he heard it crack.

"Very good," the Gestapo officer commented. He consulted the file before him. "Date of birth?"

"Seventeen July 1915." He didn't hesitate a moment.

"Place?"

"Muncie, Indiana."

"Mother's name?"

"Emily."

"Father's name?"

"William."

"Brothers? Sisters?"

"None."

"Your parents—they still live?"

"No."

He felt the weariness engulf him like a giant fist squeezing his strength from him. He knew what was coming, but he couldn't get himself to face it. Not again.

The Gestapo man leaned back in his chair. The glare from the pool of light glinted in his steel-rimmed glasses with a gleam of mockery. "Tell us about them, Lieutenant Kane. Tell us about yourself."

He *had* told them. Them. The others. All his tormentors. Over and over again. The same questions. The same answers. How many times? Forever. He began to talk. Once again. He heard his own voice as from a distance. It sounded hollow—dead. He couldn't change it. "My mother . . . she died when I was a child. I was ten. She had . . . tuberculosis."

The pink round faces of the two Gestapo officers seemed to float obscenely—disembodied—before him; indistinct, only their eyes boring into him relentlessly. His vision blurred. He squeezed his eyes tight to clear it. He tensed the aching muscles of his legs to steady them. He would go on. He *would* . . .

"My father was— He . . . he took my mother's death very hard. He was a chemist. Industrial research chemist. He . . . wanted to get away from . . . from our home after she died. He accepted an exchange position in Europe. In Denmark. Copenhagen. I went with him." He swallowed with a dry throat. His many body pains had merged into one dull ache. He was suddenly mortally afraid it would always be with him, would never leave.

"Go on!" The Gestapo officer's shrill voice cut into him.

He started. Had he dozed off? On his feet? He clenched his fists at his sides, driving his nails into the palms of his hands. It was a delicious, sharp little pain. His mind savored it. He felt mentally braced. "We were there for two years," he went on. "I went to a Danish school. I was thirteen when we returned to Muncie."

He ran a cotton tongue over his dry lips. He'd never been a habitual lip licker. Why now? When it did no good whatsoever? He continued. "I graduated from high school, and I went to New York. To college. At Columbia . . ."

He had a sudden strange feeling that everything was receding from him. He stood alone, pain-ridden, immobile in space, numbly mouthing words into a mass of gray cotton. There was only the sound of his own distant voice and a rhythmic surge in his ears.

The pain seemed to leave him. He began to feel drowsily detached—and he kept on talking. "I majored in literature—books. Books. And languages. Communication. That's what we must do. Communicate. And then . . . he died. It wasn't even his fault. But he died anyway. My . . . dad . . . It was the other driver's fault. They . . . said so."

He felt good. He was saying the right things. His whole being felt unburdened, soothed by the stream of his own words. And he was alone.

Alone in the warm gray glow. He stopped talking. He was tired. So very tired. Perhaps the words would keep on anyway. Keep on flowing around him. Caress him.

"Kane!"

The word slammed into him, shattering his cocoon of stuporous well-being. And with it came the pain. The exhaustion. And the defiance.

He—would—not—break!

How long had it been? He tried to look at the face of the big round clock on the wall. His eyes would not focus. "Yes, sir," he said.

"You stayed in the city of New York?"

"Yes, sir." He forced himself to focus his smarting eyes on the interrogator. "I went to work. In a bookstore. In Greenwich Village."

"You worked?"

"Yes."

"Then—in the United States—you would have a Social Security number, yes?"

"Yes."

"What is it?" It was a crisp, direct question. He went blank. He *had* been given a number. What? What was it?

"Well?"

"I . . . I don't remember."

"You don't remember your own Social Security number?" There was ominous incredulity in the SS interrogator's voice.

He cast about in his exhausted brain. No use. "Sir," he said. "Everyone has a Social Security number. Nobody remembers it."

"I see." The officer obviously was dissatisfied with the answer. He bent over the file. "And where did you live?"

"On West Twenty-fourth Street. Number 429½. Between Ninth and Tenth Avenue. I had a room. In a brownstone."

He spoke quickly. Perhaps his interrogator would forget about his lapse of memory. He was suddenly incensed. Who the hell ever remembers his Social Security number?

"Brown stone? What is brown stone?"

"It's a building, sir. A kind of building. An old private home, converted into an apartment house or a rooming house. They were built with a sort of brown stone."

"I see. Then you lived in a brown stone house, yes?"

"Yes."

"And the other houses around you they were also brown stone?"

"Yes. No! No—not all. There was a big new apartment house—a whole block—directly across. The . . . London Terrace. It was . . . red brick."

The other Gestapo officer, who had been silent, suddenly leaned forward. He was a somewhat older man. He spoke in a clipped no-nonsense tone of voice. "I think we ask the lieutenant about his military service," he said. He fixed the young man standing before him with a cold stare. "You are a professional soldier?"

"No, sir." He faced the new antagonist.

"Well?"

"I . . . I volunteered . . . after Pearl Harbor. I . . . went into the Army."

"You were sent to a camp?"

"Yes."

"Its name?"

"Fort Dix. In New Jersey."

"You were commissioned?"

"Yes. After basic training I went to OCS."

"What branch of the Army did you serve in?"

"Infantry."

"Infantry?" The Gestapo interrogator leaned forward intently. "With *your* language knowledge? What *do* you speak, Lieutenant, besides English?"

"Danish, sir. And some German."

"Ah! Some German."

The officer smiled a thin smile. He glanced significantly at his colleague. Then he turned back to Kane. "It is somewhat hard to believe that the American Army would not take advantage of your . . . eh . . . special knowledge, is it not?"

"The Army does things its own way."

"So."

The Gestapo man leaned back in his chair. He studied his fingernails. He spoke almost casually. "Do you know what is the OSS?"

The young man started. This was something new. The others hadn't asked about that before. He was suddenly alert. "Yes."

"It means?"

"Office of Strategic Services."

The Gestapo officer suddenly sat bolt upright. "And they are American spies. Saboteurs. Terrorists. Yes?"

The young man stood silent.

"*You* are an OSS officer, yes?"

"No, sir. Infantry."

"So." The Gestapo man fixed him with his cold eyes. "Then, what is your infantry unit, Lieutenant?"

There was only a slight hesitation.

"Seventy-ninth Infantry Division."

"Good. Very good." The officer did not take his eyes from him.

His shoulders sagged. The fatigue washed through him in numbing waves. Nothing mattered any more.

"You will stand at attention!" The interrogator's voice was sharp.

He straightened up. It didn't matter. Sooner or later he'd keel over.

The officer with the steel-rimmed glasses contemplated him. He motioned toward a straight-backed wooden chair.

"You must be tired, Lieutenant," he said, his voice almost kind. "Why don't you sit down?"

All at once he was aware of how near collapse he was. Every bone in his body whimpered for relief. The hard stiff-backed chair looked like paradise. Now that it was going to be possible for him to sit and rest he suddenly knew he couldn't stand up for another minute. He swayed toward the offered chair.

"*No!*"

The sharp command shocked his stupefied brain.

"You will *stand!*"

He looked with dull incomprehension at the older Gestapo interrogator. Stand?

"Sit down!" the other officer ordered.

"*Stand!*"

"*Sit!* That's an order!"

His mind whirled. Oh, God, what were they trying to do? He *wanted* to do the right thing. But . . . how could he? What *was* it? The conflicting orders beat on his battered mind. "Stand!" . . . "Sit!" He felt reason ripping, tearing from him. "Stand!" . . . "Sit!" . . . "Stand!" . . . And finally the thundering command, *"Obey!"* But . . . what? *What?* WHAT?

His tortured mind seethed, but he was suddenly aware of a tiny part of him standing aside, observing. Calm and calculating.

There was . . . something. Something from his training. Eons ago. Trying to break through to him. A problem. A hypothetical problem he'd been given. A problem with no acceptable solution. But he'd *had* to make a choice. What was it? He suddenly knew.

Problem: You are driving a truck on a narrow road only wide enough to accommodate your vehicle. On your left is a steep embankment rising straight from the road. On your right is a deep ravine dropping off immediately from the road shoulder. In the back of the truck are twelve of your men.

You round a bend in the road. Sitting in the middle of the road is a small child. You cannot drive around it. You cannot stop the truck in time.

Question: Do you swerve, sending the truck into the ravine? Or do you not? Do you save your men? Or the child? Or both? No solution. There was no solution, but there was only one thing to do.

Run over the child.

He focused his watering eyes on the two enraged Gestapo interrogators confronting him. Without a word he pulled himself into an attitude of attention.

And stood.

The officer with the steel-rimmed glasses glared angrily at him. With quiet malevolent menace he said, "I ordered you to sit down, Lieutenant! Are you deliberately disobeying?" His shrill voice rose in anger.

"No, sir. Obeying."

"Explain!"

"I was ordered to stand at attention, sir."

"*I* ordered you to sit down!"

"Sir. I was already under orders to stand at attention when I was given the order to sit down. I am obeying the first order. It cannot be countermanded, except by an officer of superior rank. Sir, from your insignia both you and the other officer appear to be of equal rank. However, sir, the other officer, who gave me my first order, seems older. I assume that he, therefore, has seniority."

Some of his tension left him. That was it. He'd made his choice. He'd run over the child.

Dimly he was aware that this new team of interrogators was different from the others. They were pulling something new on him in their efforts to break him down. Confusing him with utterly unreasonable, impossible demands. Humiliating him, bringing him to a point where he could no longer think.

And then?

The older interrogator spoke again. "You said you lived in a brownstone house in Greenwich Village."

Wearily he was about to agree. A tiny synapse in his tired brain snapped shut. A warning alarm flashed. Wait!

"No, sir," he said. "I *worked* in Greenwich Village."

The officer looked up quickly. "What? You are changing your story?"

"No, sir. That's what I said before."

"Impossible! Have you been lying to us?"

"No, sir. No."

"Then what *is* the truth? Did you *work* there, or *live* there?

"I worked there, sir."

"Don't lie to us again."

"I didn't lie, sir."

The officer gripped the table with his two hands. He leaned forward, suddenly dangerous. "You are calling *me* a liar?"

"No. No, sir!"

"Then *who* lies? Answer me! *Who?*"

Rage built up in him. God damn it, it's unfair! What the hell *do* they want from me? I've told them the right things. Don't they *know* by now?

At the same time he wanted to scream his frustration at them . . . and to plead for reason. For compassion. But he knew he had to cope in other ways.

"I must have been . . . unclear, sir. I *worked* in the village. I *lived* on Twenty-fourth Street."

"You are quite certain now?"

"Yes, sir."

"Perhaps you should be a little more careful with your answers in the future." It was the interrogator with the steel-rimmed glasses. The man's whole mien was provocatively overbearing.

The young lieutenant felt the fury rise in him, threatening to explode.

It took all his willpower to control himself. He trembled. Not from fatigue alone.

The older Gestapo officer gave a dry cough. "Tell me, Lieutenant Crane, what—"

"*Kane*, sir. Robert Kane. First lieutenant, 032—"

"Yes, yes." The Gestapo man interrupted him curtly. "Tell me, Lieutenant Kane, what is your favorite meal?"

His stomach suddenly contracted painfully. "Meal, sir?"

"Yes. Food. Food, Lieutenant. What is your favorite?"

His mind was all at once filled with a phantasma of foods. He felt ravenous. "Steak, I guess."

"With potatoes?"

"Yes, sir. With potatoes."

"How do you prefer it? Rare?"

Startled, he realized incredibly that his mouth was watering. He swallowed. "Medium rare, sir."

"And what do you like to drink with it? Wine? Beer?" The question came from the younger of the two interrogators.

The lieutenant turned toward him. "I . . . I like beer, sir."

"Ah, yes. There is nothing like a glass of nice cool beer, is that not so?" The Gestapo man reached over and poured himself a glass of water from a carafe on the table. He drank deeply with evident pleasure.

The young man watched, unable to tear his eyes from him. He tried to swallow. His dry tongue stuck painfully to the roof of his mouth.

The Gestapo officer looked at him speculatively. "Perhaps you would like a glass of water, too?"

He poured another glass and set it at the edge of the table. "Here. Take it."

He hesitated. He stared at the glass. It filled the room. It was another trick. Dammit, he knew it was another trick. But he'd never before in his life craved anything as avidly as he did that glass of water. The inside of his mouth crawled in anticipation. Yet . . . he hesitated. He could not face another disappointment, another rebuff.

"Go on, take it," the Gestapo interrogator urged him. He was smiling, watching the young man before him. His steel-rimmed glasses shone with reflected light. The lenses seemed impossibly large.

"Take it! . . . Take it!" His soft voice was persuasive. His spectacles hypnotic. "Take it!"

The young man reached hesitantly toward the tantalizing glass. His hand trembled. Water. He'd never seen anything as clear, as fresh, as desirable. Almost . . . almost, and his hand would touch it.

And he would drink.

"Lieutenant Kane!" The older Gestapo man spoke quietly. "There is no reason you should be permitted to drink, is there? No. Not now." His voice grew cold and harsh. "I shall give you a direct order *not* to drink. Lieutenant! *You will not drink!*" He leaned back in his chair comfortably.

The young man stiffened. Slowly he withdrew his hand. He stared mesmerized at the glass of water. His face was a waxen mask.

"My colleague has given you an order, Kane," the older Gestapo interrogator continued. "*I* have given you an order. Now, obey!"

He wanted to scream. He knew if he did he'd never stop. Why didn't they shout at him? Yell, bellow, red-necked with rage, as they did before? It would be easier. This disquieting calmness confused him. It forced him to think. And he did not want to think. He hated their calm, their restraint, their composure. It was so different from the destructive turmoil raging in *him.*

Do nothing. Just do . . . nothing.

No. If he did, they *had* beaten him. And he would *not* be beaten. He knew that it took just one tiny crack in the defensive armor he'd built around his mind. One small defeat, and the collapse would soon be complete. He hated them. He'd never known hate could be so all-consuming, so . . . stimulating. He *had* to best them.

Imperceptibly his hand moved toward the glass. He felt it quaver. He clenched it as hard as he could—and once more reached toward the glass.

"Of course, this time it is not a question of . . . eh . . . seniority, is it, Lieutenant?" The older Gestapo man smiled pleasantly at him.

His hand hesitated only a fraction of a second. Then he closed his fingers around the glass. He was startled at the cool, smooth feel of it. Carefully he lifted it off the table. With rapt fascination he watched the tiny waves ripple on the water's surface as he held the glass in his unsteady hand. He stared at it. It was no longer a glass of water. It was the deadly weapon in a grueling duel of wits. He meant to use it. He had to. He meant to win.

With a quick, determined motion, as if he were afraid his own hand would not obey him, he poured the water back into the carafe. For a brief moment he stared at the empty glass. His sense of loss was overpowering. Then he placed the glass on the table.

The older man sighed, much like an exasperated parent over a recalcitrant child. "Now, Lieutenant. Who ordered you to do that?" His voice was mildly reproving.

He stood silent. He knew he'd need time before he could trust his voice. Then he said, "Sir . . . sir, I was ordered to take the glass. I did. I was ordered not to drink. I did not."

He was certain that at that moment he'd never felt more physically exhausted, more mentally spent—or more triumphant. He had not given up. He had acted.

The younger Gestapo officer rose from the table. He walked around it to stand in front of the young man. He was smiling. "You think you are very clever, do you not?" He nodded amiably. "Well, Lieutenant, we think so, too. I think we shall reward you."

He turned to the table. Once again he poured a full glass of water. He held it out to the young man. "Here. Take it. Drink it!"

For a moment their eyes met. Then with a sudden fierce move the young man grabbed the glass. He'd give them no time for counterorders. In the same jerky motion he brought the glass to his mouth. Water spilled over the rim and ran down his fingers. Down his chin.

But he drank.

He imagined the effect to be immediate. Perhaps it was.

The Gestapo man took the empty glass from him. He looked closely at the young man. Their eyes locked briefly. "Fine," the interrogator said with a smile. "Very fine!" He turned back to the table and refilled the glass from the carafe. Again he held it out to the young man. "Here. Have another glass."

He took it. This time he drank slower, enjoying every drop of the cool liquid as it soothed his parched lips, his mouth, his throat. And again he emptied the glass.

The other interrogator joined them. He smiled agreeably at the young man. "My colleague is most generous, is he not?" he asked. He took the empty glass. "Perhaps I, too, should . . . eh . . . reward you, no?" He turned to the table, filled the glass once more and held it out to the young lieutenant. "Here," he said. "To your health!" He smiled.

The young man shook his head. "Thank you," he said. "I've had enough."

The smile suddenly vanished from the interrogator's face. "Drink it!" he snapped, the friendliness gone from his voice. *"Drink!"*

An icy shock of realization surged through the young man. With grim certainty he knew the intentions of his tormentors. Oh, God, no! Please, no!

"Drink it!"

With shaking hands he took the glass of water. He drained it. He felt nauseated. His empty stomach rebelled against the sudden flooding. He fought down the rising bile.

With deliberately elaborate gestures the Gestapo man refilled the glass, dwelling on every move. "I do not wish to be thought less generous than my colleague," he said. "Here. I, too, must insist you have a second glass." There was unmistakable menace in his mockery.

The young man took the glass. His hands trembled, and water slopped over the edge.

"Careful, Lieutenant. We do not want to waste a drop of it, do we?"

He drank. He forced the liquid down. He was bleak with despair. All of a sudden he was desperately conscious of the pain caused by his swollen bladder. So fast? Perhaps he only imagined it. But he knew with absolute certainty that he could not continue to control himself. That's what they wanted. The ultimate humiliation. The degrading moment when he was forced to relax and let his bladder empty itself. Where he stood. At attention. Faced by his disdainful tormentors.

The glass was empty.

He was hardly aware that it was again refilled—"One more for good measure!"—and once again he managed to drain it.

He was waiting. Waiting for the moment when he was finally beaten. As he must be. He knew that his defeat would be not merely the inevitable debasement, the total humiliation. That was only window dressing. No. His defeat would be absolute.

The two Gestapo men returned to their seats. For a while neither said anything. They merely watched the young man standing before them.

Their faces were intent as they observed their specimen.

Finally the older interrogator spoke. "Have you had enough? I think you have. Tell us your true identity."

"Robert . . . Kane. First lieutenant. United States Army."

Was that *his* voice? He did not recognize it.

The two Gestapo officers looked at each other. They glanced toward the two unseen men in the shadows, but nothing was said. Finally the older interrogator broke the silence. "Lieutenant, the charade is over. You have done well."

He stood mute.

"Do I understand you correctly, Lieutenant?" The Gestapo officer's voice was ominously low. "You are challenging us to . . . to proceed?"

He made no reply.

For a moment the interrogator stared at him. His expression was enigmatic. Then he shrugged. "Very well. The choice is yours." He picked up the receiver from a black phone on the table. "*Wache antreten!*" he ordered curtly.

He replaced the receiver. He looked somberly at the exhausted young man before him. He sighed. "You know what to expect." His voice was flat.

Yes. He knew. They'd told him they had one final way to break his spirit. They had advised him to avoid being forced to endure it. For his own sake.

Behind him the door opened. He heard the clicks of two pairs of heels snapping to attention.

"Take him," the Gestapo interrogator said. His voice was totally dispassionate.

He felt his arms being seized in firm grips. Dimly, through a mist of fatigue, he was conscious of two SS men, one on each side of him. His burning eyes rested for a brief moment on the two black-uniformed interrogators at the table. They sat erect, motionless, like two figures in a wax museum chamber of horrors.

Before the two SS guards turned him away, he glanced at the big round lighted clock on the wall. But he couldn't make it out. The numerals, the clock hands, the second sweep swam together in a jumble of imagery. All he knew was, it showed eternity.

And they marched him away.

They had shoved him roughly through the door. He'd heard it slam shut behind him, and a heavy bolt being rammed home.

For a moment he stood, swaying slightly, waiting. There was not a sound to be heard. He took stock. He was alone.

The room was not large, more like a big cell. There were no windows, but two doors. The one he had just come through and another in the opposite wall. The room was so dimly lit from a single light source in the unusually high ceiling that he could barely make it out. In the middle of the place stood a wooden table.

He turned back to the door that had been bolted behind him. No use even trying it. On the wall next to it was a sign. He walked to it. In German it proclaimed, IT IS STRICTLY FORBIDDEN TO URINATE ON THE FLOOR!

The swollen pain in his gut suddenly stabbed through him. Urgently he fumbled his pants open. For a brief moment he was unable to do anything. He had a flash of panic. *He'd gone too long!* Somehow he couldn't— And then he let go.

He relieved himself against the wall under the sign, totally emptying his distended bladder. It was one of the greatest satisfactions he'd ever had— almost a sexual experience. He felt enormously disburdened.

Again he looked around. His eyes were gradually getting used to the gloom. He walked to the table—and froze. On it lay a gun. A Walther 7.65. And six rounds.

He picked up the gun. He examined it carefully. It was in perfect working order. At once he loaded it.

Why? Were they "testing" him? Again? What did they expect him to do? Kill his guards when they came for him? *If* they came for him. They might not come at all. Kill himself? Hardly. Not with six rounds—unless they expected him to miss the first five times.

He grinned mirthlessly. He was still exhausted beyond comprehension, but this new challenge had rekindled some of his stamina. And he could at least move again. He walked toward the door on the opposite side. He studied it. If there was a way out of the cell, this had to be it.

He looked closer at it. It seemed like an ordinary door. There was no keyhole. A bolt on the other side? The door hinges didn't show. Good. The door would open outward.

Once again he let his eyes search the room. The door in front of him was the only possible way out. He knew it. So did they.

What was on the other side?

He cocked the Walther. Suddenly he gave the door a violent kick. It crashed open. Immediately he flung himself through, hitting the floor on his gut, the gun held in both hands stretched out before him. In the same instant there was a volley of shots from the Stygian darkness in front of him. He thought he could "feel" the bullets whiz over him. He heard them slam into the imperious sign on the wall behind him.

He did not fire. He had no target. Only blackness.

He was shocked. He had not really expected to be shot at. It *was* only a test, wasn't it? He felt suddenly drained. They *were* shots? His mind began to lose itself in confusion, doubts, uncertainties.

He lay still, gathering his thoughts, his strength. The blackness before him was not absolute after all. A long narrow corridor stretched ahead of him. Weak dim lights studded the high, inaccessible ceiling.

He listened. He watched. There was no sound. No movement. He waited. He was in no hurry. This time, whatever "games" they wanted him to play would be played at *his* discretion. He needed all the trump cards he could get.

It *was* a test. Had to be. A test subjecting him to the greatest enemy of all. The unknown. He had to keep his mind as alert, as rational as possible, even though he was exhausted to the point of impotence. That, of course, was part of their game—a game designed to weaken him, to torment him, to break him, but not to destroy him. It would not make sense to kill him. Not this way.

He stood up. He locked the gun firmly against his abdomen. All right. He'd play their damned game. He wished he could obliterate the last vestige of doubt gnawing at the edge of his mind.

Slowly he started down the corridor. He moved with incredible stealth and silence, his every sense stretched to its ultimate alertness. The last superbright blaze of a light bulb—before it burns out.

The corridor made a turn, widening into a more spacious area. Cautiously he entered. The gloom seemed to deepen.

Suddenly there was a small noise. He whirled toward it. In the same instant he saw a dim figure leap at him. Instinctively—without the time loss of thought—he sprang aside, and still clutching his gun locked in firing position, he faced the lurching figure and fired two rounds.

He heard the dull thuds as they hit. The figure swept by him. It turned and came for him again.

His mind whirled. He nearly pumped two more of his precious rounds into the attacker. He stopped himself in the last split second. No. It was not possible. He *knew* he'd hit the man. Two rounds. As he'd been trained to do. Always two rounds. For stopping power. He held his fire as the figure came at him and once again brushed past. It stopped and swung back toward him. He grabbed it.

A dummy. With two bullet holes squarely in its chest, hanging from a wire in the ceiling.

He let it go. It hung there, slowly spinning in the gloom.

A game. He had been right. He felt enormously gratified. His analysis had been correct.

He gave the mutilated dummy a contemptuous push. It dangled lifelessly from its noose.

He felt confident. He had it made. Slowly he crossed the open area. On the other side the narrow corridor continued. He peered into it. It was without any light at all. He entered. He made his way slowly, walking close to the wall. At any moment he expected something to happen.

Nothing did.

He kept himself at maximum alertness. Something *had* to happen. He was so tense the muscles in his shoulders started to cramp. With an extortionate effort he forced himself to relax. It lasted only a few seconds. He was too keyed up; his suspense had mounted to unbearable proportions.

And—nothing—happened.

Every fiber in his aching body screamed for action. Any action. He was fully aware that he was spending himself at a breakdown rate. He knew he could not sustain it for long. But he could not help it.

The pitch-black corridor seemed to go on forever. Was there no end to it?

Suddenly his foot slipped on the floor. He caught himself against the wall —and froze. Cautiously he bent down. On the floor was a small pool of a slippery, viscous ooze. He tested it with his fingers. It felt familiar.

An icy chill knifed through him. He knew what it was. Overcoming his revulsion, he brought his slimy-moist fingers up to his nose. He gagged. It was blood.

A . . . game?

He was aware of his heart beating wildly. His imagination shrieked and howled with myriad nightmare thoughts. *A game?*

He stood up. Edging along the wall, he stepped over the fetid puddle and sidled away as quickly as he dared. Too quickly. Suddenly his foot hit an obstacle on the floor. A soft, unyielding obstacle. He knew at once what it was. He saw it more clearly in his mind than if the corridor had been flooded in a blaze of light. He did not have to stoop down, stretch out his hand . . . and touch. But he did.

It was a man. He seemed to be clad in the same prisoner clothing as he himself was. He was cold. He was dead.

The lieutenant straightened up. He flattened himself against the wall, instinctively seeking its solid protection. His heart beat wildly. He had a twinge of annoyance that he couldn't control it. He felt profoundly threatened. It wasn't the shock of finding the dead body. He could cope with that. It was the disturbing frustration of not knowing what it meant. Why?

What were they doing to him? Who was this . . . man?

Things were happening that he no longer could explain rationally. Totally unexpected things. He'd thought he knew exactly what would happen to him, step by step. But he'd been wrong. He hadn't anticipated . . . this.

Was he wrong in everything else? He'd been so sure. He no longer was. He felt a desperate urge to get away from the corpse on the floor. Go back?

For a split second he had an overwhelming impulse to run back the way he came. The way he knew. Back to the cell. Back to the bolted door, to hammer on it, call out to his guards, plead for an end to his ordeal. Rather than go on into the unknown darkness. Not knowing. . . . He hated himself for it.

He went on. In the distance the corridor seemed to get lighter; he could make out a faint glow coming from the side, as if the passage made a bend. He deliberately stepped out into the middle of the corridor away from the deceptively protecting walls. Slowly he walked toward the dim light.

Suddenly there was a quick rustling sound directly behind him. Keeping his gun locked against his abdomen, he at once fell to one knee, twisting around to face back. In the same instant that he heard the dull thud as something—or someone—hit the floor from above, he fired. Two rounds. He heard them slam into their target. He didn't move. There was dead silence all around him.

Without rising from his crouch, he slowly inched himself toward the huddled form he could glimpse lying in a crumbled heap on the floor. Had he killed someone? He *had* to know. He reached out. The skin crawled on his hand. He touched.

He fought down a scream erupting in his throat—and suddenly realized that the form on which his hand was resting was not human. It was a large sandbag.

Absent-mindedly he fingered the two holes in it from which the sand trickled in steady silence. He shivered. He knew he had reached his breaking point. The seesaw turmoil created in his mind would snap whatever control his exhaustion had left him.

He had lost.

From the depths of his mind a cold, savage fury began to build, sweeping away his dark fears, his fatigue, his doubts. Only one driving thought remained: *Win!* However brutal, however maddening or merciless the game, WIN!

He stood up. He still had two rounds left in his gun. He turned back toward the faint light in front of him. Resolutely he began to walk toward it.

The corridor made a sharp turn. Once again a single weak light source from above cast a dim light. Coming from the deeper darkness, it was enough for him. He could see. In the distance, ahead of him, the passage came to an end at a door. It was closed.

He began to walk toward it. His mind seemed incredibly clear. With lightning speed it retraced every move that had brought him here, it ticked off distances, directions, calculations like a built-in compass—as it had been trained to do.

He *knew* where that door in front of him led!

With grim anticipation he moved toward it, gun ready. He was vaguely aware of another closed door to his right. As he came abreast of it, it suddenly flew open. Instantly he whirled toward it. In the shadows in the room beyond he saw the figure of a man, crouched menacingly, a gun locked before him—aimed directly at his guts!

His finger instinctively tightened on the trigger, but in the same split second his mind countermanded his instinctive action. He froze. For a full moment he crouched immobile before the open door, his eyes never wavering from the figure facing him. Then he slowly sank to one knee.

His opponent made exactly the same move.

He was looking at his own reflection in a giant mirror!

He stood up. His mind was coldly, dangerously clear. Quickly he glanced toward the door at the end of the corridor. He knew what he had to do.

There were still two rounds left in his gun. He had not wasted them shooting at his own harmless mirror image. Quickly he removed them. Then carefully he reloaded the gun, keeping one round in his clenched fist.

Then, abruptly, he fired, shooting the bullet into the floor; and immediately after the shot rang out, he hurled the gun itself at the huge mirror. With a sharp report it cracked, shattered and crashed to the floor in myriad pieces.

At once he strode to the heap of glass shards. Impatiently he kicked them aside and picked up the gun. With his one remaining round he loaded it.

He was ready. He walked to the door at the end of the corridor. He looked down at the gun in his hand. It trembled. With an angry force of will he made it stop.

One bullet. He'd make it count.

Exploding into action, he aimed a savage kick at the door. With an ear-splitting crash it flew open. He was through, into the room beyond, even as the door slammed into the wall.

Instantaneously the scene before him etched itself on his burning mind. The big round clock with its lighted face on the wall. Four men standing like grotesque statues around the table: the two Gestapo interrogators, one with steel-rimmed glasses, one older, and the two men from the shadows, one in the uniform of an SS colonel, the other a civilian. All four staring at him in frozen shock.

He lifted his gun from its locked position in front of him and aimed it with slow deliberation directly at the SS colonel.

The officer's face grew ashen. The tension in the room was a tangible thing. Not a word was spoken.

The older Gestapo officer was the first to regain his composure. He straightened up. "I congratulate you," he said. "You are very clever. You determined exactly where you were. Admirable." He smiled thinly. "But . . . now you are bluffing."

The gun pointed at the SS colonel never faltered.

"Come now. We know you are bluffing." The officer was obviously becoming impatient. "We have been listening. Six rounds. Two in the swinging dummy, both hits. Two in the deadfall. Hits. Two at the mirror" —he smiled his thin, unpleasant smile once again—"one hit, one miss! Six rounds." He stepped from behind the table and held out his hand. "Give me the gun!" His voice was sharp with absolute authority.

The young man didn't even glance at the officer. His gun was still aimed straight at the SS colonel. He extended it slightly before him. It did not waver.

"For God's sake, man!" It was the interrogator with the steel-rimmed glasses. His voice was a hoarse whisper.

The young man did not seem to hear him. His eyes bored into those of the SS colonel.

Then suddenly he whipped his gun aside—and fired his last remaining bullet into the big round face of the lighted clock on the wall! The explosion was thunderous in the confinement of the room. The clock shattered and went dark.

The four men stood in stunned shock.

The young man walked briskly to the Gestapo officer. Crisply he clicked his heels and handed him the gun. *"Zu befehl,* Herr Sturmbannführer!" he said. He stood at attention. Every fiber in his body ached. Every cell in his brain seethed with strain. But he was elated.

He had won.

The SS colonel turned to the Gestapo officer. *"Der Personalbogen,"* he ordered.

The Gestapo man handed him the file folder from the table. *"Jawohl,* Herr Kommandant!"

The SS colonel took the file. He opened it. He addressed himself to the civilian. There was obvious respect in his voice. "His name is Rudolf Kessler. Obersturmführer. Waffen SS."

He looked at the young man standing stiffly at attention before him. His eyes held undisguised approval. He turned back to the civilian. "As you have seen, Herr Gruppenführer, he has mastered his cover identity to perfection. His stamina—both mental and physical—is extraordinary"—he glanced toward the dead clock on the wall—"and his ability to function under stress obviously phenomenal!" He looked at the young Waffen SS lieutenant. "Obersturmführer Kessler, you may sit down," he said.

The young officer kept looking straight ahead. *"Danke,* Herr Kommandant," he said. "I shall prefer to stand." He'd be damned if he'd give his interrogators the satisfaction of knowing how close to collapse they'd brought him. He'd *stand,* dammit!

The civilian turned his full attention to the young man before them. He began to walk around him slowly, studying him. The commandant read from the dossier: "Rudolf Kessler. Born July seventeen, 1915, in Linz, Austria."

The young Waffen SS lieutenant listened to the clipped, direct voice of his superior officer. It seemed to come from far away, but the officer himself was right there in front of him. He was mildly amused. He couldn't understand how it could be. . . . Linz, Austria. Yes. He'd always been proud of being Austrian. Like Adolf Hitler. Like the Führer himself. Austrian.

The commandant went on reading from the dossier: "Father, Wilhelm, served as Feldwebel in the Imperial Austro-Hungarian Army during World War One. Wounded and taken prisoner of war by the Italians at Battle of Piave River, June, 1918. . . ."

. . . He remembered the scars. His father had shown them to him. The only war decorations I'm really proud of, he'd said. The bullet had gone right through the lung. The scar in the chest was small and round. The one on the back much larger and ragged. He remembered putting his finger on it in awe. It felt smooth and glossy—like the wax paper in which his favorite candy came wrapped. His father had told him about the battle. About crossing the river with General von Bojna's army and beating the Italians back; about the downpour of rain that bogged down the advance and forced the Austrians to retreat, only to find that the flooded river had washed away the bridges they'd thrown across, trapping them; about the Italian counterattack, and the bullet that smashed through him. He'd fallen at the river's edge. The rushing water kept washing over him, keeping him conscious. The . . . water. His eyes were drawn to the carafe of water on the table. It was still half full. The memory of his swollen bladder suddenly flooded his mind. He had a sharp urge to urinate and a flash of alarm before it left him as abruptly as it had come upon him.

The commandant's voice was a distant drone to him: ". . . Mother, Erna, died August, 1920. . . ."

. . . Mutti. He hardly remembered her. He'd been not quite five years old when she died. He thought of her as a large round-faced woman, always warm, who would envelop him in soft arms and a moist, pungent odor, which came to mean protection and comfort to him. Comfort. Rest. The pains in his tired legs shot up across the small of his back. If only they wouldn't cramp. Not now. He had to stick it out. He *had* to.

The commandant's voice again broke in on his rambling thoughts: ". . . Rudolf accepted for foster home placement by the Danish organization to aid needy Austrian children after the war, called Wienerbörn— Vienna Children. Arrived in Denmark September, 1920. Placed as foster child in home of Helga and Jens Peter Rasmussen, a childless couple, in Copenhagen. . . ."

. . . He had not understood. He had been frightened. First his father went away, and he remembered his mother crying all the time; and then she was gone, too. He felt abandoned. A lot of strangers had shunted him from place to place and finally put him on a big train that traveled away forever. He had not been able to understand the speech of the people in whose home he found himself, and he thought he would have to be different from everyone else for the rest of his life. But Helga and Jens Peter were warm and understanding people, and he soon looked upon them as family. He had a natural gift for languages, and he was young enough to talk on and on in this new tongue without being embarrassed about any mistakes he made. Soon he was playing with the Danish children as if he'd always been one of them . . .

". . . Enrolled in Danish School Vestre Borgerdyd, Copenhagen, 1921. Allowed to remain with Rasmussen family beyond normal time limit, for four years, due to the fact that there was no family in Austria to accept responsibility for him. . . ."

. . . The Rasmussens lived in an apartment house on St. Knudsvej Street on the third floor. There was a little garden in back, and here the boys had built a shack out of old crates. It was their fort. Here they became cowboys and Indians, acting out the stories they were all reading. His biggest hero had been "Leatherstocking." They even had a totem pole painted in many colors.

He got on well with the other boys; he liked them, except one. His name was Holger, and he kept teasing him and calling him a no-good refugee from a coward country that had been beaten in the war. He called him a stupid foreigner who couldn't even speak right. But he got his revenge. It still made him feel good when he thought about it. Like now. It had been just after his ninth birthday. His foster parents had given him three kroner to buy anything he liked. He bought two dog pistols. They looked just like real ones, but they could only shoot harmless blanks that made a deafening noise. People used them to scare off dogs that would chase them when they were riding their bicycles. He and his friends had played Mohicans, and they had captured Holger. They tied him to their totem pole and told him they would torture him like real Indians did. They told him they would make him blind and deaf and push him out into the middle of the street to be run over. They blindfolded their enemy and tied his hands. It had made him feel good to see how scared Holger was. He'd fixed his two new dog pistols to the totem pole, one on each side, right next to Holger's ears, and shot them off. Holger had screamed. They had marched him around the yard and then turned him loose, still blindfolded and still with his hands tied. He thought he was in the middle of the street and about to be run over. He stumbled about sobbing and pleading with them, and it was the funniest thing he'd ever seen. He laughed and laughed and laughed. And Holger couldn't see anything and he couldn't hear anything—even when they shouted at him. He only cried. It had been great. They finally let him go, and he ran home. He never saw him again.

The guns had done a *prima* job. The guns . . . The *guns!* He had a flash of panic. Where was the gun? He'd had a gun. What had he done with it? Where was it?

Then he remembered.

He was aware of the civilian behind him. He had a strong urge to turn around, but he kept his position at attention.

The commandant turned a page in his dossier. "Father released from Italian prisoner of war camp, recuperated from his wound, October, 1924. Returned to Linz, where employed as state forester. Rudolf, aged nine, joined his father two months later. . . ."

. . . He suddenly felt a shiver of cold. . . . He had been ten years old. His father was taking care of a *Staatsjagdrevier* near Linz, and the two of them lived in the little *Forsthaus* provided. He knew his father was eager to make a good hunter out of him. He had promised to take him rabbit hunting as soon as he could handle a shotgun, and he had promised him his first buck when he turned twelve.

But he could not wait. He wanted to please his father. He wanted to show him he was big enough. Early one morning he had taken his father's shotgun, the one with the fancy carvings on the barrel. He had gone out into the early morning fields. He was going to show his father. He was going to shoot a rabbit. All by himself. The grass was tall and wet with dew, and his shoes and socks got soaked. And then he saw it. A faintly seen gray figure sneaking through the tall grass. His heart beat wildly. He brought up the shotgun, fighting the weight of it. And he fired. The creature screamed a hideous shriek, which knifed through him with terror. And it did not stop. It kept on screaming and thrashing about. He was petrified. He threw the gun away and ran to the screaming rabbit.

Only it was not a rabbit. It was Mausi. It was his cat—his Mausi! And he loved her. And now she was screaming and writhing in agony. Agony he had inflicted upon her. When she saw him coming toward her, she tried to run away, but her entrails were spilling out, and she got her hind legs caught in them. And she kept screaming. He tried to pick her up and she bit him and scratched him. He did not notice. Only her screaming. He thought he would lose his mind. He realized that only one thing could help her. Death. And it was up to him to give it to her. It was his doing.

He put her on the wet ground. He took a large stone. And he smashed her head—smashed it until the screaming stopped. . . . When his father found him, he was sitting in the grass, bloody with his own and Mausi's blood, hugging the mutilated cat carcass to him. But he was dry-eyed.

His father had insisted that he go hunting rabbits with him the very next day. He could not be permitted to nurture a fear of guns, a fear of hunting, of killing. Like a rider thrown from his horse, he had to mount again at once. He had not the strength to protest. He had been certain he would never kill anything again. But he got over that. There had been more hunting, more killing, and soon it meant nothing to him at all. He was not afraid of death, of killing. He could cope with that. . . .

The civilian came around in front of him. He went to the table and sat on the edge of it. He did not take his eyes from the young SS officer but watched him intently as the commandant continued reading.

". . . Subject's education continued at Linz Gymnasium. At age fourteen he joined the Austrian Hitler Youth. Attended the Reichsparteitag in Nuremberg, 1929, and the Reichsjugendtag of the NSDAP at Potsdam, 1932. . . ."

. . . He would never forget it. It had been a stirring adventure he felt certain would always be a high point in his life. He'd written about it in his diary: "Potsdam, 2 October 1932—the Greatest Experience of My Life!"

In his mind's eye he could see the Gothic script marching along each pale blue line on the pages of the composition book he had used. He would always remember those words, words of pride and of glory, as he confided his feelings to his diary:

For many days thousands upon thousands of German boys and German girls from all the provinces of Greater Germany have streamed into town, this town of the heroic Prussian Warrior King, Frederick the Great. It is awe inspiring.

At dusk every road and every path leading to the giant stadium seems alive with youth. The swastika banners fly high in the wind over the gigantic arena which we cover with our multitude. Torch bearers arrive, their firebrands blazing, and brilliant searchlights illuminate the mighty dome of heaven. We are thrilled at the splendid grandeur, almost reverent. . . .

The Führer is to speak to us!

We wait with an impatience that will hardly be denied.

At last He is at the podium.

Our exultation knows no bounds! The roar of our homage fills our world. We are in His presence. *Our Führer.* The one whose name we bear in pride—*Hitler Youth!* The one for whom no sacrifice is too great.

And He speaks. To *us.* The Youth of Greater Germany.

We listen. Impassioned. He speaks as a leader to his faithful followers, as a father to his children. His words shall forever remain emblazoned upon our hearts.

Others may mock and laugh, he says. But *you* are Holy Germany's future; *you* are her coming people, and upon *you* shall rest the fulfillment of what we so solemnly struggle for today. Already as boys and girls you have dedicated yourselves to our New Germany. You remain true. Rewards which no one can give you today shall be yours tomorrow. Germany awaken!

The tumultuous ovation we give our Führer must be heard

throughout Germany. Throughout the world! Our spirits soar with the rocketing fireworks and explode with them in a burst of radiance. And it is over. . . .

. . . For a brief moment his attention returned to the close, windowless interrogation room and the droning voice of the commandant reading his dossier. But he knew his thoughts would go back to that day long ago. . . .

. . . Slowly they had started back to their tent city from the stadium. It was then he had met Elsa.

She was sixteen. A BDM—Bund Deutscher Mädel. Her thick honey-yellow braids were wound around her head, and her bright blue eyes sparkled with the excitement of the moment. He loved her at once.

They walked with their arms around each other in eager closeness and unity. Soon it was not enough. They found a little barn, half filled with new-mown grass. The scent was an intoxicating opiate.

He felt near bursting with excitement, with ardor and desire. He was seventeen years old and he felt he was at last *a man*. He desperately wanted to *act* the man. Elsa was as ready as he, and the grass was soft and yielding. He held her tight.

Elsa. . . . She would be his first woman. His very first. He caressed and kissed her small thrusting girl-woman breasts, and she was eager for him. He was hot with passion. He crushed her young body to him. He strained against her. He was *a man*. . . . But so tense, so pent up was his want that at the very first intimate man-woman contact he lost control. Completely. Even before having entered the aroused girl.

He was humiliated, crushed. He begged her for another chance; a few minutes' rest and everything would be all right. She said nothing, but he could feel her frustration . . . and contempt. They lay side by side in silence in their fragrant crib. And the exhaustion of the eventful day proved too great. He fell asleep. . . .

At precisely five o'clock the next morning he was jolted awake at the sound of a thousand trumpets rousing the great tent city nearby to the new day. He at once looked around.

Elsa was gone.

He hurried back to his section. No one had missed him. With his comrades he marched past the Führer himself in step to stirring martial music with swastika flags flying proudly. He pushed the memory of the night from him. It had been unimportant. The important thing was the fact that he, Rudi, was part of Germany's future!

It was all there in his diary. He still had it among his possessions. In it he had also written about Elsa. But that page was torn out. . . .

He was suddenly aware that the commandant was addressing *him*.

"All right, Lieutenant. You would not wish to sit down?"

. . . He snapped out of his reveries. He had to watch himself. "If it pleases Herr Kommandant," he said crisply. "I am fine."

The commandant gave him a searching look. "As you wish." He resumed reading: "On leaving the Hitler Youth in 1933 upon reaching the age of eighteen, subject had reached the rank of Bannführer. He graduated from Linz Gymnasium and became assistant to his father in the State Forestry Service. In 1934 he left Austria and went to Munich. Here he worked in various capacities. He joined the NSDAP and was loyally active in party affairs. Enlisted in the SS Verfügungstruppe in 1937. Served meritoriously during the period of the Austrian Anschluss, March, 1938. Subsequently won rapid promotion in the Waffen SS, being commissioned first lieutenant in 1939. Distinguished himself in combat during Polish Campaign, September, 1939, while serving in March Combat Group Bock of the Fourteenth Army under Generaloberst List of the Southern Army Group, commanded by Generaloberst von Rundstedt. At the annihilation of the Polish Sixth Division, Cracow Army Group, at Cracow, and the annihilation of the Polish Twenty-second Division, Przemysl Army Group, at Krasnik. Commendations attached. Later, during the defeat of France, he was instrumental in halting a tank counterattack at Dunkirk, for which action he won the Iron Cross First Class, twenty-one May 1940. . . ."

. . . He felt a touch of pride. He always did when he thought of his Iron Cross.

The Engländer had launched an armored attack at Arras in an attempt to break out of the closing Dunkirk trap. No one had expected them to try anything so foolhardy, and the encircling troops were taken by surprise. He, Rudi, had been manning a machine gun position at an auxiliary weapons distribution point, the MG 34 guarding a crossroad, when a column of British infantry tanks came lumbering down the road.

He thought fast. He grabbed a *Granatwerfer* 36, and while his fellow machine gunners in vain tried to halt the enemy tanks, he ran to a small depression in the field flanking the tank column. A direct hit by the lead tank on the MG position obliterated it, leaving the tanks a clear road ahead. But as they started forward, he was ready. Firing the light mortar single-handed, he destroyed two of the tanks and damaged a third while the raking machine gun fire from the tanks probed for him. He delayed the advance of the column long enough for reinforcements to arrive and rout the remaining enemy armor. He was proud of his action, and he could still remember the dull plopping sound of enemy machine gun bullets slamming into the ground inches from his place of concealment. He remembered, too, with pride that he had not been afraid—only elated. He had been certain nothing would happen to him. Not to him. . . .

The civilian walked to the table and began to make notes in a small black notebook as the commandant read on briskly: "Because of subject's high intelligence quotient and aptitude for foreign languages he was transferred to Military Intelligence School in 1941. Studied military intelligence procedures as well as the Danish and English languages, graduating in the top five percent of his class. Because of his special knowledge of Denmark and the Danish language, subject was assigned to the Protectorate High Command in Copenhagen, Denmark, in December, 1941, at the first signs of organized underground resistance. His mission: to perform undercover work under supervision of the Gestapo and Abwehr III—Counter Espionage—which organizations needed reliable agents who could pass for Danes. Letters of the highest commendation for his work during this period from SS Standartenführer Bovensiepen, Chief of Gestapo, and High Administrator SS Obergruppenführer Dr. Werner Best are hereto attached. . . ."

. . . He vividly recalled his first undercover assignment after being attached to the counterespionage organization in Copenhagen. It had been the first time he had returned to Denmark after his childhood stay with the Rasmussen family. It had been strange, but he did not let mawkish feelings of sentimentality interfere with his duty.

It had taken him only a few weeks to become completely acclimatized —a "Dane."

He had infiltrated a group of young saboteurs dramatically calling themselves "Torshammer," after the avenging weapon of the Norse god Thor. One of the members had been suspicious of him. He had talked the others into making certain he was a native born Dane. They had given him a menu to read. It was an old trick. It had been used in the First World War, too. Only someone born and raised in Denmark could pronounce the ridiculous sounding name of the national Danish desert that appeared on every menu, a sort of red fruit pudding served with cream. Only a native Dane. Or a Vienna Child. He had no problems. *Rødgrød med Fløde* had been his favorite when he lived with his foster parents.

The Torshammer group had been assigned the destruction of a small factory producing ball bearings for the German aircraft industry. The operation had been well planned, but he had not been able to warn his superiors in Abwehr III before the action was carried out. He still remembered his surprise at the fantastic sight of the building's entire roof, intact, shooting straight up into the air and crashing down, obliterating the machine shop. It had been a Sunday, and not a soul had been in the factory.

The saboteurs were elated, but the Gestapo had picked up every one of them within the hour. They were secretly executed by a firing squad. The Nazis were not yet ready to admit that there was serious trouble in their "showcase" protectorate.

The Gestapo had asked if he wanted to watch, but he had found some excuse. He always felt a little ashamed of that. It *had* affected him. He had known them all. Well. But he had been able to shake the uneasy feeling quickly. He knew they had thought of themselves as patriots, and he reluctantly admitted to himself that had he been in their shoes he probably would have acted as they did. But he was not. And they were, of course, enemies of the Reich. They deserved their fate.

Still, he liked the Danes. They were Aryan, after all. They were close to being German. He sometimes even had admired their audacity in the face of superior force. Like that little fellow on the street in Copenhagen. A nobody. A bookkeeper or something like that. . . .

A German staff car had caught fire and was burning fiercely. A group of Danes stood around doing nothing but watching and looking rather pleased. He had come upon the scene but could, of course, do nothing lest he give himself away.

Suddenly this little fellow had come running up. He had a pail in one hand and a bicycle pump in the other. He filled the tiny pump from the pail and gave a single squirt at the burning car. After a while he squirted again, and repeated the action every now and again. The car kept blazing merrily.

He had no longer been able to contain himself. The little man's effort was so pitifully ridiculous. He walked over to him and asked, "Do you really think that is doing any good?"

"Of course," the little fellow had answered, squirting the flaming car once more. "It's kerosene!"

He chuckled to himself. He had to admire that kind of spirit. . . .

. . . "Yes, Lieutenant?" It was the commandant.

Yes? Had he chuckled out loud? He must have. He had to be careful. He could not afford to lose himself in daydreams. His mind was too tired.

"Nothing, Herr Kommandant. Sorry, Herr Kommandant."

He forced himself to listen attentively to the droning voice of his superior officer as he continued reading: "In 1943 subject, Rudolf Kessler, was recruited for the Sleeper Agent program following reactivation of that undertaking earlier that year."

The colonel looked up from the dossier. "It should be noted, sir," he said, "that the withdrawal of Kessler from his undercover work in Denmark at the height of Danish underground terrorism and his transfer to the Sleeper Agent program was effected only over severe protests by the authorities in the Danish Protectorate. However, Berlin felt that the Sleeper Agent undertaking had priority. Sleepers placed in foreign countries prior to the war have proven enormously effective, as for instance the Sleeper who caused the French liner *Normandie* to capsize and burn in New York Harbor in 'forty-two. An exceedingly successful operation, sir. The agent, having become a naturalized American citizen, had lived in Chicago, working as a hairdresser, until he was activated and charged with the *Normandie* mission. Also in—"

"I *know* the importance of the Sleeper Agent program, Colonel!" the civilian interrupted curtly. "Continue!"

"Of course, sir. . . . Subject arrived at Schloss Ehrenstein training school in September, 1943," he read. "Basic training and indoctrination completed September, 1944. Special language, social and psychological studies for Sleeper activity in the United States begun October, 1944, with special tutoring in the American dialect and contemporary expressions." He glanced at the civilian. "The tutor was a native born and educated American from the city of New York," he said with obvious self-satisfaction. "We arranged to obtain him from the American Bund. He was, of course, of great value to the project, providing the subject with what is called 'slang' in America."

The civilian nodded impatiently.

The commandant continued: "Subject's code name: Rudi A-27. Readiness tests completed"—he looked up from the dossier—"as of . . . now, sir, eighteen April 1945."

He closed the file and handed it to one of the Gestapo officers. He turned to the civilian. "Rudi A-27 has at this moment full knowledge of our extensive preparations for a Sleeper Agent network coast to coast in the United States. He is the top agent so far graduated from Schloss Ehrenstein." He looked straight at the civilian. "Shall we continue?"

"By all means."

The commandant turned to the two Gestapo officers. "You are dismissed."

The officers came to attention. Two pairs of heels clicked as one; two arms shot out stiffly as the men chorused "Heil Hitler!" and left.

The civilian walked over to stand directly in front of Rudi. There was no friendliness on his hard face, no compassion in his cold voice. Only deadly determination. "You have impressed me, Obersturmführer Kessler," he said. "Although I do not appreciate melodramatics."

Rudi stood stiffly at attention. He kept his silence. He wondered about the civilian. He was obviously a man of consequence. Great consequence. Rudi was tense, his numbing fatigue all but forgotten. He felt certain the next few moments would be the most important in his life.

The civilian continued: "You have been selected for a highly special top secret mission. It will be dangerous. Are you willing to undertake such a mission—no questions asked?"

"Yes, sir." He did not hesitate.

"You have sworn your oath of loyalty to your Führer, of course."

"Of course, sir."

"Repeat it!"

He drew himself up. He forced his exhausted mind to remember the words. "I swear to you, Adolf Hitler, as Führer and Reichschancellor, loyalty and valor. I vow to you, and to those you have named to command me, obedience unto death, so help me God!"

"Good. Remember it. It is the single most important fact in your life." For a moment the man stared searchingly at the young officer before him. "We shall use your training, Lieutenant, your cunning and your stamina to the last vestige of it, do not fear. We shall use your special knowledge of the United States of America and our network there. We shall use *you*, any way we see fit. Understood?"

"Yes, sir!"

"You will now make yourself ready to leave here. Leave Schloss Ehrenstein. Your commandant will brief you regarding your transportation. Your final mission briefing will be in Berlin. You will be there within three days. The day of the Führer's birthday. You will keep this in utmost secrecy. That is an order! You are dismissed."

He turned away from the young officer without acknowledging the inevitable "Heil Hitler!" salute. As soon as he heard the door close behind Rudi, he picked up the telephone on the table. Brusquely he gave the operator a number. He waited. Then he spoke into the receiver, carefully holding it so that it did not come in contact with his face.

"Heil Hitler! Here is Brigadeführer Arnold. Put me through." He listened for a moment, his face clouding in anger. "No!" he snapped. "I must speak with him *personally!*" Again he listened, scowling. "I am not interested in listening to excuses!" His voice became ominously calm and flat. "Your name and rank, please?"

He wrote quickly in his notebook.

"I trust, *Colonel* Lutze, that you realize that the responsibility for *any* consequence, however grave, will rest with you alone if I do not get to speak with the Reichsleiter within the next sixty seconds!" He listened, a thin, malicious smile on his lips. "I shall wait." He waited. Impatiently he drummed his fingers on the tabletop.

The commandant watched him in silence. He started to look toward the wall clock—but remembered. Instead he glanced at his watch.

Less than forty seconds had gone by when Arnold spoke into the phone: "Herr Reichsleiter? Heil Hitler! . . . It is in order. We have found the perfect subject. He will report to you in Berlin on April the twentieth. . . . Heil Hitler!"

He hung up. He turned to the commandant. "You will see that Kessler reports for his briefing at the Führerbunker in Berlin at the specified time. Without fail!"

"Yes, Herr Brigadeführer."

"You will proceed at once with the final dissolution of the Sleeper Agent project and the closing down and evacuation of Schloss Ehrenstein."

"It will be done."

The civilian nodded. "You are to be congratulated, Colonel. You have turned out an excellent man for a mission of vital importance for the survival of the Third Reich."

"Thank you, Herr Brigadeführer. May I ask, to whom shall Kessler report in Berlin?"

"To the Reichsleiter personally. Reichsleiter Martin Bormann."

The colonel pulled the dossier to him. He opened it. For a moment he contemplated it. Then, in a meticulous hand, under the code name Rudi A-27, he wrote:

Kokon

PART 2

21–29 APRIL 1945

1

Her eyes hated him.

She was a pretty girl. Perhaps twenty-six. Her blond hair, drawn back tightly, was gathered by a thin blue ribbon at the nape of her neck and allowed to hang loosely down her back. Her tanned face was fresh and soft, but her troubled eyes were dark with hate. More than hate. Suspicion. Uncertainty. And fear.

Thomas Jaeger knew the look. Knew it well. He had seen it cloud the bleak faces of countless suspects, male and female, young and old, military and civilian, from the shores of Omaha Beach through Normandy and Luxembourg, across the Rhine and through the heartland of Germany to this little Bavarian town of Grafenwöhr nestled in the forest clad mountains twenty-five miles southeast of Bayreuth. Here his Counter Intelligence team, one of the six teams of CIC Detachment 212, had set up shop only the day before, even as the place was being secured by elements of the 11th Armored Division.

Grafenwöhr was a town like so many others in Bavaria. Picturesque, colorful, distinguished only by the presence of a huge German Chemical Warfare Service dump concealed in the woods surrounding it. Stacks and stacks of incendiary bombs and poison gas projectiles. The Ordnance boys had estimated over three million of them. Enough to wipe out all of Europe.

The girl had wandered into town—she, her girl friend and her little boy, who was four years old, healthy, cute—and obviously pure Aryan.

Their clothes, though of good quality, were dirty and bedraggled. They said they came from the Czech town of Pilsen, some seventy-five miles to the east, and had been on the road for days, carrying their scant belongings with them, in an effort to reach their home town of Bayreuth before being cut off and trapped by the rapidly advancing Russian troops.

He believed them.

But it was CIC routine to screen everyone who crossed the line from enemy-held territory, military or civilian. And there were literally thousands of them.

The front was beginning to break up. Hitler's thousand-year Third Reich lay gutted, cut in half like a chicken carcass on a butcher's block.

The situation was unpredictable from hour to hour, from village to village. Fierce resistance and heavy firefighting, especially where Waffen SS troops were in command, were still the order of the day. And yet in some sectors the hordes of surrendering German troops were so great it became impossible to handle them. As in Grafenwöhr.

Columns of Nazi troops, crowded onto their own vehicles, fully armed and under the command of their own officers, rumbled through on their way to the rear and captivity—with a single GI as both guide and guard. German staff cars, trucks and Volkswagens rubbed fenders with American half-tracks, 2½-ton trucks and jeeps on the narrow roads. Ramrod German officers with white armbands reading LIAISON OFFICER WITH U.S. ARMY shared the streets with American MP's, and field orders were issued in both English and German by American and German commanding officers. Tom had seen one entire battalion of Nazi troops marching smartly through town, unguarded, carrying a white sign before them as if it were a conquered enemy standard: THESE ARE PW'S. DIRECT TO NEAREST CAGE. So many individual soldiers were trying to give themselves up that nobody could find time to bother with them—even when they anxiously accosted the GI's, holding out their paybooks and literally begging to be taken prisoner. The Americans would just point to the rear and order them to march.

Mixed in with the hectic military traffic came German civilians fleeing Czechoslovakia before the Russian onslaught; petty Nazi officials, who only weeks before had been the haughty masters of Sudetenland; dependents of the occupation forces; and others who thought it best to seek safety from the "savage Slavs."

On foot, crammed into all kinds of vehicles, pushing carts or bicycles, they streamed into the little Bavarian town. They were ordered to stay off the main roads so as not to impede military traffic, but this rule was constantly violated. It was the duty of the CIC to screen this flood of people before allowing them to proceed farther into Germany—behind the American lines.

The girl sitting so tensely before Tom and his partner, CIC agent Larry Scott, was one of these fugitives.

They had interrogated her companion first. Her name was Liselotte Greiner. She had answered their routine questions satisfactorily. Her papers were as valid as any, and her story had been plausible. She was obviously intelligent, but her handsome face had seemed hard. Perhaps it was only a resentful animosity she could not conceal. But she had been in complete control of herself, even a little haughty.

They had not liked her. But it was not their job to like or dislike their subjects. Only to screen them. They had been all set to send the two girls on their way after the usual cursory examination which under the circumstances constituted a screening.

But Tom had felt uneasy when they started questioning the second girl. Her name was Maria Bauer. Where her companion had been composed, she was nervous. Where they had seen only hostility and venom in the eyes of her friend, here there was also fear. Where the other's face had been only hard and resentful, hers was also vulnerable and fearful.

Tom recognized his nagging feeling of uneasiness. He knew what it meant. A hunch. A hunch that all was not as it seemed. A hunch that his subject was concealing something. A hunch that could not be explained logically but which was a familiar sensation to every seasoned interrogator. Seldom wrong, it had to be followed up.

He glanced at Larry. His partner met his glance and nodded imperceptibly. He, too, felt it, Tom realized.

Many subjects were nervous and ill at ease under interrogation. It was normal. But this girl had something to hide. Something she was in deadly fear they would discover.

Tom once more studied the little gray *Kennkarte* in his hand. It was the standard German identification card. It seemed in order, crisp and clean. He looked at the date of issue: 17 September 1943. He frowned. "When was your *Kennkarte* issued to you?" he asked. His German was perfect.

The tip of the girl's tongue flitted between her dry lips in a darting motion. "On September seventeenth, 1943."

Perhaps that was it, he thought. Perhaps that was what had alerted him, nudged his subconscious into kindling his hunch. The girl had fished out her identification card from a large purse she nervously clutched to her. It was in too good a condition to have been treated like that for more than a year and a half.

"You've had this card since then?"

"Yes."

Slowly he turned the card over in his hand. Thoughtfully he examined it. "It's in pretty good shape for being that old, isn't it?"

Again the tip of her tongue darted swiftly between her bloodless lips. "I . . . I didn't carry it with me for a long time after I got it," she whispered. "I . . . I left it at the house."

Tom looked questioningly at her. "In Pilsen? In a strange town? You *do* come from *Bayreuth*, don't you?"

"Yes."

"And you didn't think it necessary to carry your German identification card with you—in *Czechoslovakia?*" His tone of voice eloquently conveyed his incredulity.

"No." It was barely a whisper.

"What would you have done if you'd been picked up?" Larry asked suddenly. "Or had an accident?"

The girl looked quickly toward the source of this new thrust. "I . . . I don't know," she whispered. "I . . . never thought . . ."

Tom frowned at the *Kennkarte.* There was . . . something. But, dammit, it would take the whole bag of tricks, no doubt, to get at the truth. Time. And time they did not have. There were hundreds of others still to be screened. Hell, he thought, what kind of Mata Hari could this frightened kid be, anyway? There might be another way to get to her. A quicker way.

He smiled at her. His voice was friendly and relaxed. "Very well, Frau Bauer. Your papers seem to be in order." He gave the *Kennkarte* back to her. He watched her closely.

The reaction he expected did not come. The tenseness in the girl's face did not change. The fear in her eyes did not diminish.

He was puzzled. He had been sure she would relax once her identification had been accepted. He watched her. Watched her slender hands unconsciously twisting and untwisting the heavy shoulder strap on the bag she clutched to her.

Something else?

"Frau Bauer!" His voice was suddenly sharp. "Give me your bag!"

There was a barely perceptible gasp from the girl. The blood drained from her face, leaving her tanned cheeks a sickly gray.

Something else . . .

Without a word she handed him the bag.

He took it. He turned it upside down. Its contents spilled out upon the table. The girl watched, mesmerized. He moved the objects about. A large comb. A purse with a little money. A purple hair ribbon. A lipstick. Handkerchief. A small pocket knife. A piece of paper with several safety pins attached. A child's toy whistle. A fountain pen. And . . . ah! There it was.

He picked it up. A solid gold medal, twice the size of a silver dollar and many times as heavy, with a bas-relief religious motif embossed on both sides.

He had found the "something else."

The medal must represent a fortune to her, he thought. Her only means of starting a new life for herself and her boy, once back home in Bayreuth, the only concrete hope in her nightmare world.

It explained her extreme nervousness. She was simply afraid he'd liberate the only thing of value she possessed. He felt sorry for her. His guilt feelings began to stir again. Angrily he suppressed them. He knew damned well how irrational they were.

He handed the heavy gold piece back to the girl. "Here," he said, his voice reassuring. "You'd better hold on to this."

She took the coin. Her fingers touched his. They were cold.

So certain had he been that he'd found the reason for her uneasiness that he almost missed her reaction. Or rather, *lack* of reaction. The girl did not relax. She showed no relief as she held the gold medal tightly clenched in her fist.

Tom shot a glance at Larry, but his partner's attention was on the release report he'd already begun to fill out.

Tom felt his pulse quicken. He had misread the girl completely. He suddenly knew he had to follow through. He scooped up the rest of the girl's belongings and dumped them into her handbag. He gave it to her.

She seemed to relax. She clutched the bag to her. She even looked a little smug as Tom unhurriedly reached over and picked up the release form filled out by Larry. He appeared to study it, but his thoughts were racing.

It was not the medal, not the gold value of it that concerned the girl. He was sure of it. It was easy to verify.

He looked up at her. He smiled. "That's a very interesting medal you have there," he commented. "Let me see it again." He held out his hand.

At once the girl dug into her bag and came up with the gold medal. She handed it to Tom. *"Bitte,"* she said.

She watched him as he looked the coin over. But there was no anxiety in her large eyes. Rather a certain . . . expectation, a seeming eagerness to please her interrogator. Deliberately Tom put the coin in his pocket.

The girl sighed. It was more a sigh of relief than of concern. The gold medal meant nothing to her. He was certain of it now. It had to be something else.

The bag itself!

He suddenly reached over and grabbed the bag from the startled girl. He spilled its familiar contents out onto the table. Quickly he examined the empty bag. He tested the seams, felt the lining and ripped it open. Hidden beneath it was a folded piece of paper. He slipped it out.

The girl had uttered not a word. Ashen-faced, she sat in her chair, an unnatural rigidity stiffening her young body, her eyes dark with fear and shock.

Tom unfolded the paper. It was a letter-sized document. Official. It was headed, GEHEIME STAATSPOLIZEI. GEHEIME KOMMANDOSACHE—GESTAPO. TOP SECRET!

It was a routine document. Tom read it quickly. It dealt with the transfer of a certain SS Standartenführer, Gestapo Colonel Wolfgang Steinmetz, from Prague to Pilsen on special assignment. It was dated two weeks before.

Tom was puzzled. It made no sense. Why would she be carrying a document like that? Hidden in the lining of her purse? He passed the document to Larry. He picked up the completed release form and slowly tore it in half. His eyes bored into hers. "Who is this Colonel Steinmetz?" he demanded. "Why are *you* carrying his transfer orders?"

The girl's lips trembled, but she remained silent.

Larry pushed the Mandatory Arrest and War Criminals Wanted List across the table to Tom. His finger stabbed a name: STEINMETZ, WOLFGANG (39) SS STANDARTENFÜHRER. The colonel was a wanted man. A very much wanted man!

Tom picked up the field telephone. He cranked the handle. "This is Agent Jaeger," he said into the mouthpiece. "CIC Detachment 212. Get me Captain Elliott, Sixteenth Field Hospital. They're in Kemnath."

He waited. The girl was staring at him. She did not understand his words, but she knew it was her fate being decided.

"Ell?" Tom spoke with sober quiet. "I need to borrow one of your nurses. . . . No, no. A body search. We've got a subject here, a girl. She has to be searched. Thoroughly." He listened for a moment. He frowned. "Oh, come on, Ell. You can shake one of them loose for a few hours. I'll send a jeep for her."

Again he listened, his face grim. "Okay, Ell. I got you. Thanks." He hung up and turned to Larry. "No go."

"Dammit!" Larry sounded thoroughly disgusted.

"The Twenty-sixth ran into a pocket of SS. Beat the hell out of their forward units. They can't even spare an aspirin." He looked at the girl sitting tensely before him. He stood up. "Let's get on with it," he said.

They went over every inch of every stitch of clothing the girl possessed. Systematically they searched the girl herself. Things can be concealed in many ways. There are seven orifices in the female body. Each can afford a place of concealment. They did not miss any of them.

The girl endured the humiliating ordeal in stoic silence. She let herself be manipulated like a manikin. She seemed totally, inexorably resigned.

It was a distasteful, a degrading experience. For all three of them. But it was not in vain. Taped to the instep of the girl's right foot Tom found a second *Kennkarte*. It had the same picture, the same description, the same vital data. It was the ID of the same girl. Only the name was different. It was Maria Steinmetz. Frau Wolfgang Steinmetz!

Tom stared at the card. So that was her secret. The damning fact she had been so mortally afraid he'd uncover, so fearful that her very actions in trying to conceal it had given her away. How often that happened, he thought.

Mrs. Wolfgang Steinmetz. Wife of a wanted Gestapo Colonel.

He placed the card on the table. He looked at the young naked girl standing in the middle of the room, her arms hanging dead at her sides, her head bowed. He swallowed. He turned to Larry. "Let her get dressed," he said quietly. "I'll be back in a couple of minutes." He left the room.

The house taken over by the CIC team belonged to a local big shot. It was large, opulently furnished in typical Teutonic taste, situated on the outskirts of town.

The owner, his family and servants had been living in it when Tom and his teammates had commandeered it. The Germans had been given half an hour to clear out and allowed to take only the most necessary possessions. In fear and shock they had obeyed, and the CIC team had moved in. They'd stay there until they had to move on, at which time the family could return to their home.

It was routine procedure, a procedure that had been learned the hard way: Always take over a house that is occupied and kick the occupants out fast. Empty houses are booby-trapped!

Tom and Larry were using the family dining room on the main floor as their interrogation room. Now Tom stood in the large entrance foyer. For a moment he leaned against the closed door to the interrogation room. He seemed to *see* the foyer for the first time: the front door with the two etched glass panels, the grandfather clock stopped at 7:19, the ornate mahogany dresser with the bevel-edged mirror and the hanging clothes rack made of deer antlers, the rows of roebuck and elk antlers and the plaques with wild boar tusks adorning the walls.

His parents might well have lived in homes exactly like this, he thought, before they emigrated to the United States. Before he was born.

He wondered what his mother would have thought had she known that her insistence that he learn to speak the language of the old country fluently had made it possible for him to do his present job. To perform duties such as the one he'd just completed. She would not even have been able to comprehend it. Neither she nor his father. . . .

Hermann Jaeger came from a small town in Bavaria. He emigrated to America in 1910 and found employment in a watch repair shop. In 1913 he returned to his native Germany and brought back a bride, Fannerl, to his new country. In 1917 their only child, a son, was born.

Fannerl kept her Bavarian ways. She was slow to learn English, and the boy spoke mostly German at home. It was she who named her son Thomas —though it was never clear whether it was after Thomas Jefferson or Thomas Mann.

The family lived in New York City, in Yorkville. Hermann had his own little jewelry and watch repair shop within walking distance.

When after 1939 people began to equate Germans with Nazis, the Jaegers were deeply disturbed, but they could not bring themselves to leave their familiar neighborhood, although they abhorred the spreading influence of Fritz Kuhn and his Bund.

Tom went to Columbia, majoring in English and European lit. He lived at home, helping with expenses by working part time as a reader and translator for various publishers, reading books in German and writing synopses of them in English.

After Pearl Harbor and the declaration of war on Germany, Hermann changed. He withdrew into himself. He was literally heartbroken. One night he did not come home. Tom went to the shop and found his father slumped over his workbench, dead, his jeweler's eyepiece still wedged in his eye. Fannerl soon followed her husband. During her last weeks she spoke only German, as if she blamed her adopted country for having taken her husband from her.

Tom was at loose ends. He met a girl among the standees at the Metropolitan Opera. She was fun, intelligent and exciting. He desperately needed to channel his emotions, and after a whirlwind romance he proposed. He and Julie were married late in 1942.

With a German name, Julie—"American" enough to pass the strictest DAR scrutiny—soon began to feel the pressures and disapproval of her friends, especially since her "German" husband was not in the armed forces. Subtly she began to persuade Tom not to wait to be drafted but to volunteer—to show he was really an American. He did.

Because of his language abilities, he ended up in Military Intelligence Service at Camp Ritchie, Maryland, and finally in the CIC.

He had earned the Bronze Star for his work in the ETO. He had been involved in countless cases, investigations and interrogations. The Maria Steinmetz search was not his first such body search.

But he still felt unclean. It was an uncleanness he knew he couldn't wash off. And he still had not conquered the nagging feeling of guilt that worried his mind. He—a *German*—fighting his own people.

He stepped away from the door. He looked at his hands. He went to wash up.

When he re-entered the interrogation room the girl was sitting in her chair. Her handbag lay forgotten on the floor next to her, her hands were clenched tightly in her lap, and her bleak eyes stared unseeing into space.

Tom took his place opposite her. He picked up the real *Kennkarte*. He frowned at it. Why? Why, with a false ID card that could pass any inspection, had she hidden this real card on her person? Was there a reason?

Or was it just another manifestation of that peculiar Germanic trait that made it impossible for them to give up the last tenuous link to past power and glory? Was it the fear of not being able to prove conclusively to officialdom their true loyalties should the Nazis still prevail and once again seize power? He'd run into that sort of thing before. But if that were the case, what *was* the link?

Tom studied her quietly for a moment. The fact that the girl was the wife of a wanted Gestapo officer meant nothing by itself. Unless she had knowledge of her husband's whereabouts and activities. The CIC did not wage war on the families of their enemies. The fact that she had been using false papers was a relatively minor violation. One that could easily be rectified. Anyway, he suspected he knew why.

But he couldn't shake the feeling that in this frightened, humbled girl with all her vulnerability there was hidden a greater, a more dangerous secret.

He also instinctively knew that she would not be easy to break, despite her deep apprehension. She would have to be handled with special care. He decided that the soft approach would be the best. He had a quick thought that his decision was prompted by his feelings of pity for the girl because of the traumatic suffering he had been forced to inflict upon her. He dismissed it. His choice was the correct one.

He glanced at Larry. He spoke in German. "I think Section eighty-seven, Paragraph nine applies in this case. Agreed?" he asked crisply.

It was their own special code. It simply meant Let's use the good-guy/bad-guy routine. You be the bad guy.

Larry picked up on it immediately. He scowled. "Of course," he snapped. He turned to the girl. He stared at her. Coldly. "Now, *Frau* Steinmetz," he said, his voice sharp with the ring of malevolence. "It is about time that you come up with some real answers. You hear me?"

The girl cringed.

"You *are* the wife of a Gestapo colonel, are you not? An SS officer? A wanted war criminal?" Each epithet was rapped out with hateful vehemence. *"Answer me!"*

The girl winced. "Yes," she whispered almost inaudibly.

"You *were* using false papers, a criminal offense, were you not?"

She nodded.

"I want to know *why!* I want to know everything *you* know. About your husband. Where he is. What he does. And I want to know it *now!* You understand?"

The girl stared at her clenched fists in her lap. She remained silent.

"Answer me!"

She flinched as if physically struck by Larry's shouted demand. "I . . . I don't understand what you mean," she whispered. "I know nothing. Nothing at all." Her voice was unsteady.

"Well, Frau Colonel Steinmetz," Larry said caustically, *"I* think you do!" He leaned across the table, his face close to hers. "And I *will* find out!" He smiled nastily. "Don't think that the fact that you are a woman means anything to us," he said in an ominously quiet tone of voice. "It does not. *You* should know that," he finished with a smirk.

He suddenly grabbed the girl's chin and lifted her face. His eyes stabbed at hers. "So help me, Frau Gestapo Colonel Steinmetz"—he savored each word and spat it out as if offended by its taste—"I'll get every bit of information you have out of you! I'll grab hold of your brain, *Frau Gestapo Colonel Steinmetz,* and I'll squeeze it until every drop of knowledge oozes from it!"

Tom had been following the performance closely. He knew it was an act, and yet he felt genuinely disturbed. He shook the feeling off. He could not afford it. You did not last long in the ruthless world in which he functioned if you allowed yourself to become personally or emotionally involved with your subjects. For any reason.

He frowned. He looked concerned. He had *his* part to play. He touched Larry on the arm. "Larry," he said soberly, "take it easy." He spoke in

German as if unaware of the fact. It seemed completely natural. He lowered his voice to a confidential murmur, yet loud enough for the girl to overhear. "Don't you think she's gone through enough right now?"

He gave the girl a sympathetic look. He turned back to his partner. "Why don't you take a break? Let me talk to her for a while. . . . Go on."

Larry glared at him. Without a word he got up and stalked from the room, slamming the door behind him.

For a moment neither Tom nor the girl spoke. She sat rigidly, her hands clasped tightly before her, her head lowered.

Then Tom began to talk, quietly, reassuringly. "Frau Steinmetz," he said, "you must realize that it is best to be cooperative. For your own sake. For the sake of your little son."

He waited for a brief moment, then he went on, almost reluctantly. "Look, I . . . I really shouldn't suggest this to you, Frau Steinmetz, but I do feel . . . regretful for what we had to do to you. . . . Look, my partner is determined to find out *something* from you. He is a hard man, Frau Steinmetz. . . . Why don't you—" He hesitated, then seemingly made up his mind. "Look, you could tell us some unimportant facts perhaps— something that can't harm your husband. I know you can't do that. Just . . . anything, to satisfy him."

He knew only too well that once a subject begins to talk, to give any information at all, it becomes increasingly easy to get the next fact. And the next. Until there are no secrets left.

He stood up. He walked behind her. She tensed. He placed his hand gently on her shoulder. He felt her shiver. "Why don't you talk to me, Frau Steinmetz. Perhaps I can help you. I should like to."

In that moment he actually loathed himself, and yet not for a moment did he doubt that what he was doing was necessary—and right.

"The war is over, Frau Steinmetz. Soon there will be no more killing. No more suffering. You and your boy are alive. And whole. Perhaps your husband is, too? Soon you may all be together again. And happy." He spoke quietly, convincingly. "Even if your husband will have to face justice, perhaps be interned for a while, it won't be forever. Think of it, Frau Steinmetz. Don't spoil it by being unnecessarily stubborn. Think of it. Think of yourself. Think of your little boy."

He watched the knuckles grow white as the girl clenched her fists almost convulsively. He felt the suppressed sobs shake her body. He went back to sit across from her again. "Frau Steinmetz," he said softly.

She looked up slowly. Her eyes were moist with unshed tears brimming at her lids.

"Where is your husband?"

She looked haunted. She did not speak.

"You don't have to tell me anything you don't want to," he said. "Just . . . tell me what you can. How did you come here? Why did you use the false *Kennkarte?* Why?"

"Because . . . they told me to." It was a mere whisper. But it was a beginning.

"Who? Who told you to?"

"The Gestapo."

And slowly, haltingly the girl told her story.

She was indeed the wife of Colonel Wolfgang Steinmetz—and proud of it. He was a good man. A good soldier. A good German. The false *Kennkarte* had been given to her by the Gestapo in Prague. That's why it could not be detected as a forgery. It was the real thing except for the name. She had been ordered to use it. She had been told that all members of the families of Gestapo and SS officers were put to death by the enemy. Perhaps tortured. She never doubted it. Had she not heard it said over the radio by Dr. Goebbels himself? She had nightmares thinking about her little boy being killed. Or tortured.

She had been told to destroy her real identification card, but she had not been able to do it. It had been the final link to her true identity, as the document pertaining to her husband had been the last concrete link to him.

Flat-eyed, lifelessly she told her story in a low, monotonous voice. She had been caught. The wife of a Gestapo colonel. Using forged papers. She would be executed. She—and her son. She was convinced of it. It is what the Gestapo would have done. . . .

Tom listened to her in silence. It was not a new story. He'd heard it before in every conceivable variation.

The girl fell silent.

"Where is the Colonel now?" Tom asked gently.

Her expression did not change. She was beyond reaction. "I do not know."

"When did you last see him?"

"Not for many weeks."

"What was the special assignment on the Gestapo order you were carrying?"

"I do not know."

"What were your husband's duties in the Gestapo?"

"I do not know."

I do not know. . . . I do not know. . . . I do not know. . . . The same answer delivered in the exact same flat tone of voice. Over and over again. There was no way of reaching her.

To herself, her person, her existence, her actions mattered no more. She was dead.

Larry joined them. Together the two CIC agents tried to convince the girl that she would not be killed. That she would not be tortured. That her son would not in any way be harmed. That her beliefs were wrong, the result of Goebbels' propaganda and Gestapo lies.

They could not reach her behind her flat, drawn mask of total resignation. Patiently they explained to her that she would have to go before a Military Government court in the morning on a charge of using falsified identification papers. She might be fined. She might not. A travel permit would have to be issued. But she would be allowed to go on. To Bayreuth. Home. With her son. No harm would come to either of them.

She would have to spend the night in jail. Not imprisoned by American troops. No. In the local German jail. Among her own people. Her boy would be with her friend. They would be put up at the *Gasthaus* for the night. In the morning they would all three be on their way. She listened, empty-eyed. They were not sure she heard them.

It was late. They decided to wait until morning to interrogate the other girl, Liselotte Greiner, once again. They had little hope of getting any information from her. Tom felt certain that both girls knew more than they would admit. They were lying. But, then, they might also be telling the truth. They would try to find out. In the morning. . . .

In the morning, early, Tom was awakened by an insistent banging on the door to his room.

"Yes?" he called groggily, fighting his way up from a deep sleep.

"Sir!" It was Sergeant Pete Connors. "You're wanted on the phone. It's the jail. It's urgent!"

He was wide awake at once. He hurried to the interrogation room.

It was the German jailer. *"Bitteschön! Bitteschön!"* His pleading voice sounded panic-stricken. "Please! Please come to the jail. Please come at once!"

Tom and Larry were there in less than ten minutes. The elderly German jailer looked gray-faced and sick. He hurried them to a cell, the cell that held the Gestapo colonel's wife. He opened the door. She was there. Hanging from the bars in the window on the opposite wall. Dead. Even in the lonely cell she had been forced to listen to the lethal words of Goebbels and the Gestapo. And she had believed.

The jailer was a kind man. A considerate man. A man of compassion. He had taken from the girl all her belongings, as was the regulation. Anything with which she might have harmed herself. But he had allowed her to keep her comb. And her handkerchief. And her large bag to keep them in.

The girl had torn off the shoulder strap, and it had become a hangman's noose.

When she had stepped up on the bench fixed to the wall under the barred window, the strap had been just barely long enough to be tied to one of the bars and knotted tightly around the girl's slender neck. In desperate determination she had stepped off the bench to hang from her macabre gallows until she strangled to death.

Profoundly shaken, his stomach a sudden leaden knot, his throat a swollen lump, Tom stared at the girl.

He put her there. . . .

Staring glassy eyes which seemed to strain to escape their sockets. A blackish bloated tongue protruding obscenely between small white teeth. Purple-blue splotches on her puffy face and her bare arms, and a pair of grotesquely pointing, stiff legs on the side of the rough wooden bench that had served as her gallows platform.

He—put—her—there.

"Oh, my God!"

Tom heard Larry's shocked, hoarse-voiced exclamation as if through a cocoon of cotton. He had to turn away. But he didn't. He had gone too far with her, he thought in bleak self-recrimination. He had driven her to this. And for what! His dread-dark guilt feelings were never more ravenous, threatening to devour his very being. He felt his sanity ripping loose. But he kept himself staring at the girl. Slowly he forced himself back to reality and reason.

He had not killed the girl. The stinking, rotten lies of the stinking, rotten Nazi bastards had killed her! He breathed deeply. He began to think clearly once again. He looked away from the girl. And he saw it. It was written on the scrubbed, worn surface of the tabletop fastened to the wall. A message:

"Leb wohl mein Liebling, weitermachen!—Farewell my darling, carry on!"

He walked over to the girl. He examined her more closely. She had had nothing with which to write her last words. She had had nothing with which to get at the only means of writing them—her own blood. She had been determined. She had bitten open a vein on her wrist.

Farewell my darling . . .

Slowly he returned to the table. He stared at the message. The blood-ink had dried a dirty brown.

In his mind's eye he saw the grim desperation with which the despairing young girl had gone about her ghastly task. Again he felt an overwhelming flood of pity wash over him.

He stared at the pathetic message. And suddenly the guilt-created haze obscuring his mind swept away. The message! He should have seen it at once. The girl, for all her youth and appeal, *was* the loyal wife of a war criminal. A dangerous Gestapo officer. And she admired him. She had died only because in her own warped mind she had conferred upon her American enemies the same unholy, inhuman ways of her own rotten system. She had obviously been lying all the time. Undoubtedly she had known her husband's whereabouts. She might even have been in on his future plans, and judging from the man's record they would surely be worth discovering.

The proof was right there in front of him. On the tabletop. Written in her blood. The message.

For whom was it meant? Obviously not her friend. She would not call her "my darling." Not her young son. It was not worded right to be for him. It had to be meant for her husband. And, if so, she must have known it would be delivered to him.

Only one person could do that!

He heard Larry order the shaken jailer to cut the girl down and take her away. He whirled on them. "No!" he said sharply. He despised himself for saying it. "Leave her!"

The telephone receiver felt leaden in his hand. He had an irrational hope that, somehow, he wouldn't get through. But presently he heard the voice of Sergeant Connors. "CIC."

He sighed. "Pete," he said. He hardly recognized his own voice. "Get over to *Zum Grünen Kranze*. The *Gasthaus*. Round up the Greiner woman. Leave the kid. Bring her over here. To the jail. On the double!"

Pete didn't even sound surprised. "Okay," he said cheerfully. "Be there in a few minutes."

Tom replaced the receiver. He stared at it as if it shared a guilty secret with him. He got up.

Liselotte Greiner was brought to the jail exactly seventeen minutes later. It had seemed an eternity to Tom, waiting in the dingy little office of the jailer with Larry and the uneasy German.

Sergeant Connors ushered her in. She swaggered arrogantly into the room, confidently aware of her good looks. Insolently she ignored Tom's offer of a chair. "Why have I been brought to this . . . this *place?*" she demanded to know. She looked around with obvious distaste. "Surely I am not under *arrest!*" Her mockery was brazen.

She seems so damned sure of herself, Tom thought, it might be a cover-up for a real sense of apprehension. He fervently hoped so. He came straight to the point. "Where is Colonel Steinmetz?" he snapped.

The girl did not move a muscle. Almost derisively she said, "I do not know *what* you are talking about."

Tom was taken aback. He had expected some reaction. He had been watching her closely. Watching for those little involuntary telltale signs that betrayed so much. There had been nothing.

He thought quickly. The girl was clever. She would have prepared herself for just that question. When her companion had been detained she would have realized that she had been made to talk, that her interrogators had found out about her Colonel Steinmetz. She was too clever to run away without a proper travel permit. That would only have thrown suspicion on her, and she would have been hunted down and brought back. All she really had to do was to stay put—and keep her mouth shut.

He looked at her, his set face grim. He had a chilly sensation. It was true. The fanatic Nazi women were ten times harder, ten times more ruthless than their male counterparts. He had run into many of them from the concentration camps. This one—she would not break easily. If at all. He grew tense. He had no choice. He nodded to the jailer.

The man started. *"Ja-jawohl,* Herr Hauptmann Jaeger," he stammered. *"So-sofort!* At once!" He hurried out.

The girl stared at Tom, venom in her cold eyes. "Jaeger," she repeated pointedly. "A *German* name!" She smiled a contemptuous smile. "I thought your German was too perfect for an *Ami!"* She looked him up and down, a withering appraisal. "A *German!* Betraying his own!" She made a mock exaggerated gesture of spitting on the floor. *"Ptui!"*

Tom sat perfectly still and quiet, but his pulse raced and roared in his ears. Damn the bitch, he thought savagely. Damn her soul to hell! He stood up. "Come with me, please," he said pleasantly.

They walked briskly down the corridor toward the cell. Tom kept his eyes on the girl. She's a cool one, he thought with grudging respect. If she's the least bit concerned, she doesn't show it.

The jailer waited by the open cell door. His sallow face looked chalky. He averted his eyes from the girl coming toward him.

Tom stepped aside. His mind was icy with the knowledge of what he was about to do. But he *had* to know. He was powerless to spare the girl. He could not allow even the possibility of a deadly agent such as Steinmetz going into action behind the lines. Without a word he motioned the girl through the open door.

She took one step into the cell—and stopped dead. Her hands flew to her mouth, and a shocked cry of anguish escaped between her clenched fingers. Her eyes—strained open and black with horror—were riveted upon the grisly sight before her. For an eternal moment she stood rooted to the spot, then she slowly reeled back to sag against the stone wall. Her arms fell lifeless at her sides. She pressed her head back against the rough stone, her mouth open in a hellish silent scream. Great rending sobs shook her body, but she seemed unable to tear her eyes from the misshapen bloated body of her friend hanging grotesquely on the wall before her, staring back at her with frightful bulbous eyes.

Tom didn't take his eyes from the stricken girl. His own heart beat wildly as he watched her go into hysterics. He could feel the cold sweat running down his armpits. He stepped close to the dread-possessed girl. "You *know* Colonel Steinmetz?" The question was shot at her, grating in the silence.

She was totally unaware of him.

He grabbed her shoulders and shook her. "Answer me!"

She was utterly oblivious to anything but the turgid monstrosity on the wall. She could not wrest her eyes from the sight confronting her. She was on the verge of total physical collapse from shock.

Tom stepped in front of her, blocking her field of view. He slapped her face sharply.

The girl focused her burning eyes on him as if seeing him for the very first time.

"You *know* Colonel Steinmetz!" It was no longer a question. It was a statement of damning fact.

The girl stared at him with glazed eyes. She no longer had a will of her own. She no longer commanded her mind. The shock had drained her of every control. "Yes." Her voice was a shriek of excruciating horror.

"Who is he?"

"My . . . brother."

"*Where* is he?"

"In . . . Bayreuth."

"You were meeting him there?"

"Yes."

"When?"

"April . . . April twenty-fourth."

"What are his plans?"

"Fight . . . fight . . . the Americans."

"How?"

But the girl did not answer. She lapsed into silence. The stark abysmal horror in her eyes shone with near madness. "You . . . you did that to her," she whispered in abject terror. "You . . . did . . . that."

She stared straight ahead. He knew she saw herself on that wall. Her horrified eyes sought out his. "You . . . killed her." And finally her strength broke. She collapsed at his feet.

In the Führerbunker in Berlin, that maze of impenetrable shelters deep in the earth beneath the Reichschancellery, protected by six feet of dirt and sixteen feet of concrete, Adolf Hitler, Führer of the Third Reich, had celebrated his fifty-sixth birthday on April 20, the day before.

It had been a quiet celebration. Many of the top Nazis had paid their respects: Goebbels, Himmler, Göring, Von Ribbentrop, Doenitz, Raeder, Jodl, Krebs, Speer, Eva Braun and, of course, Martin Bormann.

Bormann had been impatient to get the ceremonies over and done with. He had met the young man sent to him from Schloss Ehrenstein, Obersturmführer Rudolf Kessler.

He had been impressed. He knew the vital importance of the mission that was to be entrusted to the young man. He was impatient to begin. There was much to be done, but fate had conspired to keep him from doing it, with delay after delay.

The military conference following Hitler's birthday had not broken up until three A.M. Saturday. And immediately thereafter the exodus began, making it necessary for Bormann to observe and record. Like rats deserting a sinking ship they fled in the dark of night. The cream of the Thousand Year Reich: Himmler, Göring, Von Ribbentrop, Raeder, Doenitz and Speer.

Stripping their flashy badges of high rank, their glittering medals and ribbons, the gaudy golden braid from their uniforms, they fled.

Bitterly he thought how appropriate was the term he'd heard used to describe the exodus: *"Die Flucht der Goldfasanen—*The flight of the golden pheasants."

Then at 11:30 Saturday morning the Berlin center had been hit by the first Russian artillery barrage, forcefully bringing home how close was the enemy, how desperate the situation. The Brandenburg Gate was hit. The cupola of the burned-out Reichstag collapsed. The city's center had become the front line.

And finally, in the evening, Hitler had ordered an all-out last-hope counterattack on the Russian forces in the northern suburbs of Berlin, an attack to be mounted by SS Obergruppenführer Felix Steiner and his group from their positions in the Eberswalde on the flank of Von Manteuffel's Third Panzer Army.

Bormann knew it was a self-deceiving exercise in futility, but it nevertheless demanded his attention.

Finally he had been able to break free, and the young SS officer had been ushered into his presence a second time. It was late in the evening, Saturday, April 21, 1945. The final briefing of Rudi A-27 had begun.

2

The picturesque Bavarian town of Bayreuth, home of the Wagner festivals, had been taken by the 11th Armored Division, fighting with the 26th Infantry, on April 14, ten days before Tom arrived at Iceberg Forward to report to his commanding officer in the CIC, Major Lee, Herbert W. Lee. XII Corps had been in Bayreuth since the 21st.

The town had been severely damaged in the fighting, and the people were having a rough time of it. The retreating Wehrmacht had stripped the town of food before pulling out.

Tom felt oddly familiar with the place as he drove through the streets. His father had been a great Wagner fan, ever since he had attended a Bayreuth Festival performance of *Parsifal* with Fritz Vogelstrom in the title role. That had been in 1909, the year before he emigrated to the United States. He'd never stopped talking about it. It had been a magnificent performance. An unforgettable experience, according to Hermann. Tom recalled how his father's eyes had shone with remembered pleasure and excitement. The production had been under the direction of Siegfried Wagner himself. The son of Richard Wagner. Imagine! It had been breathtaking. Tom had listened to his father's famous "Wagner Festival Story" many times. He wished he could hear it again.

He looked at the shrapnel-scarred houses, many still with their white sheets of surrender fluttering submissively from empty windows, as he drove through the shell-cratered streets. He was conscious of feeling the loss of his parents more keenly than he had in a long time.

He passed Villa Wahnfried, the home of Richard Wagner and his family. Richard was buried on the grounds, he knew. The house looked undamaged from the front, but the entire back was caved in.

He wondered about the Festspielhaus, site of the Wagner festivals. He knew all about it. His father, naturally, had been an expert on the subject. The edifice was built following Wagner's own brilliant ideas to be the perfect showcase for his operas. And it was. Situated on a hill at the end of a broad avenue of trees, it overlooked the entire town.

He suddenly had an irresistible urge to find out if the famous opera house was still standing. He spotted a couple of MP's, one of them a sergeant. He stopped the jeep. "Hey, Sergeant, come here a moment!" he called.

The MP's sauntered over. "Yes, sir?"

"You know the Festspielhaus?"

"The . . . what?" The sergeant looked blank.

"The opera house on the hill. The Wagner theater."

The sergeant saw the light. "Oh, yeah! That big barn of a place." He frowned. "What about it, sir?"

"Is it still standing?"

The soldier looked at him, puzzled. "Sure. Not a scratch on it."

"Thanks."

He drove off. He felt foolish. But he also felt better. The Festspielhaus had been a sort of shrine to his father. He was glad it had not been destroyed.

The Ring, he thought. The very first performance at the Bayreuther Festspielhaus had been *The Ring*. How strangely ironic that the last part of *The Ring* was the opera *Götterdämmerung*—"Twilight of the Gods."

He suddenly felt depressed. It was all those damned thoughts about Wagner. About opera. That's how he'd met *her*, after all. Julie. He felt a pang of bitterness. Then anger. Damn the woman! Why did she have to write to me? he thought. Why did she have to tell me those things about Julie? Damn her!

He still had the letter in his pocket. Crumpled and dirty by now. He knew parts of it by heart. *Those* parts. Even to the spelling errors:

. . . I am working for your wife as a cleaning lady. . . . I think you should know wat sort of things do go on in your house you not beeing heer and all. . . . But I just want to say that your wife she is playing around if you know what I meen. . . . I think it is a crying shame you

beeing over there fitting for us. . . . Yours truly Daisy Jones.
PS. I find your APO adres on your letter to her.

His first impulse had been to tear the letter up. Forget the whole thing. But he couldn't. However much he wanted to ignore it, he couldn't. He did not *want* to believe it true. But he knew it was.

Perhaps his marriage to Julie had been a mistake. Brought on by all the wrong emotions. His loss. His loneliness. His need. The hectic times of war. The fun she'd been to be with. The good times in bed. All the wrong things.

But he'd hoped to be able to make a real marriage out of their relationship once he returned home. Maybe he still could.

If he could only forget about that damned letter . . .

He pulled up at the Iceberg Forward dismount point. For a moment he sat behind the wheel of his jeep. He had to snap out of it. He could not afford to dwell on his own troubles now.

Herbert Wadsworth Lee, Major, USA, commanding officer of CIC Detachment 212, was a portly man. The few fellow officers who did not like him for reasons of their own called him fat, although never to his face. Lee himself insisted it was all muscle, but he never explained to what use he put the muscle around his middle that looked like a well-stuffed ammo belt. He came from Atlanta, Georgia, and had played halfback for the Georgia Bulldogs. He spoke with a trace of a soft Southern accent.

Tom had looked him up in his office at Corps Headquarters. "What about it, Herb? Any objections?"

The CO looked at him. He frowned. "Haven't you got anything more important to do? In your own area?"

"How do you know *this* isn't important?"

"How do *you* know it is?"

"Fair question." Tom contemplated his superior officer. The CO had won his promotion in the CIC by being one hell of a good agent.

"Look, Herb," he said. "It's a hunch. Didn't *you* have them when you were in the field? When you were working—instead of loafing behind a desk?"

Lee looked at Tom. He envied him. He did miss the action, the feeling of excitement, of accomplishment, when a case was broken. Sure, he'd had hunches. And he'd followed them.

"Still seems like a routine operation to me, Tom," he said. "You got all the dope needed to pick up the guy. From that girl. His sister, wasn't it?"

"Yes."

"Where he'd be. When. A description of the man. What else do you want? They'll sweat his mission out of him back at AIC. Why not let the MP's handle it? What's so damned special?"

Tom had a fleeting vision of the Gestapo officer's dead wife hanging on the wall. "I want to be there when they take him," he said quietly. "I want to see the man. Hell, you know that most cases we crack we never get a chance to follow through. We don't even know most of the time *what* happens to a case once we hand it back. Well, this one I want to know about!" He looked straight at the major. "Come on, Herb. Make the damned call!"

Lee sighed. "Okay. I guess I'll never get rid of you if I don't. And I've got to get back to my Japs."

Tom looked startled. "Japs?"

"We've got thirty-five Jap prisoners here. Second Cavalry picked them up at Zwiesel."

"*Japs?* Here?"

"Say they're diplomats. Come complete with wives and kids. They all speak English. So damned polite they make you puke." He picked up the phone. "Don't know what the hell I'll do with them. Pass them on back, I suppose."

He spoke into the phone. "Give me Corps MP's. Captain Forrester." He waited. Then: "Jack? . . . On that Gestapo colonel, the Steinmetz stakeout. . . . Right. . . . One of my agents, Tom Jaeger, will call the signals. . . . Sure, Jack, I know your boys can handle it." He grinned. "I guess Tom has a personal ax to grind. . . . Good deal!"

He hung up. He turned to Tom. "You got the ball. Don't fumble it."

Ludwigsstrasse 17 was a four-story apartment house. The building had received a direct hit, and the entire corner had collapsed, leaving a huge wedge-shaped gash that made a mockery of the sign painted in white on the still standing part of the wall: LUFTSCHUTZ—AIR RAID SHELTER. The floors from the exposed rooms above hung precariously, drooping over the edges. In the rubble below, pointing in every direction but straight up, Corps signposts had already sprouted like toadstools on a rotten log: ICEBERG FWD . . . IPW 79 . . . 820 MP CO . . . 461 MED COLL CO . . . 676 EGR L EQUIP CO . . . 93 SIGNAL BN . . . 2 BAN 101 INF . . . 17 ARMD GP (CADC) . . . and the inevitable ROCKSPRINGS, TEXAS, 5729 MILES.

The building had caught fire and was gutted. Black soot fingers pointed accusingly upward from each empty window socket.

It was the place where the wife and sister of Gestapo Colonel Wolfgang Steinmetz were supposed to meet him. The time: 24 April at 1200 hours, a time selected by the colonel to avoid any possible curfew imposed on the townspeople.

Tom had requested a detail of eight MP's and one MP noncom for the stakeout. He wanted to take no chances. Steinmetz could not be permitted to give them the slip.

He had gone over his plan of action with the men carefully. He had determined a spot for each man, out of sight, covering the entire area. Once inside the building, Steinmetz would not escape.

He himself would keep the main entrance on Ludwigsstrasse under observation. The noncom, Sergeant David Rosenfeld, would be around the corner keeping an eye on the side entrance and the side street.

It was 1000 hours. Two hours before H-hour. They were in place. They were ready. Waiting . . .

Sergeant Rosenfeld was holed up behind a shattered basement window in the house across the street from the target building. He had a clear view of the street and the side entrance to Ludwigsstrasse 17. He felt keyed up. He touched the sergeant's stripes on his sleeve. Only yesterday he'd sewn them on! And already today he was in charge of eight men and an important mission. He, David Rosenfeld himself—in person! Sergeant David Rosenfeld, commanding! Well . . . after that CIC guy, of course.

He'd show them. He wanted desperately to carry out his first real command job without a hitch. Right down the old groove, all the way. He would, too. He shifted the walkie-talkie lying on the sill next to him. He'd checked in with the CIC agent minutes before. He knew his instructions: Report anything out of the ordinary—but stay off the button unless there is something to report. Clear enough.

He looked up and down the street. There was some civilian traffic, all on foot. Mostly women and elderly men, an occasional kid or wounded ex-Wehrmacht soldier in his stripped uniform. No one paid any attention to the gutted corner building.

He glanced at his watch. 1012 hours. He had a long wait. . . . He shifted again. He positioned himself so that he had optimum sight lines down the side street, to his left. He even thought "optimum sight lines." He liked the word "optimum." It sounded so . . . official. Important.

He had considered it carefully. That was the direction from which the suspect would be most likely to show. Anyone coming from the other direction would have passed the CIC agent. If it was the suspect, he'd probably have been spotted.

He mentally went over the description of the German officer once more: six feet one inch tall. A hundred and eighty pounds. Blond hair. Blue eyes. Thirty-nine years old. And how many Krauts did that description fit? he thought wryly. Well, anyway, it eliminated three-foot dwarfs with triangular heads.

He settled down to wait. . . . It was 1109 hours. Sergeant Rosenfeld yawned. Gawd, being on stakeout was boring. He looked at his walkie-talkie. There hadn't been a peep out of the damned thing. And he hadn't used it. He peered down the street.

There were only a few Germans abroad. Half a dozen women hurrying along, heads down, carrying cloth bags; an old man making his way toward Ludwigsstrasse; and way in the distance he could make out someone pushing an old baby carriage. A man. He seemed to be wearing a woolen cap, and a Wehrmacht greatcoat flapped around his ankles. He was working his way slowly down the street, occasionally stopping to pick up something, to examine the rubble and debris lining the street and to peer into old boxes and crates and piles of trash.

Rosenfeld knew what he was searching for. Anything of use. Anything salvable. Anything to eat. And that rare treasure, a discarded GI cigarette butt. In that ascending order of importance.

He was not the only one. The war had made scavengers of all.

The man with the rickety baby carriage was getting closer. He was tall. Six feet one inch? It was impossible to tell the color of his hair, but he had a dirty blond beard stubble. So . . . who didn't? Age? Impossible to say.

Could be thirty-nine. Or forty-nine. The man looked tired and worn. He limped slightly.

Sergeant Rosenfeld watched him suspiciously. Should he report him?

The German stopped almost directly opposite Rosenfeld. He hobbled to the curb and laboriously bent down to pick up something. A butt? Probably. He seemed to be looking for a match in the pockets of his ragged greatcoat. He came up empty handed.

Rosenfeld had a sudden urge to throw him a book of matches. He grinned. A great way to lose those stripes!

The German rummaged around and fished out an old tin box from a burlap bag he carried on a strap over his shoulder. Carefully he placed the butt in it. He put his hands over the small of his back and stretched painfully. Then he started off down the street again. His limp seemed more pronounced. He stopped. He looked pathetically defeated. Dejected. He pushed his baby carriage close to the wall and awkwardly eased himself down to sit on the stone step of the ruined side entrance to Ludwigsstrasse 17. He placed his face in his grimy hands, leaned his elbows on his knees and rested.

Sergeant Rosenfeld watched him tensely. He picked up the walkie-talkie. He'd better report the old man. His finger was on the button. He would speak in a low voice. He hesitated. So . . . what was to report?

An old Kraut scavenger taking a break? So . . . the CIC agent would come running over to take a look. Commotion. Just as the real suspect turned up! Great! He'd really have fucked things up then.

Okay. He'd wait. See what the old man was up to. Likely as not he'd be on his way soon. He put down the walkie-talkie.

But the agent had said *anything* out of the ordinary. Maybe he *should* report the old man. He could always say he didn't think he was of any importance. Leave it up to the CIC agent. He tensed.

Across the street the German raised his head and peered narrow-eyed at the sun beating down on him. He slowly moved into the shade of the doorway—all but lost in the shadows.

Okay, Buster, Rosenfeld thought, that does it. He was about to pick up the walkie-talkie again when he saw the other man. He was coming down the street. He wore boots. Military boots. He had on some sort of uniform, stripped of all insignia. A gray peaked cap. On his right sleeve was an armband. It read, POSTAMT BAYREUTH.

The man carried a clipboard. He looked—and acted—"official." At each house he'd stop and make a notation. He was only three houses from Ludwigsstrasse 17. He fit the description of SS Colonel Wolfgang Steinmetz. No doubt about it.

Rosenfeld hardly dared breathe. It could be him! He didn't take his eyes off the man. One house away. Rosenfeld picked up the walkie-talkie. His hands were sweaty. This was it.

The man stopped at the side street entrance of the target house. He paid no attention to the resting forager in the doorway. He made a note on his clipboard and quickly strode down the street to Ludwigsstrasse, disappearing around the corner.

Rosenfeld was so disappointed he could taste it. Shit! he thought in disgust. He'd been so sure . . . He looked over toward the side entrance. The old baby carriage still hugged the wall; the man could just be made out sleeping in the shade of the doorway.

Should he report him? No. Hell, what kind of sergeant would he be if he couldn't handle a crippled old scavenger without hollering for help? He'd wait . . . and watch. . . .

It was 1231 hours when Sergeant Rosenfeld's walkie-talkie sputtered to life. Thirty-one minutes past H-hour.

It was the CIC agent. Jaeger. "Sergeant? Anything on your side?"

"No, sir. Nothing."

"We'll give it another thirty minutes."

"Okay, sir."

"Keep your eyes open. He could still show up."

"Right."

"Jaeger, out."

"Rosenfeld, out."

Half an hour later Sergeant Rosenfeld saw the CIC agent with two of his MP's come around the corner and walk toward him.

Well, that's that, he thought. Nothing but a wild-goose chase. He felt let down. Some big assignment! He stretched. He picked up his walkie-talkie and ducked out of his hiding place. He met Agent Jaeger just outside the basement entrance.

The officer glanced at him. "Nothing?"

"Nothing. Not a damned thing, sir." He gave a crooked grin. "Unless we're looking for a baby buggy and an old rag picker!"

"*What* rag picker?" Tom was at once alert.

Rosenfeld was startled at the instant change in the CIC officer. He had a quick pang of apprehension. He should have reported that fucking old fart! He should have . . . He grew sober. "Just an old bum, sir. Scavenging around. With an old baby buggy." He nodded across the street. "That one. Over there."

Tom looked quickly. "Where's the man?" he snapped.

"Asleep, sir. He's . . . sitting just inside the doorway." He strained to see into the shadows. The man was still there. Wasn't he?

Tom stared at the darkened doorway. He thought he could see a figure slumped against the wall. He felt the familiar chill of tenseness shudder down his back. He turned to Rosenfeld. His voice was low, intense. "How long has he been there?"

Rosenfeld was clammy with misgivings. God damn it all to hell, he cursed to himself, he'd gone and fucked up his first assignment. But good. He said quickly, "A couple of hours, sir." He thought fast. "I didn't want to roust him. It would've given the show away."

Tom looked at the frightened young soldier. No use chewing his ass now, he thought.

"Get to your men, Sergeant. Tell them to move in. *Now!*" He turned to the two MP's. "You two. Come with me!"

Rosenfeld took off down the street. Tom and the MP's ran to the doorway of Ludwigsstrasse 17.

Tom knew what he'd find before he was halfway across the street. What had appeared to be the figure of the old scavenger sitting hunched against the wall in the shadows was only a couple of scorched pieces of lumber, lent credence by the presence of the old baby carriage just outside.

The scavenger was gone.

They found him on the second floor of the building. In a room facing the rear courtyard. He was asleep.

When Tom, closely followed by the two MP's, burst into the room, his gun tightly locked against his abdomen and aimed at anything he would face, the startled man sat up in alarm and cowered against the cracked wall.

"Up!" Tom snapped. "On your feet!"

The man scrambled to obey. He looked bewildered and frightened.

"Hands on top of your head. Move!"

The man quickly clasped his hands on top of the old wool cap he wore. He stared at Tom.

"Search him," Tom ordered the MP's. "I'll cover you."

The soldiers began to shake down the dazed man. He stood stock still.

Sergeant Rosenfeld came into the room. He took in the scene in an instant. He felt enormously relieved. The old pisser had not got away! He quickly grew sober. It was no thanks to him. He turned to Tom. "I got a couple of men on each exit, sir."

Tom didn't take his eyes from the captive. "Very good, Sergeant," he said.

The soldiers had finished their search. One of them came over to Tom. "He's clean, sir." He handed the agent a small thin booklet. "Here are his papers."

Tom took the booklet. It was a *Soldbuch*—a Wehrmacht soldier's identification and paybook. He glanced at it. The man was supposed to be one Hans Moser, ex-Feldwebel in the Wehrmacht.

He had expected nothing else. A name means nothing. Papers can be forged. But not so easily a physical description: six feet one inch. Blond. Blue-eyed. A hundred and eighty pounds. Thirty-nine years old. It was the exact description of the prisoner. And of SS Colonel Wolfgang Steinmetz.

Tom stepped closer to the man. He watched him intently. "You are under arrest," he said firmly, "*Colonel Steinmetz!*"

There was absolutely no reaction from the captive except a bewildered stare. "I . . . I do not understand." The man looked confused, apprehensive. Was it apprehension caused by a situation he did not comprehend? Or the fear of discovery?

"You *are* SS Standartenführer Wolfgang Steinmetz, are you not?" Tom sounded exasperated. Impatient. "We *know* you are!"

The man shook his head. "Feldwebel Moser, Hans. One, four, oh, two . . ." he began intoning automatically. The hands clasped on his head shook slightly.

Tom watched him with a frown. He thought fast. He was convinced the man was lying. He was certain he was not what he pretended to be. A real scavenger would not have left the baby carriage with all his treasures in it unattended outside. And he had fielded his attempt to shock him into revealing himself beautifully. The man was good. Damned good. If he couldn't be broken fast—*now*, when he had been caught off guard—he'd *never* break. He had to play rough.

What was it Lee used to say? Never hit a man when he's down. Kick him. He took a deep breath. "It's no use, Colonel Steinmetz," he said with deceptive calm. "We *know* who you are. We know why you are here." He looked directly into the man's pale blue eyes. "I have a message for you. Written by your wife. . . . Before she died!"

The German's eyes briefly widened. The muscles in his jaws momentarily corded. That was all. It was enough.

Tom had known what he would see. That unmistakable "look" of perfect control abruptly jolted—and just as quickly regained.

For a moment the two men stood facing each other, eyes locked. Then the German slowly turned and walked to the window. In silence he stood staring into space.

Maria . . . It was over. So soon. He had given himself away. Like a novice he had given himself away. He knew the reaction he had been unable to check had not gone unnoticed by the American officer.

He had taken a calculated risk. And lost. Everything. When he became aware that the building was surrounded and he was being watched, he'd tried to brazen out his disguise. A decrepit old scavenger, sleeping off his fatigue in an empty house. Why not? There were countless thousands of them. But the odds had been stacked against him. He, too, was dead.

Without turning around, he finally asked, "My . . . son?" His voice was dark and low.

"With your sister. He's all right."

The German turned to face Tom. He was once again in control of himself. But something had burned out in his eyes. His gray face was slack. "My wife," he asked softly. "How did she die?"

Tom had a quick mental glimpse of the misshapen corpse obscenely dangling from the cell window bars.

"She . . . killed herself, Colonel. Rather than talk." He stopped. What was the use of telling the man the whole truth? What use were the gory details now?

Steinmetz seemed to stand a little straighter. A good woman, his wife. "You said a message?"

Tom nodded.

She had been right. She had known her husband would get her message. But she had not known that it would be delivered by him, her hated enemy.

"She asked you to . . . carry on," he said quietly.

Steinmetz looked away. "What will happen to me now?" It was a question of simple curiosity.

"You will be taken to Army Interrogation Center, Colonel, where they'll question you. We know you are on a special mission. They'll find out exactly *what* back there."

Steinmetz smiled, thin-lipped, with his mouth only. "I doubt it." He searched in vain for an insignia of rank on Tom's uniform. There was none. Only two officer's "US" emblems were visible on the American's collar. Curious. But the man was obviously an officer.

"I doubt that, Herr Offizier," he said, his voice oddly lifeless and flat. "I am only a very small cog in a very great machine. A great undertaking. Greater than you can ever imagine. An undertaking you will never know. That you cannot stop!"

An alarm suddenly shrieked in Tom's mind. He leaped at the German. "Grab him!" he shouted. *"Grab his jaw!"*

But he was too late.

Steinmetz bit down hard. In his mouth the false tooth containing the cyanide was crushed. For a split moment his eyes seemed to bulge from their restraining sockets, staring with desperate triumph at Tom. His face contorted in agony; his whole body was wracked by a violent convulsion, and he fell heavily to the floor. A savage spasm shot through him. His legs jerked once. Once again. He was dead. And with him the secret of his mission.

Tom stared at the body sprawled at his feet. He should have known. God damn it! He should have known!

He turned to Sergeant Rosenfeld. The young soldier looked stricken. You and me, buddy, Tom thought bitterly. We both fucked up. But at least your fuck-up was corrected. Mine can never be. . . . "Have Graves Registration pick him up," he said curtly.

"Yes, sir."

Without looking back, Tom started to walk from the room. Rosenfeld hesitated. Should he speak up? Or should he let well enough alone and keep his big damned mouth shut?

"Sir!" he said.

Tom turned to him. "What is it?"

Rosenfeld bent over a stack of debris lying in a corner of the room. He pulled an old burlap bag from under a pile of broken plaster. He held it out toward Tom. "This bag, sir." He swallowed. "The . . . the colonel, that is . . . the rag picker had one just like it. In the street. He doesn't now. Maybe . . . maybe this is it?"

Tom was at his side in two strides. He took the bag from him. He spilled the contents out onto the floor. Quickly he glanced at the odds and ends of junk. Nothing. He picked up a small tin box. He opened it. It contained half a dozen dirty cigarette butts. But under them was a piece of paper. Folded. He dumped the butts and pried the paper out. He unfolded it. He stared at it.

There was the official embossed Nazi emblem—the eagle, wings spread wide, holding the oak-leaf wreath with the swastika in its claws.

"*Führerhauptquartier,*" the date line read—"Führer Headquarters—*den* 7. April 1945." And printed underneath: "*Geheime Kommandosache*— Top Secret."

Two prominent black stamps had been affixed:

GEHEIM
[Secret]

CHEF-SACHE!
NUR DURCH OFFIZIER!
[Command Order!
Officer Courier Only!]

Tom read on:

Der Reichsleiter hat nachfolgenden Befehl an den Standartenführer Steinmetz, Wolfgang, gegeben . . .

The Reichsleiter has given SS Colonel Steinmetz, Wolfgang, the following order:

1. Col. Steinmetz is hereby relieved of all further Gestapo and/or

SS duties. The Colonel will from above date be responsible to the below signed only.

Heil Hitler!
Bormann

Tom reread the document. He felt a hell of a lot better. At least they didn't come away completely empty handed. Something big *was* up!

He glanced at the young sergeant. Not a total loss after all, he thought. He does have powers of observation. And he can use them. Good man— once he gets a little experience under his ammo belt. He felt quite benevolent toward the young noncom. It was easier to overlook his earlier fuck-up now that things were looking up.

He examined the document in his hand once more. "Why the hell didn't he burn the damned thing?" he thought aloud.

"He probably couldn't," Rosenfeld ventured.

"Couldn't?" Tom looked at him.

"When I saw him on the street, sir," Rosenfeld explained, "he was looking for a match to light one of his butts." He grinned. "He was fresh out!"

Tom nodded. He knew it. The guy is okay. Knows how to observe. How to put two and two together.

"For the want of a match . . . Eh, what, Richard?"

Rosenfeld looked puzzled. What the hell was that supposed to mean?

Tom read the document once more. At the bottom of it was a referral indicator: *"Betr: KOKON."* He stared at the letters: K-O-K-O-N.

What the hell did that mean? Had to be initials. Like NSDAP. Or CIC, for that matter. The letters meant nothing to him. He'd never run across them before—in that context. He had no idea what they could stand for.

Of course, they did form a word. A German word: *Kokon.* The word for "cocoon." It meant nothing.

C-O-C-O-O-N . . .

It was well past midnight, but Obersturmführer Rudolf Kessler could not sleep.

Even deep in the bowels of the earth the crashing thunder of the Russian artillery barrages sporadically pounding the city above could not be escaped. But that was not what kept Rudi awake.

It was KOKON.

He had glimpsed the word written on his *Personalbogen,* when Reichs-leiter Bormann had been studying it. He had read it upside down, as he had been trained to do. It had been automatic. He had wondered what it meant. Now he knew!

His mind was seething with the fantastic implications of the plans, the bold ingenuity of the momentous project he'd been made privy to.

His briefing was progressing slowly in the hectic atmosphere of the Führerbunker. Bormann was constantly in demand, and the Reichsleiter insisted on briefing Rudi personally. No detail could be wrong. No possibility overlooked.

There was a constant coming and going of some of the most important personalities in the Third Reich. Armament Minister Albert Speer had arrived—and left early that morning, looking grim and drawn. Top Wehrmacht and SS officers had departed to conduct relief operations from outside the beleaguered city.

Rudi did not much care for life in the bunker. There was an inescapable air of tension and strain. But not the stimulating tension born of excitement and challenge. It made him feel uneasy. The only person who had time to be pleasant and cheerful was Fräulein Eva Braun. He liked her.

He had also actually seen the Führer himself. Adolf Hitler. But he didn't like to think about it. He had been deeply shocked. The Führer had looked old. Gray and weakened. His eyes burning with a deep inner agony. He seemed a broken man. Rudi had been profoundly moved. His Führer. Slowly giving his very life for his people. Against overwhelming odds.

Even some of his own closest comrades apparently had betrayed him.

Rudi had overheard a conversation between Bormann's aide, Standartenführer Zander, and the secretary, Fräulein Krueger, that Reichsmarschall Göring was a traitor to his Führer and his country.

Bormann himself had spent much feverish time in trying to combat Göring's treachery, and he'd heard Zander telling Fräulein Krueger, when he emerged from a long meeting between Hitler and Bormann, that Göring was finished. Bormann "got him!" he'd said.

Rudi had been gratified. Traitors to the Führer and the Reich should be destroyed. Ruthlessly. No matter who they were.

He was lying on his bunk. Occasionally the bunker lights flickered, and he found himself listening for the steady hum of the power diesel engine among the many noises and sounds of the shelter.

It was obvious to him that it was only a matter of time—and not much time—before the Third Reich no longer could defend herself against the combined might of the rest of the world that had ganged up on her. It made *his* mission that much more vital, and he was anxious to complete his briefing and be on his way.

KOKON . . .

The more he thought of the nature of his mission, the more apt he found its code name. *Kokon*—the cocoon. That masterpiece of mimicry. The primordial, the simplest, the most effective and successful of all methods of protection. The source of a great, a wondrous change. The implications of the code name were mind-staggering. Martin Bormann himself had coined it. It was perfect.

3

"Dammit! Nobody's ever heard of that KOKON crap of yours, Tom. Drop it. Get back to work."

Major Lee sounded annoyed. He was. Corps CP had moved from Grofenwöhr to Schwarzenfeld at 0800 hours. They were supposed to be open for business at 1100. The CP had taken over a barrackslike housing development on the edge of town. Square, squat buildings, rows of wood-shuttered windows and gabled dormers set into peaked roofs. Major Lee found the quarters assigned to him completely inadequate. He always did. He found moving a colossal pain in the ass, and this time Corps had been in Grofenwöhr only two days—hardly enough time to get settled in for some serious work—when they were off again to the new quarters at Schwarzenfeld. The war was moving too damned fast.

Throughout the housing complex reigned that organized confusion that made it possible for the entire Corps HQ to move thirty miles from one town to another and become fully operational in less than three hours.

The room to be occupied by CIC looked a cluttered mess. Major Lee was standing in the middle of the disarray directing a minor army of GI's bringing boxes, crates, files and equipment to place in the cramped space where Lee prescribed.

Tom knew from past observation that order would miraculously uncoil from the chaos. Lee had a phenomenal memory of what was contained in his voluminous files and had definite ideas where everything was to be placed. It always turned out to be the most efficient solution. Tom was used to his CO's short-tempered irritation when in the process of exercising his gift.

"So nobody has run across KOKON before," he said. "I find that even more intriguing, Herb. Something new."

"Hell, Tom. Don't waste any more time on it. It's probably nothing but some local letter designation."

"Maybe. Maybe not"

He watched Lee check a file drawer and order the GI's to get it the hell out of his office and dump it on the IPW's where it belonged. Were they color blind, for Christ's sake? Couldn't they see the tags were wrong? Dammit, get on the ball!

He grabbed a large map tube from another soldier. "Give me that!" he barked. He plunked it down on his desk. The tube had a broad red stripe painted around it. It was known as "Herbie's Drawers."

Tom knew all about it. Contrary to popular belief, the tube did not contain a Confederate flag but a Nazi flag. It had been the personal standard of a German general—the first general captured and interrogated at Corps, an interrogation conducted by Lee himself. The flag had been in the general's staff car, and Lee had claimed it as his personal loot.

It was about two by three with twin points and a thick silver-cord fringe all around. On the red silk a huge iron cross had been embroidered in black and real silver thread, with a grim Teutonic eagle in the center holding a swastika. The workmanship was fantastic—equally impeccable on both sides of the flag. A black and silver swastika adorned each corner, and the heavy silver thread and brocade gave a hefty body to the whole damned thing. It was magnificent.

Lee carted it along in the specially marked map tube wherever Corps moved and tacked it up on the wall—in the john.

Tom persisted. "What about Prague?" he asked.

"Not a damned thing about Prague. Get out of here, will you? Go catch a spy or something!"

Tom ignored him. "It's the only lead I have, Herb. The fact that Steinmetz and his family were stationed in Prague prior to his KOKON assignment."

The major appeared not to be listening. He sent a GI scurrying for a more comfortable desk chair—". . . even if you have to liberate it from the AC of S!" he shouted after the man.

"You did ask the IPW's and the MP's to let you know if they got anybody fresh from Prague?" Tom persisted. "Herb? You did, didn't you?"

"Yes, yes, yes, dammit!" He bellowed at a couple of men appearing in the doorway lugging a field desk, "Blue tags, you idiots! *Blue* tags in here. Open your damned eyes!"

The men hastily disappeared. Lee turned to Tom. "I've got to be operational in twelve minutes," he said with exasperation. "The Twenty-sixth has just reached Straubing. Biggest town we've taken in some time. Crammed with regional Nazi offices. There's stiffened SS resistance and the damned Danube bridge is blown. It's a whole new ballgame. I need your damned KOKON like I need a fifteen-yard penalty!"

A GI came up to him. "Phones are in, sir. And operating."

"Okay."

"Well?" Tom asked.

Lee stopped short. He glared at Tom, his face grim. "Nothing," he said. "Drop it!"

"I'm staying on the case, Herb." Tom sounded determined.

"*What* case?" Lee's voice was a minor roar. "There *is* no fucking case! Get it through your thick skull, Tom. *You got no case!* Forget that KOKON shit!"

The field telephone rang shrilly.

Lee grabbed it. "CIC. Major Lee," he barked angrily into the mouthpiece. He listened for a brief moment.

"No, dammit!" he exploded. "I don't want your fucking PW! Give him to the IPW's. Or throw him back! I don't give— What?"

He listened. He frowned. He scribbled a note on a scrap of paper. "Hold him!" he snapped. He banged the receiver down.

He looked sideways at Tom. "You are the luckiest SOB I know," he said sourly. "Where's your team located now? Grafenau, isn't it?"

Tom nodded. "Right."

Major Lee handed him the scrap of paper. "Switch of signals. The MP's are holding a PW. They claim he's fresh from Prague."

Tom snatched the paper. "Thanks, Herb." He turned to leave.

Lee stopped him. He was suddenly serious. And quiet. "Look, Tom," he said soberly. "I mean it. I hope you don't get dumped for a loss. I hope it pans out. But if it doesn't, I want you to drop that KOKON thing. Understood?"

Tom nodded. "Understood, Herb." He grinned. "You know," he observed, "I've got another hunch! I think it *will* pan out!" He hurried from the room.

Grafenau was nestled cozily in a shallow valley at the foot of Frauenberg in the Bayrischer Wald—the Bavarian Forest. The cupola-topped church-tower and the step-parapeted tower of the *Rathaus*—the town hall—on Oberer Stadtplatz vied for dominance over the skyline of the idyllic little postcard town. Grafenau had been taken only the day before after token resistance and scattered *Panzerfaust* fire.

Tom's CIC team had taken over a farmhouse on the outskirts of town, a rough-walled two-story building with a wooden balcony running the length of the house on the outside. A huge pile of unevenly cut logs was stacked directly in front of the main door, providing easy access to the firewood—as well as good protection from stray bullets.

The MP's had set up shop in a house on the steep main street of the town itself, close to the centrally located *Rathaus*.

When Tom arrived at the house that served as MP Headquarters it was already past 1400 hours. He was at once directed to the room used as an office by the Detachment CO, Captain Frank Williams. The captain himself was examining the PW, he was told.

Tom was about to knock on the door—when he froze. From the room beyond came the sound of a series of muffled thuds. A voice, unmistakably American, could be heard: "Talk, you fucking Kraut! *Talk! Talk! Talk!*" Each "talk" was accompanied by a dull thud.

He flung the door open. The sight before him etched itself indelibly on his mind in a split instant. In the room stood a young MP captain. In his right hand he had a Nazi dagger. A *Reichsarbeitsdienst*—Reich Labor Service—dagger. Holding it by its bone-handled eagle-head grip, he used its sharp point to prod at a large barely healed wound high on the right shoulder blade of a man standing before him. Stripped to the waist, his hands bound behind him, the man stood facing the wall, toes touching the floorboard. The blood from his opened wound ran steadily in small tortuous rivulets down his sweat-soaked back. His spasmodic breath was an unbroken chain of low moans.

Over and over again the MP officer snarled at the prisoner: "Talk! Talk!

Talk!" And with each word, using his free left hand, he rammed the man's forehead into the wall. Hard.

Tom felt cold rage well up in him. He did nothing to repress it. In two strides he was in back of the MP officer. Roughly he grabbed him by the shoulder and whirled him around. With the hard edge of his hand he dealt a numbing blow across the man's forearm. The ornate dagger clattered to the floor. Savagely he kicked it aside. He seized the officer's jacket with both hands and hurled him with all his might across the room.

The officer rammed backwards into a chair, tumbled over it and slammed against the wall with bone-rattling force. For a moment he slumped there, dazed, staring at the hard-breathing Tom towering over him.

"You fucking bastard!" Tom said in hoarsely whispered fury.

Slowly the MP officer climbed to his feet. "What the hell's the matter with you?" he asked shakily. "You crazy or something?"

Tom stood silent, trying to calm himself. Williams stared at him. His eyes narrowed unpleasantly. "You're in trouble, soldier," he threatened darkly. "One fucking heap of trouble. Striking an officer!" He glared at Tom, hatefully. "I'll see they throw the damned book away at your court-martial!"

"Be my guest."

"You bet your sweet ass!" Williams glanced at the PW at the wall. He had a quick surge of black hatred for the enemy soldier—witness to his humiliation. He pushed it aside. For now. He studied Tom. He was rapidly getting hold of himself. "What the hell are you trying to prove?" he demanded.

"What the hell are *you* doing? Torturing a PW!" Tom countered, his voice savage. He turned toward the prisoner at the wall. His eyes widened in revulsion and shock.

The PW had turned around. He was leaning weakly against the wall. His forehead was a mass of bleeding holes where a nail, placed in the wall at the exactly calculated height, had jabbed into his brow every time Williams slammed his head against the wall. His deathly pale face was streaked with runnels of blood oozing from the wounds. His hands tied behind him, he was trying to blink the blood from his eyes. One spot on his forehead was so gutted with holes that a flap of skin had torn loose and hung limply down over one eye.

The man looked straight at Tom. His face was a mask of pure pain. The red-streaked mask of a clown made up in hell.

"You—fucking—bastard!" Tom's voice broke. He stared at Williams, his eyes not believing what they had seen.

"*Why?*" Williams strode to the table. He snatched up a *Soldbuch* lying on it. He thrust it at Tom. "Look, you dumb asshole!" He stabbed a finger at a word in the booklet. "*Totenkopf!* Read it! Right there. *Totenkopf!* That damned well means death's-head!"

He banged the *Soldbuch* down on the table. "And you and me both know what those *Totenkopf* bastards are. Concentration camp guards, that's what! Murdering, sadistic swine every one of them!" He nodded malevolently toward the trembling PW. "Don't go bleeding your fucking heart for *that* Kraut shithead. This is a picnic to what *he's* used to dishing out!"

Grim-faced, Tom picked up the *Soldbuch.* He glanced at it. He gave the MP officer a withering look. "When the hell did *you* get over here, you miserable son of a bitch? Yesterday?" His voice was dangerously low. "Didn't you *read* this? The man belongs to the First SS Totenkopf Infantry Regiment, SS Panzer Grenadier Division Totenkopf!"

"That's what I damned well said. *Totenkopf!* You think you Intelligence prima donnas are so damned smart. It doesn't take a lot of brains to figure out what kind of prick this Kraut is. He's got it coming. In spades!"

"Brains!" Tom glared at the MP officer. "You've got crap where your brains ought to be!"

His face mirrored the virulent contempt and fury that raged in him. "This man is an *Infantry man,* dammit! He belongs to a Waffen SS Division *named Totenkopf!* He's a Pole. A damned lot of conscripted foreign-born troops were put in the Waffen SS by the Nazis. This man does *not* belong to the SS *Totenkopf VERBAND,* you blasted idiot. He's a soldier, *not* a concentration camp guard!"

Williams glared back at Tom. "He's a fucking Kraut prick!" he said.

"You have no right—"

"This is *my* office, dammit!" Williams interrupted him. "*My office!* You hear? Here the customer is always wrong. And *I* do what I goddamned well please!"

"You're no better than the worst of them." Tom's abysmal contempt was explicit.

Williams reddened. "Listen you—" He glared at the two US officer's emblems on Tom's collar tabs. "What the hell *is* your rank?"

"My rank is none of your goddamned business, *Captain!*" Tom growled in cold fury. "You know damned well it's confidential. But I got news for you, *Captain.*" He made the word sound like a curse. "I'm sure as hell not outranked *now!*"

Williams glared at him with murderous hate. Tom stood his ground.

"Get out of here, *Captain!*" He felt himself tremble with anger and disgust. "Get out, and leave me alone with this man." He took a step toward the MP officer. "And I hope to God you do prefer charges! I'd like nothing better than to see this whole stinking, rotten affair come out in a general court-martial!"

His face a pinched mask of barely contained fury, Williams turned on his heel. Tom glanced at the blood-tipped *Reichsarbeitsdienst* dagger lying on the floor. The inscription on its gleaming blade flashed into his mind: "*Arbeit Adelt*—Work Makes Noble."

Not always, he thought bitterly. Not always. . . . He nodded toward the dagger. "And take your filthy plaything with you," he said contemptuously.

Williams stopped. "Shove it!" He spat out the expletive vehemently. He gave the dagger on the floor a violent kick. It flew across the floor to bury its point in the floorboard with a sharp thud. Williams stalked to the door. He slammed it as hard as he could behind him.

Tom untied the prisoner's hands. He gave him his handkerchief to stem the flow of blood from his forehead. The man seemed in a daze. Tom knew it would be impossible to interrogate him on the spot. He was in no condition to respond coherently. Later.

But he had to verify that the man actually did come from the Prague area. He had to know. Once more he glanced at the prisoner's *Soldbuch*. There was no indication of his last station. He turned to the shaken man. "Your name is Michal Swiderski?" he asked. His voice was calm and kind.

The man started to nod. He grimaced with pain. He spoke. "*Ja.*" His voice was weak with agony.

"You are Polish?"

"*Ja.*"

"You served in the Waffen SS. As a corporal. Correct?"

"*Ja.*"

"Where was your last assignment?"

"Prague."

"What were your duties?"

The prisoner licked his gray lips. "Guard . . . duty," he whispered.

"Guarding what?"

"Headquarters." The man swayed on his feet.

Tom grabbed his arm. "Sit down," he said. He righted the chair over-turned by Williams. The prisoner sank into it.

Tom gave him time. He looked at him intently. "Headquarters?" he prompted.

"*Ja,*" the prisoner murmured. His face behind the scarlet streaks of blood was gray. He was going into shock. Tom held his breath, tensely waiting for the prisoner to continue.

"We were . . . guarding . . . Headquarters . . . of the Luftwaffe High Command. In . . . Prague." The man closed his eyes. He looked on the verge of passing out.

Tom expelled his pent-up breath in a rush. It tasted sour. A reminder of MP Captain Williams, he thought caustically. He felt a rising excitement. The PW might—just might—be the link he was searching for. KOKON *could* be connected with the German Air Force High Command.

He looked at the prisoner. The man needed attention. Badly. Just one more question. "What happened to the Luftwaffe staff officers?" he asked.

"They . . . fled Prague. . . . We . . . we were told . . . to get to the *Ami* lines . . . and surrender."

Tom's mind raced. He knew of no high ranking Luftwaffe officers cap-tured in the sector. Where were they? Still in the area? Why? What connection—if any—did they have with KOKON? A host of questions urgently presented themselves.

But the PW was beyond giving any further information. Until later.

Tom took the man by the arm. He helped him to his feet. "Come on," he said quietly. "You need to be looked after. I'll see to it."

For a brief moment the two men's eyes met. Then the prisoner lowered his head. His eyes had been filled with fear.

Captain Williams was waiting outside the door with an MP corporal when Tom emerged with the trembling PW. "This man needs medical care," he snapped curtly. "And he needs it now!"

He turned the PW over to the corporal and faced Williams. "I want him taken to the aid station. I'll follow." Without waiting for acknowledgment he turned on his heel and walked away.

Tom was following the MP jeep as it sped down the country road. The jeep ahead of him was driven by the MP corporal. The PW was slumped in the seat next to him. Captain Williams sat uncomfortably rigid in the back seat, a Tommy gun across his knees, guarding the prisoner.

Tom was impatient. Angry. That SOB Williams had screwed up everything. If it hadn't been for his degenerate conduct with the PW, the man would already be giving Tom all the information he so avidly wanted. He had a gut feeling that he was onto something. Something important. And the PW in the speeding jeep ahead was the key.

The lead jeep suddenly slowed down for a half-filled shell crater on the road. Tom put his foot on the brake. Suddenly he saw the PW lurch from the slowing jeep. He fell to the ground and rolled head over heels in an unchecked heap, arms and legs flailing. Miraculously he got to his feet. At once he began to run. Run from the road. From the jeep. From the MP's. Run into a newly plowed field. Stumbling across the deep, fresh furrows . . .

And he saw Williams stand up in his jeep, now stopped dead. He saw him raise his Tommy gun.

His anguished cry of protest was drowned by the staccato thunder of a prolonged burst of fire from the submachine gun.

In the field the PW fell—dead before his tortured body hit the soft dark earth.

Tom brought his jeep to a screeching halt up against the MP vehicle. He leaped from his seat and ran to Williams. His heart raced with rage, and frustration, and bleak impotence. He stopped—barely keeping himself from tearing the MP officer from his deadly perch and beating him, beating him, beating him with his bare fists.

Williams wore a smirk of self-satisfaction on his lips. He turned to Tom. "I suppose *now* you'll tell me it is not my duty to shoot an escaping prisoner!" He gave a short unpleasant laugh. "Try it!" He looked out toward the still body among the plow furrows. "So much for that Kraut bastard," he observed with cold finality. He turned to the corporal. "Go pick him up," he ordered. "We'll take him back to GR."

Slowly, without a word, Tom turned away and walked to his jeep. It was over. He dismissed Williams from his thoughts. The man was not worth the bother. He had done all the damage he could. Tom was certain the officer had not killed the prisoner because of his ineffectual escape attempt. He could so easily have been recaptured. No. That was not the reason. But the man had witnessed his tormentor's humiliation. His disgrace. He could not be allowed to live. That was the reason.

Whatever it was, the result was inescapable. His only possible link to KOKON was a dead one.

How ironic, he thought bleakly. When for once his bad-guy/good-guy routine was on the level, it had not been believed.

Major Lee was finally right. He had no case.

It was 1620 hours when Tom walked into the big central room used by his team. Larry was making coffee on the big black stove. He took one look at Tom. "You look like you could finish this whole pot in one gulp and then some," he commented dryly. "It'll be ready in a couple of minutes.

Tom grunted. He went straight to the Uninvestigated Case Report File and began flipping through the cards. He knew he had to put KOKON out of his mind before it became a goddamned fixation. The only way he knew of doing that was to get involved in another case at once. Okay. So that's exactly what he'd do. KOKON was out. He'd made his deal with Lee. He'd stick to it.

If only he could rid himself of that nagging feeling of missing something. Something big.

Larry brought him a canteen cup filled with steaming jet-black coffee. "Here," he said. "Coat your tonsils with this. It'll put hair on 'em."

"Thanks."

Tom pulled a case card. "Anything new and fascinating?" he asked. "I'm looking for a good and juicy case." He read the card. "What's this 'shot fired, vicinity Oberwiese'? Looks like your scrawl."

Larry took the card. "Yeah. Came in a few hours ago. Some AAA captain"—he squinted at the writing—"Slam . . . Sloan. Captain Robert

Sloan. He reported a shot fired in the woods in the mountains. Near some godforsaken place called Oberwiese. Some kind of mountain pasture. He seemed to think it was enormously significant. Why, beats me."

He consulted the card once again, not without difficulty. "His outfit is the 459th Anti-Aircraft Artillery Battalion. They're stationed just outside Regen."

"Where the hell is Regen?"

"Little burg north of here. About twelve miles. It was supposed to be secure two days ago. Maybe that's why Sloan's got a case of itchy crotch. It's on the main highway from Prague." He grinned. "You can't miss it!"

Tom looked up quickly. "Okay," he said. "I'll take it."

Larry shrugged. "No one's going to fight you for it. It's no blue-ribbon ballbuster of a case, if you ask me."

"I'll run up first thing tomorrow morning."

"Who do you want to team up with?"

"You."

"Thanks a bunch!" Larry returned to the stove.

Tom looked at the card. He began to decipher Larry's scrawl. Regen. First town in Germany on the main highway from Prague.

Okay, he'd stick to his deal with Major Lee. He'd take on a new case. Lay off KOKON. The Regen case seemed as good a bet as any. He fingered the card in his hand. He wasn't really hedging that bet—just because Regen was on the Prague highway.

Larry turned to him from his chores at the stove. "Hey! What happened to that hot KOKON deal of yours? Anything?"

Tom shrugged. "Kaput," he said.

4

The black and white sign next to the open farmyard gate read, HQ MAESTRO CHARLIE—code name for the 459th AAA AW Battalion. The farm, a drab group of gray squat houses and barns placed squarely around the spacious cobblestoned farmyard, was located on the outskirts of Regen.

The town of Regen was a scant ten miles from the mountainous Czech border. Lying in the valley of the Regen River at the crossing of two main highways, one running east-west, the other north-south, it was of greater importance than its size would indicate.

It had suffered a severe shelling by tanks of Combat Command B, 11th Armored Division, on April 24th, and the town had been entered and secured by that unit and by the 21st Armored Infantry Battalion the same day.

It was 0715 hours when Tom and Larry parked their jeep in the farmyard, which was cluttered with a conglomeration of farm machinery and military equipment.

Captain Sloan, an intense, humorless young officer not given to wasting time with polite chatter, came straight to the point.

He had reported the single shot, heard coming from the woods near Oberwiese, for reasons he proceeded to detail in a clipped, methodical manner.

One, no American troops were in the area at the time in question. Two, as per Army directives all firearms and other weapons had been confiscated from the German population at the time the area had been secured. Consequently there should have been no shot fired in the vicinity.

Since a shot *was* in fact fired, and not by a GI, certain questions became paramount. One, who fired it? Two, how did the subject firing the gun obtain it? Three, for what purpose was the shot fired?

Two prime possibilities suggested themselves. One, a local inhabitant had concealed and retained a firearm against the specific orders of the occupation forces. If so, why? Two, a subject or subjects unknown had infiltrated the area since it had been rendered secure. If that was the case, who were they? Why were they armed? What was the purpose of the shot?

These questions obviously all had to have answers—and the answers had to be found.

Examined in this light, the seemingly inconsequential matter of a single unaccounted-for shot having been fired in the forest took on more significance, and he, Captain Robert Sloan, felt it incumbent upon him to report the incident at once to the CIC for proper investigation.

Tom and Larry exchanged glances.

The investigation would be carried out. Immediately.

Oberwiese was not on the map.

The two CIC agents had to get directions from the local *Bürgermeisteramt*—the mayor's office. The *Bürgermeister* himself, who had been allowed to remain in office—at least temporarily—nearly fell over himself in his efforts to be helpful.

Oberwiese was the residence of the *Staatsforstmeister*—the state forester and game warden—in charge of the state hunting preserve that comprised the mountain forest area between Regen and the border. The *Forstmeister* and his family lived at Oberwiese, but no one in Regen had been in contact with the man, or anyone else from the place, for several weeks.

A dirt road—little more than a wagon trail—snaked up into the mountains.

Larry was disgusted. The whole thing would turn out to be no more exciting than the tit on a ten-year-old. The man at Oberwiese was a gamekeeper. A hunter. He was used to shooting game. Very likely he needed it to feed his family. He probably kept back a gun for just that purpose, when his weapons were confiscated by the U.S. troops. As simple as that. And as boring. But they were this far. Might as well check the place out.

The road suddenly forked. An old weatherbeaten signpost leaned on one leg. OBER IESE, 2 KM, it announced. A bullet hole had neatly obliterated the W.

The shot? The famous single Oberwiese *shot?*

Tom stopped the jeep, and Larry jumped out to examine the signpost. He shrugged wearily. The hole was obviously months—or years—old.

Oberwiese turned out to consist of two main buildings—a house and a barn—and several more or less ramshackle coops and sheds.

The forester, his wife and four children—two girls and two boys between the ages of nine and thirteen—lived in the main house. But obviously the barn was occupied as well.

Larry stayed with the jeep, keeping an eye on the barn. Tom went to the house.

The forester, Hans Kampers, was a round-faced man with pale blond hair bristling the top of his head, shaved high above the ears, and a small toothbrush mustache. He was smiling from ear to ear, showing bad teeth stained by tobacco. He was lying in a huge bed, nearly hidden by the soft mound of a gigantic featherbed. His entire family was gathered apprehensively around the desperately grinning forester, who all but sat at attention and saluted when Tom strode into the stuffy, overheated room.

The man greeted Tom with effusive deference. It was an honor for his humble home to be visited by an American officer. He would, of course, at once get up to greet him as befitted his rank and importance if it should be required, but he had regrettably been bedridden with a broken leg for over a week.

He tried to throw off the featherbedding to let his leg bear witness to his words, but it became a losing battle. He snapped his fingers, and at once his two boys jumped to haul back the voluminous bed covering and show off their father's bandaged leg.

"It has kept me here," the man said plaintively, "in bed. A man like me, who is always up and out in my *Revier* before dawn. Here. On my back. For many days now."

Tom believed him. The room stank of his confinement. "You are the *Forstmeister?*" he asked quickly. He was anxious to get his stay over with and get into the fresh air again.

"*Jawohl*, Herr Offizier!" the man said proudly. "Staatsforstmeister Hans Kampers, Staatsjagdrevier Regen, at your service!"

"You own a gun?"

"Three, Herr Offizier." The man beamed broadly. "Two shotguns. A Kettner, double barrel, and a Merkel, over and under. That one is wonderfully carved. Also a rifle. A Mauser." He suddenly looked resentful. "It is, however, an ill luck that has befallen me, Herr Offizier. My guns have all been taken from me."

"By whom?"

"By the *Amis*—" He caught himself hastily. "By the Americans. I have here a receipt signed by the American sergeant. Also with his rank. He leaned over toward a nightstand next to the bed, trying to wrestle a drawer open. It was stuck. He could not get the right leverage. Again he snapped his fingers, and again his boys jumped to assist. The older one handed his father a piece of paper.

The forester in turn handed it to Tom with a ceremonious flourish. "Here it is."

It was the receipt for three guns, property of a state official. It was signed by a sergeant from the 21st Armored Infantry, two days before.

Tom gave it back to the *Forstmeister*. "Any other guns?" he asked.

The German looked shocked. "Other guns?" His round face became indignant. "Of course not, Herr Offizier. I would have given them to the soldiers. As they commanded me to do." The smile returned to his moon-shaped face. "It is only temporarily. It was explained to me. I am a state official! I shall have my guns returned to me. Any day."

"Who lives across the street?" Tom asked.

The *Forstmeister* looked surprised. Then he smiled broadly. "In the barn! *Ach ja!*" He shook his head. "They are refugees. Civilians. They have no place else to go. I let them stay."

"Who are they?"

The man frowned in concentration. "There is a woman. The widow of a Wehrmacht officer. And her son. There is Fräulein Ilse, and there are two ex-Wehrmacht soldiers—Gefreiter Beigel and Unteroffizier Joachim." Automatically he counted on his fingers. "Five. Five of them."

Two women, a child . . . and a discharged army corporal and sergeant.

"How long have they been here?"

The German shrugged. "Many days. They came just after I broke my leg." He made an elaborate gesture of spitting on the floor. "Pfui! *Zum*

Teufel damit!—The devil take it!" He grinned. "They are harmless!"

"Who fired the shot here yesterday?" Tom asked suddenly.

The man started. "We did not," he said emphatically. Instinctively his whole family drew closer around him, their frightened faces all turned toward Tom.

"We heard it, naturally. One shot. I even said, Who could that be shooting in the forest? In my *Revier?*" He looked at his wife. "Did I not say that, *Schatzi?*"

The woman nodded solemnly.

"Yes, I did," the forester said firmly. He looked at Tom.

The matter was settled.

The group of refugees from the barn stood silently, resentfully before the two CIC agents, their sullen faces trying not to betray their hostility too overtly.

Tom knew it was there. He knew why. He and Larry represented the enemy—an enemy responsible for the discomfort they suffered, for their loss and the uncertainty of their future. That had to be the worst of all. The uncertainty.

He had examined their papers—all as acceptable as any in the disrupted world of German bureaucracy. The *Soldbuchs* of the two soldiers seemed in order; the *Kennkartes* of the civilians appeared genuine. There was no reason to suspect that they were not exactly what they claimed to be: people, uprooted and flung about by the whirlwind of war. No reason at all.

Tom contemplated each one of them in turn.

Gefreiter Beigel, Anton, forty-seven. A large heavyset man with a ramrod posture and a coarse-featured, cold face. Unteroffizier Joachim, Dieter, forty-three. A scholarly-looking man, slightly stooped. Perhaps a former schoolteacher. With steel-rimmed glasses, and on the verge of baldness.

Both ex-soldiers still wore their field-gray Wehrmacht noncom uniforms, with all insignia removed. They still had on their heavy hobnailed military boots.

His uniform, Tom thought, the last thing a defeated soldier gives up. Only after his weapon—and before his life.

Had Tom been confronted with two German noncoms of the relatively advanced ages of Beigel and Joachim when he first became operational as an investigator, he would have been at once suspicious. A forty-seven-year-old corporal would have been, to say the least, unusual.

But not now. Not at this stage of the war. Men of even the slightest military use were now either drafted into the regular army or forced to serve in the Volkssturm, where it was not uncommon to find men in their seventies fighting side by side with boys of twelve. A forty-seven-year-old Wehrmacht corporal no longer aroused his suspicion.

The older woman, the officer's widow, was matronly and stiff, her pinched face grim. Her thirteen-year-old son stared relentlessly at the two enemy officers, his expression vacillating between fear and hatred.

Fräulein Ilse, Ilse Neumann, was a pleasantly plump blond girl in her twenties, with a soft, sweet face. She had served as a Wehrmachthelferinn —a German WAC—with a communications outfit. She stood close to Gefreiter Beigel, as if seeking protection in his manly stature.

Tom and Larry had screened the five refugees. Their stories had been plausible. Just vague enough to make them sound legitimate. The investigation at Oberwiese had proven unproductive. The mysterious "Oberwiese Shot" remained mysterious.

Captain Robert Sloan, 459th AAA, was not the slightest bit perturbed that the investigation in Oberwiese had produced no concrete results. He had made his report. As a consequence an inquiry had been made. That was the important thing. The incident was closed.

But Tom was dissatisfied. He hated the idea of an investigation that turned up absolutely nothing. Although he did concede to himself that this was actually never the case. Every investigation produced *some* information, however obscure. It was a word for which he had great respect: information. Information invariably led to more information, and information was the lifeblood of any battle, be it a battle of guns or of wits. He knew that somewhere along the line in his questioning of the Oberwiese crew he had gained some information of value.

But what? He did not know. It made him uncomfortable. He decided to try to salvage some of what otherwise would have to be logged as unproductive time. There was one way of doing it.

Every outfit billeted close to the front maintained a temporary civilian detention enclosure. A sort of guarded catch-all compound to hold anyone not able to identify himself properly, or who for one reason or another had made himself suspicious. Here such detainees awaited screening and disposition.

The 459th AAA was no exception. The unit's detention enclosure was located at a farm a short distance away. Periodically CIC checked these detention cages in search of mandatory arrestees, war criminals and other subjects dangerous to the security of the U.S. armed forces. The two CIC agents would inspect the battalion's enclosure. Might as well. They were there. At least their trip would not have been a total waste.

Tom had worked out a special procedure for such inspections. Usually among the detainees in custody in any given compound there would be a discharged Wehrmacht Hauptfeldwebel—a master sergeant—with the gruff voice and manner of a real DI. Tom would single the man out and give him specific instructions, and the German noncom would take over while Tom merely watched. It was surprising how the Krauts jumped to the orders of one of their own!

Bellowing his orders, the sergeant would line up the men. Scowling and cursing, he would dress the motley crew for inspection. He would inform them that a war criminal wanted by the Americans was known to be hiding in their ranks and that the American Intelligence officer had come to arrest him. He would then smartly turn the inspection over to Tom.

As Tom slowly walked along the rows of men standing stiffly at attention, observing them closely, he could literally pick out every one with something to conceal. These men would be given thorough interrogations. Tom had apprehended numerous subjects using his Wehrmacht sergeant.

There were about a hundred detainees in the 459th AAA enclosure. Tom and Larry selected their sergeant—a big ruddy-faced bruiser of a man with his right hand missing and a voice that seemed to originate in his groin and rumble up through his barrel chest.

The sergeant lined up the men, and Tom and Larry walked along the rows inspecting the detainees mustered in the enclosure. A cold drizzle began to fall. Some of the detainees huddled against the chilly wetness. They would be the civilians who had no military training, Tom thought idly. Others stood at attention, oblivious to the weather. The ex-soldiers. A lot could be learned from very little. All you had to do was open your eyes.

As Tom walked along the line of men he looked briefly, searchingly into the face of each one of them. The trick was to appear as if you knew some deep, dark secret—pointing an accusing finger at just that one man. Tom had the look down pat. In his wake he left a string of captives, each worrying why *he* had been singled out for a penetrating all-knowing stare. Larry, following behind, would note each man whose concern seemed greater than normal. It was a crazy system. But it worked.

The detainees of the 459th AAA cage were true to form. All ages and all sizes; well dressed and in rags; well groomed and imbedded with the grime of defeat and retreat; ex-soldiers in stripped uniforms and civilians in every conceivable kind of clothing—an embroidered Bavarian jacket, a fur-collared ankle-length overcoat, a near-new tan trench coat, or no coat at all. But all of them apprehensive and hostile.

Only one man was obviously more apprehensive than the situation demanded. A small youngish man with eyes that avoided contact and hands that trembled slightly.

They ordered the burly German noncom to dismiss the men and to bring the shaky suspect to the little hut that served as quarters for the enclosure guard detail.

Larry took over the interrogation. "You know who we are?" he demanded brusquely.

The little man oozed the sweat of fear. *"Ja."* He nodded. "American secret police."

Larry looked fierce. Had to play the part bestowed upon him, after all. "Your papers!" He held out his hand.

With quavering hands the little German began a fidgety search through his pockets, coming up with a collection of dog-eared cards and smudged, crinkled papers.

Nervously he poured out a stream of words, giving the CIC agents his entire story, while gathering his ID from his numerous pockets.

He was a war correspondent. For a big important Swedish newspaper. He was born in Sweden of Swedish parents and was a Swedish subject. But his parents had moved to Germany when he was a small child. He had never been to Sweden, and he only knew a few words of the language. He had sent in his stories in German. To a large Stockholm paper. He had been on the Eastern front when it collapsed before the Russian onslaught, and he had secured permission from American front-line troops to travel into

Germany. He had been on his way to seek out and report to the proper military authorities when he had been picked up as a travel violator and thrown into the American concentration camp.

His voice took on a plaintive whine. He had *told* them who he was. That all he wanted was to go to Sweden to join his parents who had moved there just before the war.

Quite a story. Just unconventional and unbelievable enough to be true. And the man's papers and ID corroborated his statement—including the obviously valid travel pass issued to him by a U.S. Infantry unit commander.

Tom contemplated the little man. Was his story true? Or at least partially true? Which meant, of course, partially untrue, as well. Any interrogator believes only half of what he's told. A *good* one knows *which* half to believe! Okay, which was which? It *was* possible that his papers were genuine. It was also possible that they had been issued to him to go with a carefully planned cover story. It *was* possible that he'd been able to con an American Infantry officer, and it *was* just the sort of procedure a clever agent might adopt in order to get to the destination of his mission unmolested, realizing that without proper permits he'd be in constant danger of being picked up.

Larry was about to hand back the man's papers to him. Tom stopped him. He turned to the German. "You are a writer," he said pleasantly. "A journalist. Must be interesting."

The man started. Then he beamed nervously at Tom. *"Ja,* Herr Offizier," he agreed, head bobbing. "Most interesting."

"How long did you work for that Swedish newspaper?"

"Three years, Herr Offizier. Three years—plus."

"All through the war. Must have been a little difficult, getting your stuff to Sweden?"

"Not at all, Herr Offizier. It was routine."

"You used the mail?"

"Yes. Sweden is a neutral country. There is no difficulties with mail. It is quite efficient."

Tom nodded. "I see. And I suppose they could send their checks back to you. In payment. And you had no trouble cashing them?"

"No trouble, Herr Offizier. There is very good business relations between Sweden and Germany."

"Did the paper use a lot of your material?"

"Yes. Many stories. Many first-hand descriptions."

Tom nodded. He handed the man a sheet of paper and a pencil. "Here," he said. "Write the name of your paper for me. I'd be interested."

"*Jawohl,* Herr Offizier." The man wrote, meticulously printing the words.

Tom took the slip of paper. He glanced at it. Suddenly he began to laugh. At first he tried to hold back, but he soon capitulated. He laughed till he felt the tears gather in his eyes.

Larry looked at him, dumfounded. The German stared uncomprehendingly. But then the color began to drain from his pinched face as he began to suspect.

At last Tom turned to Larry. "Hold on to his papers," he said. "That little bastard goes back to Army Interrogation Center. They've got the time to get the *truth* out of him!"

The German shivered. He seemed to shrivel. He stammered. "The . . . truth? But . . . I . . . I *have* told the truth!"

Tom suddenly dropped the merriment from his face. He glared at the cowering man. "Have you?" he snapped icily. "Stop lying! *Who* and *what* are you?"

The German tried to moisten his thin, dry lips. "*Ich . . . verstehe nicht,*" he whispered. "I . . . do not understand."

"*That* I believe," Tom said with scathing contempt. "You're too goddamned dumb! A war correspondent! A man who for three years plus has been sending stories to his newspaper in Sweden! And cashing checks! And you don't even know how to *spell* the paper's name!"

For once the little man's eyes stayed riveted to one spot. He stared at Tom. "But . . . I—"

"*But,* my ass! You made a very stupid mistake, my friend. A very *German* mistake."

He held out the paper on which the man had written the name of his Swedish publication. "Look at it! Look at what you wrote!" He stabbed a finger at the words SWENSKA DAGBLADET.

The German stared at the paper, his face an uncomprehending mask. He looked up at Tom almost pleadingly. He was unable to utter a word. He kept shaking his head in utter incomprehension.

"You don't get it, do you?" Tom gave a short mirthless laugh. "Well, I'll explain it to you. You wrote the name of your damned paper all right, the *Swedish Daily Paper*"—he pointed to the first word on the paper— "but you used a W in *Svenska* instead of a V! A *V*, you dumb bastard! That's what it *should* be." He looked at the man with disdain.

"You have never written a fucking line to that paper. You have only *heard* the name of it. You have never *seen* it written. On checks—or anywhere else! You think because W is pronounced as V by your *Master Race*, and V as F, it's got to be the same in every other language! Well, it's not. In Swedish a V is a V—and sounds like a V! If you had been a correspondent for the *Svenska Dagbladet*, you'd damned well know that, even if you are a fucking German!"

The little man stared at Tom with eyes widening with growing horror and shock. He began to shake uncontrollably. He sank down in a chair and buried his face in his hands.

The two CIC agents watched him. They could almost see the thoughts churning convulsively within his head. He'd been trapped. Trapped by one tiny overlooked detail. What else had he overlooked? Where else had he slipped up?

Larry took him roughly by the shoulders and hauled him to his feet. "Okay," he growled. "*Now* let's have your real story!"

Half an hour later they gave up.

The man was so frightened, so shattered, that he was incoherent. They could get nothing from him. All they knew was that he could not be connected with that damned Oberwiese shot. He'd been right there in the 459th AAA detention enclosure at the time the shot was fired.

Larry looked with utter disgust at the broken man. "We might as well give him to Sloan to transport back to AIC," he said. "Maybe he'll calm down by the time he gets there. Right now he's so damned scared, he'd go into a panic at the sound of his own fart!"

They turned the German over to a guard and started back to the battalion HQ. The drizzle had stopped. Larry was driving. Curiously he glanced at Tom. "How the hell did you know about that Swedish bit?" he asked.

"I guess my bout with European lit in college wasn't a total loss." Tom grinned. "I studied Lagerlöf and Söderberg. And Strindberg. His collection of short stories—*Swedish Fates and Adventures*. I didn't speak Swedish, of course, but I did look at the original titles. Strindberg's *Fates* was called *Svenska öden och äventyr*. And *Svenska* was damned well spelled with a V!"

"I'll be damned!" Larry shook his head. "My study of Swedish is limited to *skoal!*"

"What more do you need?"

"Right now a good cold reason for showing off my entire Swedish vocabulary!" He grew sober. "I think we could both do with a little liquid cheer. It's been a pisser of a day, that's for sure." He lapsed into silence.

Tom suddenly felt glum. A pisser of a day was right. They'd gotten exactly nowhere with the Oberwiese shot investigation. And his secret hope of running into a Prague lead—okay, a KOKON lead—had petered out into a big fat nothing. One lousy suspect was all they had to show for their efforts. And *that* was below par for a detention camp screening.

He still had the nagging feeling of having overlooked something. At Oberwiese? At the AAA compound? Interrogating that fake correspondent? Some . . . clue? That was something else. Clues. How the hell did you know when you missed one? The clues that broke cases weren't exactly neon signs that lit up when you got within a mile of them. They were stupid *little* things. They didn't stand out from the tedious sea of trivia like some Loch Ness monster rising from the calm surface of a lake. The hell they did. They were little things that could have perfectly reasonable, logical and damned obvious explanations. They could be perfectly innocent. Or—they could not.

A hell of a lot depended on that little word: *or*. Sometimes the difference between freedom *or* arrest. Joy *or* anguish. Life *or* death.

All because of one damned little clue. One little mistake. Like a sentimental clinging to the wrong object. A missing match. A mix-up of organizations in some bastard's mind. A misspelled word. So what *had* he missed?

They were driving past the detention compound. He glanced at the barbed-wire enclosure with the barn that served as shelter for the detainees.

One damned little clue. Something that meant nothing at all. *Or* everything. He suddenly sat bolt upright. He knew what it was that kept nagging him. That one little out-of-place clue. The belt! The goddamned belt on that guy's trench coat! *The crease was wrong.*

He was suddenly excited. His depression vanished. He *knew* he was onto something. He turned to Larry. "I got it!" he exclaimed.

"Keep it."

"Turn back into the compound. I just figured out what's been bugging me. I want to take a look at those jokers again!"

The burly German noncom did not allow his bewilderment or his annoyance to show on his grim, expressionless face. In no time he had the detainees lined up for inspection once more. The ominous uncertainty and apprehension of the waiting men hung like an ill-omened mist over the detail.

The man in the tan trench coat stood at attention in the second row. Tom went straight to him. He stared at the belt on his coat. The belt was too big. An extra hole had been made in it for the leather-covered buckle to fit into. But halfway along the leftover tongue was a crease, the indented mark of the buckle. The coat had been worn by a large man. It was almost new. How had it come into the possession of this detainee? How did he come by it here, in the middle of nowhere?

He suddenly felt uncertain. It probably meant nothing at all. He'd made a damned fool of himself. It was just another one of those stupid little things that had a perfectly logical explanation.

"Take off your coat!" he ordered. The man obeyed. He looked confused.

Tom grabbed the coat from him. He stared at it. He turned the collar inside out and examined the back of it. Quickly he turned to the blank-faced noncom. "That man," he snapped. "Bring him to the hut!"

He looked once more inside the neck of the coat. The haberdasher's label read, W. NEZVAL. PRAHA.

Prague!

Leutnant Meister, Emil, discharged, had nothing to hide. As far as he was concerned the war was over. He talked freely.

Yes, he had come from Prague, only a few days ago. He had been an officer, a statistician, on the staff of the Luftwaffe High Command. It had been a dreary, discouraging job. He had fled the city with the rest of the staff officers, but like most of them he had not surrendered to the Americans. He correctly guessed that all General Staff officers, regardless of rank, had a high priority on enemy wanted lists. By losing himself in the flood of refugees he had hoped to escape a lengthy stay in some PW camp. He shrugged. It had not worked.

The coat? It had been given to him by his commanding general as a sort of parting gift.

Where was this general? And the other General Staff officers? He did not know. All he knew was that he and a few other officers had crossed into Germany from Czechoslovakia together and gone their separate ways.

"You know who these officers are?" Tom asked.

"I do."

"I want you to make a list. Every officer from the Luftwaffe General Staff that crossed with you. Understood?"

"Understood."

"I also want you to list the code names or letter designations of every project you worked on during the last six months. Is that understood?"

"Yes, sir."

"Go to it."

The list of code names and letter abbreviations was not long. Tom's eyes raced down the paper. There was no KOKON. He frowned at the lieutenant. "Have you ever heard of a project called KOKON?" he asked. Or, K-O-K-O-N?"

The man shook his head slowly. "No," he said. "I have not."

Tom had a twinge of disappointment. He dismissed it. "Do you know an SS colonel named Steinmetz? Wolfgang Steinmetz?"

"No. I do not." He handed Tom the list of General Staff officers. It, too, was quite short.

Tom glanced at it. He read it once more. Heading it were three high-ranking officers: Generalmajor Anton Beigel, Generalmajor Dieter Joachim, Oberst Eugen Cornelius.

The crew in the Oberwiese barn had just been handed one hell of a promotion!

Tom and his teammate had brought a small detail of men from the 21st Armored Infantry with them when they returned to Oberwiese. The GI's were guarding the Oberwiese barn crew while Tom and Larry interrogated the suspects one by one.

The two CIC agents had questioned stubborn suspects before. But never a group as blindly obstinate as the five improbable refugees from the barn.

They told them they knew their true identities. They brandished their indisputable evidence before them. They confronted them with the list of General Staff officers headed by the name Anton Beigel. But despite it, and despite looking and acting the prototype of a Prussian Junker officer, Beigel imperiously insisted he was a discharged corporal. He practically ordered the CIC agents to believe him. It was *his* word against that of some inferior detainee, he claimed. What was more, his papers proved his true identity. It was there in black and white. Who would dare doubt the written word against the irresponsible say-so of some nonentity? No contest was conceivable, of course. He categorically refused to admit to what was obviously fact —that he was indeed Generalmajor Anton Beigel.

Joachim followed suit.

The matronly officer's widow hardly deigned to open her mouth. When she did, it was to deny any knowledge of or connection with Beigel and Joachim, or for that matter any interest in them—a couple of enlisted men. It was bad enough that regrettable circumstances forced her to share the shelter of the barn with them.

Her son had been brought up just right in the Hitler Youth. It was all he could do to keep from spitting in his interrogators' faces.

Their last chance was Ilse Neumann, the ex-Wehrmachthelferinn. They had her brought to the harness room where they had established their interrogation area. A rough workbench served as a desk, a couple of bales of hay as chairs for the agents.

Tom's voice was cold, matter-of-fact as he explained to the girl that she was considered not a civilian refugee, but a prisoner of war, as were the two soldiers. Her German discharge papers, dated within the last couple of weeks, could not be considered valid. He informed her that as a PW she was entitled to all considerations due that status, all the obligations—and the serious consequences of resisting such obligations. As a PW it was her duty *not* to withhold the name, rank and serial number of any military personnel.

The girl listened in silence, staring straight ahead.

"I want to know," Tom demanded firmly. "Beigel and Joachim. They are both generals on the Luftwaffe General Staff. Is that correct?"

The girl swallowed. "I do not know," she said. She kept her eyes from his.

Wearily Tom studied the girl. She was obviously deathly afraid. And she was lying. He knew it. And she in turn was well aware of that fact. The question was Why? What could possibly be accomplished by the ridiculous charade? Still, she was the only one who had betrayed any area of weakness. It had become evident that she and Beigel were more than just fellow refugees stranded in the Oberwiese barn.

Could she be bluffed? It was worth a try. He reached over and on the margin of the paper lying in front of Larry he scribbled an R.

Larry glanced at it. He stood up and walked from the harness room.

The girl watched him apprehensively.

Tom gazed at her steadily. He said not a word. Together they waited in silence.

With every passing moment the uneasiness of the girl mounted.

Larry returned. He carried a musette bag fetched from the jeep. He sat down at the bench. He took out a bunch of large yellow tags with a short piece of string attached to each one. Unhurriedly he began to write on one of the tags.

Still not a word was spoken.

Ilse was pale. Her large blue eyes were dark, filled with fear. They flitted from one of the grim CIC investigators to the other. She began to tremble.

Larry finished his writing. He stood up. He walked to the fearful girl. Without a word he tied the tag to a button on her blouse front. It hung like an evil tarot of death on her ample bosom. He looked over at Tom.

"One last time, Fräulein. Will you tell the truth?" Tom asked the girl.

"I . . ." Her voice broke. She cleared her throat. "I . . . have."

Tom shrugged. "Your choice," he said, his voice flat. He nodded to his comrade. Larry rummaged in the musette bag. He came up with a big red pencil. He turned to the girl, and on the PW tag he wrote a large red R.

Tom stood up. He looked at the girl with obvious pity. "I am sorry," he said, compassion in his voice. He turned to leave.

"Please!" Ilse pleaded, her voice husky with alarm. "Please, Herr Hauptmann." She glanced at the tag. "What means this?"

Tom turned back to her. He spoke kindly. "It is a PW tag, Fräulein."

She looked at him, fearfully questioning.

He explained. "You are considered a prisoner of war. A PW. This tag will accompany you wherever you go from now on. It states your name, the time, the place and circumstance of your capture. It is routine."

Again she looked at the tag. She lifted her hand toward it. She could not bring herself to touch it. "And . . . this red R?" she whispered. "What means it?"

Tom turned away. He hesitated. Then he said, "Russia."

She had known. Yet she blanched. *"Russia!"* she repeated automatically. Tom turned back to her. His face was angry. "You chose it, Fräulein!" he said savagely. "It is your own doing." He stopped. He went on. "You will be turned over to the Russians. For interrogation. Possibly internment. In Russia. Or Siberia. We have a quota of prisoners we must turn over to them. We give them the ones who choose not to cooperate with *us."*

Ilse was ashen-faced. She swayed slightly on her feet. She stared with dread at Tom. "And . . . the others," she said. "You will mark them with a red R too?"

"Yes." He turned on his heel.

"Wait!" It was a cry in the wilderness. A cry of utter despair.

He turned back to her.

"I . . . will cooperate," the girl whispered. "Please do not send us to *them*. Any of us."

"Well?"

She stared at the PW tag. The big red R filled its yellow face. She clenched her hands before her in unconscious supplication. She squeezed them until her fingers showed white.

"Gefreiter Beigel is Generalmajor Anton Beigel, OQu IV. . . . Deputy Chief of General Staff, Intelligence, OKL—Oberkommando der Luftwaffe, Field Echelon, Prague." The damning words were delivered in a flat, lifeless voice. She added, "I . . . I was his secretary."

"Joachim?"

She nodded. "Generalmajor Joachim."

"You will repeat exactly what you have just said to Generalmajor Beigel's face." It was a statement, not a request.

"Ja," she said.

He looked at her. The tears were running down her cheeks. She could not know, he thought. She could not know that his reluctant disclosure of a Russian "quota" was pure fabrication.

The prisoners stood in a defiant group, guarded by the GI's, when Tom and Larry brought Ilse face to face with them. The girl was deathly pale, her eyes dark with despair, focusing on nothing.

Tom placed her directly in front of Beigel. The man fixed his blazing eyes upon her. She shivered. "All right," Tom ordered harshly. "Repeat exactly what you told us."

The girl's mouth worked. But no sound emerged.

Beigel stood as if hewn in granite. His eyes bored into those of the terrified girl. The power emanating from him was a tangible thing. Starting at his bullneck, protruding from his tunic collar, his face flushed a deep, angry red as he stood immobile.

Twice the girl tried to speak. Twice the man's blazing eyes silenced her.

Tom knew what she was going through. Face to face with her comrades, she had to betray them. She thought by denouncing them she would save them from a fate of unspeakable horror. Them—and herself. It was a soul-wrenching choice to be forced to make.

At last she cried, a cry of pure anguish, "I told you nothing! I only said what you wanted to hear. I was frightened. *I—told—you—nothing!"* She put her hands to her face. She sobbed.

Beigel moved not a muscle.

Tom and Larry walked to their jeep. Larry was carrying the musette bag. He called it "the bag of tricks." It was. It had been successful once again. With no result.

Tom was angry. It wasn't strictly necessary to get confessions from the two officers. His evidence was strong enough. Their identities could be checked out, in time. Damn them! Thick-skulled bastards! Well, their obstinacy had rubbed off on him. He'd be damned if he'd send a couple of suspects back to AIC without confirmed identification!

And there was something else. The third name on the list. Colonel Eugen Cornelius. The prisoners had refused even to admit any knowledge of such an officer.

Beigel was no fool. Autocratic, pig-headed, yes. But no fool. He must know he was fighting a losing battle. It could only be a matter of time before the facts would emerge. Then, why? Was he fighting a holding action? Buying time? For what? Had it something to do with Cornelius? With that damned shot in the forest?

He made up his mind. He *had* to get to the bottom of the whole mess before calling it quits. He felt better, having come to a decision.

Larry tossed the musette bag into the jeep. He gave a short laugh. "You know," he said, "if it weren't so funny-peculiar, it'd be damned funny-ha-ha!"

Tom grinned. "I've had enough of the ha-ha. Let's go on to the peculiar."

"How? We've threatened the bastards with fire and brimstone. Or more specifically, with the firing squad and the Russians. What the hell's left?"

"Forget about that phony crew in the barn." Tom looked toward the main house. "Let's go to work on the jolly forester. No holds barred!"

"Okay," Larry said. "I'm with you. But how the hell do we crack him?"

"We don't," Tom countered tersely. "We let them do it."

Larry looked startled. "Them?"

"Beigel and his buddies." Tom nodded toward the barn.

For a moment Larry stared at him, nonplused. Then he brightened. He shook his head. "You're some kind of devious bastard!" he said. "But you go straight for the jugular!"

Tom grinned. "You better believe it!"

Gathering her children around her, the forester's wife scurried ahead of the two agents as they marched to her husband's sickroom. The family clustered apprehensively around the bed.

Tom swept the somber group with a benevolent glance. He turned to the forester. "Herr Forstmeister," he said pleasantly. "We shall be leaving now. We have finished our investigation here." The entire family relaxed visibly. Tom continued. "We want to thank you for your cooperation."

The forester's grinning geniality returned. He sat up in his bed. *"Selbst-verständlich!*—Naturally—Herr Offizier." He beamed with servile heartiness. "Anything we can do. Anything!"

"Fine." Tom started to leave. He turned back to the bedridden man. "As a matter of fact," he said, "there is one thing." He looked at the forester. "As an important state official, Herr Forstmeister, you can be of value to us."

The forester sat up even straighter in his bed. *"Jawohl!"* he snapped.

"We are leaving you in command here," Tom continued. "You will be in charge of Oberwiese and the surrounding area. Responsible to the CIC."

"Ja-wohl!" the man barked. He preened with pride. He shot a stern glance at his two boys and snapped his fingers. At once they stood stiffly erect.

"Zu Befehl!" the man said. "At your orders!"

"Very well," Tom said. His manner changed subtly. His voice took on a ring of officer-to-officer confidentiality.

"You know, Herr Forstmeister," he said candidly, "we actually did think we had a pretty important case here. We had been led to believe that Gefreiter Beigel and Unteroffizier Joachim were really *generals* in disguise. Hiding out. With a colonel named Cornelius." He smiled. "Of course, they denied it."

He did not miss the quick glance of sudden apprehension exchanged between the forester and his wife, but he took no notice of it. He gave a little laugh. "We tried to trick them," he confessed. "We told them it was *you* who had informed on them!"

The forester's mouth fell open. He stared at Tom.

The woman's face drained to a sickly gray. Instinctively she clasped the two youngest children to her. She turned to her husband. "*Gott im Himmel!*" she breathed. "Oh, my God!" She crossed herself.

The man swallowed with obvious difficulty. "You . . . you told them . . . *I* . . ." The words croaked from him.

Tom shrugged. "Well, they didn't fall for it. And since it's not true, it's of no consequence." Briskly he went on. "You should have no problems with them Herr Forstmeister. We told them we were going to investigate further. Put a little fear of God in them." He smiled pleasantly. "They'll behave." He turned to leave. "*Grüss Gott,*" he said.

Ashen-faced, the forester stared after the two CIC agents. "Wait!" he cried hoarsely.

They stopped. They turned back toward him. He stared at them with terror-filled eyes.

"You cannot leave us here with them," he whispered. "Please! They will kill us!"

"Who?" Tom snapped.

"Beigel . . . Joachim." The man's voice was on the verge of cracking. "It is true, what you said. They *are* generals! They *are* hiding. They . . . they will kill us if they think *we* gave them away!" He swung his legs from under the featherbed to sit on the edge of his bed, every muscle in his body taut. His two boys rallied to him. "*Bitte,*" he implored. "Please. We—"

Tom interrupted him coldly. "You knew the two soldiers in the barn were General Staff officers!"

The forester stood up. He was oblivious of his broken leg in the heavy soiled bandages. He took a step toward Tom. "You do not understand, Herr Offizier," he pleaded. "They threatened us. They said—" He held out his arms to encompass his family. "My family . . ." He blinked at Tom, beseeching him to understand.

For a moment Tom stood in silent, frowning thought, the sole target of the anxious stares of the forester's family. He looked searchingly at each one of them in turn. Finally he turned to Larry.

Solemnly Larry nodded his head.

Tom gazed straight at the agonized forester.

"Perhaps," he said slowly, "perhaps under the circumstances we might . . . overlook your forgetfulness. *If!* If you tell us all you know, now!"

The woman quickly turned to her husband. "Please, Hans! Please!" she begged.

The German looked at his four children. And his wife. All anxiously watching him. He sighed. He turned to Tom. "What do you wish to know?" he asked heavily.

"Where is Colonel Cornelius? Where are the others?"

"Somewhere in the forest. I do not know where."

"How many are there?"

"About . . . a dozen. Maybe more. They often come here for food. Late in the day."

"Are they armed?"

"Yes." The German looked away.

It suddenly made sense. The whole absurd masquerade suddenly made a hell of a lot of sense. All Beigel had to do was stall. Stall until Cornelius and his troops came to Oberwiese. Late in the day. The Germans could make short shrift of them all: Larry, himself—and their half dozen unsuspecting GI's!

"When do they come here?" he asked.

"At dusk. Usually."

He glanced at his watch. It was 1317 hours. There was time. He glared at the German. "I think you had better tell us *where* Colonel Cornelius is, Herr Forstmeister," he said. There was unmistakable menace in his voice.

The man shook his head. He looked wildly at his wife. "But I do not know. *I swear it!"* The man looked terror-stricken. A film of the thin greasy sweat of fear coated his pallid face. For a moment there was not a sound in the sour-smelling room.

The next move was up to Tom. . . .

Suddenly the younger boy stepped in front of his father. Big-eyed, big-eared, bucktoothed and barefoot, his grimy lederhosen looking as if he'd been born in them, he planted himself firmly before the CIC agent. *"I* know where he is," he said, staring straight up at Tom. "If you will promise not to hurt Vati and Mutti, I will show you."

The woman looked thunderstruck. Her hand flew to her mouth. "Otto!" she exclaimed.

The forester put his hands on the boy's shoulders. He drew him back close to him. "He is only nine, Herr Offizier," he said in quick defense of his son. "He did not know. He . . . he likes to go into the forest. To play *Jäger*—hunter. He may have seen something . . ."

Involuntarily Tom started at the sound of his name. That's what he was. A hunter. A hunter of his own people. And there before him his latest prey, run to ground. For an instant he felt unclean. Then his rational mind prevailed, and he shook off the intrusive thought. It had no base in cold reality.

He bent down on one knee in front of the boy. His eyes on the level with the child's, he said, "Thank you, Otto." His voice was kind and serious. "You can be of great help. To us. And to your parents."

Otto grinned widely. His large buckteeth seemed to light up his entire face.

Quickly the CIC agents laid their plans.

Two men were assigned to guard the group from the barn, keeping them inside. Two men were given sentry duty. And two men were sent off to Regen with orders to bring back reinforcements. On the double!

Tom gently questioned Otto.

With his small-boy curiosity, Otto had followed Colonel Cornelius into the forest one day, pretending in his game of playing hunter that the officer was a wild animal to be stalked to its lair without being discovered. Although he had not actually seen the bivouac area of Cornelius and his men, he had a good idea where it was.

In less than an hour two squads of men from the 21st Armored Infantry barreled into Oberwiese, and with little Otto as a guide Tom and Larry took their search party into the woods.

In silence they followed a narrow path winding up a gentle slope among the thick evergreens. After half an hour's walk they came to a clearing where the slope leveled off. At one edge of the open plot a large bare rock formation thrust up through the grassy ground. A perfect landmark.

Otto stopped. He pointed to the woods across the clearing. "In there!" he whispered, his eyes shining with excitement. "That is where the colonel went."

Quickly Tom and Larry deployed their men. Skirting the open ground, they quietly, cautiously infiltrated the woods ahead, while a disappointed Otto was ordered to stay hidden where he was.

Tom walked carefully, watchfully through the forest undergrowth, wending his way around clumps of brush and overgrown rocks. On both sides of him he could see GI's stealthily moving forward, searching and probing.

He made his way around a thicket of shrubs. Suddenly he stopped short. He stared. Dug into the ground directly in front of him was a big camouflaged tent, so skillfully placed and concealed that it blended perfectly with the forest floor and underbrush. One more step and he would literally have tumbled down upon the heads of his quarry!

At once he held his hand high. Around him the GI's stopped in place. Tensely they watched him. He pointed to the hidden tent. He motioned his orders, and quietly the men surrounded the area, weapons ready.

The damp air hung heavy among the silent trees. There was no motion to be seen, no sound to be heard.

Suddenly Tom shouted at the top of his voice, *"Rauskommen! Los! Hände hoch! Los! Los!"*

At once the GI's all around the area took up the cry: "Come out! Hands up! Get going! Out! Out! . . ."

The effect was instantaneous. The big tent in front of Tom literally heaved and shook with the sudden motion within. Bumps and bulges rippled in quick succession across the motley surface as the startled men inside leaped up and lurched against the canvas. A short distance away the astounding performance was repeated at another hidden tent. Tom had not even seen that one.

From the two tents men in blue-gray uniforms came tumbling out. For a moment all seemed utter chaos. Soldiers stumbled about in complete confusion, hands on their heads or raised high in the air, looking for the omnipresent enemy. Weapons were forgotten. Not a shot was fired. The Germans had been taken completely by surprise.

They were quickly rounded up to form a bewildered group huddled in the small clearing between the two camouflaged tents, surrounded by GI's.

Tom stepped forward. *"Achtung,* Sondergruppe Cornelius!" he called aloud—"Attention Special Unit Cornelius! Generalmajor Anton Beigel, Deputy Chief of Staff, Intelligence, Oberkommando der Luftwaffe, has ordered you to surrender! You will obey his command without resistance!"

The prisoners shifted uneasily. Tom looked them over. "Which one of you is Colonel Cornelius?" he demanded.

A small gray-haired man stepped forward. "I am Colonel Cornelius," he said calmly.

Tom motioned him over. He indicated the group of prisoners. "Is that your entire command?"

"Yes."

"How many?"

"Eleven officers. Six noncommissioned officers."

"All from the Prague Field Echelon of the Luftwaffe General Staff?"

"Yes."

Larry joined them. "The count is seventeen," he reported to Tom.

Tom nodded. "It tallies." He turned to Cornelius. "Who is your immediate superior officer?"

Cornelius looked startled. "The general, of course. Generalmajor Beigel."

"At Oberwiese?"

"Yes."

Larry was studying the calm Luftwaffe officer. "Why are you and your men camped out here, Colonel?" he asked. "Why are you not with General Beigel?"

Cornelius turned to look at him. He smiled. A condescending smile. "Cornelius, Eugen. Oberst. *Fünf, drei, neun—*"

"Oh, shit!" Larry interrupted him in disgust. "Skip it!"

Cornelius at once fell silent. But the little smile did not leave his lips.

"That's all, Colonel," Tom said curtly. "Rejoin your men."

Cornelius clicked his heels. With a slight bow he gave a military salute. He turned on his heel and deliberately walked toward the group of men in the clearing. He had been correct. He had been courteous. But he had also given the unmistakable impression of mocking the two Americans.

The agents watched him. Tom found himself wondering about the man. He was an unusual officer. He seemed more a scholar than a soldier. Not at all like Beigel. And he was in complete control of himself. What had his function been on the General Staff? His assignment? He had countless questions to ask the man. But this was not the time. Not the place. Patience. Patience is the weapon of a hunter. More so, a hunter of men.

Larry was scowling after the German with annoyance. Suddenly he grinned. "Hey, Tom," he said, nodding toward the prisoners. "You see what I see?"

Tom looked closely at the group. One of the men had turned toward the approaching colonel. He stood attentively, as if awaiting any orders the colonel might give. He wore the distinctive peaked Luftwaffe field cap. On his uniform tunic the Luftwaffe emblem, the flying eagle gripping a swastika in its talons, soared proudly over his right breast pocket. The insignia of rank on his collar tabs showed three hash marks, like stylized birds in flight, on a light brown background. A Feldwebel. An intelligence noncom.

"How about it?" Larry asked. "Nothing I'd like better than to put the screws to that SOB Beigel!"

"Why not," Tom agreed. "Let's have a little talk with that eager-beaver sergeant."

It was late afternoon when the search party and the prisoners returned to Oberwiese.

Guarded by the entire detachment of GI's, the captives were marched to the open yard area between the two large buildings. They were ordered to fall in and stand at attention. From the gamekeeper's house the forester and his family, joined by Otto, watched with misgiving and awe.

When the prisoners were assembled the little group from the barn were brought out. Not one of them reacted visibly to the sight of the Luftwaffe PW's standing stiffly at attention in the yard.

Larry stepped forward. In a loud, booming voice he gave the order. "Feldwebel Bergman! Make your report!"

From the ranks of ramrod prisoners the Feldwebel stepped forward.

Smartly he wheeled and marched to the center of the column. Again he made a precise turn and with firm, measured strides he all but goose-stepped to stand directly in front of Beigel, the self-styled corporal. His hand shot up in a stiff-armed Nazi salute. His heels clicked together with the sharp crack of a shot. In a loud, firm voice he said, "Herr Generalmajor! Heil Hitler! I beg to report that Sondergruppe Cornelius has surrendered!"

It was worth it!

Beigel turned red as an overboiled crab. His eyes, glaring at the hapless Feldwebel with venomous malevolence, bulged dangerously in his crimson face. His whole massive body shook with suppressed fury and impotence. His fists clenched in rage at his sides. His tightly compressed lips worked in frustrated anger. But he said not a word. Suddenly he whirled about, and utterly disregarding the GI guards, he stalked stiffly and heavily to the sanctuary of the barn, closely followed by two GI's.

It was a most satisfying reaction. Dammit, it was worth it!

"Cornelius, Eugen. Oberst. *Fünf, drei . . .*"

It's got to be the thousandth time by now, Tom thought wearily as the tired voice of the German officer droned on. The man spoke slowly, deliberately. Each separate, familiar syllable hit Tom's mind with the sting of a whip biting into a cringing spot already raw from countless prior lashes.

He let the officer finish his tedious litany, trying to shut out the deadly drone. He needed the time to think. He glanced at Larry. I wonder if I look as beat as he does, he mused. From the way I feel, probably worse.

Larry was glaring at the German officer through eyes narrowed in anger. He took a short breath, on the verge of a sharp remark, but caught himself in the last instant. Unconsciously he pressed his lips together in a thin, hard line. He looked away from the monotonously droning German.

Tempers were growing short, Tom realized. They were exhausted. All of them. It was no good. An interrogator has to have a fresh and alert mind. It is his greatest advantage over a tired, benumbed suspect. His best weapon in the battle of wits. Interrogator and suspect should never be on equal footing.

He quickly reviewed their situation. It was well past 2300 hours. For over six hours he and Larry had grilled Beigel and Cornelius. The guttural sounds of their names, their ranks and their serial numbers whispered mockingly in every cell of their brains. It was all they had learned.

After preliminary interrogation of the prisoners at the AAA Battalion HQ in Regen, Tom had decided to take General Beigel and Colonel Cornelius to Grafenau for further in-depth interrogation while the subjects were still newly captured. It was the best time to achieve a breakthrough. The other captives, headed by General Joachim, had been left with Captain Sloan for transportation to Army Interrogation Center.

All except Ilse. She had begged them to be allowed to accompany Beigel. She had admitted that a close relationship existed between them, and she was obviously very concerned about his fate.

Tom thought it over. The girl was not a mandatory arrestee. She had told them her true identity. Her presence close to Beigel during his interrogation might be an advantage. A further pressure on the man. He had agreed.

Ilse was waiting anxiously in one of the many rooms of the large farmhouse taken over by the CIC in Grafenau.

But neither Beigel nor Cornelius had talked, despite every interrogation pressure and trick Tom and Larry could muster. Except for that damned incessant name-rank-serial-number routine!

Tom had notified Major Lee and told him the two General Staff officers would be brought to Corps HQ the following morning. He'd assured him they'd have all pertinent information necessary by then.

Like hell they would. Name. Rank. Serial number. That was all they had. After six hours of intensive interrogation, they were no further than they had been at Oberwiese.

Larry had wanted to arrest the German *Forstmeister* as well, back there. For concealing mandatory arrestees. Tom had talked him out of it. It would serve no useful purpose, he'd argued. Had that been his real reason? Or was he leaning over backward to salve his haunted conscience by giving the Germans a break? Larry had given him a funny look as he agreed to leave the gamekeeper alone. Had it been a look of suspicion? A knowing look of scorn?

Of course not. Angrily he derailed his bleak train of thoughts. It took him nowhere. It was his own stupid twin-edged sensitivity, damning himself if he did, and damning himself if he did not.

He looked up at the prisoner.

". . . *acht, vier,*" the colonel finished.

Tom stood up. He walked over to the big stove and poured himself a canteen cup of hot black coffee.

Larry joined him. "Call it a day?" he asked.

"Might as well." Tom glanced toward Cornelius sitting silently at the rough wooden table in the *Bauernstube*—the big combination living room, dining room and kitchen of the farm, used by the agents as an interrogation room. "Those two bastards are not about to crack." There was grudging respect in his voice. "We'll have to take them to Corps. Let the IPW's work them over before sending them to AIC."

"Hell of a note!" Larry sounded thoroughly disgusted. He was. They wouldn't hear the last of it for the rest of the goddamned war.

"We'll take them back in the morning," Tom said. "Seven hundred hours, okay?"

"Okay."

Tom nodded toward Cornelius. "Secure him for the night, will you? I'll go tell the girl. She'll want to go along."

He looked at the coffee on the stove. He reached for it. He stopped. Hell, he didn't want coffee. What he wanted was a good night's sleep.

On his way to his quarters he stopped at the room where Ilse waited. He told the girl to be ready to leave early the next morning if she wanted to accompany Beigel to Corps HQ.

She looked at him with her large, anxious eyes. "They . . . they told you nothing," she said. It was neither a statement nor a question. She stepped close to him.

He remained silent.

She wet her lips. *"Es sieht schlecht aus?"* She looked deeply concerned.

Tom nodded gravely. "Yes. It looks bad."

He was suddenly acutely aware of her scent. The fresh smell of clean-scrubbed girl. He turned abruptly from her.

The cat's-paw noise that woke him was almost imperceptible. But he was at once wide awake. The sound had come from outside the door to his room. His hand quietly found the gun hanging in its holster on the wall side of the bed. The hard, cold feel of it in his hand was reassuring. He listened.

He looked around the room. He had left the heavy wooden window shutters open, and his eyes were used to the dim silver-blue light that seeped in through the curtains.

Again there was a slight scraping sound. He tensed. Someone was lifting the iron latch on the door. He brought the gun in front of him. He aimed it at the door. He lay still, breathing evenly. He saw the door open. A silent figure stepped quietly into the room, closing the door softly behind. He knew at once who it was. Ilse. He did not move.

The girl stepped closer to his bed. She was barefoot. She wore a GI blanket wrapped around her like a coarse toga. She stopped. Slowly she spread her arms. The blanket parted in front of her and slid off her shoulders to crumble at her feet. She stood before him naked.

He did not move. He felt the blood pound in his ears. His eyes drank in the girl standing wraithlike at his bed. She was beautiful. The sweet softness of her face was echoed in the round fullness of her generous breasts and the curves of her firm hips. The silver-blue light made her pale smooth skin shine with a gleaming life. Her blond hair cascaded over her smooth shoulders. Little rays of light from the window shone through it and tipped the fine soft hair at the apex of her long legs with silvery gold.

He sat up.

She did not move. "Please," she whispered softly. "Please. I will be . . . good for you. Please."

He swallowed. His whole being suddenly ached with want for the girl standing in unconcealed beauty and desirability at his bed. He longed to take her in his arms. Press his body to hers. Touching every inch. Bury his face in the soft arc of her neck.

She took a step closer. She held out a hand to him.

He got up. For a moment they stood looking at each other. Then he reached out to her and took her in his arms. He crushed her to him.

She yielded gently to his hungry need, eyes closed, head lifted up.

He snuggled his face against the cool velvet of her throat. He felt her hands caress his naked back, her nails dig into him with tender savagery. Oh, God, how long it had been. How long . . .

He felt himself grow tense and swell in a flood of throbbing desire. The musky scent of woman was overwhelming. He wanted her with every fiery fiber of his body and mind. Slowly he moved away from her.

She trembled.

He put his hands on her shoulders, glistening in the pale light with the moisture of excitement. He looked searchingly into her huge luminous eyes, which were watching him with uncertainty.

And he knew. He knew why she had come to him. He knew it was to try to save the man she loved. The general. Beigel. And he knew he could not take her.

He picked up the blanket from the floor. Gently he placed it around the girl's shoulders. "You are lovely, Ilse," he said. His own voice sounded strange to him. "Go back to your room. I will not harm your general."

Two large tears welled up in Ilse's eyes, brimmed and slowly ran down her cheeks, turned into drops of mother-of-pearl by the faint light. Suddenly she seized Tom's hand. She brought it to her lips. She kissed it. "Thank you!" she whispered. And she was gone.

For a while Tom stood quiet, silent. Alone. He felt empty, in turmoil —and yet at peace. For how long?

He had wanted her so much. So very much. He lay down on his bed. He knew he would not be able to sleep. Not for a long while. He tried to analyze himself. Coldly. Clinically. His body had taken in a damned good-sized shot of adrenalin. It would take hours to absorb. But he had not taken the strain and exertion of the last few days into account. In less than twenty minutes he was deep in a fitful sleep.

He knew without turning around that it was she. Ilse. Lying in bed beside him. He reached his hand back. She was soft. And warm. And silken. He turned to her.

Her skin was luminous, shimmering in the silvery light. She smiled at him. She whispered, "Tom . . ."

He held her. He felt her lips against his. Her naked breasts pressed against him. He thought he would burst asunder. His eyes sought her lovely face—*and he recoiled!* It was Julie's face. *Julie.* It stared up at him. Ghastly gray. Cold. Hard. Hateful. He tried to pull himself away.

She clung to him.

He grew frightened. Desperately he fought to tear himself from her embrace, but her arms were like steel bands welded across his back, her legs held his in an iron grip. He squirmed. He struggled.

She laughed. A cruel, scornful laugh that shrieked in his ears.

He screwed his eyes shut. He tried to close his ears. In vain. He still saw her. He still heard her. He cringed in horror.

Abruptly the mocking laughter stopped.

He opened his eyes. He looked down upon the sweet face of Ilse. He felt her hands gently stroke the back of his neck. He sobbed.

His want, his need for release, reborn, washed over him, banishing all else. He felt himself melt into her. His whole being draining exultantly into hers.

Her arms encircled him. Tighter . . . tighter.

He could no longer breathe. He tried to call out to her. He could not. He could not utter a sound. He shivered in terror. He fought against the icy embrace in desperate impotence. The force that was strangling his very life would not let go.

His mind shrieked in abject panic. Ilse! Julie! Help me! Help! *Hilfe! Hilfe!* German? *German?*

He chilled. The strident, scornful laughter pierced his mind. He heard the sickening, grating sound of his very bones being splintered and crushed, traveling through his mangled flesh to his tortured brain. He screamed. But not the whisper of a sound was heard. Julie . . . Ilse . . . But he knew it was neither.

He was being crushed into nothingness by a far greater force. Into . . . nothingness.

5

He woke with a start, bathed in sweat. For a moment he lay completely still, allowing his racing heart to seek its normal rythm. It had been a nightmare. A malignant, mind-chilling nightmare.

He got out of bed. He glanced at his watch—0517 hours. It was just beginning to get light.

There was a pump in the farmyard with good cold water. He needed it. In a couple of hours he'd be taking the two German General Staff officers to AIC. Cornelius and Beigel.

He suddenly felt cold. He frowned. Beigel. Had *he* been in his dream? He shook it off. He could not remember. But he did remember the girl. Ilse. And that had been no dream! He smiled to himself. Damned lucky fellow that SOB Beigel!

Generalmajor Anton Beigel, OQu IV, Deputy Chief of Staff, Intelligence, Oberkommando der Luftwaffe, sat in stony Junker stiffness on the rough-hewn wooden bench placed against the wall in the *Bauernstube*. He looked unrelenting and forbidding. Close at his side sat Ilse, her lovely face pale and wan. Cornelius, somber and preoccupied, sat a little way off by himself. They were waiting. Waiting uncertainly, apprehensively.

Larry and Sergeant Pete Connors were at the big kitchen stove pouring steaming coffee for themselves when Tom entered. He went to join them.

"All set, sir," Pete greeted him. "I've got a three-quarter-ton coming over from the MP motor pool with a driver and a guard. You and me can take the jeep. Okay?"

"Okay."

Pete glanced at his watch. "Should be here in a few minutes." He drained his cup with obvious pleasure and put it down. "I'll alert you when they arrive." He left.

Tom looked toward the prisoners watching him from their station on the bench. He caught Ilse's eyes. She looked away. He poured himself a cup of coffee. Larry always did make a hell of a good cup of coffee. Strong— and scalding hot. Cautiously he took a sip. He walked over to the Germans. "Good morning," he said pleasantly.

They chorused a polite, distant reply.

He turned to Ilse. "I hope you had a comfortable night, Fräulein Neumann," he said.

The girl looked up at him, her eyes big and fearful.

He smiled to himself. I won't give you away, honey, he thought. Don't worry.

"Yes. Thank you," she said in a small voice.

"Good." He smiled. He took another sip from his steaming cup. The aroma rising from it was delicious.

He was suddenly aware that the eyes of all three Germans were riveted on the cup and its fragrant contents. Of course! They had probably not had *real* coffee in ages. Ersatz by *any* name has only one taste. Bad. The prisoners were obviously very much aware of the tantalizing smell that drifted toward their eager nostrils. Even the imperturbable Beigel began to get restless.

Tom turned away. Beigel was no fool, and Tom did not want him to discern the kernel of an idea that had begun to germinate in his mind. He walked to the table and sat down. Leisurely he drank, obviously savoring the strong black coffee. He glanced toward the three Germans sitting in rigid discomfort on the bench. "We still have a little time," he said pleasantly. "Would you like to join us in a cup of coffee before we hit the road?" His tone of voice was quite casual.

Involuntarily the Germans tensed. For a moment they sat in utter silence. Then Ilse and Cornelius looked at Beigel. He kept staring straight ahead.

Tom drained his cup. He walked to the stove and began to pour himself a refill. The aromatic steam rose in enticing swirls. "You got enough Java in that pot, Larry, for a little extra?" he asked.

"All you want."

Tom turned toward the Germans. He held the steaming cup out toward them.

"How about it, Herr Generalmajor," he asked. "It may be a pretty cold trip."

Beigel turned to him. *"Ja. Danke,"* he said curtly.

Soon the Germans were seated at the big table with Larry and Tom, cups of rich hot coffee before them. *Real* coffee! Almost reverently they sipped the black brew.

Tom could almost see the stiffness and tenseness melt from them as they warmed and relaxed. It was the crucial moment. If he was to establish any kind of rapport with them outside of that infernal name-rank-serial-number shit—especially with Beigel—he'd have to tread softly.

He began by talking about the beauty of the Bavarian countryside—the hills and mountains clad in verdant evergreens.

They agreed.

Larry fished a pack of Luckies from his pocket and lit up comfortably. He pitched the pack onto the table before the Germans. "Help yourselves," he offered.

The two men stared at the tempting pack of cigarettes. Then, with a quick motion, Cornelius picked it up. He flipped out a cigarette and offered it to Beigel. The general hesitated—then took it. *"Danke."*

Larry pitched a book of matches to Cornelius. The colonel lit the cigarette for Beigel and took one himself. It did not occur to him to offer one to Ilse. German women did not smoke. The Führer frowned on it.

The smoke wafted up and mingled with the fragrant tendrils of steam from the coffee to embrace the little group in a mist of well-being.

Tom went on talking. "Bavaria is so different from northern Germany," he said. "Not only in looks. The people. Even the language. It always amazes me that there is such a tremendous difference between the German spoken in, let's say Prussia, and the dialect spoken here in Bavaria—only a couple of hundred miles away!"

Cornelius smiled. "Bayrisch is indeed a language all its own," he agreed.

Tom looked at Ilse. "Am I right?" he asked. "In Bavaria a pretty girl, instead of being *eine hübsches Mädchen,* is called a *Muckerl?* And her pretty eyes are *Guggerl* instead of *Augen?"*

Ilse blushed prettily.

Cornelius laughed. "Quite correct!" He looked at his cigarette with obvious appreciation. "And a *Zigarette* is called a *Schpreiz'n!*"

Tom and Larry joined him in his little laugh. Tom turned to Beigel. "Berlin, too, has quite a distinctive dialect, isn't that so, Herr Generalmajor?"

"There are many different dialects in Greater Germany," Beigel said stiffly. "They have never interested me. *Hochdeutsch*—High German—is our national tongue."

Tom nodded. "I quite agree. A national language *should* retain its purity." Tom soon had the German officers engaged in give-and-take conversation. He talked of Germany's great contributions to literature, to art and to science.

They agreed.

He talked of his father's and his own admiration of Wagner and his operas. Those grand, sweeping, forceful masterpieces of glorious music.

Again they agreed with him and told him why he was right.

He sipped his coffee. "Germany *is* a beautiful country," he said quietly. "And a country of great contradictions."

They looked at him.

"A country that can produce men like Goethe and Schiller. Holbein and Dürer. Like Wagner and Beethoven. Gutenberg and Keppler. You name them. Beauty and wisdom." He paused for a brief moment. They were all watching him. "And at the same time a Hitler, a Goebbels and a Himmler." He shook his head thoughtfully. "A strange people indeed."

Beigel reddened. "Nonsense!" he snapped. "You are being selective. You are not speaking of the German people. They were misled!"

Ilse drew in her breath sharply. Cornelius gave Beigel a quick penetrating look.

Tom ignored them. "Misled?" he said. "By whom? A handful of Nazis?"

"Not all of us agree with everything the Nazi party stands for. It is obvious. The leadership made mistakes. Certainly the Supreme Command has no military acumen."

"Hitler?" Tom interjected.

Beigel ignored him. "Of course mistakes were made. Strategic mistakes in the conduct of the war. Mistakes at home. Do not blame the German people."

"Why not? Why did the German *people* follow the Führer? And carry out his every order blindly?"

"They had no choice."

"No choice? Why not?"

"They could not object. Even in matters they did not condone. We— they were forced to support the Reich."

"How?"

"Through fear." Beigel frowned. "Yes. Fear. Fear of what would happen to them if they did rebel."

"Fear? I think not."

Sternly Beigel fixed him with questioning eyes.

Tom's mind was racing. I've got him, he exulted. He felt exhilarated. I have him interested. So far he has only mouthed the standard I-was-no-Nazi platitudes. But he is interested. He is arguing with me.

"Not fear, Herr Generalmajor," he said. "Terror."

Beigel dismissed it with an impatient wave of his hand. "It is the same."

"It is not. Fear has led men to great accomplishments. Terror never. It is totally negative. Unless you have felt it grip you many times, you will freeze before it. The best you can hope for is to learn to cope. To survive, quite simply. Or you learn to treat it as fear. Terror is a poison without an antidote, but fear can be conquered if you act. If you don't spend too much time thinking about it, but act. Action is the only antidote."

Beigel glared at him. "You cannot know," he growled. "You *do* not know. Circumstances forced—"

"Circumstances!" Tom interrupted. "What circumstances forced your leaders to take the path of terror and violence they did? To hurl the whole world into war!"

"It is a well-known fact! The unjust, the impossible Treaty of Versailles left Germany no choice!"

"That's a lotta bullshit! The same tired old excuses, Herr Generalmajor. It does not hold water."

Beigel glared at him. He was getting angry.

Good, Tom thought. Let him. "True," he went on. "Germany lost the war in 1918. But the peace treaty was not tough enough! This time—this time you have been beaten for good! The German military machine is kaput, once and for all!"

Beigel bristled angrily. "The military could have *won* the war! Against *all* its enemies, had we not been crippled by dilettante civilians!"

"Like Hitler?"

Beigel clamped his jaws shut, his face dark.

Tom went on. "Hitler's Third Reich is totally kaput, Herr Generalmajor. You know it. I know it. Done for. Germany will never again be a first-rate power."

Beigel spoke with dangerous control. "You are being arbitrary. You do not know what you talk about!"

"Look around you, General. Your country is in ruins. The cream of your nation's youth is spent. Your military might destroyed. Your industries, your economy shot to hell!"

"You are wrong!"

"Is he, Anton?" It was Cornelius. He looked soberly at his fellow officer. "Is he? . . . I am not so certain."

Beigel whirled toward him. "Yes! Dead wrong!" He snapped in anger. "*You* should know that better than anyone, Eugen!"

Tom's heart skipped a beat. In the flash of an instant he recognized what was happening. It was an old argument between the two fellow officers— the Junker and the "scholar." And right now—at this moment—mellowed by good coffee and stimulating conversation, the two men were completely off guard. Arguing as they had probably done so often in the past. He tensed. He knew he had to handle the situation with extreme caution. One wrong gesture, one wrong word, and the two men would be brought back to their bleak reality and clam up. He had a strong urge to look at Larry. To warn him with a glance. He suppressed it. He knew it was not necessary. And it would not have gone unnoticed by the general.

He refilled the coffee cups. The two Germans nodded perfunctory acknowledgment, as they would have if they had been seated in their own mess, Tom thought.

"We all did our duty, Anton," Cornelius continued. "We all obeyed the orders that came to us from OKW. You, too."

Beigel lapsed into silence.

Cornelius puffed thoughtfully on his cigarette.

Tom felt a surge of alarm. They were slipping away. He had to get them back. It was time to pounce. "General," he said, with just the right amount of disinterest, "you feel the colonel should know better than anyone, as you put it, that the German military is not beaten once and for all. . . . Why?"

Beigel started. He stared at Tom.

Tom met his look guilelessly. "I should have thought, as his superior officer, you would be the one to know best."

"Of course," Beigel snapped angrily. "The colonel performed his duties under my supervision. He is merely more conversant with details."

"Details? What details, General?"

Beigel waved his hand impatiently. "Of—" He suddenly stopped. He looked at Tom as if seeing him for the first time. Realizing who he was. His eyes widened. He snapped his head around to stare at Cornelius.

"What were his duties, General?" Tom persisted quietly.

Beigel's face slowly reddened. He clenched his teeth so tightly shut that the muscles stood out on his jaws.

Tom seemingly took no notice. He sipped his coffee. "From what you have already told us, General, the colonel's work pertained to Germany's capability to wage war, is that not correct?" He held his breath. Had he gone too far? Was he losing them?

Cornelius sat motionless, staring at Beigel. The general looked stricken. His jaws were grating in silent turmoil.

Ilse rose from her chair. Her soft face was pale. She went to stand by the officer's side. He did not notice.

Pleasantly Tom looked at Cornelius. Then back to Beigel. "Well?" he pressed. "That's what you told us, General. You, yourself. Isn't it?"

Incredibly the deep flush drained from the officer's face leaving it a sickly gray. He sat utterly still and motionless.

Ilse watched his inner struggle and torment with agony. He, the general himself, had just given the enemy the key to the vital information they so jealously guarded!

Beigel took a convulsive breath, as if he had forgotten how to breathe and suddenly remembered. The appalling truth hit him with the force of a two-ton bomb. *He had betrayed his trust.*

Ilse gave a little moan. "No!" she cried. "The general has told you nothing! Nor will he ever do so!" She sobbed. "But *I* will! I do not have *his* courage. *His* strength. What you learn you will learn from me!"

She turned to Colonel Cornelius. She was suddenly calm. "Colonel

Cornelius was working on a special Luftwaffe project. *The Collection and Evaluation of Information for Future War.*"

For a moment there was total silence in the room. Tom sat frozen. It was big. And it was not at all what he had expected.

Suddenly Ilse fell to her knees. She buried her face in Beigel's lap. She cried. "I had to tell them, Anton. . . . Please understand. I . . . had to." She wept uncontrollably.

The general said nothing. Slowly he raised his hand. Without looking at the girl he began to stroke her hair gently. He seemed oblivious to the others.

Tom turned to Cornelius. "You brought the documents with you? From Prague?"

The colonel nodded.

"You were under orders to preserve them?"

"Yes."

"You concealed them?"

"Yes."

"Where?"

Cornelius looked at Beigel. For a moment the eyes of the two German officers were locked together. Then the general turned aside. Cornelius sighed. He turned to Tom. "They are buried." He fell silent.

He thought for a while. He was shaken. How had he come to this? He had been so determined not to give away any military information. Only what was required. Name. Rank. Serial number. As his oath as an officer dictated. And now he suddenly found himself debating with himself how much to tell. Or not to tell. Neither he nor Beigel—nor the girl for that matter—had given away any concrete information. They could still revert to their posture of silence. Or could they? Perhaps they should never have let themselves be drawn into discussions with the Americans at all. About anything. But they had. It was too late. They *had* revealed that they were involved in a very special project of the Oberkommando der Luftwaffe. No longer were they merely ordinary officer prisoners. They were *special.* Very special. Ultimately their secret would be revealed completely; now their interrogators knew that a secret did indeed exist. And they *had* been talking. Talking freely. About many things. Somehow it did not seem so inconceivable to go on.

He did.

"We had orders to deliver our documents to a certain organization in the area. They were to be buried in a specially prepared concealment pit with the records of that organization. Once we had turned over our documents, we had orders to remain in the general area in concealment and to avoid capture and interrogation for as long as possible." He stopped.

Tom felt a rising excitement. He had difficulty keeping it out of his voice when he asked tensely, "Did your project have a code name, Colonel?"

Cornelius hesitated. Again he glanced at Beigel. The general remained silent. Cornelius nodded. "Yes."

"What was it?"

"FENIX."

Tom could taste his disappointment. But it was a fitting code name for the project that sought to aid the Third Reich to rise from defeat and explode in war once again. The Fourth Reich? Yes. It was not the code name he had hoped to hear. But it was fitting. *Fenix*—the fabulous bird that rose from its own ashes. The *Phoenix.*

"The organization you brought your documents to," he asked. "What kind of organization was it?"

Cornelius shook his head. "I do not know."

"You must have *some* idea." Tom's voice took on a hard edge.

Cornelius shrugged. "It was probably the Ordensburg. I am not certain."

Tom had heard of the Ordensburg—a Nazi party academy to train special young men for leading positions in the party. He filed away the information that the records of the organization were preserved. They should make interesting reading.

"Where exactly were the documents buried?" he asked.

Again Cornelius shook his head. "I do not know that either," he said. "The pit is somewhere on the estate of the Ordensburg. And it is a very large estate."

"Where?"

"Twelve kilometers north of Straubing. Overlooking the Danube River. On the east bank."

"Does the estate have a name?"

"Yes. Schloss Ehrenstein."

Tom went straight to the leather-cased field telephone installed in the *Bauernstube*. He lifted the receiver off the hook and turned the handle. "Iceberg Forward. Major Lee. CIC," he said briskly. He waited. Then: "Herb? This is Tom. Listen. What's the situation along the Danube about ten miles north of Straubing? . . . The east bank."

Larry had quickly brought out a map. He showed it to Tom, placing a finger on it.

"Coordinates Uncle 545425," Tom continued. He listened. "Okay. . . . Good. . . . Thanks." He started to hang up. The phone sputtered. Again he listened. Then: "The General Staff officers? . . . Yeah. Well, we'll be —" He reached down and began to crank the telephone handle spasmodically. "Hello! Hello!" he shouted into the mouthpiece. "Herb! I can't hear you. Bad connection. I'll get back to you later. Out!" He hung up. He turned to Larry. "We'll never get out of here if I have to explain to old Herb." He grinned. "Straubing is being mopped up. The area north of the town has been pretty much secured."

He glanced at the silent phone. "By the time Herb gets through chewing out the entire Signal Corps and gets on the horn, we'll be off. We've got business at Schloss Ehrenstein!"

He walked over to the three Germans. "You will be taken to Corps Headquarters for further interrogation. Sergeant Connors will be in charge," he informed them.

He glanced at Ilse. "You will be prisoners of war of the American armed forces—and you will be treated as such."

The girl's lips trembled involuntarily with her intense relief. She lowered her head.

Tom started to walk away. He stopped. He walked back to the prisoners. "One more question," he said. "Did anyone from your command at Oberwiese fire a shot two days ago?"

Cornelius looked startled. "Yes," he said. "I did."

"Why?"

The colonel cast an embarrassed glance toward Beigel. "I . . . I was getting tired of the monotony of canned army rations," he explained. "I thought rabbit stew would be a nice change." He smiled ruefully. "I missed."

Schloss Ehrenstein—Rock of Honor Castle—crowned a humpbacked hill overlooking the river, majestically dominating a huge forest-clad domain. Below, the famous "blue" Danube, flowing a muddy brown, washed the roots of the great estate. The Romany Gypsies coming from the Balkans called the river the "dustless highway." For those of them who traveled it during the mastery of the Third Reich it was a highway to hell. The hell of concentration camps.

A few miles to the north, atop another wooded hill, stood the imposing edifice Valhalla, named after the Norse mythology home of the Gods and the souls of fallen heroes. Erected by King Ludwig I of Bavaria, the ersatz Pantheon held a multitude of busts representing Germany's great, sitting perched on their shelves and pedestals timelessly staring at one another in stony silence. Here, according to the Nazi propaganda mill, the souls of those who died fighting to establish the master race would find their final hallowed resting place.

A long, winding road led to the secluded centuries-old castle itself. Along the way were signs of several abandoned guard posts and checkpoints. Whoever had occupied the mansion had obviously wanted strictly enforced privacy.

The main building of Schloss Ehrenstein was a massive edifice with a steep-backed red tile roof, several round cone-capped turrets and a large square tower topped by a squat black cupola. The spacious cobblestone-paved courtyard extending before the front entrance was surrounded by a thick, forbidding wall, and entered through a narrow tunnellike gateway.

Tom and Larry found the castle occupied by elements of an Engineer combat battalion.

A young talkative lieutenant showed them through the cavernous place. "You're just plain SOL," he said amiably. "There's not a damned thing here."

"How long have you been billeted in this godforsaken mausoleum?" Tom asked.

"Got here two days ago. The burg was deserted. The Kraut outfit that occupied the place cleared out about a week ago."

"How do you know that?" Larry wanted to know.

"The locals. I got a sergeant who *sprechen-Sie-Deutsch*. We always try to find out a little something about the place we take over. You never know." He led the way down a stone staircase to the castle basement. "Anyway," he continued, "the Krauts carted off everything that wasn't nailed down. And some that was. After that the place stood empty, and the locals went through it liberating anything that might have been over- looked. Then *we* got here."

They were making their way through a maze of corridors and passage- ways. The lieutenant paused at an open door. They glanced into a dismal empty room. Windowless, walls of bare concrete, it was depressing. On the wall opposite the door hung a big round clock, its face shattered.

"There's nothing left." The lieutenant nodded toward the mangled clock on the wall. "Nothing but junk." He walked on. "There's some sort of screwy shooting range down here, too. Place must have been a training school or something like that."

"That's probably what it was."

"Well, they sure stripped the hell out of it. I've never seen a place picked as clean as this one. Like as if one of those hordes of scavenger ants had swarmed through. Not once, but a dozen times! We've been over every damned square inch of the place. Nothing. Believe me, when my men can't find any loot, there's *nothing* to find!"

"You didn't run across any documents? Papers?"

"You kidding? Not even a used postage stamp, for crissake!"

"There was no one here at all, when you moved in?" Larry asked.

"There's an old Frau around someplace. A sort of half-assed caretaker. Only one who didn't scram. She has a room in one of the utility buildings. You can talk to her." He grinned. "But you won't get the time of day from her. She's as tight-lipped as a spinster at an orgy!"

Frau Peukert was a short, stocky woman whose graying hair, pulled tightly back into a firm bun, and round ruddy face with its straight-lipped, turned-down mouth and small piercing eyes set in a patchwork of crow's- feet wrinkles of the kind caused by a perpetual scowl rather than smile, fully corroborated her stated age of fifty-four.

She was demonstratively hostile and abrasively self-assured. Her sharp- pitched voice grated unpleasantly, and the young Engineer officer had been entirely wrong about her taciturnity. She talked. She talked a blue streak a minute.

Tom had no complaints on that score. It was *what* she said. She bitterly berated the Americans for overrunning the estate and despoiling it. She cursed the soldier vandals for taking over and defacing the venerable castle. She denounced the local farmers and villagers for robbing Schloss Ehrenstein of anything even remotely serviceable. She had been a housekeeper at the manor house itself for several years, a good one, ever since her late husband, the castle caretaker, had been drafted into the Wehrmacht. He had died a hero's death on the Russian front. She had kept the estate as immaculate as the Christ Child's crib—until foreign troops and piggish local riffraff had descended on the place.

It was not until Tom broke into her stream of vituperation and managed to ask her a direct question about the training school, which apparently had occupied Schloss Ehrenstein until recently, that she displayed her advertised reticence. Her already tight face grew tighter, and incongruously she snapped, "I have nothing to say."

Tom and Larry took turns firing questions at her. She showed no favoritism toward either of them, her only comment being a terse "I have nothing to say."

Finally Tom informed her that they knew certain records and documents were buried on the grounds of the estate, and that they meant to find out exactly *where* from her. He had expected some reaction to his blunt statement.

There was none. Except "I have nothing to say!"

She left little doubt as to what she really meant. Of course, she knew that. And, of course, she was not about to tell them anything.

But breaking the stubborn Frau Peukert not only would be difficult and time consuming. It would likely as not be impossible.

After instructing the Engineer officer to keep an eye on the woman and be sure she stayed put, Tom and Larry set out to track down the CIC team setting up in the nearby town of Straubing.

Straubing exhibited the usual chaotic mixture of fear and curiosity of a newly taken town. The familiar sheets of surrender fluttered from the windows, and empty flagpoles poked thin naked holes in the air. The signs *"Juden Nicht Erwünscht!*—No Jews!"—and other anti-Jewish slogans were hastily being removed by skittish shopkeepers from boarded-up stores and shops which sported sudden light-colored square patches on faded walls.

Small clusters of grim white-faced people huddled in the illusory safety of doorways, bleakly watching the enemy move in and take over. Nazi edicts and proclamations tacked up in conspicuous places were being replaced by stern U.S. Army curfew regulations—1900 to 0600 hours—and travel restrictions—six kilometers from home.

The CIC team had established HQ in a small inn on the outskirts of town, Gastwirtschaft Bockelmeier.

CIC agent Irwin Buter, and a young infantry noncom of German descent, Sergeant Winkler, who spoke German and had been "annexed" by the team as an interpreter, listened attentively to Tom's account of the investigations leading to Schloss Ehrenstein and the obstinate caretaker.

Buter looked at an area map. "I'm a stranger here myself," he said. "But I guess that is in our sector. You want us to take over?"

"No," Tom said quickly. "No. We'll handle it. It's . . . part of a case we're working on."

Larry gave him a curious glance.

Tom continued. "We just wanted you to know that we might be dipping into your sector occasionally. And we might call on you if we need a quick assist. But we're staying on the case."

Buter shrugged. "Terrific."

Tom turned as the door to the spacious *Gaststube* of the inn opened. A man entered. A civilian. Well built, in his early forties, with a strong, intelligent face, he was clad in typical Bavarian dress. Gray knickers, gray woolen over-the-calf socks and heavy brown tassel shoes. A green coarse-weave shirt and a plain green country jacket with brown bone buttons.

He nodded briefly toward Buter and walked straight to a table covered with papers, maps and books. He sat down and began to write.

Closely following him and taking his place on the floor beside the man was the most magnificent German shepherd dog Tom had ever seen: proud, powerful, with a gleaming black and tan coat. His bright alert eyes never left the men on the other side of the room. He sat quietly, motionless, yet leaving no doubt that the slightest hostile movement toward his master would uncoil a ferocious bare-fanged leap of instant defense.

Tom turned to Buter. "Who's your friend?" he asked.

Buter grinned. He turned toward the civilian. "Max!" he called. "Over here!"

The man stood up. The dog didn't budge. Without a glance, the man snapped a curt command: *"Zu Fuss!*—Heel!"

At once the dog jumped up and closely followed to the left of the man as he walked over to the CIC agents.

Buter made an elaborate gesture of introduction toward the civilian. "This is SS Major Maximilian Helmuth," he said. "Ex!" He grinned broadly. "And his superdog Rolf."

The major clicked his heels and bowed slightly. He did not extend his hand to the American officer. He had learned better. He remained standing, looking at the CIC agents without expression in his cold blue eyes.

"That's all, Max," Buter dismissed him.

Tom watched the man and his dog return to their table. He turned to Buter. "What the hell's *he* doing here? A Sturmbannführer making himself at home," he asked. "He's a mandatory!"

Buter smiled beatifically. He was enjoying himself hugely. "He's manna from heaven, my boy!"

"What are you on?" Larry asked. "Some kind of poison diet?"

"Just a glutton. Pure and simple." Buter looked smug. "Max is a veritable horn of plenty. We picked him up in Schwandorf. He came swaggering into our office big as life and introduced himself."

"I know that one," Tom remarked. "Another 'I-was-never-a-Nazi!' Just a spoke in the wheel. Have to turn when it turns."

"Not . . . exactly." Buter paused for obvious dramatic effect. Then: "Actually, he claimed to be Chief of Gestapo, Landkreis Regensburg!"

"You are kidding!" Larry was openly incredulous.

"He had all kinds of papers to prove it," Buter said. "Spread them out before us." He smiled in fond remembrance. "Added to the arm-long file we already had on the bastard, it made interesting reading."

"Okay, so what's the joke?" Tom wanted to know.

Buter leaned back in his chair. "Oh, we made a deal with him," he said airily.

"A deal?"

Buter nodded. "It was his idea. He very logically pointed out to us that he knew just about everything about everybody in the whole damned Landkreis who'd even as much as heard the word 'Nazi.' He proposed to deliver to us one mandatory arrestee, one wanted suspect a day, in return for his personal comfort and to be safe—both from us and from them."

"I'll be damned." Tom shook his head. "And you threw the rule book away. You agreed."

"You're damned right I agreed! I'm no latrine lawyer, but I sure as hell can spot a good deal when it comes marching right up to me."

He glanced toward the busily writing major. "Max has already been the key in cracking several tough cases. He's better than a coopful of stool pigeons. It's a good deal all around." He looked back at Tom. "He has a fair idea of what's in store for him once he's formally arrested and slapped in an internment camp."

"An exaggerated one, I'll bet," Larry commented dryly. "From observing his own concentration camps."

"So, it's deliver—or else," Tom said.

"Exactly. He knows enough about detective work and investigation procedure to realize that he has little chance of shaking us at this time, even if we do let him work with a minimum of supervision. Besides, he eats well."

He shrugged. "It may not be orthodox intelligence SOP, but it's sure paying off." He stretched lazily. "Why should I run my ass ragged when I can let some Kraut bastard do it for me? When *der Tag* comes, when his usefulness is kaput, we'll slap him in detention. Maybe his cooperation will count in his favor. Who knows?"

Tom was watching the Gestapo major thoughtfully. He turned to Buter. "Irwin," he said. "Mind if I borrow your magic major for a little quick job?"

"Help yourself. But return him in good condition. He's still got a lot of good mileage left in him."

Tom walked over to the Gestapo major. The man stood up. His dog watched Tom intently. "You are familiar with the Schloss Ehrenstein estate?" Tom came straight to the point. "On the Danube, north of here?"

A quick shadow seemed to flit across the major's face. Tom could not be sure. "*Ja.*"

"During the last few years, what was it used for?"

The major shrugged. "I am not certain," he said. "A training school for officer candidates, I believe. SS perhaps."

Tom nodded. His respect for the man's quick cunning increased. He had given just enough information. No more. No less. He had avoided the mistake of denying any knowledge at all, which would at once have made him suspect.

"We have reason to believe that certain records are buried on the estate. What do you know about that?"

"*Nichts*—Nothing."

Tom's voice hardened. "In that case you had better find out! Come up with someone who does!"

The major looked uneasy. "I . . . I may not be able to do that."

"I was under the impression that that was exactly what you are here to do!"

"Yes, but—"

"No *buts*, Major Helmuth," Tom interrupted, his voice dangerously low. "A *yes*. Or . . . if you are prepared to give it, a *no.*"

Helmuth fixed Tom with hard, piercing eyes. Tom returned his gaze steadily. He was well aware that he was being sized up. Helmuth looked away. "It . . . it may take time."

"Agreed," Tom snapped. "You'll have it. Two hours!"

Helmuth's face turned red. For a brief moment he glared at Tom. Then he said, "Two hours."

With a brief command, "Rolf! *Zu Fuss!*" he turned on his heel. Without a backward glance he stalked from the *Gaststube*, Rolf close behind.

Tom watched them leave. He walked back to the others. "Thanks, Irwin," he said.

He looked around the *Gaststube*. Most of the tables in the little country-style restaurant dining room had been pushed against the walls, some still covered with red-and-white-checkered tablecloths. Plain straight-backed wooden chairs were stacked in a corner. Only half a dozen tables were scattered about the room used by the CIC team as a common makeshift office. He turned to Sergeant Winkler. "Sergeant," he said. "I'll need an interrogation room. Private. In two hours." He glanced at his watch. "At 1630 hours. Okay?"

"Can do, sir." Winkler grinned. "Can do."

It was precisely 1627 hours when SS Major Maximilian Helmuth returned to Gastwirtschaft Bockelmeier. The frightened young girl he held firmly by the arm as he walked into the *Gaststube* had obviously been crying. Her eyes were red and puffed.

Tom and Larry were waiting for him. They watched as the Gestapo major pushed the girl into a chair. He gave Rolf a short command: *"Bewachen!—*On Guard!" The dog at once fixed his attention on the petrified girl. His lips drew back in a menacing snarl and a low growl rumbled in his throat as he watched his cringing charge.

Helmuth marched over to the CIC agents. "This is Fräulein Ingeborg," he reported dispassionately. "She was for some months an office worker at Schloss Ehrenstein."

"She has information?" Tom asked.

Helmuth shrugged. "Perhaps. She will not talk to me. But she is the only one still in the area. Except for the caretaker, Frau Peukert." He looked at Tom, flat-eyed, the hint of a sardonic smile on his lips. "But I understand *she* has already told you all she knows."

The bastard is rubbing our noses in it! Tom thought. The arrogant SOB.

Helmuth glanced at his watch. "Two hours," he said. He looked at Tom. "It is what you said, yes? I should have saved some time had I been told you already had interrogated Frau Peukert."

Tom chose to ignore him. He looked toward the girl. She sat rigidly terrified on her chair, staring wide-eyed at the menacing dog guarding her. "Call off your dog," he ordered.

Helmuth smiled a thin smile. "As you wish." He turned toward the dog. "Rolf! *Zu Fuss!*"

At once the dog broke off his watch and bounded over to stand close at Helmuth's heels. The girl sagged in her chair. She put her face in her hands. Her slender shoulders shook gently.

Tom glared at the SS major with ill-concealed distaste. "You will stay here, Major. You will hold yourself available. I will let you know if I want you." The order was impersonal. Intentionally curt.

Helmuth drew himself up. He clicked his heels, bowed slightly, smartly turned on his heel and walked off with Rolf close at heel. A performance of subservience bordering on mockery. It was not lost on Tom. He considered it a draw.

He walked over to the girl. "What is your name?" he asked.

She looked up at him, her eyes terror-stricken. "Rost," she whispered. "Ingeborg Rost."

He nodded. "They tell me, Ingeborg, that you worked in the administration office at Schloss Ehrenstein, is that correct?"

The girl stared at him, her wide eyes dark with fear and foreboding. She seemed to stop breathing. She uttered not a sound.

Sergeant Winkler came into the *Gaststube*. He walked up to Tom. "All set on that interrogation room," he said, looking with curiosity at the girl. "Best room in the inn with a fine view of World War Two!"

Tom watched the silent, frightened girl. She looked on the verge of nervous collapse. Even if she does know something, he thought, she's so damned scared she can't think straight enough to answer any questions intelligibly. To Winkler he said, "Not just yet, Sergeant. How are chances for some coffee? Strong and black?"

"Better than good, sir." The sergeant nodded toward a door. "Kitchen's over there. I'll have the coffee ready in less than no time."

As Ingeborg, sitting at the kitchen table with Tom, Larry and Winkler, sipped her hot coffee, she slowly lost some of her paralyzing fear.

Tom had deliberately stayed away from any anxiety-arousing questions as he calmly and reassuringly talked to her.

The girl was a stenographer-typist. She had indeed worked in the administrative offices of Schloss Ehrenstein, but in a strictly non-sensitive capacity. She had held her job for some five months, being assigned to it when she left the Bund Deutscher Mädel—the female branch of the Hitler Youth. She had been handling estate logistic and administrative correspondence and filing. She'd had no involvement with personnel, training or any policy matters of the organization occupying the castle. She only knew that the estate was used as some kind of school for young men, with whom she was told not to fraternize. And she knew that there had been definite SS supervision. She had been dismissed when the Schloss Ehrenstein operation was closed down.

"As a typist and file clerk you must have handled a lot of letters," Tom suggested pleasantly. "A lot of documents."

Ingeborg nodded.

He paused for a moment. He looked straight at her. "What happened to all those records and files when the organization pulled out of the castle?" he asked.

The girl tensed, her cup forgotten in her hands. Some of the old fear crept back into her eyes.

"What was done with them?" Tom pressed. "You were there to the last. You must know."

The girl stared at Tom. The color in her softly rounded cheeks, brought back by the hot coffee and carefully nurtured sense of danger past, visibly drained away.

"Please," she begged. "Please, I do not know what was done with the documents. I do not know where they are. Already I told the major." Involuntarily she flinched, conjuring up the images of the Gestapo officer and his dog. "Please do not hurt me," she pleaded. "I will do anything you ask, but please do not hurt me. I . . . I do not know." Tears of terror and self-pity welled up in her eyes.

Unsparingly Tom persisted. "Tell me what you *do* know."

She shook her head slowly in fearful, silent indecision.

Tom's voice took on a harsh edge. He leaned closer to the girl, deliberately violating the private ego space she maintained around her. "What was done with the records of Schloss Ehrenstein?" he demanded.

She strained away from him, pressing her body against the straight hard back of the chair. "I . . . I think a lot of the papers were destroyed," she whispered. "Burned."

"All of them?"

"No." She caught herself. "I . . . I do not know."

"Did *you* help dispose of any papers?"

"No."

"Did you help *hide* anything?"

It was a leading question. He knew it. It was a calculated risk. The girl was desperately anxious to find something to please her interrogator. It was a common reaction. He could only hope that her answers would be true, and not merely what she thought he wanted to hear. He waited.

"No . . . no . . ." she stammered. "I . . ." She stopped. She looked down. She was lying.

He knew it.

Abruptly he stood up. The girl's half-filled cup clattered to the table, rich brown coffee spreading in a dark stain on the tabletop. He loomed over the petrified girl. "Well!" he snapped, the last vestige of his calm and friendly manner wholly replaced by brusque exasperation. "Did you? Or did you not?"

She shrank from him. "They . . . they made me swear not to tell!" It was barely a whisper.

Tom drew back a little. "But you *will* tell, won't you?"

"Please . . ." Her wounded eyes implored him.

"Now!"

She flinched. She sat in agonizing silence for a moment. He did not pressure her. Then she went on, her voice trembling: "I . . . I helped the housekeeper, Frau Peukert. I helped her pack a large steel filing cabinet. From the office." Her voice broke. With difficulty she swallowed. The men watched her in utter silence. "It . . . it was supposed to be . . . to be buried. In the woods. On the estate." She sobbed.

"Was it?"

"Yes."

"You know where?"

"Yes."

Tom straightened up. He felt some of his tenseness leave him. He had not been aware of how stiffly he'd carried his shoulders. It surprised him. He felt elated. At last!

"What was in the filing cabinet?" he asked, unable completely to keep his excitement out of his voice.

The girl wet her bloodless lips. She looked imploringly from one of the men to the other. She fixed her huge eyes beseechingly on Tom. There was no reprieve. And the words came tumbling out. "Silk. Silk and brocade from Paris. Silverware. Gold coins. And jewelry. Stockings. Perfume. And . . . But, please, Herr Offizier, nothing of it is mine. Nothing! I swear it. I only did what I was told. It all belonged to the colonel. The commandant. *He* took it. When he was in Paris. Some of it is the woman's. Nothing is mine! Please . . . do not punish me. I . . . I was afraid. They made me swear. On my faith in the Holy Virgin. They made me swear not to tell!"

She buried her face in her hands and leaned her arms on the table, oblivious to the puddle of cold coffee smearing the smooth skin on her bare arms. She cried, partly with relief, partly with fear.

Tom looked down at her. Loot! he thought, the disappointment bitter in his mouth. Nothing but some SS bastard's damned loot! He bent down to her. He lifted up her tear-stained face. He looked searchingly at her. "Do you know of any other place where things are buried?" he asked wearily. He already knew the answer.

"No."

He believed her. Had she known, she would have talked. He took a deep breath.

The door to the *Gaststube* opened, and Buter stood in the doorway. He took in the scene around the table. "Cozy," he commented dryly. "How goes it?"

"Great," Tom said bleakly, looking up at Buter. "Just great."

"Terrific."

Tom glanced past the CIC agent in the doorway into the *Gaststube* beyond.

At a far table sat SS Major Helmuth, stiffly waiting to be summoned. Patiently, watchfully Rolf lay at his feet, eyes and ears alert.

Ingeborg followed his gaze. She shuddered.

Tom looked at her. Suddenly he drew himself up. "Hey, Irwin!" he said, new vigor in his voice. "How's the chow in this here outfit?"

"The best. We . . . ah . . . 'inherited' a well-stocked larder from the former *Inhaber*. It's in the basement."

Tom looked pleased. "I was hoping you'd say that!" He looked around him. "I could use a bite. Lead the way, Irwin."

He turned to Sergeant Winkler. "And, Winkler. Ask the major to join us." He looked into the *Gaststube*. "And, of course, Rolf!"

6

The morning of April 29th was gray and overcast. In the doorway to the Gastwirtschaft Bockelmeier Tom squinted up at the gloomy sky. He hoped it wouldn't rain.

He yawned. It had been a rough night. Hours spent in meticulous preparations. It had better work.

He surveyed the scene of activity in the courtyard before him. Several U.S. Army vehicles were drawn up at one end of the yard. Three jeeps, one of them his own, and a 2½-ton open truck. A handful of MP guards were herding a group of a score or so German PW's equipped with picks, spades and shovels onto the truck. The clanging sounds òf metal striking metal rang out in the dismal morning as the PW's manhandled their tools aboard.

SS Major Maximilian Helmuth stood by himself at one of the jeeps, a forbidding ramrod figure; Rolf sat at his side eying the activity with alert suspicion. Larry and Sergeant Winkler were poring over a map spread out on the hood of one of the other jeeps, and a few kids hung around the wide courtyard gate watching the proceedings with frank curiosity.

Agent Buter joined Tom at the entrance. "Morning," he said.

"Morning."

"Quite a show you're putting on."

"You ain't seen nothing yet!" Tom grinned. "I hope! How about coming along?"

"Is that a request?"

"Hell, no. I thought you might like to be in on the fun and games."

"Volunteer?" Buter sounded horrified.

"Why not?"

"You *must* be kidding! I haven't volunteered for anything since basic training."

"How's our little Ingeborg?"

"Still impersonating the Sleeping Beauty."

"Keep her here until the operation has been completed. Just in case."

"Will do." Buter nodded toward the Gestapo major. "How're you getting along with marvelous Max?"

"Fine. I've got him eating out of my hand."

"Yeah? Have you counted your fingers lately?"

Larry came up to them. "Ready to go," he said.

"Okay. Let's get the show on the road."

Buter raised his hand benevolently. "Good hunting!"

Forty-five minutes later the little convoy drove up to the main entrance of Schloss Ehrenstein and ground to a halt.

In the lead jeep were Tom and Larry, followed by a second jeep driven by Sergeant Winkler, with Major Helmuth and Rolf in the back. Then the 2½-ton, crammed with the German PW's and their tools. The rear was brought up by a jeep with four MP guards, weapons at the ready.

In front of the castle entrance the young Engineer lieutenant stood waiting, a detail of his men at parade rest behind him. Next to him stood the caretaker, Frau Peukert, flanked by two burly soldiers. Churlishly she glowered at the unfolding spectacle.

Tom and Larry dismounted and marched up to the lieutenant. The officers exchanged salutes, and Tom turned briskly to the woman. He wasted no time. "We now possess definite proof that the Schloss Ehrenstein documents are buried here on the estate," he declared, his voice brisk. He looked straight at the scowling woman, matching her grimness. "We are also informed that you do know *where!* If we are forced to find the records without your cooperation, Frau Peukert, you will have to bear the consequences. The serious consequences. I hope that is fully understood."

He paused significantly. Then, solemnly, he went on: "We are here to give you one last chance." Momentously he gave the two last words unmistakable capital-letter importance. He watched the woman closely. He hoped he was being properly impressive. She returned his gaze. It was difficult for him to tell just what she was thinking. Only one emotion showed through on her stony face: contempt.

"I have nothing to say," she said in her flat tone of voice. "Nothing."

Tom whirled on his heel. "Sergeant Winkler!" he called. "Dismount the prisoners!"

At once Winkler and the MP guards began to order the German PW's from the truck. With shouts of *"Schnell! Schnell!"* and *"Los!"* they formed the men in a column of twos, each man carrying a pick, a spade or a shovel.

Tom turned back to the sullen woman. "As you can see, Frau Peukert, we have come prepared," he said. "We will keep searching and digging until we find what we're looking for." He watched her closely. "And heaven help you when we do," he added portentously.

The woman's mien of confident scorn did not change. She knew perfectly well that it would take a lifetime of digging before anything could be found on the hundreds of acres of land that made up the estate of Schloss Ehrenstein. Unless . . . unless the diggers knew exactly where and how deep to dig.

She shook her head. "I have nothing to say."

He had expected it. He turned toward the jeep where Major Helmuth and Rolf were waiting. "Major Helmuth!" he called.

The major dismounted. Leading Rolf on a long leash, coiled like a lasso in his hand so that the dog trotted close by his left leg, he walked over to stand next to Tom, facing the recalcitrant woman.

"This is Sturmbannführer Maximilian Helmuth," Tom said importantly. "Gestapo."

He thought he saw a brief flicker of alarm in the woman's flat eyes. He went on. "The dog's name is Rolf. He has been trained by the Gestapo for a very special purpose." He lowered his voice and spoke with grave emphasis. "You see, Frau Peukert, we will not search aimlessly. We will not dig without method. Rolf will show us *where* to dig. He has been carefully trained to smell out where anything touched by human hands lies buried, even though weeks may have passed!"

He turned to Helmuth. "Am I correct, Major?" he asked.

"Ja!" The Gestapo officer's answer was curt.

For the first time the woman looked a little uneasy. A little uncertain. Her eyes involuntarily went to Rolf. Helmuth gave a short yank on the leash, and the dog bared his fangs and growled threateningly, never taking his savage eyes from the woman before him.

For a moment she was unnerved. But her native peasant astuteness won out. She correctly reasoned that *no* dog—Gestapo-trained or not—could possibly nose out weeks-old diggings in a fast-growing spring forest. She smelled the bluff. A thin, mocking smile grew on her lips. "Let the dog show you then," she said. "I cannot!"

He turned his back on her. "Ready to move out!" he shouted.

It was an impressive procession lined up on the grounds before the castle, facing the forest beginning nearby. At the head stood SS Major Helmuth, holding the eagerly straining Rolf on a tight leash. Behind them the column of PW's, shouldering spades, picks and shovels, led by Sergeant Winkler and guarded by the four MP's. And bringing up the rear the Engineer lieutenant and his detail of men, carrying ropes, axes and hoisting equipment.

The woman took it all in. The open derision on her heavy face had given way to uneasy apprehension. But the set of her jaw was still stubborn and firm.

Tom turned to her. "Well, Frau Peukert. Have you anything to say?"

She did not answer him. Stony-faced she stared straight ahead.

He turned to the two soldiers flanking her. "Bring her along," he ordered sharply.

Together he and Larry marched to the head of the column. Larry glanced at his partner. He looked faintly amused. "Curtain, act one," he said. "On with the play!"

"With a cast of thousands." Tom grinned. "I only hope they know how to deliver their lines!" They took up positions directly behind the Gestapo major and his dog.

"Major Helmuth," Tom said. *"Los!*—Let's go!"

At once the Gestapo officer dropped the long coiled leash from his hand, holding on only to the looped end of it, giving Rolf full rein. *"Such!"* he commanded urgently. *"Such! Such!*—Search! Search!"

With a small yelp of excitement, nose to the ground, Rolf took off. Zigzagging, he searched and sniffed the ground before them in ever widening loops. Suddenly he let out an eager bark, and tugging at the leash, he led his master toward the forest.

Falling in behind came Tom and Larry, the Peukert woman and her two guards, Winkler, the column of PW's and their MP guards, and the Engineer lieutenant with his detail of men, all half-trotting to keep up with the straining dog.

Through the forest wound the whole procession, following the convoluted zigzag track of the dog. Deeper and deeper in among the trees and brush. From time to time Rolf would yelp excitedly as he pulled on his leash in his efforts to leap ahead.

Tom gave the Peukert woman a quick glance. She seemed less sure of herself as they went on.

They were about four hundred yards into the woods when Rolf suddenly reared and barked sharply.

The major released him, and at once he streaked away on a tangent. But only a short distance. At the edge of a small clearing he stopped. Furiously he began to scratch and claw at the ground.

Helmuth ran to his dog. He clipped the leash back on his collar and held him off.

The Peukert woman had stopped dead in her tracks. She stood stock still, staring at the excited barking dog, her face deathly pale and drawn, her eyes wide in silent, incredulous terror.

Tom took her firmly by the arm. Like an automaton she walked with him. He led her to the spot on the ground that showed the scratch and claw marks of the Gestapo dog. She stared at the dog. Tom turned to the dazed woman. "Is there anything buried here?" he asked sharply.

She did not hear him.

He stepped in front of her. "Answer me!"

She shook her head. Whether in defiance or incredulity, he could not be sure. He grabbed a spade from one of the PW's. He shoved it at her. "Dig!"

She made no move. No sound. Her eyes, aghast, were riveted on Rolf.

The dog crouched before the woman, snarling and growling dangerously, deep in his throat. His ferocious eyes never left her. His bared fangs gleamed evilly above his dripping crimson tongue. Only the sturdy leash held by Helmuth kept him in check.

"Dig!" Tom repeated. "Or are you afraid of what you will find?"

The woman stood motionless, mesmerized, staring at the menacing dog as if she were looking at the devil himself.

Tom turned to Winkler. "Tell the prisoners to start digging," he ordered. He looked gravely at the woman. "You have made your choice, Frau Peukert," he said.

She shivered abruptly. She tore her gaze from the dog. She grabbed Tom's arm. "Wait!" she cried. It was a sound of soul-tearing agony. "Wait!" Her voice was deeply shaken. Unreal. *"Der Hund hat rechts!"* she murmured. "The dog is right!"

He thrust his face close to hers. Razor-eyed, he glared at her, holding her. He shot his questions at her like staccato bursts from a machine gun. "There is something buried here?"

"Yes."

"There are other burial places?"

"Yes."

"You will show us where?"

"Yes."

"How many?"

"One."

He frowned. "Only one?"

"Yes. Most of the papers were burned. Only the most vital documents were buried."

"Here?"

"No."

"Where?"

She pointed.

"In the woods. That way."

"What is buried here?"

She averted her eyes. "Only . . . personal belongings. The commandant's personal belongings."

He turned from her. "Sergeant Winkler," he called. "Have the men fall in. We are moving on to another burial spot. Frau Peukert will lead us." He turned to the woman. "On your way," he ordered.

She seemed to sag a little. Her ruddy complexion had gone sickly gray, her defiant eyes lackluster. She was thoroughly cowed. She started off into the forest.

Tom walked at her side. He felt good. His scenario was working out beautifully. It was just as well that the Peukert woman had refused to dig at the hiding place where the commandant's loot was buried, he thought. Only a foot down she would have unearthed the foot-long, arm-thick Bavarian sausage he'd placed there! The spicy, strong-smelling sausage he'd liberated from Buter's larder and spent half the night dragging all over God's half acre, laying a trail for Rolf to follow, leading to the only place where he *knew* from Fräulein Ingeborg that something had been buried! The only place Rolf could possibly have found. The Gestapo dog had played his role like a real trouper.

The second burial spot was half a mile farther into the forest. Frau Peukert pointed wordlessly to a spot between two tall pine trees, and the PW's went to work with their picks and shovels.

Grimly the woman watched the men dig into the loosely packed ground. She was deeply disturbed.

The enemy was unearthing a cache of documents never meant for eyes hostile to the Third Reich. She did not know the full import of the buried records. But she did know that their discovery by the *Amis* had to be reported at any cost, and she knew to whom. They would know what steps to take.

She knew what she must do. As soon as circumstances would permit.

An hour later a pit had been exposed, a deep square concrete shaft lined with tarpaper. In it rested three steel boxes, each twice the size of a footlocker.

Using their heavy ropes the Engineers brought up the top box. It was securely locked, and totally without markings. But on the lids of the two boxes remaining in the pit Tom could make out the flying eagle insignia of the Luftwaffe and the letters OKL—Oberkommando der Luftwaffe—Air Force High Command. The records of the Cornelius Luftwaffe project! *The Collection and Evaluation of Information for Future War.*

It was what he had come for. It was a whale of a haul! The unmarked box would be the records of the Schloss Ehrenstein school. He had the Engineers put it aside. It could wait. He was eager to take a look at the Luftwaffe documents.

Larry came up to him. Tom grinned broadly. "We pulled it off!" he exulted. "It was beautiful!" He laughed. "I'll never forget the look on that

Frau's puss. It was worth the entire price of admission!"

"Wait till she finds out about the damned sausage," Larry said. "She'll split her gut! That was some trail you laid. Even *I* could smell it!"

Tom laughed. "I wonder how many other cases have been solved by a dog," he said. "And a sausage! A Gestapo dog—and a Counter Intelligence sausage! A hell of a tough act to follow." He turned back to watch the Engineers wrestle the Luftwaffe boxes from the pit.

The bone-rattling explosion slammed into him with numbing force, shooting searing lances of pain through his ears. He whirled around while the deadly thunder still hung in the acrid air.

The Schloss Ehrenstein documents box had been opened! It was a mass of seething flame. Tom rushed toward it. The whole infernal scene instantly etched itself indelibly on his mind.

Sgt. Winkler lay writhing on the ground near the blazing box. His clothing spurted white-hot flames in several places. His face was a glistening mask of crimson ooze. His hands suddenly burned with a searing pain. With a mind-wrenching effort he forced his eyes open. He brought his pain-torn hands up. He held them to his face. And he screamed.

There—were—no—hands. Only two bloody stumps spurting his life away. It was the last sight he ever saw.

In the same instant Tom saw Larry run to the fiery box. He saw him thrust his bare hands into the flames. He heard him bellow with raw pain. He saw him tear his hands away, clutching a sheef of burning papers. He saw him hurling them to the ground, stamping out the flames.

Tom was at Winkler's side. He saw at once he could do nothing. For an instant he looked at the dead soldier. Winkler . . . Sergeant . . . a boy . . . of German descent.

He felt a sudden sharp stab of all-engulfing identification. *Of German descent.* Dead.

The boy had let curiosity get the better of him. He had been impatient. With a pickax he had forced the lock on the Schloss Ehrenstein box. But the documents it contained were never meant to fall into enemy hands. The Germans had guarded well against it. As the lock was broken and the lid pried open, a violent incendiary charge exploded, spewing jagged steel splinters and instantly setting ablaze the papers inside.

Tom ran to Larry. His partner was sitting on the ground, dazed, his hands held tightly in the pits of his arms, his face a drawn mask of agony.

Tom gently pulled Larry's hands from their inadequate sanctuary. He gasped. The hands were horribly burned. Bits of the white phosphorus from the incendiary charge—hot enough to burn through steel—had been imbedded in the skin and seared away the flesh to the blackened bone. The fingers on both hands were distended, encased in charred crusts.

Tom gagged. "You—goddamned—fool," he sobbed. His voice broke. He looked up. "Medic!" he shouted. "Medic, dammit! Medic!" He looked at Larry. His eyes smarted. It was not the smoke.

Larry numbly examined his mangled, disfigured hands. "I . . . didn't count on that damned phosphorus," he mumbled. "I guess . . . I guess I bought myself a Stateside ticket." He looked up at Tom. "Winkler?" he asked.

"He bought it. All the way."

Larry shivered. His face was growing ghostly pale. He was rapidly going into shock.

Two Engineers came running up.

"Get him back!" Tom snapped savagely. "Get him to an aid station, dammit! Get—" He stopped. He stood up and turned away. His throat was too tight for him to go on.

The Engineers hurried Larry away.

Tom watched the lieutenant and some of his men valiantly trying to get at the still blazing documents box. They managed to overturn it, spilling the contents out on the ground. They stamped on the papers furiously.

But it was too late. The incendiary bomb had done its job too well. There was nothing left but still smoldering ashes and black flakes of scorched and burned paper. Nothing. Except—

His eyes sought the papers Larry had pulled from the fire. They were lying on the ground where he had thrown them. Perhaps three or four sheets, the edges seared and browned. Numbly he picked them up. They had been bought at a terrible price.

Standing rooted to the spot he stared at the top sheet:

GEHEIM   GEHEIM   GEHEIM
[Secret]   [Secret]   [Secret]

UNTERNEHMEN SCHWEIGEAGENT
[Operation]   [Sleeper Agent]

PERSONALBOGEN
[Personal Dossier]

KESSLER, RUDOLF
RUDI A-27

Beneath the code name someone had written in a careful, meticulous hand,

КОНОN

PART 3
30 APRIL–5 MAY 1945

7

Obersturmführer Rudolf Kessler glanced impatiently at his watch. He was surprised to see that the day had come to an end. It was just past midnight. Living underground gave little sense of passing time.

He was restless. He had been waiting tensely almost an hour outside Bormann's private bunker office. He knew that when the door finally opened and he was called in, he would be facing the Reichsleiter himself —and the climax of the last few frantic days of briefing.

Time was running out. Too fast. The place was rife with rumors. They said that the Russians were only a mile away. They said they would reach the Führerbunker on May 1st or 2nd. They said that General Wenck's rescue army was still expected any hour.

Everything seemed to have been speeded up. Crazily. Even time itself. Months flew like days.

He had not liked his stay in the bunker. He felt both physically and mentally entombed. Life around him had a nightmarish quality. It made him feel constantly uneasy. Yet, never before in his life had he felt so exhilarated, so keyed up, as he did at this very moment.

His briefing on KOKON was completed. He had been instructed in everything: his own specific orders, Reichsleiter Bormann's personal plans, the innermost secrets of KOKON! He—knew.

He shifted uncomfortably on the bench. He watched the steady stream of grim people passing before him. The domed yellow ceiling lights gave an eerie, unnatural cast to the scene. It seemed to him as if all the *Bonzen* —all the big shots—in Germany were hurrying through the bunker corridors deep under the Reichschancellery. Generals, admirals, diplomats and ministers. Nazi officers of the highest ranks.

He felt a fierce pride surge through him. At this moment, he, Rudi Kessler, was more important than any one of them! Again he looked at his watch. It had been an eventful day. Before it was over it would surely be the most eventful day in his life.

Early in the morning the Führer had married Fräulein Eva Braun. The ceremony had taken place in the maproom of the Führer's private quarters. Reichsleiter Bormann had been there, of course. Rudi had not been present at the modest champagne reception afterward, but later he had congratulated the Führer with the others. He was pleased. He liked the friendly, unpretentious Fräulein Eva.

The Reichsleiter had been occupied with urgent affairs all morning, and at noon three important officer couriers, one of them Standartenführer Wilhelm Zander, Bormann's personal aide, had left the bunker on a vital mission. It was rumored that they carried copies of the Führer's personal and political testaments. He had been awed. Papers, he thought. Papers covered with the marks of the future.

Later in the afternoon he had played for a while with the Führer's Alsatian dog, Blondi, and her new litter of puppies. One of them had been his special favorite. It had reminded him of Mausi. He frowned. That was ridiculous. Anyway, it was completely immaterial. The dog had been ordered put to sleep.

Dr. Haase had given her poison while she was quietly nursing her four pups. She died almost instantaneously. So fast that her puppies were still trying to suckle her in death. Standartenführer Günsche, the Führer's personal bodyguard, carried her body in a box to the garden above to be buried. There he shot the pups, one by one, still clinging to their mother's teats.

It was too bad, he thought unemotionally. But since the order had been given to do it, it was obviously necessary.

In the evening, while the Führer had been in conference with his military leaders, some appalling news had reached the bunker. Reichsleiter-SS Heinrich Himmler had turned traitor! He had made an offer to the Anglo-American High Command to surrender Germany! Himmler! That back-stabbing *Schweinehund!*

And if that was not enough, only a few hours ago the Führer had finally received the delayed report that Mussolini and his mistress, Clara Petacci, had been caught by partisan terrorists the day before. They had been executed, their bodies desecrated and barbarously strung up by their heels. The news had depressed everyone. An ignoble end for such a valiant leader. A friend of the Führer himself.

He took a deep breath. He glanced toward the closed door.

An eventful day. A time of critical decisions. Momentous tasks. He, Rudi Kessler, was living history that would never die. But it all paled in his mind when he contemplated his own mission, yet to be carried out! KOKON.

The door to Bormann's office suddenly opened.

Rudi had expected to see Bormann's secretary, Fräulein Else Krüger, "Krügerchen—Little Krüger"—as she was affectionately called by the Reichsleiter's staff.

The man standing in the doorway was familiar to him. It was the civilian who had examined him at Schloss Ehrenstein, Brigadeführer Arnold. This time he wore his SS general's uniform. He motioned Rudi to enter.

Reichsleiter Martin Bormann sat in stocky stolidity behind his massive desk, brought down into the bunker from his offices in the Reichschancellery above. His arms were folded across his chest, the swastika armband prominent on his simple uniform. He was not an impressive man.

Rudi always felt a twinge of disillusion when he saw the Reichsleiter in person. But it was just that. A fleeting thought. He knew that Bormann's mind was the sharpest, the most cunning in Germany. He knew him to be the true heir of the Führer himself.

Arnold took his place at the side of the Reichsleiter. He placed his uniform cap on the desk: Rudi glanced at it. Once before—how long ago? —he had stood before a desk staring at the death's-head emblem on a black peaked SS uniform cap.

The meaning of the skull and crossbones flashed through his mind. "Obedience and loyalty to the Führer and to one another unto the grave and beyond!" It had been the credo of the ancient Teuton knights. He believed in it.

Bormann's small piggish eyes set deeply in his coarse-featured face fixed Rudi with a penetrating stare. "Obersturmführer Kessler," he said solemnly.

Rudi snapped to attention.

"You are about to embark upon the most crucial mission of your life."

Gravely he paused. Then he continued. "For some time now you have undergone intensive briefing. By me. By others. I should have liked to examine you thoroughly, to ascertain without doubt that you are ready for your mission. But time will not permit."

He glanced at Arnold. "Brigadeführer Arnold assures me, however, that you are a young man of exceptional abilities. Of great resourcefulness. I rely on his judgment. He and I will cover only the essential facts of your mission with you now. Understood?"

Rudi clicked his heels. *"Jawohl,* Herr Reichsleiter!"

Bormann nodded.

Arnold spoke. "You realize the enormous trust placed in you," he said solemnly. "By your country. Your people. Your Führer. And most especially by Reichsleiter Bormann himself?"

"I do, Herr Brigadeführer," Rudi said. "I shall honor it!"

"During the last few days you have been instructed in the most sacred secrets of the German Reich," Arnold continued. "Secrets that spell life or death for her future." He leaned forward in his chair and gazed at Rudi. "The Reichsleiter felt that you had to be fully and completely informed on all levels in order to function at peak efficiency. On my assurances, Obersturmführer Kessler, no restrictions, I repeat *no* restrictions, were placed on your need to know."

He leaned back in his chair. "You are already fully conversant with your duties as a Sleeper Agent. At this moment you possess full knowledge of the preparations and plans for our entire Sleeper Agent network in the United States of America. There is no need to discuss these matters further. You are well aware of the importance, of the potential value, of Operation Sleeper Agent. It was proven by our quick victory in Poland. You were there. We shall limit ourselves, here and now, to your mission for KOKON. Is that clear?"

"It is, Herr Brigadeführer," Rudi answered crisply. He began to feel impatient. He wished they would get on with their questioning. He was eager to show them that he had mastered everything he had been told. That his comprehension was complete.

Arnold went on. "I asked you once before, Obersturmführer Kessler, to recite to me the solemn oath of loyalty to your Führer, which you swore as an officer in the SS. I ask you now to do so again!"

Rudi drew himself up proudly. He delivered the familiar, stirring oath in a ringing voice. "I swear to you, Adolf Hitler, as Führer and Reichschancellor, loyalty and valor. I vow to you, and to those you have named to command me, obedience unto death, so help me God!"

Arnold leaned forward. His eyes bored into Rudi's. ". . . and to those you have named to command me," he repeated slowly, significantly. He looked at Reichsleiter Bormann, then back at Rudi. "Obedience unto death! You understand?"

"*Jawohl*, Herr Brigadeführer. And I obey!"

Arnold nodded. "*Gut.*" He sat back. "You will now recapitulate your orders. Begin with your departure from the bunker."

Rudi spoke crisply, to the point. "At a designated time I shall leave the Führerbunker and the Chancellery through the underground garages exiting on Hermann Göring Strasse," he began. "I shall proceed through the Tiergarten, through Charlottenburg to Pickelsdorf at the north end of Havel Lake. Here the bridge is being held by a battalion of Hitlerjugend. I shall then proceed south to Wannsee. From there west toward the Elbe River. I shall follow the east bank of the Elbe, heading for Hamburg and Schleswig-Holstein. I shall bypass Hamburg proper and proceed to Flensburg on the Danish border, which I have been told will be held by German forces as long as possible."

"You have calculated the length of your journey?" It was Bormann.

"Yes, Herr Reichsleiter. Four hundred and twenty kilometers, if no detours are necessary."

"You have five days."

"Yes, Herr Reichsleiter. It will be enough."

"The Schleswig-Holstein area, including Hamburg, is held by our forces. The Americans have stopped their advance on the west bank of the Elbe River," Arnold said. "Our latest information indicates that scattered Russian combat patrols have penetrated to the east bank. However, no enemy forces are present in strength."

Rudi knew. He had to run the gantlet between the American and the Russian forces until he reached territory held by the Wehrmacht. He was confident he could succeed.

"Show caution," Arnold said. "The situation is extremely fluid."

"*Jawohl*, Herr Brigadeführer."

"And trust no one!" Bormann interjected. "Not the civilians. Not our own troops. Rely exclusively on yourself."

Rudi looked at Bormann with surprise, quickly controlled. *"Jawohl,* Herr Reichsleiter."

"Reports have reached us of . . . severe action taken against suspected deserters and defeatists by roving patrols of SS troops," Arnold explained. "You may see the results hanging from several lampposts," he added. "Should they question you, search you and find your papers . . ." He shrugged eloquently.

"Your papers have been issued to you?" Bormann asked.

"Yes, Herr Reichsleiter. One set of German ID papers in my own name and rank. One set of Danish papers in the name of Rudolf Rasmussen."

He carried the German papers in the breast pocket of his uniform tunic. The Danish set was taped to the small of his back. He had examined the false papers minutely. They were perfect, including the Danish passport produced by the SS Department of Forged Documents. No one could possibly detect they were not genuine.

"After I have arrived in America I shall revert to the cover identity prepared for me by Operation Sleeper Agent." He looked from one officer to the other. "I have also been issued a sum of money in German as well as Danish currency," he added.

"Very good. Proceed."

"In Copenhagen I am to meet an Abwehr contact on the staff of Generalgouverneur Dr. Werner Best, whose name has been given me. Sturmbannführer Dettling. Gestapo. This contact will hand over to me the final list of Sleeper Agents to be deployed in the United States. I will memorize this list and destroy it. This man has also arranged passage for me to New York City in America, traveling as a Danish subject, a technical expert. As corroboration in case of any future check on my identity he has had my cover name inserted on the Gestapo list of employees of the Adler Motor Works in the Sydhavnen district of Copenhagen suspected of collaborating with the Danish terrorists who earlier in the year destroyed the plant. Sturmbannführer Dettling will give me my instructions."

He looked at Bormann. "Shall I elaborate, Herr Reichsleiter?" he asked.

"Not necessary", Bormann said. "Proceed."

"Once in America I have orders to stay in New York City. Get a job.

Settle down. This city will be headquarters for Operation Sleeper Agent, as well as my immediate mission, KOKON."

Bormann's small beady eyes fixed the young soldier standing before him. "And what, Obersturmführer Kessler, do you understand KOKON to be?" he asked, his voice weighty with importance.

Rudi tensed. His mind raced. He wanted to express his concept in the very best, the very clearest way possible. He drew himself up. "I have been told, Herr Reichsleiter, that the present conflict is coming to an end," he said. "That the war will be over within a few months." His voice grew quiet. "That Germany at this moment lies defeated." He paused. Then: "I have been told that the Führer is determined to remain in Berlin with his people. That his health, his strength, given so bounteously to the German people, will not permit him to carry on the cause of the party. But his ideals, the ideals of Nazism, of our fatherland, must be carried on, reborn. To serve this goal it is imperative that selected German leaders endure to plan and head the resurrection of the New Order. KOKON will make certain that this occurs. KOKON will assure the rise of the Fourth Reich!" He paused to collect his thoughts.

Bormann at once shot at him: "How?"

"A number of specially chosen political and military leaders will be assisted in leaving Germany and the postwar chaos certain to follow. These men will make their way to a predetermined foreign country and go underground. They will form the nucleus of a new power. They will work together for the re-establishment of the New Germany, the new world in the spirit of Adolf Hitler."

It was a bold, an inspired scheme. He felt a surge of pride swell in him. He was part of it. A vital part. He knew now that high-ranking officers and officials, realizing that the war was coming to an end, had set up highly efficient and complex clandestine escape routes by which they would be able to flee a temporarily defeated Germany. He remembered the name of one such escape route: *"Die Schleuse*—The Lock-Gate."

And he knew about KOKON. A group of the highest, most important and influential officers of the Third Reich, anticipating that escape routes like Lock-Gate would be swamped with lesser Nazis and SS officers, had set up their own highly secret, well-financed elite escape-and-concealment apparatus, KOKON—cocoon, like its namesake designed to protect, to hide, and ultimately to afford its charges the ability to metamorphose into full-fledged glory when *The Day* would come.

Like super Sleepers.

They would not seek refuge along with the masses in the obvious and therefore vulnerable places. They would hide "in the open."

He took a deep breath. "The country selected as the KOKON members' base of operations is the United States of America," he said.

"Why?" Bormann's questions were like pistol shots.

"Several reasons, Herr Reichsleiter."

Quickly he organized his thoughts. "One. It is the place least likely to be considered safe by our enemies. That very fact *makes* it safe. It is where no one will look. Some individual leaders will go to other places. South America, Egypt, Syria. The elite KOKON members will concentrate in the United States of America. Rumors will be circulated that the top Third Reich officers have taken refuge in South America. These rumors will serve as a smoke screen."

He paused briefly. Then: "Two. America, the United States, is made up of people from many European nations. A foreigner will not stand out among Americans. The KOKON members will, of course, possess perfect papers of identification and will alter their appearances. The risk of recognition will be minimal. It is a necessary risk. But people as a rule do not recognize other people out of context."

It was true, he knew. For months he had frequented the school barber at Schloss Ehrenstein. When he saw the man, out of his barber's uniform, out of his usual setting, at a theater in Regensburg, he had not been able to place him.

He continued. "The greatest care, of course, must be taken in safeguarding the identity of the Reichsleiter himself. One advantage here is the fact that the appearance of the Reichsleiter is not widely known abroad. Second, a well-orchestrated program of conflicting reports and sightings of the Reichsleiter in various parts of the world will confuse the issue. Should a genuine report be made, it will tend to be lost. No one will believe it. Also several reports will be made by persons claiming to have seen the Reichsleiter dead. Such reports will be made by members of such organizations as the SS Brotherhood and the Werewolves, as well as by individuals genuinely duped."

An almost imperceptible smile played on Bormann's lips as he slowly nodded his head.

Rudi continued. "Three. The United States of America, because of its cosmopolitan makeup, offers the greatest opportunities for the KOKON leaders to further their cause undetected." He took a deep breath. "In short, Herr Reichsleiter, safety and opportunity."

Bormann nodded in approval. "Your immediate duties upon arrival in New York?" he demanded.

"From the *Schweigeagenten*—the Sleeper Agents—in active positions, I will delegate one deputy in each of twelve major cities selected for agent activity. These deputies will prepare safe houses and safe cover identities for the arrival of KOKON members. Only I will know who the twelve are. I myself shall perform the same service in New York."

"Why only major cities?" Arnold asked.

"It is easiest to stay lost in a crowd," Rudi answered. "People in the big cities are used to dealing with foreigners. They do not notice them."

He had a flash recollection of a newspaper account that had appeared in one of the big American newspapers supplied the students at Schloss Ehrenstein. *The New York Times* it was. Two reporters, to test the alertness of the New Yorkers in time of war, had walked boldly up and down Times Square clad in full Nazi U-boat commander uniforms, and in heavy German accents had asked directions to several sensitive city projects. They had either been ignored—or given the information they sought. Not one citizen had been alerted. Not one had informed on them. Not one denounced them. The big American cities would be safe for the KOKON members!

"How will you be contacted as the members arrive?" Arnold asked.

"A method of drop contact has been established, Herr Brigadeführer," Rudi answered.

"Specify!" Bormann ordered.

Rudi glanced quickly at his superior. When I volunteer to give specifics, you reject them, he thought. When I do not, you request them. He recognized the method. He acknowledged it. No matter. He was fully prepared to answer any questions.

"*Jawohl*, Herr Reichsleiter," he said promptly. "I go to the Public Library at Fifth Avenue and Forty-second Street every afternoon at 1500 hours. I inspect page one hundred and twenty of Volume Twelve of the

Encyclopedia Americana displayed for reference. If more than one set is displayed, I inspect each Volume Twelve. On the bottom of the page I look for a code number, penciled in. I memorize it. I erase it and substitute a code for a randomly selected meeting place. A street corner in the city. The code consists of three separate numbers. One denoting an avenue, one a cross street, one a date in the current month. The rendezvous will always take place on the southwest corner of the intersection at twelve noon. The subject will identify himself by frequently scratching his right ear as he waits. I will approach the subject and identify myself by giving him his code number. He will acknowledge with the word 'KOKON.' I will conduct him to the safe house prepared for him and instruct him in his cover."

"What is your alternate plan, should you yourself be prevented from making the contact?" Arnold wanted to know.

"I shall have designated a deputy from among the agents in my city. Should anything prevent me from carrying out my duties, he will take over, in turn selecting a deputy at that time. Deputies in the other cities will follow the same procedure."

Bormann consulted a document on the desk before him. "You have been given a list of names and code numbers. How many on the list?" he asked.

"Five hundred and seventy-nine, Herr Reichsleiter," Rudi answered at once.

"What is my code number?"

"B-177, Herr Reichsleiter."

"Brigadeführer Arnold?"

"A-042."

"General Jodl?"

"J-322." Rudi's answers were instant without the slightest hesitation.

"Who is E-364?"

"Obersturmbannführer Eichmann, Adolf."

"S-253."

"Streicher, Julius."

"M-172?"

"Dr. Mengele, Joseph."

Bormann glanced at Arnold. "Proceed," he said.

"You have been briefed on the personal plans of the Reichsleiter?" Arnold asked.

"*Jawohl*, Herr Brigadeführer."

"Give the details."

"The Reichsleiter will leave Berlin in a small plane flying to Hamburg. From there he will proceed to Flensburg. Germany will not surrender with the fall of Berlin. Admiral Doenitz has orders to hold the Flensburg area as long as possible, buying the time necessary. Months . . . or weeks. It will be no longer than that before our Fatherland will be forced into final, complete surrender. Speed is essential."

He looked at the two superior officers watching him closely, listening intently to his account, looking for the slightest error. He knew he was impressing them with his thoroughness and well-organized presentation of facts. He continued.

"In Flensburg the Reichsleiter will board a U-boat, type XXI, ocean-going, *Schnorchel*-equipped. This U-boat will take the Reichsleiter to Argentina for temporary refuge, until such a time as the Reichsleiter's cover and safe house in the U.S.A. will be ready. Here he will then take his place as the head of Operation KOKON. The U-boat will later be reported scuttled in Flensburg to prevent tracing and investigation."

"Just so," Arnold said.

"Alternate plan?" Bormann asked.

"If any delay or adversity is experienced in the Flensburg area, the Reichsleiter will enter the SS military hospital at Graasten Castle in Denmark just north of the border, under assumed identity, to await later evacuation arrangements," Rudi answered.

Bormann stood up. He walked around the desk to Rudi. "Let me impress upon you one final time the unsurpassed importance of your mission," he said soberly. "KOKON has taken much time and effort to organize. But the unforeseen rapid developments in the war have badly strained our original operational timetable. We must now move forward at a faster pace than anticipated. You understand?"

"I do, Herr Reichsleiter."

"KOKON is absolutely essential for our future," Bormann went on. "If its members are forced to scatter throughout the world, no cohesive, no concentrated effort will be possible. One by one they will be hunted down by a world fearful of them. Or they will live out their lives an ineffectual waste. This must not be! The torch of Nazism must remain ablaze. That is the charge of KOKON!" He let the words melt on his tongue, savoring their aftertaste.

He stood close to Rudi. "You know the plans. You know how to carry them out. When word is received that your Sleeper Agent network has been activated and is ready to receive the KOKON members, we shall arrive."

His eyes bored into Rudi's. "You, Obersturmführer Kessler," he said weightily, "you are the key that will unlock the gateway to the *Fourth German Reich!*" He turned his bullnecked head to look at Arnold. *"Er ist bereit,"* he said. "He is ready."

Arnold rose. "Obersturmführer Kessler, you are about to take your place in the glorious history of our Fatherland!" He paused. Then: "You will leave on your mission in exactly one hour!"

Rudi snapped to attention. *"Zu Befehl!* Herr Brigadeführer," he called out smartly. "At your orders!" His hand shot out in a stiff-armed salute. "Heil Hitler!"

Arnold returned his salute. *"Sieg heil!"* he said. He turned to Bormann. Again he saluted. *"Heil!"* he said. *"Heil* the leader of the Fourth Reich!"

It was 0305 hours, April 30, when Rudi walked from Reichsleiter Bormann's office to make his final preparations for his departure from the Führerbunker. He was excited. He looked forward to action. He took a few steps into the corridor—and stopped short in shocked consternation. In the few short hours he had been in Bormann's office the entire atmosphere in the bunker had changed preposterously.

Where before the sour smell of resignation and defeat had hung in the air, and everyone had spoken in subdued whispers, loud voices, ribald singing and cacophonous dance music now assaulted his ears. Incredulously he looked around him.

Outside the office empty glasses lay scattered about on the floor among half-full bottles of beer and wine. A can of partly eaten caviar had been discarded on the bench where a scant few hours before he had been waiting impatiently, and cigarette butts and burnt matches littered the corridor, despite the Führer's strict ban on smoking!

He was profoundly shocked. He felt as if his world was suddenly crumbling. He hurried to the SS guards' room. The sound of loud, raucous laughter and blaring music beat its way through the closed door. He threw it open.

The sight that met his eyes shocked him to the core. Grunting SS guards in various states of undress lay locked in desperate copulation with naked girls, oblivious to the din and the dissolute hubbub around them. Others were wolfing down expensive delicacies, smoking and drinking, already drunk with wild abandon. Still others had passed out in drooling collapse across tables, chairs and bunks.

He grabbed an SS man staggering past him. Unconsciously he tightened his grip on the man's arm until his fingers hurt. "What the hell goes on?" he screamed at the startled man.

"Goes on?" the man repeated, looking at Rudi with bleary eyes. "Goes on?" He grinned vacuously. "Don't you know? The Führer has announced he is going to kill himself!"

Rudi tensed with shock. He let go of the man's arm as if it were suddenly a red hot gun barrel. He stared at the drunken soldier. "And *this* is the respect you show your Führer!" he screamed at the man. *"Du scheissdreck Schweinehund du!—*You shit! You dirty swine!"

"Hell, why not?" The soldier grinned. "It's our last chance. We are *all* about to die!"

Red rage flared up in Rudi, obliterating all else. With sudden fury he struck the man a crushing blow in the pit of his stomach, feeling his fist burying itself deep in the man's viscera.

The SS guard doubled over in pain. His bulging eyes stared up at Rudi in uncomprehending terror. Sour yellow vomit spewed from his open mouth as he collapsed in writhing, heaving agony.

Rudi spat on the prostrate figure. He turned abruptly on his heel and fled from the hellish scene. He slammed the door behind him. For a moment he leaned against the cold, hard concrete wall of the bunker corridor. His whole world was disintegrating.

Gradually he regained control. He had a moment of panic when the full realization of his loss of control reached his conscious mind. He could not afford such lapses. He strove to think clearly. Precisely. Analytically.

Adolf Hitler's decision to commit suicide was not entirely unexpected. He realized that the Führer was sacrificing himself rather than fall into the hands of the barbarous Russians and suffer the indignity of imprisonment.

Perhaps execution. Like Mussolini. The Führer had given Germany everything. Now he was giving her his life!

He straightened up. He stood tall. The Führer's ideals. The Führer's goals would be carried on by Reichsleiter Martin Bormann. By KOKON. The operation was now more vital than ever. And so was the success of his, Rudi Kessler's, mission! He squared his shoulders and marched proudly toward his quarters, oblivious to the debauchery going on around him.

Brigadeführer Arnold himself accompanied Rudi to the Hermann Göring Strasse garages.

Two SS guards armed with Schmeisser machine pistols were waiting for them at the garage exit. Between them stood a small old man clad in a stripped, threadbare uniform.

Arnold addressed one of the guards. "Is this the man?" he asked crisply.

"*Jawohl,* Herr Brigadeführer." The guard snapped to attention.

Arnold nodded. He turned to the old man. "Name?"

"Fischbein," the man answered, his voice shaking. "Josef Fischbein."

"What is your *Beruf*—your occupation?"

"Master engraver."

Again Arnold nodded. "Come with me."

Arnold walked the old man the few steps over to Rudi. The man stared at the young officer. Arnold watched him closely. "You know this man?" he asked. There was a sardonic taint to his voice.

The old man nodded. "*Ja.*"

"You have seen him before?"

"*Nein.*"

"How do you know him then?"

The old man licked his thin lips. "I . . . I worked on his passport. A Danish passport. At the SS Department of Forged Documents."

"Anyone else work on that document?"

"No."

Arnold contemplated the man for a brief moment. "You did an excellent job, Herr Fischbein," he said. "We are not ungrateful." He nodded toward the debris-filled street before them. "You are free to go," he said. He smiled. "*Hals- und Beinbruch!*" he said. "May you break your neck and leg!" It was the usual German good-luck wish.

The old man stared wide-eyed at Arnold. Slowly he edged toward the street. He began to walk away, glancing fearfully back over his shoulder. Then he started a shuffling run.

Rudi did not even hear the staccato bursts of fire from the Schmeissers of the two SS guards that raked across the old man's back, cutting him down and slamming him into the gutter of Hermann Göring Strasse to lie in an oddly sprawling heap of death. . . .

Rudi was staring at the city. The sight of the blazing city lying before him was like a numbing physical blow. Berlin was dying.

Under savage artillery bombardment by the Red Army forces the city was a holocaust.. Blood-red fingers of flame licked up toward the night sky, crisscrossed by a latticework of desperately probing searchlights. Ground-shaking explosions, the roar of blazing fires, the crashing of shattered masonry, the wails of fire engines and ambulances all vied with one another in their assault upon his ears.

Rudi felt his confidence drain from him. Suddenly the stirring words he'd read in the Führer's *Mein Kampf* rang out with clarion purity in his mind: "A holy fire has been lighted and out of its flames will rise the sword which will regain the freedom and the mastery of the Germanic Siegfried, and the eternal life of the German nation!"

Fire, he thought. It can destroy. And it can purify. He clenched his fists. The sword of Germany *would* be forged, ready to strike! Adolf Hitler had written *Mein Kampf* for the German people. Martin Bormann would write the sequel!

Arnold came up to him. He shook his hand. *"Sieg heil!"* he said quietly, his eyes grave.

"Sieg heil!" Rudi answered. Quickly he ducked from the entrance, ran across the rubble-strewn street, and disappeared among the splintered trees of the Tiergarten park. Operation KOKON had begun.

Major Herbert Lee, CO of CIC Detachment 212, was fretfully preoccupied as he marched across the empty lot between the two buildings occupied by Corps CP in the little town of Viechtacht. He was hardly aware of Tom walking silently beside him.

The morning was overcast, and a fine sleety snow was falling, melting almost at once on the wet, soggy ground.

He huddled down in his ample mackinaw and hurried along a little faster. Corps had moved to Viechtacht the day before in the morning. They had barely become operational when General Patton had arrived. Corps was to move at once on Linz, Salzburg and Berchtesgaden. New areas to be considered by the CIC.

And then there was the matter of General Koeltz and the goddamned Werewolves!

The French general and his staff would be showing up at Corps any time now. Later in the day General Koeltz was scheduled to tap four officers for the Legion of Honor, two one-star generals and two bird colonels. Right in the empty lot he was even now trudging through.

And only yesterday those Werewolf "warning" circulars had been found tacked up on fences and doors in town. Dated "25. 4. 45" and addressed to "all traitors and collaborators," the damned things warned them not to display the white flags of submission, not to aid the enemy, but to continue to destroy him. "We shall punish every traitor and his entire family!" the proclamation threatened. Shit! Half the town had to be sleeping in dirty sheets—judging from the amount of laundry hanging out the windows.

"Unser Rache ist tödlich!—Our revenge is deadly!" the warning promised. It was signed, *"Der Werwolf."*

He didn't give a damn whether the Werewolves were a well-trained terrorist guerrilla organization or a bunch of fanatic crackpots with a corny radio program. A bullet fired by a nut is just as lethal.

He grimaced involuntarily. It would be one hell of a mess, he thought, if a visiting French general was gunned down. In his, Herbert Wadsworth Lee's, own territory! But how in hell was he supposed to foul the pattern of that kind of thrust? He pushed on, deep in his glum thoughts.

Tom walked silently beside his CO. He had brought Larry to the aid station yesterday. Doc Elliott had jeeped over to take a look at him. It was doubtful that Larry would ever regain the full use of his hands. Unless they performed a minor miracle back in the States.

He felt depressed and angry. More than ever he wanted to follow through with the case of the Sleeper Agent operation—and KOKON.

He had spent hours with Lee going over the information gained from the few pieces of scorched paper saved by Larry. He had requested a TDY assigning him to the Sleeper case exclusively. The approval of the Assistant

Chief of Staff, G-2, Colonel Streeter, was necessary. He and Lee were on their way to see him so that Tom could present his case in person. He was well aware of his feeling of depression. He tried to shake it. He needed to be at his best if he hoped to persuade the AC of S to grant his request. It was not easy. It wasn't only Larry and Winkler that bothered him. It was also the letter from Julie that had been waiting for him at Corps.

Damn it!

"I do so hope you understand," she'd written. Like hell, he did. "My friend is a captain stationed in Washington. He has a bad back, poor dear, and he won't be able to go overseas," Julie had explained. "He comes from a very good old American family."

And she had hastened to reassure him: "We are not in any hurry to get married, you understand. Our divorce can wait, Tom. It can wait till any time you say. I certainly don't want to worry you now. I'm sure you have enough on your mind. I am sorry, Tom. . . ."

There was more. Much more. It all swam together in his mind. It was too new. He could not yet sort out his emotions. He made a conscious effort to snap out of his doldrums. His job now was KOKON.

Colonel Streeter listened without interruption as Tom briefly chronicled the events and investigations leading up to the discovery of the Sleeper Agent dossier of one Rudolf Kessler, code name Rudi A-27.

Tom was summing up. "Sir, Schloss Ehrenstein was a school for Sleeper Agents to be placed in foreign countries," he said. "Including the United States. There is no way of knowing how many were actually graduated. We only know a part of the personal history of one such agent, Rudi A-27. We know *his* assignment to be the States. We know some of his past history, some of his training." He paused.

Streeter remained silent. With a slight frown he was watching the young CIC agent.

Tom continued. "It all fits, sir. The Luftwaffe project FENIX, on future war. The Sleeper Agent program. It all points to some comeback plan for Nazi Germany. Only the meaning of KOKON is still unknown. I believe it to be part of the master plan."

He looked at Streeter earnestly. "I strongly feel that Rudi A-27 must be tracked down and captured. I am certain he is still here in the ETO. The dossier entry of his Readiness Test Completion was dated less than two weeks ago. If we can get him, he can reveal the scope and the operational procedures of the entire Nazi Sleeper Agent project. He may lead us to others, other Sleepers, perhaps already in the States. The FBI can follow through."

He looked firmly at the colonel. "Sir. Rudi A-27 *must* be captured. He is our key. We cannot allow an unknown number of enemy agents to infiltrate the United States and settle down. If we do, we may *end* the war —but we will not have *won* it!"

He stood erect. "With the approval of Major Lee, I request exclusive assignment to the case of the Sleeper Agent and KOKON."

Streeter sat a moment in silent thought, studying Tom standing before him. He looked at Major Lee, then back to Tom. "Wait outside," he said.

Tom walked over to a window in the hall outside Streeter's office. He looked out. It had stopped snowing. He tried to concentrate on the meeting with the G-2. But other thoughts intruded. Julie . . . When had he stopped loving her? Or had he? He could not pin it down. And she?

He had loved her. Deeply.

He'd spent hours the night before, after getting his "Dear John" letter —why "Dear John"? Why not "Dear Tom"?—looking through the earlier letters he'd received from Julie and kept. They seemed unreal now. . . .

He was jolted from his morose thoughts when the door to Colonel Streeter's office opened and Major Lee came out into the hall.

Tom walked up to him. "Well?" he asked.

Lee looked at him. "It's no go, Tom," he said soberly.

Tom felt angry frustration well up in him. "Why the hell not?" he exploded. "*Somebody*'d better get on it, dammit!"

"Easy, Tom," Lee said. "Easy does it."

"Sure, easy does it!" Tom shot back bitterly. "But haven't you noticed that when easy does it someone always has to do it over again? Can we afford that?"

"Sorry, Tom." Lee sounded genuinely regretful. "I sure as hell can't put the ball in play if the coach says no. Streeter feels there are too damned many . . . eh . . . unorthodox procedures involved. There is no way." He started to walk away.

Tom's mind raced. There *was* a way. He made his decision. "Herb!" he called. "Hold it a minute."

Lee stopped. He turned to Tom.

"I think I have a way, Herb," Tom said quietly.

Lee walked up to him. He shook his head. "I know that convoluted noodle of yours works in strange and mysterious ways to perform its wonders," he said. "But *this* I've gotta hear!"

"I'll take it," Tom said.

Lee looked nonplused. "Take what?"

"Remember that field commission you offered me a while back? Okay. I'll take it!"

Lee stared at him in astonishment. "Yeah," he said. "I remember. You turned it down. You didn't like the required three-year hitch that went with it."

"That's right."

Lee looked at the CIC agent with sudden interest. "Say, what the hell *is* your rank, anyway?"

"Staff sergeant."

Lee nodded.

"Here's what I want you to do, Herb." Tom spoke urgently. "Go back to Streeter. Tell him I've accepted a field commission, effective at once. It's Corps policy to give a two-week furlough. I'll take it. Now. What I do with it is my own damn affair, right? I can be as *unorthodox* as I damned well please! Okay. I need someone along. I know I can't get another CIC partner. But how about letting me have that MP sergeant that worked the Steinmetz stakeout in Bayreuth? Sergeant Rosenfeld? Just for the two lousy weeks? Okay? Herb, I *know* I can track that Sleeper bastard down!"

Lee was staring at him. He slowly shook his head. "Jesus!" he said. "You're really out to get that poor SOB."

Tom had a fleeting mind's-eye vision of the Steinmetz girl's bloated body hanging on the cold cell wall. Of Sergeant Winkler's mangled hands and face. Of Larry. "Yes," he said.

"You are nuts," Lee observed solemnly.

"It'll work."

"Yeah, but—"

"Come on, Herb!" Tom pleaded. "Do it!"

"I still think you're nuts," Lee said. "But—" He shrugged. "Well, I'll see what I can do." He sounded dubious. He started toward the door to the office of the AC of S, G-2.

Tom stopped him. "Herb," he said. "Get it! Don't be too damned catmatic."

Lee looked at him suspiciously. "What the hell is that supposed to mean?"

"What? Catmatic?"

"Yeah. Catmatic."

Tom grinned. "I thought you knew. It's the opposite of dogmatic. Pussyfooting around! Don't pussyfoot, Herb. *Go get it!*"

Lee shook himself in thorough exasperation. "For Christ's sake," he muttered as he entered Streeter's office.

Tom took a deep breath. It was done. Three years. Three more years of looking at the Bavarian landscape. It *was* beautiful. But even steak and ice cream can get monotonous. Hell, he'd stick it out. He had nothing to go home to.

His decision made, he felt a sense of loss. Of relief. Of excitement. . . .

Major Lee emerged from the office of the G-2. "Streeter says it's one hell of an unorthodox caper." He grinned. "But you got it, *Lieutenant* Jaeger!"

Tom at once started down the hall. "Come on, Herb!" he called. "Let's get those orders cut!"

The two men walked rapidly, purposefully away. The hunt for Rudi A-27 had begun. The hunt for KOKON. . . .

8

Sergeant David Rosenfeld brought his jeep to an impressively gravel-sliding stop in the walled courtyard at the main entrance to Schloss Ehrenstein. He had enjoyed the early morning ride up to the castle, and especially being waved through the checkpoints manned by troops from the Engineer outfit billeted at the estate, when the guards were shown the CIC agent's ID.

He felt important. Excited. After his piss-poor performance at that Steinmetz stakeout in Bayreuth, the last thing in the world he'd have bet on was to be assigned to work as the CIC agent's partner! By request, no less! He looked expectantly at Tom, sitting next to him.

Tom nodded toward a row of trucks and jeeps parked at the courtyard wall. Next to one of the jeeps stood a soldier. Despite the raw overcast morning, he was clad only in his OD shorts and undershirt. He was busily brushing his teeth from a canteen cup. The jeep motor was idling, the hood was up, and the soldier's steel helmet, filled with water, was set on the engine block. White steam curled up from it into the crisp, cool morning air, like the contented breath of the purring machine.

"Ask him where we can find the lieutenant," Tom said.

"Yes, sir!"

Rosenfeld jumped smartly from the jeep and strode purposefully toward the GI engrossed in his morning ablutions.

Tom stayed in the jeep. He wanted to think undisturbed for a few moments. Everything had happened so damned fast. His field commission. He savored the thought. He didn't feel one iota different. Certainly he did not look any different. His uniform still was bare of any insignia of rank, except for the two officer's U.S. emblems on his collar tabs. Exactly as he'd worn them ever since he splashed ashore at Omaha Beach, a T5.

And now he was hunting KOKON. He had exactly two weeks to track down a quarry as elusive as a lone bedbug in a sleeping bag. He had not one damned clue where to begin. Except at Schloss Ehrenstein. And that place had been thoroughly cleaned out.

There was only one remote possibility: the looters. The German farmers who had ransacked the estate. They might still have some of their plunder in their possession. It might—just might—contain a lead. Any lead.

But he'd need whatever information the engineer officer would be able to give him. Or the Peukert woman. He had to have some starting point. He couldn't interrogate every damned farmer in Bavaria. Not in two weeks.

He glanced towards his young companion. The man had already once demonstrated that he knew how to use his eyes. He sure could use a second pair. He hoped he'd come through for him.

Rosenfeld walked briskly up to the GI at the jeep. "Where can I find your CO, soldier?" he demanded.

The GI looked him over out of the corner of his eye.

"'oo 'onts 'o 'ow?" he grunted through his foaming toothbrush.

"CIC!" Rosenfeld snapped importantly.

The soldier slowly removed his toothbrush from his mouth. He rinsed it out in his canteen cup and threw the dirty water on the ground. He dipped the cup into the steaming water in the helmet on the engine block, cautiously took a mouthful and noisily swished it around in his mouth. He spat the toothpaste-clouded water onto the ground and nodded toward the main entrance. "The lootenant's probably in the orderly room, Mac. Second door on your right. You can't miss it."

"Thank you, soldier," Rosenfeld acknowledged. "Second door on the right." He turned smartly on his heel and marched back to Tom. Vaguely he felt that his first act as the partner of a CIC agent hadn't been overly auspicious.

"The Peukert dame?" The Engineer lieutenant shook his head. "You're SOL again, my friend!" He grinned. "You ruffled her feathers too roughly. She flew the coop day after you pulled that dog trick on her."

"What do you know about the locals that looted the castle?"

"Not a damned thing," the officer answered. "Except they did a hell of a job. And the Peukert dame was always bitching about them."

He thought for a moment. "Wait a minute," he said. "I do remember one name. Some farmer. The Peukert dame was especially vitriolic about him. Guess he liberated something she'd had her eye on herself."

He frowned. "Let me think. . . . Burg-something . . . Burghower. Hoffer. Hauser. Burghauser. That's it. Anton Burghauser. He's supposed to have a farm a couple or three miles from the estate. Near the village of Wörth. On the road to Cham."

It was 0837 hours when the jeep with Tom and Sergeant Rosenfeld screeched to a stop in the barnyard of the Burghauser farm, barely missing a barrel-bodied manure wagon. Tom had to put his hand on the dashboard and brace himself to keep from going through the windshield.

He glanced at Rosenfeld. He was about to make a caustic remark. He caught himself. The young soldier was obviously enjoying himself. Everything he did was done with an abundance of exuberance. Even stopping a jeep. It would be foolish to dampen his enthusiasm. It might pay off.

Both men jumped from the jeep, and Tom flung open the door to the *Bauernstube*.

The farmer and his family were having their mid-morning boiled potatoes dipped in hot oil. Startled, they looked up from their frugal meal and stared at the Americans. Three of them. The farmer. An older woman. A teenage girl.

Frowning, Tom looked from one to the other. His first subjects in the hunt for KOKON. He was acutely aware of the time limitation imposed upon him. Two lousy weeks. He had no time to waste on lengthy interrogations. He had to have his answers at once. He could not afford to handle anyone with kid gloves. The stakes were too high. Each investigation had to be played by ear. On the spur of the moment he would have to come up with the quickest, most efficient way to break his suspects—whatever the method. He had to trick them. Confuse them. Menace them. Trap them. . . . And he couldn't let them see the trap until they tripped over the cheese.

He glanced at the three Germans. Quickly he sized them up. Ceremoniously he pulled a notebook from his pocket and made a show of consulting it. He looked up at the farmer. "You are Anton Burghauser?" He snapped the question at the man, his voice cold and harsh.

"Yes."

Tom gave an impersonal nod toward the two women. "Your wife? Your daughter?"

"Yes."

Tom pointed an imperious finger at Burghauser. Sharply he beckoned him. "You! Come with me!" He flung the words at the man. "You are under arrest!"

The farmer's leathery face visibly paled.

The two women gasped. They looked stricken. Instinctively they drew together, clinging to each other, staring at Tom in bleak terror.

Burghauser slowly rose to his feet. "Arrest?" he repeated heavily. "But why?"

"Possession of US Army property," Tom shot at him. "Let's go!"

"But . . . I do not have any of your army's property," the man said in bewilderment. He shook his head. "Believe me. Nothing. There is a mistake."

Tom took a deliberate step toward the man. He glowered angrily at him. "Are you accusing me of making a mistake?" His voice was dangerous.

The farmer drew back. "No. No . . . I meant—"

"You have plunder, stolen from Schloss Ehrenstein on your premises," Tom lashed out. "Effects that belonged to the Waffen SS. Now US Army property! According to international law. Do you deny it?"

He had been watching the women closely. He saw them give each other a quick terror-stricken look.

Burghauser's weather-textured face looked ashen but grim. "I have nothing of such things here," he said.

Irritably Tom again looked in his notebook.

"You are lying," he said icily. "You have been denounced by one of your neighbors as a criminal looter." He fixed the man with razor eyes. "Do you deny it?"

Out of the corner of his eye he saw the women react. It must have been a familiar story to them. Denunciation—German against German—was commonplace in the glorious Nazi Reich.

"It is a lie," Burghauser stated.

Again Tom looked in his notebook. He seemed exasperated. "Your accuser is a Frau Peukert," he informed the farmer. "She declares that you stole some items of value from the castle."

The impact of the Peukert woman's name on the two women was obvious. Burghauser said nothing.

"Where is the loot?" Tom demanded brusquely.

"There is nothing here."

For a moment Tom scowled at the man. Then he shrugged, as if writing him off. He snapped his notebook shut and put it away. "Sergeant!" he called.

Rosenfeld had watched the scene with fascination. He had seen the CIC agent in action before, and he recognized the bluff at once. But he knew they had no concrete information about any loot, only general assumption. Would it work? He was dying to find out. He was dying to get into the act. Smartly he stepped up to Tom. "Yes, sir."

Tom lowered his voice. "Take the old man outside," he said. "Walk him around the farm."

"Okay."

"Keep your eyes open. Look around."

"Okay. What am I looking for?"

"Hopefully you'll know when you see it."

Rosenfeld grinned. "Got you!"

"Keep him covered. Don't let him pull anything."

"He won't get a chance to try."

"This is important. Five minutes after you get out there, fire one shot."

Rosenfeld's mouth dropped open for an instant. "A . . . *shot?*"

"A shot."

"What'll I shoot at?"

"I don't give a damn. You can try to hit Berlin if you like. Just don't hurt the old man."

"Okay. Got you."

"Five minutes."

Tom turned toward Burghauser. Aloud he ordered, "Take him away."

Rosenfeld drew his .45. He tried to act and look as grim and cold as Tom. Brusquely he gun-gestured to the farmer. "Get going!" he commanded. "Outside! Move it!"

Tom walked up to the two women. He looked at them with a dark, penetrating scowl. They shrank away from him.

He consulted his watch. "Your husband has exactly ten minutes to show the sergeant where he has hidden the loot. Ten minutes. If he does not . . ." He shrugged eloquently. "We do not show consideration for people who lie to us, Frau Burghauser!"

He looked from mother to daughter. Once more he glanced at his watch.

"*Nine* minutes, Frau Burghauser, for your husband to talk. Or . . . for you." He pulled one of the chairs away from the table and sat down, leaning his arms over the back. He stared relentlessly at the two women. He said nothing.

The hour-long seconds ticked by. The girl bit her lips. She was perhaps sixteen. Seventeen. Blond braids were put up in spirals over her ears. Her face was round, and her sturdy body had not quite lost its baby fat. She looked at her mother with big frightened eyes. "Mutti?" she whispered.

Her mother tightened her protective embrace around the girl. She said nothing.

Time oozed on. Tom shifted on his chair. It creaked. It was the only sound. Minutes . . . The girl began to tremble slightly.

Tom watched her. He was acutely aware of his own tenseness. The suspense centered in the watch on his wrist. He felt himself waiting for the shot. How much more heavily the pressure must weigh on them, he thought. His eyes went to the young girl again. The blouse around her armpits was wet with the sweat of fear. He felt compassion for her. He did not enjoy waging war against work-worn women and pigtailed girls still covered with baby fat.

He had no choice. Did he? He had to go by a different set of values. This time. When *does* the end justify the means? Ever?

He glanced at his watch. The women's eyes were glued to his gesture. He said nothing. The waiting had become oppressive.

Suddenly a shot rang out in the farmyard.

The girl gave a startled scream. She wrenched her eyes wide open. She turned them full on Tom in unbelieving horror. She gave a wretched little cry and buried her head in her mother's bosom. She sobbed.

Tom rose deliberately. He stood—dark, icy, foreboding—before them. He beckoned to the mother. "You!" he said, steel in his voice. "Come with me!"

The young girl clung to her mother in anguished desperation. She turned her plump, tear-streaked child's face toward Tom. *"Nein!"* she wailed. *"Nein! Nicht* Mutti!—Not Mother!" She gulped her breath between sobs. *"Es war ja nur . . . a Fotzhobl!"* she cried accusingly. *"Nur a Fotzhobl—* only a *Fotzhobl."*

What the hell is a *Fotzhobl?* Tom thought.Then the familiar surge of excitement swept through him. He had no idea what a *Fotzhobl* was. The Bavarian dialect contained a flood of words that bore no relation to German. But whatever it was, it came from Schloss Ehrenstein.

"Get it!" he snapped. "Now!"

The girl ran to a large ornately carved cupboard. As soon as she let go of her mother, the woman sank down on a chair. She sat immobile, staring vacuously into space. The girl tore open a drawer. Desperately she rummaged around . . . and came up with a small package wrapped in old newspaper.

She ran to Tom and handed it to him. "It is all we took," she sobbed. "All. That horrid woman at the castle wanted it when we found it. But Vati would not give it to her. It is a gift for Werner. My brother. When he comes back from Russia." Abruptly she ran to her mother. She put her arms around her and hugged her tightly. She cried softly.

Tom looked at the package in his hand. A *Fotzhobl . . .* He tore the paper away. Inside was a cardboard box. He opened it. In it, on a piece of yellow pressed cotton, lay a large gleaming mouth organ. A fine Hohner harmonica!

Tom had to fight down his impulse to hurl the shiny thing to the floor in his disappointment. Why the hell did those damned Bavarians have to make up their own fucking words? Why couldn't they call a harmonica a goddamned *Mundharmonika* like the rest of the Germans? A *Fotzhobl!* Shit!

He walked over to the women. "What else did you take from Schloss Ehrenstein?" he asked.

The girl looked up at him. There was hate in her eyes. And fear. He already knew her answer. She shook her head. "Nothing."

He believed her. He placed the harmonica—the goddamned *Fotzhobl* —on the table. "Keep it," he said.

He looked at the shaken girl. "Your father is all right," he said. "Nothing has happened to him."

The girl's eyes opened wide. She leaped to her feet and rushed from the room, followed by her mother.

Rosenfeld stood in the barnyard with Burghauser.

Both the women were hugging the farmer unashamedly. He looked uncomfortable at the display of emotion in front of strangers.

Tom went up to Rosenfeld.

"Did it work?" the sergeant asked eagerly.

"Yes." Tom did not feel like elaborating. "It worked."

"I may have something, too," Rosenfeld said importantly.

Tom looked at him sharply. "What do you mean?"

"Well, you told me to take a look around. So I did." He nodded toward a shack in a far corner of the yard. "That's the chicken coop," he said. "There's a chest in there. Like a footlocker. They use it as a feed bin. It's got a number stenciled on it. Like an ASN. It could be the army serial number of some Kraut, couldn't it? And it could have come from the Schloss Ehrenstein place, right?"

"Right!" Tom was already striding toward the chicken coop.

A few sleepily roosting hens put up a cackling protest when he flung open the door to the coop and began to shoo them out. The close air in the shack was heavy and sour, and the dirt floor was moist and slimy with chicken dung. In a corner stood the feed box. Tom recognized it at once as a German soldier's field chest. It was scratched and smeared with dirt. But the army serial number could be plainly read.

Tom turned to Rosenfeld. "Get that damned farmer over here on the double!" he barked.

Burghauser stood awkwardly in the doorway to the chicken coop.

Tom pointed to the chest. "Where did you get that?" he demanded bitingly. "Schloss Ehrenstein?"

The farmer stared at the chest as if seeing it for the first time. Slowly he nodded his head. "Yes," he said. "I had not remembered it." He shook his head in worried wonder. "Yes . . . The feed bin."

"Empty it!"

The farmer sloshed across the slimy floor. With his big callused hands he took hold of the chest and up-ended it. The dry chicken feed poured out onto the wet floor, slowly soaking the moisture from the fresh dung.

"Bring it here!"

The farmer placed the chest at Tom's feet.

He examined it. The inside was caked and filthy with old feed. The chest was indeed empty. He bent down to look closer. And he saw it. In the corner a small bit of blue paper was caught in a crack. He pried it loose. It was crusted with dried chicken feed. Carefully he cleaned it off. It was the torn-off stub of a theater ticket.

"Regensburger Stadttheater," he read. *"Parkett Links.* Row five, number twelve. March seven, 1945." He turned it over. On the back he could make out a penciled note: "791 SG." It meant nothing to him. Absolutely nothing.

It was dusk when Tom stood in the overheated, stuffy *Bauernstube* of a small farm on the outskirts of the village of Falkenstein, some fifteen miles northeast of Schloss Ehrenstein.

For almost ten grueling hours he and Sergeant Rosenfeld had interrogated a host of farmers and villagers in the area around the estate. One had led to another. And another. And another. He had lost count.

He had scrutinized beat-up, dented cookware and kitchen utensils, mismatched boots with worn-through soles and mended socks. Ripped and empty sandbags, odd-sized leather straps and a dog-eared copy of *Mein Kampf.* All looted from Schloss Ehrenstein. All put to some use by the looters. He had found nothing.

He had examined odds and ends of uniform clothing. Some of it he had literally taken off the backs of the new owners. Though he knew it was futile, he had searched through every pocket. He'd had to do something. There had been nothing.

He had inspected a Waffen SS belt with a broken buckle, a rusty bayonet, its tip snapped off. Torn blankets. A boxful of spent cartridges, a collection of sundry useless hardware—and a goddamned *Fotzhobl!* Nothing!

The woman who stood trembling before him, flanked by two young boys barely in their teens, stared at him fearfully. She was alone on the farm. Her husband had been killed in the Rundstedt offensive at Bastogne. She and her two boys had run the farm, with the help of two foreign laborers who had long since run off.

On the table in the room lay an assortment of items. A box of uniform buttons. Two large wooden ladles, one of them split. A sweat-soaked uniform cap, its insignia gone. And a notebook. It was empty. The first several pages had been ripped out. "That is all you took from Schloss Ehrenstein?" Tom asked.

The woman nodded.

Sergeant Rosenfeld came in from the yard. The woman turned to look at him apprehensively. "Nobody else around," he said.

Tom nodded. He addressed the woman. "You realize that if you are keeping anything back, you will be severely punished?"

She looked back at Tom. For the shadow of a split second a look of black hatred flared in her frightened eyes. Or was it stark fear? "There is nothing else," the woman whispered, her voice barely audible.

"Good." He fixed her with a baleful stare. "All the same, we shall take a look through the house. You come with me. The boys stay here." He turned to Rosenfeld. "Keep an eye on them."

The woman tensed. For a moment she seemed ready to uncoil in violence. Then she meekly let go of her boys.

Deep in his own bleak thoughts, Tom did not notice.

The woman followed him from room to room in the little farmhouse as Tom searched the family's belongings thoroughly. He found nothing of value. To him or anyone else.

At last they came to the cramped and cluttered attic. Dusty, dimly lit from one small dirt-grimed window, it was filled with junk. Under a stack of old yellowed newspapers he found a large leather-banded trunk with heavy metal hinges and locks.

He looked at the woman. "What is in that?" he asked. He tried to read the grim set to her face, the dark look in her eyes. Hate? Fear? Guilt?

He had a quick impulse to chuck the whole goddamned scene. Take the poor woman down to her sons and get the hell out of the place. "Open it," he said.

Without a word she obeyed. The trunk was not locked. On top of a pile of clothing was a heavy gray coat, a uniform coat. He lifted it out. He looked inside the collar. The label was still there: *"Vom Reichsführer SS befohlene Ausführung. RZM."* The mark of the official SS uniform.

"Who does this SS coat belong to?" he snapped angrily. "Your husband?"

Suddenly the woman erupted in a terrified stream of words. She was deathly afraid. "No! No, Herr Offizier!" she cried pitiably. "We did not steal the clothes, Herr Offizier. They were given to us. By an officer. From Schloss Ehrenstein."

She rubbed her tearing eyes fiercely with work-hardened knuckles. "I . . . I meant to tell you. I really did. But I was afraid you would take the clothes away. And we need them . . . the boys . . . we need them so badly. For the winter. *Bitte! Bitte!*" she pleaded. "Please, do not take them away from us!" She put her fists to her face and sobbed.

Tom's hands were already searching through the pockets of the SS coat. There! His probing fingers found something. A small piece of crumpled paper torn from a notebook. Quickly he smoothed it out. A few words were written on it in cramped Gothic script. In the dim light he could not make them out. He walked to the small dirt-streaked window and held the slip to the waning light, his back to the softly weeping woman.

Suddenly he heard the faint, sharp clang of metal striking metal. Instantly he whirled around. It saved his life.

The first shot grazed his arm at the shoulder, barely breaking the skin. The second went wild.

He lunged at the woman, who was standing wild-eyed, a blue-black Luger held in front of her. His racing mind took in the scene as he hurled himself at her: the disarrayed clothing in the trunk that had hidden the gun, the gleaming hinge it had hit in the haste of hauling it from its hiding place.

His hand struck the woman's arm a numbing blow. The Luger flew from her hand to clatter along the dusty floor. He stared at her.

She was oblivious of her arm hanging useless at her side. Her burning eyes blazed their hatred as she returned his stare. "You killed my husband, you *Ami* swine!" she hissed venomously. "You—killed—him!"

Rosenfeld came bounding up the stairs, his gun ready in his hand. Instantly he realized what had happened. He swung his gun to cover the defiant woman.

Behind him the two young boys came scrambling up. They flung themselves at their mother. She clasped them tightly to her.

Tom stared at her. He had felt sorry for her. He had felt guilty for having to treat her roughly. He had misread all the little signs she involuntarily had given him. Fear for hate. Guilt for vengeance! Because of his own god-damned mixed-up German-bastard feelings! He felt a mushroom of rage well up in him. A rage against himself. He had been one hell of a god-damned stupid shit! No more. To hell with the fucking Krauts!

He went back to the window. The light was getting bad. Intently he peered at the slip of torn paper. A name. An address.

GERTI GRUN
86 WENDERSTRA
REGENSBU

Regensburg. Like the theater ticket.

He started for the stairs.

Rosenfeld picked up the Luger. "What about her?" he asked, nodding toward the woman.

Tom stopped. He did not turn. "Leave her." For a moment he stood still. Then he looked back at the defiant woman clutching her two frightened boys to her. "Keep the clothes," he said.

Tom was sitting at one of the tables in the *Gaststube* of Gastwirtschaft Bockelmeier. He was making Straubing CIC HQ his base of operation for the time being. It was late, but he wanted to get his report out of the way. Early next morning he intended to go where his only clues were leading him: Regensburg.

He had briefly debated with himself if he should check with Major Lee first. Regensburg was after all in the XX Corps area. He had lost the debate. He had long since learned that if you don't ask questions you can't get no for an answer.

Anyway, both XX Corps and his own XII Corps were part of Third Army. That ought to be good enough—especially for an "unorthodox" caper!

The door from the street opened and Agent Buter came in. He spotted Tom. "Hey, Jaeger!" he said. "Have you heard the news?"

"What news?"

"I see you haven't," said Buter. He sauntered over to Tom. "Let me be the first to enlighten you, my boy."

"Be my guest."

"I've just come from CP. They've been monitoring the Kraut radio." He drew himself up importantly. "Der Führer is kaput!" he announced. "Dead!"

"Hitler?" Tom was startled.

"How many Führers do you know? According to the Hamburg radio— and I quote with great pleasure—Hitler died a hero's death in defense of Berlin! Yesterday."

"That's a crock of shingles."

"Undoubtedly. But the son of a bitch is just as dead." He started for the kitchen. "Don't strain yourself, buddy boy. The war is practically over." He disappeared through the door.

For a moment Tom sat in silent thought. At long last the end was near. He found it hard to realize. In a little while the fighting would be over. The complicated and chaotic time of settling in for occupation duty would begin. There would be sweeping changes in all CIC and other intelligence operations. It would be a time of confusion. A time when it would be all too easy for a Sleeper Agent—a Rudi A-27—to disappear!

He returned to his report. "86 Wenderstrasse, Regensburg," he wrote.

He stared at the words. Regensburg. . . . Somewhere in that city of some 120,000 Germans were the answers to his quest. He was certain of it. Tomorrow he would find out.

Regensburg—the ancient city of Ratisbon—had a bloody history of war and violence dating back to the pre-Christian Celtic settlement of Radispona.

Conquered by the Romans and fortified by Marcus Aurelius, it had become the Roman center of power on the upper Danube and had been renamed Castra Regina. Part of the Porta Praetorius, built in A.D. 179, still stood. The age-old massive limestone blocks and slabs gave an indestructible look to the town—belied by the devastation surrounding it.

Charlemagne captured the city in 788, and by the thirteenth century it had become the most flourishing town in southern Germany, an important stopover for the crusaders on their way to their holy wars.

Plague and capture and pillage razed the city during the Thirty Years' War, and by 1809, when Napoleon's invincible troops stood before her gates, the town had suffered through seventeen disastrous sieges during her strife-torn life. Once again she was reduced to ashes.

As Tom and Sergeant David Rosenfeld drove into the bomb-battered city it was glaringly obvious that history was repeating itself. The great Messerschmitt factories, targets of the massive Allied air raids, lay in ruins. On their way to town Tom and Rosenfeld had passed the last desperate attempt of the Luftwaffe to manufacture the much needed aircraft: an open-air assembly line of ME-262s strung through a field, hidden in a forest east of town.

The SS troops had blown the great Regen and Danube bridges—including the famous twelfth-century stone bridge, the Steinerne Brücke, an architectural marvel of the Middle Ages—in a wanton, futile attempt to stem the American tide. But the town wore her battle scars as proudly as a Heidelberg student his dueling scars.

The city had been taken six days before by the 65th and 71st Divisions, and as Tom and Rosenfeld drove through the narrow winding streets on their way to CIC HQ, civilians and soldiers alike all but ignored them.

On the famous Gesandtenstrasse—Ambassadors Street—damage to the old historic buildings was minor. The houses still bore the colorful coats of arms of the foreign representatives who had occupied them in happier days.

Tom glanced at the street map in his lap. Wenderstrasse was nearby. He turned to Rosenfeld. "Stop here," he said.

Rosenfeld looked at him in surprise. He pulled the jeep over to the curb and stopped.

"We can save some time," Tom said. "I want you to go on to CIC. Find out from them anything they have on Schloss Ehrenstein, on Sleeper Agents—and on KOKON." He looked down the street. He dismounted. "I'll take a look at the Wenderstrasse place," he said. "I'll meet you at CIC later. Take off!"

Rosenfeld drove off.

Tom stood alone in Gesandtenstrasse. The German civilians passing him made a more than necessary detour around him. He noticed they made a point of not looking at him. He glanced around him.

On the wall behind him a US Army flyer had been tacked up:

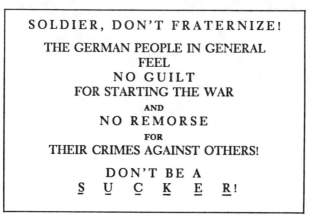

SOLDIER, DON'T FRATERNIZE!

THE GERMAN PEOPLE IN GENERAL
FEEL
NO GUILT
FOR STARTING THE WAR
AND
NO REMORSE
FOR
THEIR CRIMES AGAINST OTHERS!

DON'T BE A
S̲ U̲ C̲ K̲ E̲ R̲!

He looked away. He had never felt as conscious of his native heritage before. Furtively he watched the Germans hurrying by. None of them paid any attention to the flyer. Nor to him. He started to walk toward Wenderstrasse.

Wenderstrasse 86 was a four-story apartment building precariously propped up with large wooden beams. The ground floor was occupied by boarded-up shops; the masonry walls were chipped and gouged by shrapnel. The building had received a direct bomb hit at one corner, shearing it away, exposing the layers of empty rooms like giant honeycombs.

Tom went to the door of one of the shops. The display window had been boarded up except for one small square covered with a piece of cracked glass. He knocked on the door. He waited. He knocked again.

Finally a man's voice called, "*Wer ist da?*—Who is there?"

"I am looking for Gerti," Tom answered.

A man's face appeared at the cracked windowpane. It peered suspiciously at Tom. It withdrew. A middle-aged man with short gray bristly hair opened the door. He looked at Tom's uniform, a mixture of hostility and contempt mirrored on his sullen face. "Fräulein Grunert is in the rear," he said grumpily. "Last door on the right."

So that's her name, Tom thought. He filed it away.

"You can come through here this time," the man continued, resentment coloring his voice, "but next time use the other door. Like the rest of them do." He stood aside to let Tom pass.

Tom felt his unfriendly eyes upon him. "Thank you," he said. He wondered what "the rest of them" wanted with Gerti Grunert. He had a sudden uneasy feeling that he was about to embark on a wild-goose chase —without a shotgun.

He followed the querulous man's directions, walked down a badly lit, musty smelling corridor and found himself facing a door from behind which came muffled music from an obviously old and tinny phonograph. He tapped lightly on the door.

A feminine voice called out in passable English, "Come in, darling!"

He entered the room. He knew at once where he was. He could taste his disappointment. The room was lighted with red and amber bulbs, casting a ghastly orange glow over everything. Heavy flowered drapes were drawn across the two windows, and the air was heavy with cheap perfume. A large bed strewn with multicolored pillows dominated the room, and an old dilapidated gramophone on a mirrored dresser was grinding away on an out-of-date *Schlager*—a hit tune whose time long since had come and gone. A wad of newspaper had been stuffed into the loudspeaker to muffle the tone.

Gerti Grunert was a girl in her middle twenties possessing a certain brazen beauty. Looking at Tom with frank appraisal in her dark eyes, she uncurled herself lazily from the bed and stood up to face him. She wore a flimsy, not-too-clean pink negligee over an open-lace black bra, black lace panties—and knee-high black patent leather boots.

She shook her luxurious long brown hair seductively, planted her booted legs firmly, slightly apart, on the floor, put her hands on her hips and leaned her pelvis provocatively toward Tom. She gave a little laugh—too shrill to be pleasing. "Who are *you?*" she asked. "I do not know you."

Brazenly she looked him up and down. "But you are cute." She laughed again. "Very cute, *Schatzi!* You want to stay with me?"

It was a question to which Gerti obviously already knew the answer. She shrugged her negligee off her bare shoulders and sat down on the bed. "How did you come here, *Liebchen?*" she asked. "You have perhaps a good friend who will not mind sharing?" She laughed.. *"Ist gut!*—That's fine!"

Tom thought fast. His first Regensburg lead was not exactly what he had anticipated. But Gerti was obviously an enterprising young lady. It had not taken her long to round up a clientele among the GI's in town—fraternization or no fraternization.

She must have been in business for some time. Her name and address scribbled on the slip of paper he'd found in the coat from Schloss Ehrenstein proved that. She would have entertained personnel from the castle in the past. Perhaps she *did* have information he could use. He had to decide how best to get it out of her. And decide fast.

He scowled at her. "You are mistaken, Fräulein Grunert," he said coldly. "I am not here as a customer."

The inviting smile at once disappeared from the girl's lips. Narrow-eyed, she stared at Tom, suddenly worried.

She is not as pretty as she appeared to be at first, Tom thought. Her face is too hard. Too crafty.

"What do you want with me?" she asked testily.

"It depends," he said. "On you."

He saw the quick flicker of calculation in her eyes. What did he want? Would he make trouble? Or was he simply out to get a free lay? She was shrewd. There was something else.

She stood up. She looked closely at him. "You are not a regular *Ami* soldier," she said accusingly. "I know what their uniforms are like. Their emblems and their insignia. Officers and enlisted men. I know." She could not help sounding a little boastful. "You are"—she pointed to the single U.S. emblems on his shirt-collar tabs—"different."

He nodded. "I am."

She gave him a guarded look. She licked her red lips. "How . . . different?"

"I am an officer in the United States Army Counter Intelligence Corps," he said calmly.

Gerti's eyes grew veiled. "Secret police . . ." She turned her heavily made up eyes full upon him. "What do you want with me? I have done nothing."

"You are aware, I am sure, of the Army's non-fraternization policy, Fräulein Grunert," he said sternly. "A policy you are flagrantly violating."

She shrugged. She picked up her negligee and placed it around her shoulders. "The American soldiers, *they* come to *me*," she said brazenly. "I treat them well. Would you have me resist them?"

"I'm not interested in your activities," Tom said, his voice flat. "I want some information."

A quick flicker of apprehension flashed in the girl's eyes. "What . . . kind of information?" she asked suspiciously.

"How long have you been in business here?" he asked coldly.

She glared at him angrily. "Why should I tell you?" she demanded.

He smiled unpleasantly. "I think, Fräulein Grunert, I think you can figure out for yourself *why*," he said.

She frowned. She suddenly looked ridiculously young. "A year," she said tonelessly. She shrugged. "A few months more."

"You entertained customers from the Wehrmacht? The SS?"

She nodded.

"Were any of the men stationed at a place called Schloss Ehrenstein?" he asked.

Gerti looked up quickly. The look of alarm flitted through her eyes once again. She stared at Tom wide-eyed.

"Well?" he snapped.

"Yes," she whispered. "I . . . I think so."

"*Think?*" He fixed her with a scathing look.

"I mean . . . yes," she said quickly. "I know some boys told me they stayed at the old castle."

"That's better," he growled.

"But I know nothing else about them. Any of them." She gave him a quick glance. "What about them?"

Tom's gruff manner softened. He sat down beside her. "I'll be frank with you, Fräulein Gerti," he said earnestly. "I have a German suspect in custody. A young soldier. He has been accused of serious war crimes. He denies being guilty."

He looked at the girl. His voice grew confidential. "He says he has a brother. A brother who can prove him innocent. We do not want to punish the innocent, Fräulein. I should like to find this man's brother."

He watched the girl. She was listening intently to him. She shrewdly realized that the pressure somehow had shifted away from her. She wanted to keep it that way.

"This brother was supposedly stationed at Schloss Ehrenstein," Tom continued. "During the last year or so. His name is Rudi Kessler. Did you know him?"

Gerti shook her head. "I do not remember."

Tom suddenly returned the grim scowl to his face. Abruptly he stood up. Stiffly he glared at the girl. "As you wish, Fräulein," he said in a tone of dismissal.

Quickly she rose with him. "What the devil do you want from me?" she flared. "I cannot remember every cock who paid his twenty marks! Certainly not the marvels from Schloss Ehrenstein!" She tossed her head. "*Es war immer eine Blitzsache,*" she said scornfully. "It was always a blitz affair with them."

"Blitz affair?"

"They were always in such a damned hurry."

"Why?" he asked sharply.

"How do you expect *me* to know?" she snapped.

Tom said nothing. He merely looked at the girl, a little icy smile on his lips. Gerti suddenly looked frightened, her bravado fading away. She sank back down on her bed. "They . . . they only stopped by here to be with me on their way to someplace else," she said. "They were not supposed to."

"Where?"

She frowned at him apprehensively. "I do not know. Some meeting place. Some house . . . on Stiergasse."

"Number?"

She looked up at him, her eyes troubled. "Look," she said. "That is all I know. All. I swear it. I do not know any number. Believe me! Why should I lie to you? What is it to me?" She tried to wet her crimson lips again, but her mouth was dry.

Tom looked at the frightened girl. Her pallor of fear made the rouge on her cheeks look clownishly grotesque. He felt deeply sorry for her. But she *had* given him his clue!

"All right, Gerti," he said. "I believe you. I believe you have told me what you know."

He turned and walked from the dismal room, leaving the girl sitting on her bed. Her all-important bed. He could hardly wait to dig into his pocket and whip out the little slip of blue paper that seemed to be burning a hole in it. A theater ticket stub from the Regensburger Stadttheater.

The penciled note on the back read, "791 SG"—791 StierGasse!

Tom stood staring at a huge pile of rubble that once had been a building. What kind of a building was impossible to tell. The destruction was total. And recent. The grass and weeds overgrowing most of the rubble heaps left from the bombings were only beginning to take hold.

He was looking at Stiergasse 791. He was keenly disappointed. His only two leads had led him nowhere. He sat down on the curb across the street from the demolished house to take stock.

Rosenfeld had come up with nothing but a fat zero from the CIC. He'd sent him on to the Corps OB team, to see if there was anything in the latest Order of Battle book.

Tom himself had hunted up a set of civilian clothes with the help of the Regensburg CIC team. He'd wanted to be able to observe the house on Stiergasse as unobtrusively as possible. The jacket was too big for him, the pants too tight in the crotch. He could have saved himself the trouble, he thought bitterly. And the damned discomfort.

He gazed dispiritedly at the ruins across the street. The long late-afternoon shadows reaching down the street all seemed to point to the rubble heap as if to mock him in his defeat. For a time he sat staring at the debris. But no ideas would come to him. He was stopped. Stopped cold.

"Feuer, bitte?" The voice came from behind him. "Have a light?"

He whirled around. In the shadows of the doorway to the house in back of him stood a man. Tom had no idea where he'd sprung from. Inside? He felt in his pockets. "Yes. Here."

In the flare of the match he took a quick look at the stranger. The man was about forty. His hair was close-cropped, shaved high above the ears. He wore steel-rimmed glasses, and his small eyes behind them glinted with a curiously intent wariness as he watched Tom light his dirty gutter butt for him.

"Thanks." He puffed on his butt, holding it carefully between thumb and forefinger. He stole a glance at Tom. "I have been watching you," he said. "You are looking for something?"

Tom felt the stimulation of rising excitement course through him. His thoughts raced. He had a feeling that the encounter was not accidental.

But who was the man? What was he? He'd have to be careful. He looked at the stranger with obvious suspicion. "Why?" he demanded. "Why do you want to know?"

The stranger returned his gaze. He sized him up. "I know this place." He shrugged. "Maybe I could help you find what you are looking for."

"I have found what I was looking for," Tom said curtly.

The man grinned. It was an unnerving performance. Only his lips drew back to expose bad teeth. His eyes behind the cold steel-rimmed glasses remained icy and wary. "But not the way you had hoped to find it, I wager," he said smugly. He was watching Tom closely. "What was the number you wanted?" he asked.

Tom looked at him quickly. He hesitated just the right number of seconds. "Number 791," he said.

The man nodded. "You had business there?" he asked. "Friends?"

Tom looked at him. This sparring with words is getting me nowhere, he thought swiftly. I'll have to shit or get off the pot. "I come from Schloss Ehrenstein," he said quietly.

The stranger's eyes brightened for a brief moment behind their steel cages. Then he carefully snipped the fire off his diminishing butt with his fingernail. He looked cautiously up and down the street. "Come with me," he ordered.

Tom followed him into the gloomy hallway of the house. A narrow corridor led to the rear of the building. For a while they walked in silence, before Tom asked, "Where are we going?"

"You will see," the stranger snapped shortly. His manner had changed markedly. His posture had become decidedly military. They walked in silence for a few seconds more.

"Tell me," Tom asked. "Were you . . . expecting me?"

The man gave him a quick look. Then he coughed a mirthless laugh. "Not exactly," he said. "But ever since Number 791 was destroyed we have had someone from the cadre watch the ruins. Just in case some of you boys should show up and need a hand."

"I see," said Tom. He had a hell of a time suppressing his excitement. He knew he dared not be too curious. He was stepping along a tightrope —in GI boots! But he was getting somewhere. At last.

"Did many of us make it?" he asked casually.

The stranger gave him a quick glance. He scowled. He did not answer. Tom resolved to be more careful.

The two men left the house and began to cross the rubble-strewn back yard toward a door in a fence on the far side.

Tom tried to appear as unconcerned and incurious as possible. It was not easy. He could feel his heart pound heavily and noisily in his throat. It seemed impossible that the man walking at his side did not hear it. With growing excitement he realized that he had made contact with someone involved in the Sleeper Agent operation at Schloss Ehrenstein. He realized that he himself had been accepted as part of that operation. At least for the moment. It was a moment of utmost importance. He could not afford to lose it. And he knew he had only himself and his own powers to rely upon.

The man glanced at him. "What held *you* up?" he asked.

Tom shrugged. "I was caught in an *Ami* sweep," he said. "The damned

Coca-Cola drinkers kept me in a PW camp. I only just got away."

His companion nodded. "Yes. That happened to a couple of others." There was no suspicion in his voice.

They went through the door in the backyard fence and began to cross another rubbish-strewn yard, headed for a building on the other side.

"Where are we going?" Tom asked again.

"To see Lorenz," the man snapped. He sounded impatient.

Tom thought quickly. If Lorenz—whoever he might be—was holed up in the building they were headed for, he'd have to work fast. The man with him seemed to have accepted him. Lorenz undoubtedly would be more cautious. More inquisitive. He'd have to get as much information from his close-cropped four-eyed friend as possible.

"*Hör mal,*" he said confidentially. "Listen, I wonder if you could tell me something?" His voice was congenial with camaraderie. "I had a good friend at Schloss Ehrenstein. I wonder if he made it? Rudi was his name?"

The man stopped short. He glared at Tom, suspicion smoldering in his flinty eyes. "You ought to know better than to ask a question like that," he snapped.

Tom threw up his hands. "Hey! No offense!" he said. He felt himself go cold. Dammit, he might have fucked up the whole deal. The man was definitely mistrustful now. He'd lost him. Unless . . .

The stranger was watching him, narrow-eyed. "When did you leave Schloss Ehrenstein?" he asked slowly. "I do not seem to remember you."

"It's been several months," Tom said airily. "Things got screwed up when I got on the outside. . . ." He shrugged a gesture of frustration. "I should have known, I guess. Frau Peukert used to say that things were in a mess out there."

The man watched him speculatively. "*Ja,*" he said reflectively. "The widow Peukert."

Tom grinned disarmingly. "I guess that's why she persuaded the commandant to stash some of her loot in his safe!"

The man looked up sharply. "How did you know that?" he snapped. "About the commandant's safe?"

Tom grinned broadly. "Look, friend," he said, "what the hell were you training us for at Schloss Ehrenstein?"

The man's eyes opened wide. He barked another of his dry laughs. "*Ja!*"

he said. "That is good! Very good!" He laughed again. He started toward the house.

The yard was filled with junk hauled out from the damaged buildings surrounding it, and the two men carefully picked their way through broken furniture, scorched lumber and piles of shattered objects of all kinds.

Tom tripped and almost fell on top of a splintered long-case clock, smashed beyond salvage. "You know," he commented, "I haven't seen a clock that badly smashed up since the one in our basement shooting gallery!"

His companion's face lit up. *"Ja.* The clock!" He chuckled with evident pleasure. "The damned clock . . ." He looked sideways at Tom. "Your friend did that."

Tom stopped short. "Rudi?" he exclaimed.

The man nodded. "I was there. I was one of the interrogators. At his readiness test. That's when he did it!" He shook his head in remembered marvel. "Rudi A-27. *Das war ein Kerl!*—That was a tough one!" he said with evident respect.

Tom agreed enthusiastically as they continued toward the house. "Rudi was going to America," he said. "I hope he makes it."

"He will," the other asserted, all suspicion gone from his voice. "You can be certain of it." He nodded his head sagely. "He will," he repeated. "He was scheduled to exfiltrate by the northern route. Less crowded. Less risk. Not anything like the southern routes."

"Good. Then he is on his way."

"It is to be expected," the man agreed. "He was ordered to Berlin just before we closed down the project."

They came to the back door of the house. "Wait here," the man ordered. "I will see if Lorenz can see you." He ducked into the dark building and disappeared in the shadows.

It was his chance.

Already he had wangled important information out of the Schloss Ehrenstein cadre watchdog. He realized he'd been able to con the man only because of the limited time they'd spent together. It would be different with Lorenz. He knew he could not survive a thorough questioning.

He was alone. He could take off. Now. And be safe. But, if he did, he'd alert them and the whole damned Sleeper Agent organization to the fact that he was on their trail. They undoubtedly had alternate plans for all their missions. They would activate them. And all his work would go down the drain.

However, if he did stay, he might be able to learn even more from Lorenz, who was quite obviously on a higher rung of the Schloss Ehrenstein ladder than four-eyes. Could he get away with it?

Not bloody likely! The prudent thing to do was to scram. Right now.

He stayed.

"Lorenz is not here," the man said when he returned for Tom. "We will wait for him." He led Tom down some stairs to a large basement room. A kerosene lamp glowed faintly. He turned it up.

Tom looked around. The place appeared to be lived in. It had been provided with furniture obviously gathered from many sources, battered but sturdy. Several rolled-up canvas cots were stacked haphazardly in a corner, and a large carved wooden bed with a colorful quilted spread stood to one side. Several doors, all of them closed, led to other areas. Or did they serve as escape hatches?

The man took out his cigarette butt and relighted it. With his own matches, Tom observed wryly. "He will be here shortly," the man said. "It is almost curfew time." He peered with regret at his cigarette butt. It was getting too small to hold. Carefully he snuffed it out. He fished a small metal box from his pocket, tore the paper from the butt and spilled the rest of the loose tobacco into his box. He sighed. "Schloss Ehrenstein was never like this, was it?" he said plaintively. He snapped the box shut and put it away.

"You think *he* is from Schloss Ehrenstein, do you, Scharf?" The icy voice came from the stairs leading down into the basement.

Tom spun around. He took one look and he knew he didn't have a chance. The cards had been stacked against him all the time.

The man who stood near the bottom of the stairs was middle-aged with short gray bristly hair. It was the hostile shopkeeper of Wenderstrasse 86 who had let him go through his place to see Gerti Grunert!

In his hand he held a small black pistol. It was pointed steadily and directly at Tom's gut.

Irrelevantly he noticed that the gun was an *Ehrenwaffe*—an honor weapon. That intricately carved Walther 7.65 given by Adolf Hitler personally to the highest ranking Nazis only. Lorenz obviously was a formidable opponent.

The man called Scharf looked startled. "He is, Lorenz, he is!" he protested quickly. "He knows all about the place. He knows—"

"You are a damned fool!" Lorenz interrupted sharply. "How much have you told him?"

"Nothing! I—"

"Never mind. It is of no consequence." He gave the man a withering look. Then he turned his eyes on Tom. "We meet again!" he said sardonically.

He turned to Scharf. "I saw this man. Today. He came to question that little whore Gerti. Only then he wore an *American uniform!* With only U.S. officer emblems on his collar. You know what that means, Scharf, do you not?"

Scharf looked stricken. He edged away from Tom.

Lorenz looked at the CIC agent with contemptuous disdain. "Did you think we would not be warned after you so clumsily tried to dig up our records?" he asked, his voice brittle with sarcasm. "You give us little credit."

"Frau Peukert," Tom conceded.

"She is a loyal German." Lorenz allowed himself a thin, malicious smile. "You have been stupid. Very stupid. Since the time we were warned, we have, of course, had everyone who could possibly be linked to our operation under constant surveillance by our cadre personnel. Including that brainless little slut you visited."

He smiled again. A chilling grimace. "You should not have tangled with *us*, American," he said derisively. "You are out of your league." He paused portentously. "Fortunately, you will not live to regret it!"

Tom's thoughts were spinning in his head. Lorenz was obviously in love with the sound of his own voice. That fact might save his life. But he would have to act before it would be too late for any action at all.

Out of the corner of his eye he was aware of the heavy wooden bed to his right.

Exploding into sudden motion, he flung himself for the cover. Even as he was hurtling through the air, his hand groped for and found the gun in his shoulder holster beneath the ample jacket.

He sensed rather than saw Scharf draw his gun, and as he crashed to the floor behind the bed he sent two rounds slamming into the chest of the German.

He dropped.

In the same instant he heard the sharp report from Lorenz's gun, and the split-second whine as the slug shot over his head to bury itself in the wall behind him.

He pressed himself down behind the shelter of the bed. In front of him, in the middle of the room, he could see the body of Scharf sprawled on the floor. Lorenz, at the bottom of the stairs, was hidden from view.

Suddenly Scharf moaned. He stirred.

Tom tensed. His gun held steady, he watched the wounded man trying to sit up.

Suddenly two shots rang out thunderously in the confinement of the cellar room. Scharf's face disintegrated hideously in splattering crimson. Lorenz had made certain he would never talk again.

Tom felt the sour bile rise in his craw. He swallowed. For a few seconds he lay motionless. Then, slowly, carefully, noiselessly, he began to turn himself around until his head was where his feet had been.

Quietly he lifted one foot. Galvanizing into action, he gave a deliberate violent yank on the quilted bedspread with his raised foot.

In the same instant he catapulted himself forward, clearing his head and shoulders at the opposite end of the bed. Even as he did, he slammed two shots at Lorenz's position at the foot of the stairs.

He hit nothing. Lorenz was not there. For a moment he listened tensely. There was not a sound. Cautiously he stood up. Every muscle fiber alert, he looked around.

On the floor Scharf sprawled in crimson death. Lorenz was gone.

Regensburg was dark. Silent. Empty of its people. Only grim patrols mounted by the occupying forces moved through the deserted streets. It was long past curfew.

The figure that moved stealthily, with soundless caution, through the warped and twisted metal beams and girders, the mangled machinery and the bomb-blasted brickwork of the gutted Messerschmitt factory, seemed nothing but a shadow with a furtive life of its own.

Deep in the ruins a makeshift shelter had been erected, looking little different from other piles of rubble.

Cautiously, with whisper movements, the figure approached. It was a man. He stopped at the shelter. Quickly he knocked on a large slab of fire-blackened wood serving as a door. Once . . . twice . . . once again. He waited.

Presently the slab was pushed aside a few inches.

The man outside spoke, his voice a tense whisper. "It is Lorenz," he said. *"I have a target!"*

10

Rudi was cold. He had been soaked, crossing the canal during the night, and he had taken off his uniform jacket to let it dry out. He had checked his German ID papers. They were not damaged. They were safe in the breast pocket of his jacket, wrapped in their wax paper. He'd need them to cross the border into Denmark, still under German control. He shivered.

It was barely dawn, and the day promised to be cold and raw. It had been raining, and the ground was soggy and wet. He was sitting on an overturned wheelbarrow behind a barn, resting. The farm was just outside a small village he'd passed earlier. The black-and-white road sign said, GROSS WITTENSEE. He had looked it up on his map. He was still more than seventy kilometers from the border.

"Verflucht!"

He was a full day behind the schedule he had set up for himself. Everything had gone well for the first couple of days. He had been heeding the warnings of Brigadeführer Arnold and Bormann himself. He had avoided all contact with anyone, civilian or military. And he'd had no trouble ducking the enemy patrols he'd spotted on his way along the Elbe River.

He had succeeded in slipping between Hamburg and Lübeck, as the British forces were closing in behind him, cutting across the peninsula. All day Wednesday, the 2nd, he'd heard the battle raging around the town of Lübeck. Seen the flashes of artillery fire on the horizon. It had died down. He assumed that Lübeck had fallen. Hamburg, perhaps, as well. Maybe even Berlin. But *he* had gotten through. He was on his way to the Danish border.

Then, near Segeberg, some fifty kilometers from the Kiel Canal, the goddamned motorcycle—a BMW, 600cc he'd commandeered at Wannsee when he set out—had broken down. It had taken him all the rest of the day and most of the night to make it to the canal—on a stolen bicycle.

Here, he'd had to abandon the bike. He couldn't get it across. And he had made it on foot to his present position, on a broken wheelbarrow behind a ramshackle barn, on a run-down farm near a lousy little village. Still seventy kilometers from the goddamned border. Shit!

He had decided to abandon his cautious back-road approach and make it to the main highway to Flensburg. There was a lot of military traffic headed for town. He'd take a chance. Try to hitch a ride. It was the only way he'd make it in time.

He was hungry. He'd already scrounged around a bit on the farm and found a few vegetables. He'd dumped them into the little sackcloth bag he carried for such foraging. Perhaps he could beat the farmer's wife to gathering a few eggs.

He stood up stiffly. He put his sack and his rolled-up jacket under his arm and walked around the corner of the barn in search of the chicken coop. Near the barn the farmer apparently was building himself a potato pit. Or beet cellar. Pieces of old lumber and mounds of dirt were scattered about.

Rudi was stepping over a heavy beam in the half light when he suddenly lost his footing on the slippery ground. He pitched headlong into the mud. His sack and jacket flew from under his arm, slid across the muddy slush, and disappeared.

He stood up. He cursed the damned farmer. His pants, his shirt were caked with dirt. He walked over to where his things had suddenly disappeared. He found himself standing at the edge of the excavation for the pit—a square ten-foot-deep hole in the ground.

In the dawning light he peered into the pit. The bottom was wet and muddy. Among a few rocks, small pieces of wood and other rubble he could make out his sack and his jacket.

He looked around. At one end of the pit stood a rickety ladder. He climbed down. His boots made unpleasant squishy sounds in the mud as he walked over to retrieve his belongings.

The food sack lay among a pile of small rocks. As he bent down to pick it up, one of the rocks suddenly sprang to life and scurried across the slimy dirt floor to cower in a corner of the pit.

Rudi jumped back with a startled cry. He stared into the dim corner. It was a huge rat. Its coat was wet and slick, plastered around its body. It crouched in the corner, staring at Rudi, with wary eyes glinting like jet-black beads.

For a split moment Rudi had felt abject fear wash over him. He glared at the rat. He felt a cold hatred take possession of him, a hatred that was the cumulation of all the shitty little things that had gone wrong. He welcomed it. The goddamned animal!

He looked around the pit. Among the debris lay a piece of rusty pipe about two feet long. Carefully, never taking his eyes off the wary rat, Rudi picked up the pipe, holding it at one end like a club. Stealthily he approached the cowering creature pressing itself in the dirt corner, deflating itself. Rudi lifted the pipe over his head. Suddenly he smashed it down on the rat. For a tangible moment the squishy thud hung sluggishly in the gray dawn. But the rat was gone. Only the mud had taken the deadly impact of Rudi's blow. The rat had scurried off.

Rudi was furious. Damned beast! He searched around. He spotted the rat crouched in the opposite corner. This time he slowly walked over—the pipe raised—and lashed out against the terror-stricken animal with sudden ferocity. Again he missed.

He was consumed with malice. Relentlessly he stalked the fleeing rat, fiercely striking out at it again and again, missing every time. Finally he trapped the desperate rat in a corner where a large boulder allowed only one way to escape. The animal's beady eyes shone with fear and hate as it watched him, coiled in the very tip of the corner trap.

He lifted his pipe, coldly staring back at the trapped animal. He savored the anticipated sight of its mangled corpse.

Suddenly the rat opened its mouth. Rudi had a fleeting glimpse of long yellow curved fangs. The animal shrieked a hideous scream and hurled itself in a steel-coil leap straight for Rudi's face.

Rudi reacted with the shock of instinct. He swung the pipe at the leaping rat. He missed. Dammit, the iron pipe was too heavy, too long for a quick swing. With profound revulsion he felt the sickening, slimy impact of the rat on his cheek. But he had acted with instinctive speed. The rat's teeth found no target.

The animal hit the slushy ground beyond him and turned at once. He whirled on it. Again the rat screamed, a hideous shriek that knifed through him with eerie terror.

For a lightning moment he had a vision of a gray figure sneaking through tall grass . . . a distant scream . . .

Mausi!

And the rat leaped. It caught hold of the front of his shirt and clung there in savage, desperate rage. He stared down into its upturned face, filthy yellow fangs exposed and pitch-black eyes gleaming with hate, straining toward his face.

In sickened disgust he slapped the creature off. He backed away from the maddened animal. In self-destructive hatred it followed him, leaped, hurtling itself upon him. Again and again. And it kept on screaming.

He was unaware of his awkward fending with the unwieldy length of pipe. Of sloshing and sliding in the slimy mud. He was aware only of his mushrooming panic. And the screaming. In growing terror he retreated from the charging rat. He stumbled against the ladder.

The ladder! It slid along the wet earth wall and tumbled onto the muddy bottom.

Frantically he bent down, feeling behind him for the fallen ladder. The rat leaped again—and he barely hit it with a backhand blow, deflecting it from his eyes.

The rat tumbled in the mire. Enraged, Rudi flung the pipe at it. He turned and grabbed the ladder. He slammed it against the dirt wall and swarmed up the rungs to the safety above.

He stood panting on the rim of the pit. He looked down into its depth. Below, the crazed rat sat up on its haunches, shrieking its frenzy at him. He was filled with black hate. He picked up a large, heavy boulder. He held it out over the rim. He let it drop. The squishy thud was the sound of death. The screaming stopped.

For a moment he stood silent. Still. He was drenched with sweat. In the chilly morning it was turning bleakly cold on his skin. Slowly he climbed down into the pit. He kept his eyes averted from the large boulder half sunk into the soggy, muddy bottom. He picked up his food sack and jacket and started back up the ladder. When he reached the top he saw the farmer. And the shotgun pointed squarely at his head.

Grimly the man motioned him up. "What are you doing here?" he asked. His voice was flat.

Rudi shrugged. Without seeming to, he studied the man. Harmless. Unless stupidity was dangerous. In his fifties. Except, with farmers it was always difficult to tell.

"I asked you what you are doing on my property," the farmer repeated. His voice was cold.

"Killing a rat." Rudi pointed into the pit. "Down there."

The farmer did not react. He motioned with his shotgun. "Empty that sack," he ordered.

Rudi tensed. He obeyed. The contents of the food sack spilled out upon the ground. A crust of stale bread wrapped in newspaper. Three potatoes. A handful of pea pods. And five small carrots. From the farmer's vegetable garden.

The man stared at the food. He took a better grip on his gun. "From *my* farm?" he asked. He already knew the answer.

Rudi nodded. He suddenly had a chilling thought. The man might turn out to be a danger after all. He might be one of those self-righteous fanatics. He might take him for a deserter! And deserters were fair game. He looked at the shotgun. It was still pointed at his gut.

He began to sweat again. "Look," he said anxiously. I know what you may be thinking. But I am *not* a deserter. I have been discharged. I have papers. Proper papers. Right here in my jacket. My *Soldbuch*—"

The farmer was not listening to him. He was staring at the carrots and the rest of the food on the ground. "Pick it up," he said.

Rudi began to put the food back into his sack.

"Five scrawny carrots," the farmer said in his flat voice. "Not much of a breakfast." He looked at Rudi. "You need something more than that. I can give you some warm milk. It will do you good. We have no coffee. We have not had coffee in . . . in . . ." He let the sentence trail away. He turned and started away. "Come with me," he said.

Rudi's mind raced. He was thunderstruck. The old goat was actually offering him food! He stopped himself short. It was a trap! He thought quickly. The farmer would feed him. Keep him happy—while he sent for the military police. The SS. That was it. And Rudi would end up swinging from a rope!

He could refuse to go with the man. And let him turn in the alarm? No go. Perhaps the man really did want to help? To give him food? And, perhaps not. He could not afford to find out.

He bent down to pick up his food sack. He fumbled his paratrooper knife from his boot—and lunged up, burying the knife blade deep in the man's kidney.

The farmer was strong. Strong as an ox. He did not utter a sound. He turned around slowly and stared at Rudi with bulging, uncomprehending eyes. And he crashed to the soggy, muddy ground at his killer's feet.

Rudi jammed his knife repeatedly into the wet ground. It would clean the blade, at least until he could do a better job. He looked at the dead farmer.

"Trust nobody," the Reichsleiter had said.

He touched the body with his boot. *He* can be trusted, he thought. Now. Had the man really wanted to help? Had he? He felt a twinge of doubt. Of regret. He dismissed it summarily.

Had he not read the Führer's words: "Conscience is a disease of life." It was true. It was weakness.

He tucked his sack and his jacket under his arm. Rapidly he walked away.

Two hours later he stood at the main highway to Flensburg. Once more he was wearing his full uniform. Traffic was already heavy on the road. He would have no difficulties getting a ride. Nothing could stop him now. The situation was fluid enough. No one would ask questions.

Besides, he did have his ID. That should ward off a search he could not afford. He felt his breast pocket. He froze. It was empty. Frantically he searched. His papers were gone! A chill ran through him. He knew where they were. At the bottom of a muddy pit with the crushed carcass of a rat.

The 106th Evac Hospital had only recently been established in the vicinity of Regen, some fifteen miles northeast of Regensburg. But it was well marked. Tom and Sergeant Rosenfeld had no trouble finding it.

Rosenfeld had finally dug up something. He had obtained no useful information from OB, but he'd talked to IPW. From their records it appeared that one interrogation team had questioned a man, a former *KZ'ler*—a concentration camp inmate. The man had been in shock and incoherent, but he had mentioned one word that struck the interrogator as odd enough to spell out in his report.

The word he had written was "cocoon." Obviously the original word in

German had been "KOKON." The inmate had been taken to the 106th Evac Hospital. He was still there.

Rosenfeld turned off the main highway onto a dirt road where a prominent sign pointed the way to the hospital. Next to it, on the shoulder, stood a little wooden roadside shrine. The inverted V-shaped roof sheltered a carved and painted figure of the Madonna. Her arms were gently, lovingly cradled before her, her eyes gazing serenely down toward the child belonging there. But her arms were empty. The Christ Child had been blasted from them, shattered to kindling by a shell fragment.

The man in the bed at first sight did not appear to be human. A skeleton. Yes. A skeleton stretched over with pallid, almost translucent skin. He lay immobile, flat on his back. From deep in their sockets his eyes stared unblinkingly upward. Eyes that were disturbingly vacuous. Burned out. His arms lay outside the covers at his side. So thin were they that each separate bone in them and in the parchmentlike hands could be plainly seen.

"I'm afraid you won't get much out of him," said Captain Sokol, the doctor who had taken them to the patient. "He hasn't been lucid for days."

He looked down at the man, a mixture of outraged anger and deep compassion on his grim face. "He is dying, of course," he said quietly. "It's a wonder he's alive at all." He looked at Tom. "He's a survivor of the Flossenburg Death March," he said.

Tom clenched his jaws grimly. He was all too familiar with the infamous, inhuman atrocity they called the Flossenburg Death March. Flossenburg had been a concentration camp some fifty battle-scarred miles to the north. The SS guards there had been determined that the inmates should not be liberated by the advancing Americans. The camp crematorium was working past capacity. The ovens could handle no more. So the SS drove fifteen thousand inmates from the threatened camp southwards on a hellish march of death.

For three days and three nights without rest they were mercilessly whipped and prodded on their torturous march. Weak and emaciated as they were, they fell by the wayside by the thousands to be murdered on the spot by their guards—if they were lucky—or simply left to die a lingering death. Toward the end of the nightmare march the brutish SS guards had been driven to a frenzy, an orgy of butchery. The accounts of the infernal atrocities committed on the march defied description.

Tom knew. His Corps area had been saturated with the pitiful survivors, holed up in ruins and rubble.

"Who is he?" he asked.

"We know little about him," Captain Sokol replied. "We could get only sketchy information before he . . . well, you can see what he is like."

He picked up a clipboard hanging at the foot of the bed. He flipped to a sheet of typed notes in back of the medical charts. "His name is Loewenstein. Dr. Loewenstein. He is supposed to have been a brilliant surgeon in Berlin before the war. He is Jewish, of course. He had first been an inmate of another camp. We don't know which one. There he is supposed to have worked with some Nazi doctors on some sort of project. We could get nothing out of him about it."

He replaced the charts. Soberly he looked at Tom. "He was picked up by elements of the Eleventh Armored Division. Along the death march route," he said gravely. "Hanging from a tree." He paused. Then, angrily: "He'd been a pawn in a game the SS had amused themselves with on their dull trip. The X game."

Tom's heart skipped a beat. He had heard about the X game. It was really a children's game. It had been played by the young Nazis being trained for duty as guards in the concentration camps.

The boys were divided into two teams, and each team was allowed to go into the camp and pick one male inmate. The pawns. The playing field was the size of a tennis court. At each end stood a tall crossbeam gallows. The two inmate pawns were stripped naked. One of them was hung by his wrists from each of the two crossbeams, his legs spread out and anchored to pegs in the ground. High in the air he hung. Spread-eagled. Forming an X. The two eager teams of boys would form in the center of the court, each team with its own dog. A magnificent German shepherd. Specially trained. At a signal shot from the SS referee the two dogs would be turned loose.

Egged on, goaded, cheered by their teams, the dogs would streak for the gallows facing them. Jaws slavering, eyes bloodshot with frenzy, they would leap and jump and snap at the pawns hanging spread-eagled above.

The winner— The winner was the team of boys whose dog first ripped off the testicles of the opposing team's pawn.

Tom shivered. He looked down at the man-shell lying motionless in the bed. A children's game, he thought bleakly. And where are the children now?

Tom bent over the man. "Dr. Loewenstein," he said gently. "Dr. Loewenstein. Can you hear me?"

There was no reaction from the corpselike patient. His eyes remained dead and empty.

"Dr. Loewenstein?" Tom repeated. "Please answer me."

"He will not respond to his name," Sokol said grimly. "I understand you have to use his . . . his number."

Tom looked at the man's wasted arms lying limply at his sides. There it was. His concentration camp prisoner number. Tattooed on the inside of his right forearm.

"Try the last two pairs of digits," Sokol said quietly.

Gravely Tom contemplated the cadaverous figure lying before him. He was deeply moved. He was about to address him in the manner suggested —twenty-nine, eighty-seven—but he could not bring himself to do it. It was an indignity, he thought angrily, an affront! Dehumanizing. It would only bring a response in kind, the response of a maltreated, browbeaten *KZ'ler.* If it brought a response at all.

It was not what he wanted. He looked closely at the emaciated man. Perhaps there was another way. "Dr. Loewenstein," he said, his voice firm and professional. "We need your help. We need your advice." He bent over him. "Dr. Loewenstein! You are needed!"

There was a faint flicker in the ravaged man's dead eyes. Almost imperceptibly his shriveled lips began to work soundlessly.

"Dr. Loewenstein," Tom repeated firmly. "Please give me your attention. Your *professional* attention, Doctor."

Slowly the man's head turned on its spindly neck, until the sunken eyes looked up at Tom.

"Your opinion, Dr. Loewenstein," Tom pressed. "Please answer me!"

Suddenly the gaunt head lifted from the pillow. The harrowed eyes focused on Tom, and in a surprisingly strong voice Dr. Loewenstein spoke. "You must make a clean incision! Not a millimeter deeper than necessary. The ink. Not far below the *stratum granulosum.* Do not use sutures. They will cause a scar. Adhesive! Use adhesive."

"Dr. Loewenstein," Tom said, his heart racing. "KOKON. What do you know about KOKON?"

"KOKON? . . . KOKON? . . . *Betreffs KOKON* . . ." the haunted man repeated tonelessly. His eyes grew dark with abject terror. He stared at Tom, gazing directly into his eyes . . . and beyond.

"I will forget it, Herr Doktor! I will forget!" he whispered in stark fear. "I will never mention the word. I will forget I saw it written on the Oberstgruppenführer's records. It is not medical. Not medical. I will forget . . ."

His voice trailed off. He turned his head and once more stared into space with empty, tormented eyes. From each corner a tiny drop of moisture slowly seeped out and trickled down his sallow face.

Tom turned away.

Captain Doctor Sokol was white-faced. He stared at Loewenstein. "Holy Moses!" he said quietly. "Ink! *Tattoos!*" He turned to Tom. "I'd heard rumors," he said, obviously shaken. "They said that some of the concentration camp officers collected tattoos . . . cut off the inmates. God!" He looked in horror at his patient. "Is . . . is that what *he* did?"

"No," Tom replied, his face grim. "Not Dr. Loewenstein."

He looked down at the skeletal man in the bed. He knew now what kind of special work the Berlin surgeon had been required to perform. He had been forced to remove, without leaving any telltale scars, the identifying blood-type tattoos that only the SS bore on the inside of their upper left arms; remove them from high-brass Nazis. Nazis, like an Oberstgruppenführer—an SS general. Four stars. Whose records bore the notation "Re. KOKON."

He looked at Sokol. "No," he said. "Loewenstein's tattoo removals were much more practical."

He was an expert. An expert in demolition. He had taught the course at Schloss Ehrenstein—high explosives. Time fuses and delayed-action devices. Detonator caps and explosive cord. Grenades and mines. Incendiaries. And, of course, booby traps. The works.

He especially liked the booby traps. Their use was limited only by the inventiveness and ingenuity of their user.

Lorenz had fingered *the target* for him as the *Ami* officer left the CIC billet earlier that morning.

He'd had one hell of a time not losing him and his driver, following them in his run-down woodburner produce truck. In fact, he *had* lost them.

He had taken a chance, when he had seen the hospital's roadside signpost, and turned in. And he had spotted the target's jeep in the parking area.

He had required little time, undisturbed, and he had had it. He smiled contentedly as he slowly drove his old truck back toward Regensburg. He was pleased with his work.

A good booby trap does not have to be complicated. The simpler the better—and the easier to install. The trick was to be supercautious. Leave no trace that would give the show away.

The booby trap in the target's vehicle was simplicity itself. He had used two grenades for good measure. The *Stielhandgranate 24*, the type of hand grenade called a "potato masher" by the *Amis*. They should know!

He'd wedged them into the spring under the front seat on the passenger side of the jeep and wired them in place. It was where he had observed the target would be sitting. He had removed the safety caps from the ends of the handles, carefully freed the two grenade rip cords and tied them together, extended them and fastened them at the other end to the right front wheel.

It was simple. As soon as the vehicle moved, the cord would be wound up and pull the rip cord, setting off the grenades. It would work. That, and his own little personal refinement! There would be no survivors.

The woodburner sputtered. *Verdammt nochmal!* he thought irritably. It offended him deeply to have to depend on such inferior equipment. . . .

Tom and Sergeant Rosenfeld came from the hospital. They walked briskly toward the dismount point parking area, where they had left their jeep. It had been drizzling during the night and the ground was still wet.

"Where to now, sir?" Rosenfeld asked.

"Corps," said Tom. "It's time to go see Major Lee." He grinned. "They're moving to Grafenau this morning. Should be just about ready to settle in when we get there. I'm sure the major will be overjoyed to see us!"

They reached the jeep. Tom started to get in.

"Wait a minute," Rosenfeld said. He walked over and looked at the seat on the passenger side. "Someone in the motor pool left a piece of a used gasket on the seat," he said. "No use getting oil on your pants."

He looked. He frowned. "I saw it when you got out before," he said. He searched the seat. The floor. "It's not here." He looked concerned.

"Don't worry about it," Tom said. "Let's go."

"I saw the damned thing," Rosenfeld insisted. "It was there. Someone's been monkeying with the jeep." He suddenly looked disgusted. "Shit!" he exclaimed. "The rotor! Someone's pinched the distributor rotor! Dammit! I should have removed it myself."

He walked to the front of the jeep and lifted the hood, grumbling. "What the hell is this war coming to, anyway? You can't even keep your jeep from being stolen from under your damned nose. You remove the fucking rotor, and some joker comes along with his own and drives off in your vehicle!"

He examined the distributor. He looked puzzled. "The damned thing's still there!" he said.

"Okay, let's go," Tom said. He was getting impatient. He took his seat in the jeep.

Rosenfeld slammed the hood. "Yeah," he said. "But *someone's* been fooling around with the jeep." He started for the driver's seat. He suddenly stopped short. "Holy shit!" he whispered.

Tom turned to him. "What's the matter?" he asked sharply.

Rosenfeld stared at the ground. Then at Tom. "Sir," he said, his voice shaky, "I . . . I wouldn't move around too much. I . . . I think . . . I think the jeep may be . . . booby-trapped!"

Tom felt a quick drain of blood, and his heart began to pound. "Why?" he shot.

Rosenfeld pointed to the ground. "Because of that," he said. "That's no GI boot that made that print. That's a Kraut military boot!"

Tom looked. In the soft wet ground of a dried-up puddle was the impression of a boot. The imprints of the hobnails in the heavy soles stood out like muddy pockmarks. It was a German boot.

Tom's skin crawled. He sat precariously perched on his seat. He glanced at the ignition switch. Was that it? Would the jeep have blown up if they'd tried to start it? Or . . . what?

He was not a booby-trap expert. He had taken a brief course at ASC in Shrivenham in England while waiting for D-Day, and he knew that the damned things could be set off by a variety of methods. Push, pull, pressure, release, electricity—and any combination thereof you could dream up. And he knew the cardinal law: You never know *which* methods you are dealing with, until the damned thing blows up.in your face.

Tight-lipped, Rosenfeld stared at Tom. "That's why that oil gasket is gone," he said. "The Kraut cleaned up too good after himself!"

Tom's mind whirled. "David," he said to Rosenfeld, his voice taut. "Get to the motor pool. Fast. Get a tow truck. Have them bring a rope. And something heavy. A mortar base. Anything."

"But, you—"

"No buts! Move!"

Rosenfeld took off.

Tom sat perfectly still. He could feel the cold sweat of fear pool in his armpits and trickle down his sides. He stared in morbid fascination down at the seat. The skin in his crotch felt hot and sticky. He made a conscious effort to organize his spinning thoughts. As long as he sat motionless, the booby trap would not detonate. That much was clear.

But if it *were* there, he *could* have activated the detonator mechanism when he sat down on the seat—ready to go off when he got up and released the pressure of his weight from it.

It would have to be that. A pressure-release-type booby trap . . . or an electrically triggered trap set to go off when the jeep was started up.

He could think of no other possibilities. But he also knew they were there.

The weapons carrier arrived within minutes. It brought a thirty-foot tow rope and a heavy steel ammo box hastily filled with old nuts and bolts. One of the two motor pool mechanics who arrived with it and with David Rosenfeld cautiously peered under the jeep from every vantage point he could get.

"I don't know," he said dubiously. "It could be booby-trapped, all right. There's a little piece of wire hanging down from under the right seat. Looks new. Clean. That's all I can make out from here."

"Okay," said Tom. "Now listen." He wet his lips. He ignored the sweat forming on his forehead. "The damned jeep isn't worth taking the risk trying to find and dismantle the trap. I want you to tie the tow rope to it. Play it out as far as you can. And haul the jeep to some place where it's safe to blow it up. Got that?"

The men nodded. They moved quickly to obey.

Rosenfeld asked, "But what about you?"

"Give me that ammo box," Tom said grimly.

Rosenfeld handed him the heavy steel box. Tom placed it carefully in his lap. Its weight seemed to press him into the jeep seat itself, although every cell in his body was straining to avoid contact with the fatal spot. Death might be inches below.

"Take cover!" he snapped. "All of you." He looked at the ammo box. "I'll try to slide off the seat," he said to David. "I'll keep the weight of the box on it. If it *is* a pressure-release-type mechanism, that might do it." He looked at the men. "Now. Move it!"

The men at once ran to take cover behind the weapons carrier.

Tom took a deep breath. His last? . . . He looked down at the steel ammo box. All of a sudden it didn't seem to have any weight at all.

Slowly he slid himself across to the outside of the seat. Carefully he lifted the heavy ammo box from his lap and placed it on the seat beside him. Inch by inch he moved his right leg out of the jeep and planted it on the ground. Gradually, sweat stinging his eyes, he put his weight on the free leg, gingerly sliding the ammo box toward the center of the seat. Bit by bit he shifted his entire weight onto his leg on the ground.

The seat creaked tinnily. For a split second Tom's heart stopped. An overwhelming urge to throw himself to the ground shrieked in his mind. He resisted it.

Slowly, cautiously, he extricated his left leg from the jeep. He was on the ground. He was free. He ran to join the others at the weapons carrier.

"Okay," he called. "Get ready to move it out!"

The mechanics jumped into the truck and started the engine.

"The damned thing may not be booby-trapped at all," Tom said. "Move it out anyway."

The weapons carrier started up slowly. It took up the slack in the tow rope, and the jeep began to roll. It traveled about a foot. The sharp click of the grenade primers going off was drowned out by the laboring engine of the weapons carrier. The jeep rolled another six feet.

Suddenly there was an earth-quavering explosion. The jeep was catapulted into the air on a ragged pillar of fire and crashed back to the instantly scorched ground, a mangled mass of scrap. For a brief moment it burned intensely with an unnaturally bright flame before the gas tank blew with an ear-numbing roar.

Someone had wanted to be absolutely certain that the destruction of both vehicle and occupants would be total. Someone had packed incendiary material around the explosives and the tank!

In the instant of the blast, Tom and Rosenfeld were hit by a paralyzing shock wave of pure force and slammed savagely to the ground. Both men instinctively curled up, protecting their heads with their arms from the rain of debris that hailed down on them.

It stopped. Cautiously Tom looked toward the blazing jeep. All was quiet, except for the roar and crackle of the seething fire. He stood up. His legs felt like jelly encased in tissue paper. He stared at the burning jeep.

It is that important, he thought. The protection of Rudi A-27 and KOKON is that important. It must be carried out at any cost. He looked at Rosenfeld, dazedly picking himself up.

The young sergeant stared at the fiery destruction. "Je-sus Christ!" he said.

Tom went over to him. "Thanks," he said soberly. He tried a half-successful grin. "If you ever again see me about to get an oil spot on my pants, feel free to speak up!"

3 May 1945

SUBJECT: CHRONOLOGY AND ANALYSIS OF KOKON
TO: OIC, CIC DETACHMENT 212

I. CHRONOLOGY

1. On 24 April 1945 the capture of a subject, SS Standartenführer Wolfgang Steinmetz, was effected in Bayreuth, 0 755520. On top secret orders in his possession appeared a referral: KOKON. The meaning of this designation, either a code name or a letter abbreviation, is unknown. No previous mention could be located by this investigator.

2. On 29 April 1945 the records of an OKL project, "The Collection and Evaluation of Information for Future War," code name FENIX, were recovered on the Schloss Ehrenstein estate nr Straubing, U

545425. Records of the organization having been billeted at this estate were also located. This organization was a German Sleeper Agent project. The records of the project were destroyed except for the partial personal dossier of one Sleeper Agent, Rudi A-27. On this dossier appeared the notation: KOKON.

3. On 30 April 1945, the CO of CIC Det 212 placed Agent Thomas Jaeger on TDY status to investigate the Sleeper Agent Rudi A-27 and KOKON, by authority of AC of S, G-2, Col Richard Streeter, effective immediately.

4. Following developed leads, Agent Jaeger proceeded to Regensburg, U 208540. Here former Sleeper Agent project cadre personnel was contacted. The following Information was obtained:

a. Sleeper Agent Rudi A-27 was scheduled to exfiltrate Germany via "the northern route."

b. Rudi A-27 had been ordered to Berlin just before the training phase of the Sleeper Agent project was terminated.

c. Trained Sleeper Agents still in Germany were afforded vigilant protection and aid by former cadre members.

5. A further informant was located by Sgt David Rosenfeld, XII Corps MP, on TDY with Agent Jaeger. The subject was interrogated at 106 Evac Hosp, vic Regen, U 943555. The informant indicated that he had assisted in surgically removing the SS blood type tattoo from high ranking officers. He indicated that he observed, written on the medical records of one such officer, name unknown, the word KOKON.

II. ANALYSIS & CONCLUSION

1. It is believed by this investigator that KOKON is the code name for a special project designed to preserve the Third Reich, or reactivate it, by protecting and harboring high ranking Nazi officers and officials. The facts pointing to this conclusion are:

a. The interrelationship of FENIX, a study to enable Germany to wage future war, and the Sleeper Agent project, a mission to place Nazi agents in foreign countries.

b. The fact that high ranking Nazi officials were involved in preparation for personal and permanent concealment.

2. It appears to this investigator that the Sleeper Agent Rudi A-27 plays a key role in the execution of both the Sleeper Agent project and KOKON, for the following reasons:

a. The word KOKON was written on his dossier.

b. He was ordered to Berlin.

c. Vigorous action on the part of the Sleeper Agent project cadre members was undertaken to assure his continued safety.

3. The following facts were learned from the partial dossier of Rudi A-27:

a. He spent time in Denmark as a "Vienna Child," living with a family named Rasmussen in Copenhagen, address unknown.

b. He was active in occupied Copenhagen during 1941/43, doing undercover work for Abwehr III.

c. He was recruited for the Sleeper Agent project in 1943.

d. He was trained for evacuation to and operation in the United States of America.

e. His Readiness Tests were completed 18 April 1945.

4. It seems evident to this investigator that the Sleeper Agent Rudi A-27 at this moment is on his way to carry out his mission. It is believed that he will exfiltrate Germany via "the northern route," ie through Denmark, with which country and language he is familiar. It is believed he received special briefing in Berlin regarding both his Sleeper Agent mission and KOKON.

III. RECOMMENDATION

1. It is recommended that this investigator be authorized to pursue and capture the Sleeper Agent Rudi A-27 before that agent can make his way to the United States of America, and there disappear.

Thomas Jaeger
Special Agent
CIC Det 212

Major Herbert Lee looked up from the report. For a moment he studied Tom, sitting across the desk from him. He shook his head. "I might have known," he said with heartfelt exasperation. "I've hardly had a chance to warm the seat of my chair, and you blow in and dump *this* in my lap." He waved a deprecating hand at Tom's report.

Tom started to speak, but Lee held up his hand. "Tom, I *know* what you're going to ask," he said. "The answer is no! N. O. Period. *No!* One little word."

"Never heard of it," Tom said straight-faced.

"How in hell can I send you off to Denmark, for Christ's sake?" Lee exploded. "The Krauts *still* run the place, you know."

"It wouldn't be the first time we've operated behind enemy lines, Herb, and you know it."

"Sure. But Denmark is British territory. I've got no authority—"

"Hell, there *are* liaison officers—"

"Have you any idea of the red tape it would take to—"

"Go color blind, dammit! Or paint it green. A nice, bright green for *go!*"

Thoughtfully Lee stared at the report on his desk "The damned thing is," he said quietly, "you do have something here. Something that *could* turn out to be goddamned important."

"I know, Herb," Tom said urgently, pressing into the breach. "Rudi *could* reach the States. The whole project *could* work. Hell, we've *got* to nail him. Now. Before he gets out of the ETO. I've *got* to go to Denmark. Don't you see? I don't even know if the Rasmussens are in on the whole damned thing. Suppose they are? They could be of vital importance to the bastard. We've *got* to know!"

Lee remained silent, pensive.

"Look, Herb," Tom said gravely, "fix it up with the British. Get me on a plane. This afternoon. They've got C-47s at the airfield near Cham, ferrying in supplies. From the Ninth Troop Carrier Command. On their way back they can easily fly me up to Bremen. In British territory. There's an RAF field there." He eyed his CO earnestly. "How about it? How about the British?"

Lee studied Tom. He snorted. Slowly he shook his head. "Well," he said hesitantly, "I guess I *could* throw a pass in their direction—if I can dig up an eligible receiver."

"Okay, coach. You're great!"

"Sure," Lee said sourly. "I'm too fucking popular. It's the story of my life." He stood up. "Even in OCS everybody hated me because I was too damned popular."

Tom grinned. "One more thing, Major Popular, sir. David Rosenfeld. The MP sergeant."

"What about him?"

"He's earned himself another stripe, Herb. In spades."

"Okay. He'll get it. Write him up." He waved his hand at his office, still in disarray from the moving. "You can park your ass here," he said expansively, "while I see what I can do."

"You kidding?" Tom got up. "I've got to get my gear together."

"You seem damned sure of yourself," Lee observed dryly.

"Not of me, Herbie baby!" Tom grinned. "Not of me. Of *you!*"

Squadron Leader Charles Barlow, RAF, had taken over the erstwhile offices of the chief of maintenance located in a hangar on the airfield outside Bremen. He wanted to be close to where the action was. The field had been cleared and repaired after the bitter week-long fighting and heavy resistance that the XXX Corps of the British Second Army had run into, before the city fell on the 26th of April. It was now fully operative.

The Gauleiter of Bremen had issued a stern proclamation calling on the townspeople and the defending troops to resist to the last—and then he himself had cleared out while his city was being demolished by the desperate fighting and accompanying massive air raids.

When Squadron Leader Barlow had seen the destruction and carnage that the wanton, senseless proclamation had caused, he'd had dreams of glory about getting his hands around that Gauleiter chap's throat and squeezing. Just squeezing. The mere thought of the man still got a rise out of him.

. The RAF officer studied the four other men seated in his office.

Flight Lieutenant Campbell, Flying Officer Saunders, the American liaison officer, Captain Michael Holland, and the young Intelligence agent, Thomas Jaeger, one of the American CIC lot, who had just told them one whale of a story.

"That's quite a yarn, old chap," he said mildly. "Quite a yarn." He shrugged. "But then, why not, eh? The world is half bloody crackers after all." He contemplated Tom. "What can *we* do for you?"

Tom leaned forward eagerly. "I need assistance, Squadron Leader," he said. "All the cooperation I can get. Authorization. Information. Transportation. You name it."

"Not to worry," Barlow said. He looked at Captain Holland. "Mike tells me it is quite important. Must make *him* happy." He grinned disarmingly. "Give him something to do, eh? Put him through his paces now and then.

Or he'd just be kicking his heels." He turned back to Tom. "We should like to keep him around, you know. Makes a splendid fourth." He grew sober. "Now. What specifically can we do for you?"

Tom had been waiting for it. He knew exactly what to say. "Four main points. Authorization. Special gear. Transportation. Contacts."

"That's it then?"

"Right," Tom said. "Specifically, I need permission and authorization to operate in Denmark, in a British zone of operation. I need Danish civilian clothing, currency and some sort of ID. I need to be flown to Denmark and dropped, preferably tonight. Time is vital. And I need a reception committee at the drop zone and a contact in Copenhagen."

Squadron Leader Barlow nodded slowly. "So you do," he agreed. "We can bloody well get you your permission, your authorization, and all that. We can send a signal to London. No trouble." He thought for a moment. "As for your gear, we can have you kitted out for your mission right here. All you have to do is sign a chit, right?"

"Of course."

"As for transportation, we shall have to check with SOE."

Tom gave him a questioning look.

"Special Operations Executive," Barlow explained. "Have to see if anything is laid on for tonight, you know." He turned to Flying Officer Saunders. "Saunders."

"Sir!"

"See to it, will you, please? And the signal to London."

"Right." The officer left.

Squadron Leader Barlow fixed Tom with an inquiring stare. "About the drop," he asked. "I presume you do have jump training, old boy?"

For a flash of an instant Tom was back at the Marine base at Quantico, Virginia. Parachute jumping had been a request course during his training. He had been excited and curious. He had requested it. For several days he and a few other MIS candidates had trained at the Marine base, jumping from the tower, learning to guide the chute, to land, to roll, to control the chute on the ground. Then one sunny afternoon he'd made two training jumps from one thousand feet. He did not remember the first one. He'd been too excited. But afterward his neck had been red where the risers had slapped him as the chute opened, and his shoulders were sore from the opening jerk. On the second jump he'd come down so hard he'd been convinced his teeth had all been rearranged in his mouth.

"Yes," he said.

"Excellent." Squadron Leader Barlow sounded satisfied.

"What about a contact in Copenhagen?" Tom asked.

Barlow shrugged regretfully. "Haven't a bloody clue," he said. He turned to Flight Lieutenant Campbell. "I say, you must have an idea, Campbell. Used to be involved in that sort of thing, right?"

"Yes, sir. Flew a couple of missions."

"We need someone with the proper spirit, what? Imagination."

Campbell thought for a moment. "What about Sven, sir? Sven the Mole?"

Barlow's face lit up. "Capital idea, Campbell," he said. "Rather an active bloke, I understand."

"Bit more than that, I'd say."

"You're damned right!" Mike Holland broke in. "He heads one of the most effective groups of Freedom Fighters in Denmark."

"Right," Barlow said. He turned to Campbell. "Tell Saunders to arrange it."

"Yes, sir." Campbell left.

"Who is this Sven?" Tom asked.

"Go ahead, Mike," Barlow said to Captain Holland. "Earn your blasted keep. Tell him about the 'Mole.' "

"Okay," Mike said. He turned to Tom. "Sven is quite a character. He didn't get the code name 'Mole' for nothing. He was involved in one of the damnedest, most incredible underground projects—and I do mean underground—pulled off in any of the countries occupied by the Nazis. I'll make it short and sweet.

"It started back in September of 1944, when the Germans in Copenhagen, in the confusion of a fake air raid alarm, disarmed the entire Danish police force and marched on the King's palace, where the King was in residence, killing anyone who tried to stop them. At the palace itself, Amalienborg, they were finally driven off, but it became too damned apparent that King Christian and the members of the royal family were virtually prisoners in the palace and couldn't be evacuated in case of danger.

"A group of Danish patriots decided to do something about that. Among them, Sven. During the next several months they pulled off a stunt you won't believe.

"The Krauts were stationed in buildings completely surrounding the royal palace. Every approach, every exit from the place was heavily guarded by German troops. There was only one possible way of creating an avenue of escape. An underground tunnel running from the palace to the city outside—literally under the very feet of the Nazis!

"And the crazy Danes did it! They moved tons and tons of dirt. They had powerful air compressors force gigantic two-ton pipes of reinforced concrete five feet in diameter through the earth, creating a hundred-foot-long tunnel smack under the Kraut billets! Whatever noise the Germans picked up and complained about was innocently blamed on the ancient royal plumbing.

"Every damned bit of equipment—electric pumps, hoists, wheelbarrows, tools, machinery and God knows what—was smuggled past the Germans' noses. Getting construction materials—especially cement—was the biggest problem. The only construction the Nazis allowed was on their own fortifications.

"And this is where Sven comes in. He'd been working on the project. He assured the builders that he'd get them their cement. Little by little. But they'd get it.

"He figured the only place to scrounge the cement was from a Nazi construction site. He borrowed a horse-drawn wagon from a friend who had been pressed into service on such a project, figuring that he could get away with stealing a sack or two of cement, off and on, to keep the project going.

"The first time he tried it, he'd just loaded a sack on his wagon and was about to drive off with it when a Kraut voice shouted at him. 'Halt!' He damned near dropped off his seat. With his heart in his throat, he turned around. A German officer stood next to his wagon glaring menacingly at him. He had an instant vision of himself tied to a stake facing a firing squad.

" 'What the devil do you think you are doing, you lazy Danish dog?' the Kraut hollered at him. 'You think you will hold up our work by carrying only one sack at a time! Sabotage! Against the Reich! You are lucky I do not have you shot! Get that wagon loaded. Full. At once! And be on your way.'

"You'd better believe Sven needed no second order to obey that command! He damned near broke his back heaping sacks of cement on his wagon."

Tom laughed.

Mike continued. "Sven worked as hard as anyone on that fantastic tunnel. The passage was finished in January, and the Danish Crown Prince Frederik himself tried it out.

"Sven, who'd been active in the underground practically since the country was occupied, formed his own group of Freedom Fighters. He called it *Muldvarpen*—the Mole. Sentimental, I guess. He and his group have been extremely effective."

He looked at Tom. "That's the Sven we think would be the man for you." He glanced at Squadron Leader Barlow. "Right?"

"Rather."

"I'm sold," Tom said.

Flight Lieutenant Campbell entered. "All is in order, sir," he said. He consulted a note in his hand. "There is a mission laid on for tonight. Take-off at 0100 hours. A routine drop in Norway. Sten guns, Mark Twos. Ammunition. Field dressings. PE. That sort of thing. No personnel. They're not exactly keen on it, but they'll detour across Denmark. Drop Agent Jaeger near Copenhagen. The time of the drop should be about 0430 hours. They're sending the Mole a signal to have a reception committee on hand."

Barlow nodded. "That's it then." He looked at Tom. "Get your gear together. As soon as you're ready, Flight Lieutenant Campbell will fly you over."

Tom looked puzzled. He eyed Campbell. "Are you flying the mission to Norway?" he asked.

"Good Lord, no, old chap," Campbell said. "We don't fly that sort of job from here. I'll pop you across the Channel. There's a field near Norwich. You'll take off from there."

"That's all we can do from here," Squadron Leader Barlow said. "Except wish you bloody good luck!" He eyed Tom quizzically. "I'm afraid you'll need it."

Rudi was fully alert as he walked quickly through the empty field. He was surprised at the utter quiet and stillness of the night. Flensburg, the center of much last-moment military activity, was only ten or twelve kilometers to the east.

He had discarded his uniform tunic and picked up an old work-worn jacket and a soiled cap in a barn at a farm just outside the village of Wallsbüll. He had freed his Danish papers from their place of taped concealment in the small of his back and placed them safely in his pants pocket.

He was now Rudolf Rasmussen. Danish subject.

He estimated he could be only a kilometer or two from the border. He looked up into the gloomy night sky. He wondered if he would be able to tell when he had actually crossed. Ahead he could make out the black, ragged silhouette of a forest. That would be Frøslev Forest. In Denmark.

He felt a surge of bitter irritation. That damned rat! If it hadn't been for that *verschissene* beast he would not have had to take the risk of sneaking across the border. He could have walked right through the German checkpoint. He would have had his German ID. Without it, with only his Danish papers, he dared not risk it. He was forced to make it across clandestinely, without being spotted.

He looked at his watch. It was just past 2300 hours. Within the hour he would be across the border.

The forest was dark and silent. Rudi had not seen or heard anyone. Only once a German motorcycle patrol had roared past in the distance. He had hit the ground and had not been seen.

The border had been nothing but a fence, no different from other fences around the fields in the area. A short distance into the woods he'd come across a dirt road. He knew he had crossed the border. A signpost read, FRØSLEV. It was written in the Danish alphabet.

It was the third time in his life he'd crossed the border into Denmark. The Danes had a saying: *"Alle gode Gange tre*—Third time, best time." He fully expected them to be right.

He walked rapidly along the road. He stayed on the grass-covered shoulder to muffle his steps. Ahead, the road made a sharp turn around a thicket of spruce trees. He rounded the bend—and stopped short.

Before him, not twenty feet away, a man stood at the roadside relieving himself against a bush. Nearby a bicycle leaned against a tree.

Rudi at once took in the scene. The man wore a uniform. An unfamiliar uniform. He carried a sidearm. A Danish border guard. He shot a glance at the man's gun. He'd have to bluff it out. *"God Aften,"* he said pleasantly, in impeccable Danish.

The man nodded. *"Go' Aften."* Unperturbed, he finished his business. Meticulously he buttoned up his pants and stepped back onto the road. He peered at Rudi, his head slightly askew. "And what might you being doing here, my friend?" he inquired.

Rudi slowly walked toward him, sizing him up. Late forties. Slow-moving. Sturdy. Farmer type. . . . If he could only get close enough.

"Have to be in Frøslev first thing in the morning," he said. "Thought I'd get an early start."

Again the man nodded ponderously. "Come from Broderup?" he asked.

The map of the area flashed in Rudi's mind. "Sofiedal," he said. He stepped closer.

The man bobbed his head again. "It is a fair walk," he commented.

Rudi was only a few feet from him. He took another step. Now!

Suddenly the man exploded into unexpected action. Rudi felt rough, powerful hands grab his left arm, twist it, whirl him around and seize a breaking grip on his little finger.

The sudden pain stabbed up through his arm. Involuntarily he cried out. He felt as if his finger was about to snap. He thought quickly. Something had tipped off the border guard. What? He dismissed it. It was not important now. Important was to get free from the crippling finger grip.

He tried to pull his hand away. The grip instantly tightened. The pain shot through him.

"Naa, naa, naa," the man said calmly. *"Ta' den med Ro!*—Take it easy!"

Rudi fought down a groan. Then he quickly thought better of it. He groaned in agony. "Please!" he whined. "Please! It hurts."

"That's better," the guard grumbled amiably. "You behave, and we two will get along together just fine." With his free hand he reached for a pair of handcuffs hanging at his belt.

Rudi's mind whirled. Somehow the pain in his hand made his thoughts sharply clear. He could not let the guard get the cuffs on him. He had to break free. His mission could not end here.

He let out a little cry. "What the devil is the matter with you?" he whimpered. "You're breaking my finger!"

"Not yet, my friend," grunted the guard. "But I will if you try anything."

"But why?" Rudi complained. "I haven't done anything!" He let the plaintive whine hang between them.

"Then you have nothing to worry about, have you?"

The guard had the handcuffs in his right hand. He brought one cuff up to snap on Rudi's wrist. For a moment his grip on Rudi's finger seemed to slacken.

Savagely Rudi yanked his hand away. He felt the guard exert a sudden vicious pressure. He felt his finger snap. The pain shot up through his arm to stab lances of searing agony into the back of his eyes.

But he did not flinch. He leaped clear. In the same motion he bent down and drew his knife from his boot. When the startled guard lunged for him, he rammed the knife up into the man's chest cavity, instantly wrenching the handle sideways to inflict the greatest possible internal injury with the slash.

The guard died on his feet—but not before his astonishment had registered in his wide-open eyes.

Rudi looked at his mangled hand. It throbbed painfully. The little finger had snapped completely in the joint next to the knuckle. He had known it would happen, but the choice between capture and a broken finger had been no choice at all.

He glanced at the body of the border guard. Fair enough, he thought sardonically. Your life for my little finger. He felt no animosity toward the dead man. He felt nothing.

They had taught him not to hate when he killed. Killing was not personal.

He grabbed hold of the body and rolled it into the ditch. It emitted a ghastly hollow groan as the air was forced from its lifeless lungs.

He sat down on the ground next to the bike. He examined his throbbing finger closely. The sharp splinters of broken bone protruded through the torn skin. The finger hung loosely from his hand, as if it did not belong there at all. He took his knife and stabbed it into the ground several times to cleanse it of the drying blood from the guard. It was the second time in one day, he thought.

He knew what he had to do. He suddenly felt ridiculous. He remembered all the superpatriotic films of incredible heroics he'd seen back in Regensburg. Ufa's *Hitlerjunge Quex, SA Mann Brand* and *Hans Westmar—Einer von Vielen* with Emil Lohkamp. They, too, had gritted their teeth grimly, and courageously done what had to be done!

Shit!

He'd always felt a little contemptuous of the audience, raptly devouring those films and their obvious message. He did not need such crutches to be certain where his allegiance lay.

He wiped the knife blade on his pants. The finger would have to come off. It was as simple as that. It would be less of a handicap to cope with a stump than with a painful broken finger done up in a damned awkward splint. He lifted the knife. He clenched his jaws. Hard.

What the devil; the loss of a little finger is no big deal. The knife was poised.

He stopped. Suddenly he hurled the knife onto the ground with an angry oath. He could not do it.

A missing finger was a mark of identification no one could overlook! He could not saddle himself with that kind of handicap. Not he. He looked closely at his finger. He would *have* to set it. Splint it. Bandage it.

He crawled into the ditch and rolled the body of the border guard onto its back. He searched.

A pencil. It would do as a splint. The man had a handkerchief, but it was soiled. It would only cause infection. A piece of his shirt . . .

He began to pull at the dead man's clothing. In the back pocket of his pants was a bulge. He felt for it and brought out a partial roll of toilet paper. He grinned.

Border-patrolling obviously did not afford all the comforts of home.

He unrolled about five feet of the paper. It was the closest he could come to sterility. He used part of the clean paper to cleanse the wound. It hurt like hell. But he knew the worst was yet to come.

He wiped the pencil as clean as he could. He placed it and the roll of toilet paper within easy reach. He frowned. Something else was needed. He looked at the dead man again. He picked up the soiled handkerchief—and again discarded it.

He looked at the man's feet. He wore heavy boots laced with long laces. He untied one of the laces and laid it next to the pencil-stub splint and toilet-paper bandage.

He took a deep breath. He grabbed hold of the dangling finger. He pulled.

He was unaware of the sharp little cry that escaped his throat. His eyes burned with the tears of raw agony, and a searing pain shot fire through his whole body. But he felt the broken bone snap together. The grating sound almost made him vomit.

Quickly he grabbed the pencil stub and placed it tightly against the straightened finger. Keeping all his fingers on his left hand straight and stiff he clamped them together and pressed the edge of his hand against his thigh. The pencil stayed in place. The finger remained fixed.

He took the clean toilet paper and wrapped it around his little finger and the pencil-stub splint. Then he tied the shoelace on tightly, winding it around and around until his finger was encased in a brown cocoon. He stood up.

One more thing. Once more he went to the dead border guard. He took the man's handgun from its holster and put it in his belt. It was risky carrying a gun. It was a risk he was willing to take.

He frowned down at the body. An alarm bell was clamoring in his head. He could not shut it off. What had tipped the man off? Curfew violation? Something else? Something he had overlooked? Something that might betray him again? He stared at the dead man. He would get no answers from him.

Or would he? Quickly—one final time—he went through the man's pockets.

In his inside jacket pocket he found a folded map, soiled and cracked in the creases. It was a map of the area. He held it close. He could barely make out the writing on it.

Along the border an area had been shaded in red pencil. He read the legend: RESTRICTED AREA.

He felt a weight lift from him. That was it. That was why the guard had jumped him. No other reason.

He threw the map on the body. Without another glance at the dead border guard, he picked up the bicycle and began to pedal down the dark night road.

Rudi A-27 had arrived in Denmark.

11

Tom's legs were getting cold. The wind seemed to penetrate to the very marrow of his bones. He was sitting on the edge of the hole cut in the floor of the aircraft fuselage. In less than a minute he'd plunge through the belly of the plane—like a calf being dropped by a pregnant whale. He wondered why the British didn't use a side door to jump from, like he'd done in the States.

He let his eyes sweep the plane. Everything stood out in indelible detail. Almost as if his mind strained fully to absorb this last impression.

Last?

The plane was a De Haviland Mosquito XVI. With complete clarity he remembered every single word they'd told him about it. It was their smallest bomber: wing span fifty-four feet, length forty feet. It was powered by two Rolls Royce Merlin 73 engines of 1290 horsepower each. He was conscious of them laboring through the night sky, although their speed was probably not much over half the maximum of 408 miles per hour.

He glanced at the parachute static line, its metal snap-on ring firmly attached to the jump cable.

His mind was filled with detail. Was it to shut out other thoughts? Thoughts of . . .

He stared deliberately at the two lights above him. The red light was on. The pilot had begun his run-in to the drop zone. He was aware of the jump master, a young British NCO, standing close behind him. He rather felt he was there to give him a good shove if he froze on the jump signal.

He would not.

He had an irresistible urge to glance down into the dark night void rushing past below. They had warned him not to. Keep your eyes on the lights, they'd said. Over and over again. Keep your eyes on the lights.

He looked down. . . . He was hurtling through black space. The air shrieked past his ears. He was plummeting through the Stygian darkness. He waited for the jerk of the opening chute. It did not come.

An icy thought lanced through his mind like a flash of lightning. The truth screamed through his very being: *He had roman-candled!* The chute had not opened! He was plunging toward oblivion. In mute terror he waited for the deadly impact that would obliterate his very thoughts. . . .

He suddenly heard the voice of the jump master bellow behind him: "Go!"

He tore his eyes from their hypnotic stare into the beckoning darkness and looked up at the lights before him. The jump light shone green.

With both hands he pushed off and instantly plunged into the black void. At once he felt himself gripped in a fist of pure force. Tensely he waited for the life-assuring jerk as the static cord played out taut and ripped the canopy free from his backpack to fill with air and billow open above him. Each split second was an eternity.

His last-minute instructions, his long-ago training, the remembered experience of his two jumps, all tumbled about in his mind: You will be dropped from two thousand feet. You will be on the ground in two minutes. You will be blown horizontal to the ground the instant you drop from the plane and fall into the slip stream and the chute is ripped open.

The chute is ripped open.

He suddenly felt a violent jerk. His chute was free. Open! He felt a surge of wild elation. He glanced up. He saw nothing.

For a split moment his heart stopped, then he remembered—when the canopy is fully open you will swing under it. You will begin to oscillate. You will check the oscillation by tugging on the two risers in the direction of your swing.

He reached up above his shoulders. He grabbed hold of two of the webbed risers. He looked up. Above him he could make out the cone of suspension lines and the fully opened canopy. It was a beautiful sight.

He suddenly remembered the plane. He listened for it. Only faintly could he make out a distant, disappearing drone.

He was alone. He tugged at the risers. Gradually his swing lessened, and stopped.

He looked down. The darkness had given way to a murky grayness. He could make out the ground far below. The earth was rushing up to meet him. That was it. There was no sensation of falling. He was suspended, utterly alone, in space—and the entire massive planet was rushing headlong up to meet him in a crushing embrace.

And there, faintly glowing, three pinpoints of light. His reception committee. Far off to the right. Too far.

When you are stable, you can guide the chute in any direction you wish. Pull on the risers in the direction you want to fall. The canopy panels on that side will be partly collapsed. You will slip in that direction. How fast depends on how much you collapse them. And for how long. Try to land facing in the direction of drift. Not with your back to it.

If you can see the ground before you land, you can soften your landing impact by giving a sudden strong pull on all four risers when you are about fifteen feet above ground. The air in the chute will momentarily be trapped and you will make a soft landing. But count on your landing as being like jumping off the roof of a slow-moving freight train!

He looked for the three points of light. They were still too far to the right. He pulled on the appropriate risers and felt himself slip toward the lights.

Suddenly, farther to his right, four bright lights blazed to life! Headlights. In the same instant the sound of motors starting up reached him. The three pinpoint lights at once disappeared.

Tom felt his blood freeze. He had never in his life before felt so alone, so exposed, so helpless. His mind raced.

The drop had been discovered.

You can slip in any direction you wish.

He grabbed the left risers. He pulled them down toward him and held them. He felt the chute slip away from the glaring headlights below and gather speed until he was aware of the air whistling past his ears.

Below was a small forest. It was dangerous, but he would have to land there. The black treetops rushed up toward him.

When should he check his fall? Now! He let go the risers. The slipping stopped, but he was drifting rapidly. The next instant the top tree branches reached for his legs. Instinctively he closed his eyes.

If you have to land among trees, keep your legs together, pointed down. Keep your arms at your side. Pray you won't be knocked out. And hope you will not be caught dangling too high to get down!

He felt the tree branches tear at him, batter and whip him. The world was filled only with the sounds of breaking, splintering branches and tree limbs, and the ripping of cloth. Suddenly there was a shoulder-wrenching jerk. And silence.

He opened his eyes. He was dangling about ten feet from the ground. He punched the opening mechanism on his harness, slipped out and dropped to the turf below.

For a moment he stood listening, breathing heavily. Then he took off in a steady trot, away from the distant sound of approaching cars.

CIC Agent Thomas Jaeger had arrived in Denmark.

He was running silently along a narrow path in the hushed night forest. He realized his situation was desperate. Somehow, the drop had been discovered. By accident? Or . . . by betrayal?

He had missed the reception committee. He had no one to turn to for assistance. He was alone, unarmed, in a country occupied by the enemy, a country whose language he did not understand or speak. On the tenuous trail of a cunning, superbly trained adversary.

He knew he had an impossible task before him. He did not dwell on it. His primary job now was to evade his pursuers and find a safe place of hiding. He ran on, trying to put as much distance between him and his landing spot as he could.

The path snaked like a pale gray ribbon through the dark forest. Suddenly, ahead of him, a figure jumped from the shadowy brush on the edge of the wood and planted itself firmly in his way. The unmistakable outline of a submachine gun was pointed straight at him.

He stopped. There was a small noise behind him. He whirled around. Behind him was a second figure. And a second gun, aimed at his gut. He froze.

Automatically his right hand tensed in anticipated action. Then it hit him. He had no gun. He suddenly felt as if an abysmal cavity existed where his shoulder holster ought to be. He felt utterly naked. Totally vulnerable.

Slowly the two figures moved toward him. The guns never wavered from him. He watched them tensely, every sense alert. Two young men. Clad in dark sweaters and dark pants, their faces grim and warily hostile. They stopped a few feet away on either side of him.

From the underbrush a third figure emerged. Also clad in a dark sweater and pants. It was a girl. Her challenging breasts outlined by the tight sweater could not be denied. She stepped up to Tom. *"Hvem er De?"* she asked coldly. *"Hvad gør De her?"*

Tom thought quickly. The three were obviously not Germans. Were they part of the reception committee? Freedom Fighters? Or members of the Danish Nazi Corps preying on the underground for their masters? No. They did not look like traitors. That was ridiculous. What does a traitor look like?

He decided he had to take a chance. "I do not speak Danish," he said calmly. "I am an American Counter Intelligence officer. I was just dropped. You must have heard the plane."

He looked straight at the girl. He was struck by her clean, open features, her huge blue eyes, which stared at him with icy suspicion. In the darkness of the night her clear, fresh skin seemed to shine with a luminescence of its own.

"I missed my reception committee," he said.

The girl studied him impassively. "You will come with us," she said. She spoke with a strong Danish accent. "You will do as we say." She nodded toward the two men. "Klaus and Holger will not hesitate to shoot you."

Tom shrugged in resignation. Damned suspicious Danes. He had no time to play their cloak-and-dagger games. "Okay," he said irritably. "Let's get on with it."

In silence they marched him through the woods to a dirt road nearby. In the brush four bicycles were hidden. They had obviously been expecting someone.

Tom kept quiet.

The girl pointed to one of the bikes. "Can you ride it?" she asked.

"Of course," he snapped.

For half an hour they rode in silence along deserted back roads. They passed only a few dark houses. Finally they came to a tiny wooden cabin, brightly painted. White with red trim. In the small plot of ground around it several kinds of vegetables grew luxuriously, neatly set in row upon row. Numerous tiny plots and cabins exactly alike edged the dirt road. It was just dawn as they entered the cabin.

"What now?" Tom asked.

"We wait," the girl said.

"Look," Tom said in exasperation, "if you are part of my reception committee, say so, dammit! I came here to meet Sven. Sven the Mole. I'm on an important mission. I don't have time to play games!"

The three Danes remained silent.

"What the hell's the matter with you?" Tom demanded angrily. "Don't you believe me?"

The girl looked at him, her eyes serious. "Perhaps," she said. "Perhaps not."

"Let me prove it, dammit! Take me to see Sven!"

The girl said nothing.

"What the hell are we waiting for?" Tom growled.

"You will see."

He glared at the three grim Danes. Forcibly it struck him. They were the captors. He, the captive! He did not like being on the other side of the fence.

The two men walked over to a rough wooden bed standing at one end of the room. They moved it aside. Carefully they pried up a couple of floorboards beneath. They took out two guns that appeared to Tom to be German Walthers and placed the Sten guns in the hiding place. They replaced the bed. They settled down to wait.

The man called Klaus glanced at his watch. He nodded to the girl sitting at the window.

She stood up. "We go," she said.

They took him outside. It was already bright daylight. He looked at his watch. It was just past 0630 hours. A hell of a way to start the day.

The girl came up to him. "You will ride with us," she said. "You will not be stupid. Or you will be dead."

He did not answer her. He had already decided to play out their game. It was the only one in town.

They rode in single file. The girl led the way, followed by the man called Holger and Tom. Klaus brought up the rear. The two men had casually let Tom see their guns stuck in their belts under their sweaters before they had started out. The implication had not been lost upon him.

They quickly left the area of the little cabin plots. Victory gardens, Tom surmised. And presently a side road took them to a main highway. It was at once apparent why his captors had imposed the wait to exactly this hour. The road was filled with bicyclists. Men and women. Literally thousands of them. Riding their bicycles to work in the city.

Tom and his escort entered the stream of traffic. They could have had no better cover.

Tom's uneasy incertitude grew steadily as, surrounded by their protective shield of bike commuters, he and his watchers rode into the city of Copenhagen. Who were his captors? Where were they taking him? Why?

As they turned from one picturesque city street into another, they were suddenly confronted with a small column of uneasy-looking German soldiers marching toward them, their coarse field-gray Waffen SS uniforms looking disturbingly out of place.

Stony-faced, the Danish bicyclists steered around them. Tom's skin crawled. The enemy. So close. So damned close. He watched the hunched back of Holger riding in front of him. Had it tensed?

They rode past the sports stadium and the lakes to the center of town, Kongens Nytorv—the King's Newmarket, dominated by the impressive Royal Theater.

Here they turned down Nyhavn. It was the sailors' part of town. Sailors from the world over. Old, colorful buildings, some dating back to the eighteenth century, lined the murky canal that led from the square to the docks. Once stately and important, they now housed a conglomeration of cheap flamboyantly named taverns and dives, small questionable hotels and an assortment of tattoo parlors. At night the area was a rowdy, bawdy playgound for the pleasure-seeking rabble of the sprawling port. In the cold light of early morning it looked merely seamy and tawdry.

They stopped at a gaudily painted little bar with one of the most jaunty names of all, The Scarlet Mermaid. The man sitting at a table in the back of the dingy bar was alone in the room, except for a fat unshaven man in shirtsleeves and a shabby soiled apron halfheartedly cleaning up the sordid debris of the night before.

The girl and Klaus walked Tom to the waiting stranger. Holger stayed outside. For a moment Tom and the other man measured each other in mutual appraisal.

The man at the table was about Tom's age. He had a shock of dark brown hair that obviously defied discipline, and broad shoulders. His features were large and softly rounded, contradicting the promise of strength beneath. Cold, calculating eyes glared at Tom. There was no friendliness in them. No trust. He spoke. "Sit down," he said curtly. "I am Sven."

Tom felt instant relief flood him. "I'm Tom Jaeger," he said. "Christ, am I glad to see you!"

"Are you?" Sven commented coldly.

Tom tensed. "Dammit!" he growled. "You *know* who I am." He took a step toward Sven. At once he was aware of quick movement behind him to his right. He looked.

Klaus was holding his Walther in his hand. It was aimed at Tom.

He felt a surge of frustrated anger. "Shit!" he said with profound disgust. "What the *hell's* wrong with you people?" He turned to Sven. "Don't you realize, dammit, I have no time for stupid games!"

"Stupid," Sven said, his face grim. "If we were stupid, my friend, we would not be alive to mistrust you now!" His voice took on a sharp edge. "I said sit down!"

Tom sat. "Listen," he said. "I—"

Sven broke in at once. "*You* listen," he snapped. "And we two can save a lot of time. That is what you wish, no?"

Tom nodded. Sven spoke English with the same clipped accent as the girl, he noted. Somehow, it didn't have the same charm. "Say your piece," he said angrily.

"You must understand," Sven said. "We must be sure that you are who you say you are. You do not know the situation here. We do. The war may well be ending. But not for us. Not yet. The Gestapo, and the SS, have stepped up their actions against us. The *Hipos*, the Danish traitors, are doing all they can to help them. The German commander, General Lindemann, has ordered his occupation troops to fight to the death."

He looked grimly at Tom. "No. It is not over, my friend. Only a week ago the Nazis executed nine of us. Betrayed by traitors who said they were friends. And you will have that we accept you without question?"

Tom looked gravely at Sven. His frustrated anger was slowly leaving him, being replaced by a grudging respect for the Danish Freedom Fighter. "You—your people—saw me dropped," he said. "From an RAF Mosquito bomber."

"We saw *someone* dropped. That is correct. But—*was it you?*"

Tom looked startled.

"Understand, my friend. It has happened before. We must be absolutely sure. Other groups, perhaps less vigilant, have been betrayed by someone they accepted as a friend." He eyed Tom searchingly. "In your case, we were told by London to expect an American. That signal could—could, mind you—have been intercepted by the Germans. The drop was made. Of course. We saw it. But was that because the Germans wanted us to? The drop was also discovered. Was that by a routine patrol? Or were they waiting? In any case, we missed one another. Later, Tove and Klaus and Holger discovered you. You say you are the American. You will have papers that prove it. But, can we be certain? The Germans are clever in making false papers. Can we be sure you are not someone substituted by them for us to find? And to trust?" He let the questions hang heavily in the sour smelling barroom.

Tom cursed silently. The man was right. He was absolutely right. He knew he would have acted exactly the same way had their positions been reversed. But how the hell could he convince them?

He suddenly knew. "Sven," he said urgently. "I can prove to you that I am the one you were expecting. When I was in Squadron Leader Barlow's office at the RAF arranging for the drop, they told me why you are called the 'Mole.' I know about the King's secret passage. From the palace. I know about your wagonload of cement!"

Sven shot a quick glance at Tove and Klaus. He turned to the fat man cleaning glasses at the bar. "Søren," he said. *"Sig til Holger, at han skal komme ind."*

The fat man nodded. He picked up a broom and went out the front. He stayed outside, sweeping down the sidewalk, as Holger joined the others in the bar.

In low tones the four Danish Freedom Fighters conferred earnestly. Then Sven turned to Tom. He looked at him gravely. "You have a right to know," he said. He nodded toward the girl. "Tove says to trust you." He glanced at Klaus and Holger. "They think we must make certain. I agree with them."

"But—"

Sven held up a restraining hand. "The Germans probably know about the Amalienborg tunnel by now. It is no longer important." He frowned.

"The story about the cement I was myself stupid enough to tell to others. It could easily have become known to the Germans, too." He studied Tom. "We must have *real* proof," he said. "Proof that you *are* the American agent sent to us. We must check you out with London."

"How?"

"By radio."

"How long will that take?"

Sven shrugged. "A day. Perhaps two."

"I don't have a day or two!" Tom protested bitterly. "The man I'm after will be gone by then. He *must* be caught before he can get out of the country. I need *your* help to find him. And I need it *now!*"

Sven nodded. "And *I* need to be certain. *I* need to know that my group will not be betrayed."

"How will you verify me?"

Sven looked at him. "We want you to tell us something. Something that *only* you, and the RAF officers with whom you talked, can possibly know. You will give us a phrase. One sentence. We will transmit it to London. If that sentence could only have come from the man they sent, they will acknowledge that fact. If they do, we help you. All the way. If they do not . . ."

Tom's thoughts whirled in his mind. Something from his meeting with the British? Something only the people present at that time could know? What? Hell, how was he supposed to remember. His mind was blank. He could think of nothing.

Anger born of frustration began to build in him once more. Dammit! They were being too damned cautious. Unreasonable as hell. He'd told them everything. He'd laid his cards on the table—

Something suddenly snapped in his brain. Cards! What was it the squadron leader had said? About the American liaison officer? Captain Mike Holland?

He knew. "Send this," he said. "Mike makes a splendid fourth."

Sven looked at him. "That is all?"

"That's all."

"They will understand?"

"They will." Tom was gratified at the look of puzzlement in Sven's eyes. Good! Let *him* wonder for a while. No reason to explain to him that

Squadron Leader Barlow in a lighter moment had opined that he wanted to keep Captain Mike Holland around because he made a good bridge partner!

Sven called to the fat man outside on the sidewalk. "Søren!" The man joined them. For a moment the Danes conferred.

Something was nagging Tom's mind. What if he really had been a German plant? Hadn't Sven laid himself and his group wide open for reprisals already? Hadn't he given away a lot about himself? And his Freedom Fighters? This meeting place, for instance. Would he have done it if he really mistrusted him? Or . . . had he other plans?

Tove came over to him. "I am sorry," she said. "But Sven is right. He has the responsibility for all of us. As soon as London says you are okay, he will do everything for you."

"Perhaps too late," Tom said bitterly.

For a moment their eyes met. It was an oddly disturbing moment for Tom. The girl was different from anyone he'd ever met. She had taken off the little beret she'd been wearing. Her short-cut hair clung like a downy golden cap around her lovely face, lifted to look up at him.

Sven came over. "You will stay here," he instructed Tom. "Søren will look after you. You will not leave. If you try, we will know you are a German informer. You understand?"

"I understand."

"We shall make things happen for you, my friend. As speedily as we can." He started to leave. He turned back to Tom. "I will do this for you," he said. "Just in case you truly *are* a friend!" He smiled. His smile was surprisingly open and boyish.

"I am meeting with my group now. I shall alert them all. The moment we know about you, the moment you check out, all shall help." He nodded to Søren, who took up a position close to Tom. Sven and the others left.

Tom stared after the departing Freedom Fighters. His mind whirled. He *knew* he could not wait for clearance from London. He *knew* Rudi A-27 would be gone long before. He *knew* he could not continue his investigations without help. He *knew* he had to have the cooperation of Sven and his group. He *knew* he had to have it now!

He started to walk back into the dismal bar, his head lowered in resignation. He passed the fat man, Søren. Suddenly he whirled. With all his might he savagely slammed both his fists into the fat man's stomach. The man gasped. He gagged. His eyes strained to escape their sockets in shock. He fell to his knees before Tom.

With a quick rabbit punch across the neck Tom knocked him out. At once he ripped off the man's dirty apron. He tore it to shreds. With feverish speed he tied the man hand and foot and stuffed a piece of greasy cloth into his mouth, securing it with part of the apron string. The unconscious man snorted his breath noisily through flaring nostrils.

Tom grabbed the bulky man by his feet and dragged him behind the bar, then ran for the street. In the distance he could see the Freedom Fighters on their bicycles, just entering Kongens Nytorv, the golden-capped head of Tove bobbing in their midst.

He grabbed a bicycle leaning against the wall. It was a woman's bike. He had no time to notice. At once he set off in pursuit. He pedaled furiously to catch up with the little group, careening his bicycle over the uneven cobblestones of the street. As he reached the square, he saw his quarry turn into the street on the far right.

He suddenly felt outrageously conspicuous on the woman's bicycle. Utterly exposed. If Sven or any of the others should turn around, he'd be spotted at once. He needed something that would change his appearance. Something that would make him blend into the familiar street scene rather than stick out like a clown in a funeral procession.

He was passing a hotel. A young man was just dismounting from his bike in front of it. He carried a beat-up black leather shoulder pouch and wore an official-looking cap with a round emblem on the front. On the pouch was imprinted *"Kgl. Telegraf."* A bicycle messenger.

Tom screeched to a stop next to him. In a low, gruff voice he snapped at the startled boy, *"Halt!"*

The young man froze.

"Gestapo! *Sonderdienst!"* Tom barked at him in German. "Emergency! I am commandeering your bicycle." He grabbed the messenger's black bicycle and shoved the woman's bike at him. "Your cap, too." He snatched the cap off the young man's head and slapped it down on his own. Fiercely he scowled at the befuddled messenger. "Don't make a sound!" he threatened. He started off on the messenger's bike. He hoped he had been convincing. He had.

The young telegraph office messenger stood staring after him in stupefied silence, holding on to the discarded woman's bike.

Tom turned into the street he had seen Sven and the others enter. He glanced at the street sign. Just in case. "Store Kongensgade." He craned his neck. He could not see the others. He raced down the street, scowling from under the black-peaked messenger cap. There they were. Ahead of him.

He slowed down. He stayed back, losing himself among the other bike riders on the street, looking around as if searching for an address, but keeping Sven and his companions in sight.

They had reached an older part of town—apartment houses, three- and four-story buildings—when the four Freedom Fighters stopped, dismounted from the bikes and pushed them across the sidewalk, disappearing into a narrow arcade in one of the buildings.

Tom stopped. He parked his bike at the side of the street, one pedal resting on the curb, as he had seen other bikes parked. He walked to the door in the building in front of him and appeared to be checking the house number. He kept the arcade where the four Freedom Fighters had entered in view.

No one came out.

Purposefully he walked toward the arcade. It was an old building. Beyond the arcade was a small courtyard and across it was the rear building of the apartment complex. Outside, in a rusty metal rack, several bicycles were parked. He thought he recognized the one belonging to Tove.

Quickly he crossed the yard to the front door. He tried it. It was open. He entered.

It was a three-story walk-up building. On each landing were two apartments. One on the right. One on the left. Six apartments. Which one?

He started up the stairs. He looked at the nameplate on the door of the apartment on the second floor, left: HANSEN. It meant nothing.

He rang the bell. For a moment nothing happened. Then he heard a door open and footsteps approach.

A voice called, *"Hvem er det?"*

He had a momentary flush. He recognized the voice. It was Tove. He said nothing. He knocked on the door. He placed both his hands on his head. He waited.

There was a brief silence, then the door was cautiously opened, and Tove's face appeared in the crack. Her eyes opened wide and her soft lips drew apart in astonished shock.

He grinned. "Hi, Tove," he said. "Mind if I come in?" He pushed past her into the narrow hallway beyond.

Across from him was a door. It was ajar by a couple of inches. Quickly he strode to it and pushed it wide open with his foot.

The scene before him seemed frozen in time, like a stop-action motion picture effect. There were about a dozen young people in the room, mostly young men, some women, every one of them staring at Tom in stunned surprise. He saw Sven and Klaus and Holger—and the several guns trained menacingly on him. He was acutely aware of Tove behind him.

He kept his hands on his head. He stepped into the room. "Hello, Sven," he said.

Sven was the first of the Danes to regain control of himself. Curtly he snapped at Klaus. "Klaus!" He nodded sharply toward the door.

Klaus at once hurried away.

Sven turned to Tom. "What the devil are you doing here?" he demanded icily.

Tom returned his gaze. A lot depended upon his answer. Whatever he said, he knew it would sound melodramatic. But life *is* melodramatic. There *is* a time and a place for melodrama. Perhaps this was it. The time and the place to go all the way. "I came to be accepted," he said quietly. "Or killed."

The silent tension in the room seemed stretched beyond its limit. The eyes and attention of all were riveted on Tom.

He gazed steadily at Sven. "You were concerned, Sven, that I might be a German informer, sent to betray you and your group," he said. He looked around him. "If I were, this house would now be surrounded by Gestapo and SS!"

Slowly he took his hands from his head. No one stopped him. "Instead," he said. "Instead . . . I am alone. Unarmed. I come as a friend. I seek your help."

Klaus came hurrying into the room. Sven at once shot a questioning glance at him. Klaus shook his head. *"Der er ikke nogen,"* he said. "Nobody there."

"How did you get here?" Sven asked suspiciously.

"You forget. I can ride a bicycle, too."

"Søren?"

"He'll have a tender belly, but he's okay."

"How did you know we were in this apartment?"

Tom grinned wryly. "I didn't. I tried them all. One at a time." He took off the borrowed cap. He threw it on the table. "It's amazing how stupid a telegraph messenger can be!"

Sven began an angry retort.

"Hold it, Sven!" Tom interrupted firmly. "I think now it is time for *you* to listen to *me!*"

Sven glared at him. He shrugged. "We listen."

"Good. Here goes," Tom said. "I told you I am on the trail of a man. I am. A dangerous man. Right now, perhaps the most dangerous man alive."

The Freedom Fighters listened intently.

"I believe he is here. Now. In Copenhagen. But he will not be here for long. And he *must* be caught. I cannot do it without your help, and I cannot wait to be cleared by London."

He looked soberly around him at the grave young faces of the underground fighters. "I came here," he said, "alone. Unarmed. To prove to you that I *am* the American agent you expected. And not a German informer. If my purpose had been to capture this entire group, you would now, all of you, be prisoners of the Gestapo!"

He looked directly at Sven. "But that was not my purpose. Believe me now, Sven. Accept me. You know what your alternative is."

For a long moment there was utter silence in the room. Tom felt as if a thousand eyes were boring into him, examining him, probing him, as if he held a host of deadly secrets.

Sven regarded him solemnly. Suddenly his tension left him. "I accept you," he said.

Tom took a deep breath. He had won.

"But here," Sven continued, "here it must be unanimous. All of us must accept you." He looked gravely at Tom. "You understand, my friend? If one of us here, only *one* of us, feels that it is still necessary to check with London, it will be done."

Tom nodded grimly.

"I, then, vote yes," Sven said firmly. He turned to Tove. "Tove?"

"Yes."

"Holger?"

"Yes."

One by one he called the names of the Freedom Fighters. One by one they answered him. Yes.

One man was left. Klaus. Sven looked at him. "Klaus?"

The man frowned. He hesitated. "One question, Sven," he said, his voice strained.

"Ask it."

Klaus thought for a moment. "A bomb can be set to go off at a specific moment," he said haltingly. "At a moment when it will inflict the heaviest damage." He looked at Tom. "What . . . what if this man is like such a bomb? Waiting for the moment he can wreak the greatest destruction? Bring others down with us?"

All eyes were fixed on Tom. Silence hung heavy in the room.

Tom turned to Klaus. "Klaus," he said quietly, "right now, perhaps within days, a far greater act of destruction than anything any of us can possibly inflict is about to happen. The final destruction of Hitler's entire Third Reich. What damage that I could not already have done can I do before then?"

Klaus stared at him for a few seconds. "I vote . . . yes," he said.

The tension broke. The Freedom Fighters crowded around Tom. He sought out Tove. Their eyes met. She looked radiant.

Sven came up to him. He shook his head. "You took a very great chance, my friend," he said.

Tom grinned. "Not so damned great, Sven. I figured you really didn't believe I was a German stool pigeon. Or you would not have revealed as much as you did to me."

Sven frowned. "Revealed? What?"

"Oh, come on, Sven," Tom said. "Your names. The hiding place in the little cabin. Your meeting place in the bar. You would not have let me see all that if you really thought I was a German plant."

"You are wrong," Sven said soberly. "Dead wrong."

Tom frowned at him.

"The names mean nothing. They are code names. We would not have gone near the cabin until we knew you were all right. And the hiding place under the bed is booby-trapped."

"But . . . the bar?"

"We have never been there before. We will not go there again. The Scarlet Mermaid never opens until well after noon. No one is ever there before that time. If the Germans had questioned the owner, he could have told them nothing. Except that his establishment had been broken into. And he could have shown them the broken lock on the back door."

Tom grew sober. "And Søren?"

"Yes, Søren," Sven said seriously. "He is a patriot. But he does not work at the Mermaid." He nodded. "He did take a chance. It is as he wanted. You may have given him a sore belly, my friend. He always *had* a courageous heart." He looked at Tom. "Søren would have taken you to a hotel room. A few houses away. He would have waited with you until we had had our reply from London."

"Jesus," Tom muttered. "You had me covered six ways to Sunday."

"Now," Sven said briskly, "what can we do? This man you must find— who is he? Is he a Dane? How can we locate him?"

Tom was at once businesslike. "His name is Kessler. Rudolf Kessler," he said. "But he will not be using that name. He is an Austrian."

He looked from one to the other of the young underground fighters. "I have only one lead. It may be enough for us. The man was brought up here in Copenhagen. He was a Vienna Child. He speaks Danish fluently. He worked here for the Gestapo during part of the occupation. As an informant against the underground."

A stir rustled through the young people.

Tom looked at Sven. "I know the name of the family that took him in as a child," he said. "I do not know where they live. Nor if they are still alive, in fact. I want you to find them for me. One family that through the years from 1920 to 1924 had a Vienna Child named Rudolf Kessler in their home. Use any records available to you."

He paused. "The name is Rasmussen. Jens Peter Rasmussen."

It had not changed, except for the changes of age. Rudi stared at the nameplate on the door. The white porcelain had yellowed. The ornate black lettering was chipped. And the edges of the plate screwed onto the door were marred with smears of old paint. But the name still read, J. P. RASMUSSEN.

Gestapo records had shown that the Rasmussen family still occupied the little third-floor-right apartment on St. Knudsvej Number 5A.

Rudi had walked through the little side alley and looked into the yard in back. The bike sheds had been rebuilt, and the tree with the swing was gone. The little garden was still there. But not his fort. Not the totem pole with his dog pistols. Not his childhood. . . .

He reached for the turning handle that would ring the bell inside. He could feel his heart beat ponderously. Every cell in his body ached to turn away and leave. But he had to go through with it. His mind was a flood of rushing thoughts. . . .

He had arrived in Copenhagen earlier in the day. Once out of the restricted area, he'd had no difficulties making his way to the Danish town of Aabenraa. There he had taken a train to Copenhagen. It had been as simple as that.

He had at once reported to his contact, Sturmbannführer Dettling, at Gestapo Headquarters. Dettling had handed over to him the final Sleeper Agent list. It was now safely taped to the small of his back, where once his Danish papers had been concealed. In time he would memorize it.

But Dettling had also given him some catastrophic news. He had been blown! His cover had been compromised! Before he'd even had a chance to go into action. Through some idiotic fluke a damned American Counter Intelligence agent had blundered across part of his Schloss Ehrenstein *Personalbogen.*

The enemy now had his real name: Rudolf Kessler. They knew he had been reared in Denmark. They knew the name of the Danish foster family: Rasmussen.

It would not be difficult to deduce his cover name—the name in which all exfiltration arrangements had been made, the name he would use until he could adopt his final cover in the USA, the name on his Danish identification papers: Rudolf Rasmussen.

It *had* to be assumed that the cover name no longer was safe. All exfiltration plans made had to be scrapped. An alternate plan had been activated. He would be briefed later in the day. . . .

His hand touched the metal bell handle. It felt depressingly cold. He rang. Presently he heard soft footsteps approach. Slippers. She still wore them.

The door opened. A small gray-haired woman with a soft, solemn face looked up at Rudi.

"Lillemor," he said quietly. "Little mother."

The woman's clenched fist flew to her mouth. Her eyes filled with the instant tears of joy. She threw her arms around him. "Rudi!" she sobbed. "Rudi!"

He felt a chill knife through him. Gently he disengaged himself from his foster mother.

"Kom ind!" She beamed. *"Kom ind, min Dreng!*—Come in, my boy!" She pulled him into the flat. With radiant, tear-bright eyes she stared at him. "Oh, but you look fine!" she exclaimed. She hugged him again.

He took her by the shoulders. *"Lillemor,"* he said earnestly. "Where is *Far?"*

She grew sober. "He is gone, Rudi," she said quietly. "He is no longer with us, rest his soul." She looked at him, her eyes round with wonder. "But . . . how is it possible you are here?" she asked.

"I need help, *Lillemor."*

"Help?" She was at once concerned. "Are you in trouble?"

"No, *Lillemor,"* he said quickly. "I do not have the time to explain. Not now."

"What can I do for you, Rudi?" she said simply.

He touched his clothing, still the old soiled jacket he'd picked up at the farm. "I need clothing," he said. "I thought . . . *Far,* but—"

She looked at his clothes, seeing them for the first time. "Yes," she said brightly. "I still have one of *Far's* suits. I . . . I kept it. His good blue suit." She looked critically at Rudi. "It will perhaps be just a little big for you, my boy. But you try it, yes?"

She hurried across the room to a closet, her slippers making a soft, homey rustle on the floor. She brought out a man's blue suit. "Here," she said. "You put that on, my boy. I will make you something to eat. You must eat!"

She had come alive. She was fussing over her boy. The years had rolled away. "I will make you some *Smørrebrød,* Rudi, the kind you like." She smiled fondly at him. "I have some of your favorite *Leverpostej!* And home-made *Asier!*" She bustled off toward the kitchen. "You put on *Far's* suit," she said.

He looked after her. He felt cold. Quickly he shrugged out of his old clothes. He dressed in Jens Peter Rasmussen's good blue suit. It smelled faintly of camphor. It *was* a little too big. But it would do. He transferred his papers to his new jacket. And the gun—the gun he'd taken from the dead border guard—he stuck in his belt.

He looked around. The cushion was lying on the worn, brown velvet sofa. He remembered it. *Lillemor* had embroidered the sentimental epigram on it herself. For *Far:*

LYKKE MELLEM TO MENNESKER
ER SOM DEN DUNKLE NAT
STILLE, MEN MED TUSINDE
LYSE STJERNER BESAT

Happiness between two people
Is like the ebon night,
Still and silent, yet with a thousand
Stars in shining light.

He picked it up. He could feel the cold sticky sweat staining his armpits.

"Here you are, my boy," Mrs. Rasmussen called cheerfully as she entered with a little tray. "*Rigtig Leverpostejmad*—real liver paté sandwiches and milk! Enjoy it, love."

He stood in the middle of the room, the little embroidered cushion clutched before him.

She bent down to place the tray on the little coffee table.

He did not want her to know. He did not . . . It *had* to be.

She turned her head toward him, her face glowing with happiness.

Now! The shot was muffled by the little cushion with its message of love. The slug tore into his foster mother's back, ripping through her lung. For a split second he looked into her eyes—an abyss of incomprehension. Of anguish.

She crashed across the tray with her offering of affection to her foster son and slid onto the floor. She lay still.

He turned away. He couldn't bear to look at her. But, *verdammt noch-*

mal, he'd *had* to do it! He'd had no choice. No choice at all.

The American agent who'd gotten his stinking hands on his dossier had sealed her fate. *They* would have tracked her down. *They* would have made her talk. She could have given them too much information. Too much intimate information about him. It could not be allowed. She could have described him too well.

It had been only three years since he had seen her last. While he had been working for Abwehr III in Copenhagen. In the beginning. He had been curious to see the foster parents of his childhood. Just once. He had pretended he'd been in Denmark on vacation.

He suddenly remembered the snapshot. She had taken a snapshot of him standing with his foster father. Urgently he looked around. The photo album. There. On the buffet. He tore it open.

There was the picture he'd taken of the two of them. And the one of *Lillemor* alone. Smiling. And an empty space. Four empty photo corners —and a blank space. The snapshot of him was gone.

He slammed the album shut. What could she have done with it? Her purse! Maybe she carried it in her purse. Quickly he looked around. He found the purse on a little side table in the hallway. He spilled out the contents. There was no snapshot.

He thought fast. He did not have the time to search the entire apartment. What the hell had she done with the damned picture?

No need to panic. It was not important. If it was found, no one would connect it with him, out of context.

He went to the telephone. He picked up the receiver. He asked the operator for a number. He waited. Then: "Dettling?" he said. "It is done."

He listened for a moment.

"Yes," he said. "Wolff." He hung up. Suddenly a small sound sent an icy chill grating through him. He whirled toward the grotesquely sprawled body of his foster mother.

Her eyes were open. Accusing. They stared at him. She moaned, a small gurgling sound. She was still alive.

He grabbed the little cushion. Across its tender embroidered motto ran an ugly scorched streak. Somehow his gun was in his hand. He stepped behind her, away from the accusing, bewildered eyes. He *had* to. It was up to him. He looked down at her.

Her hair was spilled in gray disarray around her head. *Gray, like Mausi.* . . .

He fled.

The little flat across the yard, second-floor-left, in the old apartment complex used by Sven and his group of Freedom Fighters, had been a busy place since Tom had walked in on them. It had become the base of operations for the search for one Jens Peter Rasmussen, foster father.

One by one the searchers reported back to Tom and Sven:

City Hall records controlled by the Germans, not accessible without long-term preparation. Negative.

Telephone records inconclusive. Negative.

The special records of Centralkontoret for Wienerbørns Ophold i Danmark—the Central Bureau for the Residence of Vienna Children in Denmark—impounded by Germans. Not available on short notice. Negative.

Utility records inconclusive. Negative.

It was Tove who finally came up with a lead. A friend of hers worked in the Municipal Public Schools office. She was able to cut through bureaucratic red tape and examine the records herself.

For the years 1921 through 1924 a Vienna Child named Rudolf Kessler was recorded as having attended Vestre Borgerdyd school in Copenhagen. Foster parents: Helga and Jens Peter Rasmussen. Address: St. Knudsvej 5A 3. th. No up-to-date address change recorded.

It was a few minutes before 1700 hours when Tom, accompanied by Sven and Klaus, walked in the front entrance of Number 5A St. Knudsvej Street. They were excited to discover that the nameplate on the door to the third floor apartment, right still read, J. P. RASMUSSEN. Tove's lead had paid off.

Tom and Klaus positioned themselves on either side of the door. Sven turned the bell handle. Inside, the old bell made a rasping sound. They waited. There was no response. Sven looked at Tom. Tom nodded. Cautiously Sven tried the door. It was unlocked. Slowly he pushed it open. Tom peered into the little hallway beyond.

The first thing he saw was the purse, its contents spilled out on the side table. Someone had been at the Rasmussen place before them.

Quietly, cautiously they entered the apartment. They found Helga Rasmussen still sprawled on the floor in the parlor, her clothing soaking up the blood from the pool beneath her. They at once examined her. She was still alive. Unconscious.

"Shot," Tom said grimly. "Through the lung. She won't last much longer without help."

Sven turned to Klaus, his face tight. "Call Falcks," he snapped.

Klaus hurried to the telephone.

Tom looked questioningly at Sven.

"Falcks Redningskorps," Sven said. "Emergency service." He looked at the woman, his eyes haunted. "The bastards," he growled.

"Who do you think did it?" Tom asked.

"Gestapo. *Hipo. En Stikkergruppe*—a squealer group. They are all murderers," Sven answered bitterly.

"Or . . . Rudi," Tom said quietly.

Startled, Sven looked up at him.

Klaus joined them. "They'll be here," he said.

Sven nodded. "We had better get out of here before they come."

"Whoever was here," Tom said, "was looking for something. Let's take a quick look around. See what we can find."

"Okay," Sven agreed. "We have a few minutes." He stood up. Klaus disappeared into one of the other rooms. Tom started for the hallway. Suddenly they froze.

The unholy sound they'd heard had been a faint gurgling moan. The sound of desperate agony. Helga Rasmussen had regained consciousness. They knelt beside her. She tried to sit up.

"Don't move, Fru Rasmussen," Sven said, his voice soft and assuring. "We have sent for help."

She looked up at the two men leaning over her. Pink froth colored the corners of her mouth. Black grief her eyes. She made a valiant effort to talk.

"Don't try to say anything," Sven said. "We shall speak with you later."

Weakly she shook her head. *"Nu,"* she whispered. *"Vigtigt*—Now. Important . . ."

Sven and Tom looked at each other. Sven cocked an ear. No sound of the ambulance yet. "What is it, *lille Frue,"* he said compassionately.

"Ru-di . . . *min* . . . *søn,"* she breathed. *"Ikke* . . . *min* . . . Rudi—not my Rudi." Somehow, by sheer expression in her whisper, she made the same name spoken twice sound like two different people.

Tom and Sven were at once alert. They glanced at each other. "Talk to her," Tom said tensely. "Tell me later."

Sven nodded. He looked earnestly at the woman. *"Mener De, der er to Maend?"*

She screwed her eyes shut for a moment in anguish. *"Nej,"* she murmured. *"Han . . . har forandret sig . . ."*

"Skød han Dem?"

"Ja . . ." She looked toward the hallway. *"Telefon,"* she wheezed. *"Han . . . ringede . . ."*

"Hørte de Nummeret?"

"Husker det—ikke helt . . . Kun—fem, ni . . . To sidste Numre . . ."

Sven shot a grim look at Tom. He started to speak.

Helga Rasmussen stopped him. *"Et Navn,"* she mumbled. *"Dettling . . ."*

Sven tensed.

The woman went on. She was getting weak. It was a laborious effort. *"Rudi . . . tog Fars blaa Tøj,"* she whispered, using her waning strength with increasing difficulty. *"For . . . stort . . . for ham . . ."* She coughed a rasping, gurgling cough. The pink foam at her mouth bubbled obscenely. She closed her eyes.

Sven stood up. He looked angry. "Here it is," he said. He spoke quickly, tensely. "Rudi shot her. She says something has changed him." He clenched his jaws. He looked down at the woman, his eyes dark. "He must have left her for dead," he said. "It is a miracle she is not."

He looked back at Tom. "She overheard him make a telephone call. She only remembers the last two digits of the number he asked for. They are the last digits of the telephone number of the new Gestapo Headquarters in St. Annae Palae! She heard him mention a name. Dettling."

He paused significantly. His voice grew harsh. "We know there is an SS Major Dettling at Gestapo." Again he looked down at the mortally wounded woman crumpled pitifully on the floor. "She said Rudi took her husband's blue suit," he said, profound compassion in his voice. "She said it was too big for him. . . ."

Suddenly Helga Rasmussen spoke again. "Wolff," she breathed almost inaudibly. "Wolff . . ."

Tom shot a quick glance at Sven. He shook his head. Suddenly he tensed. Faintly in the distance the wailing horn of an emergency vehicle could be heard approaching.

Klaus came in. "Nothing," he said. "They're coming."

Sven nodded. He bent down close to the suffering woman. "Help is coming now," he said softly.

She stared up into his face. Her eyes had an oddly imploring look in them.

"Ru-di . . ." she faltered. She stared at the two men with pain-glazed eyes. "Ru-di . . ."

With superhuman effort she moved her hand toward her throat, inching it along her blood-soaked chest. Higher. Higher. The hand stopped. It would never reach its goal.

Quickly, gently Tom opened the top button of her blouse. A thin gold chain hung around the neck of Helga Rasmussen. He pulled it out. On the end of it was a locket, the size and shape of a half dollar.

The loud ululating clamor of the emergency horn came to a wailing stop. The ambulance had arrived.

Sven grabbed Tom by the shoulders. "Come on!" he said urgently. "We must get out!"

They ran from the room. As they heard the emergency crew pound up the front steps, they ducked out the kitchen door and ran down the back stairs. They hurriedly crossed a little garden, scaled a low fence, and didn't stop until they were in the yard of the building next door.

Tom looked at the locket clutched in his fist. He opened it. On one side of it the kindly, dignified face of an elderly man looked out at him. Jens Peter Rasmussen. Helga's husband. On the other, on top of the faded picture of a thin, earnest little boy, was a cut-out snapshot of a grinning young man.

Rudi A-27 had a face!

Tom and the two Danish Freedom Fighters were making their way toward Gestapo Headquarters.

If Rudi had made a call to Major Dettling, he might well have gone there. Now that they knew what their quarry looked like, they might spot him. Wearing his new oversized blue suit!

The streets of the city were tense with barely contained excitement. The suspense was mounting minute by minute. Rumors ran rampant through the restless, ever-shifting crowds. Posters and placards appeared almost magically in shopwindows, on walls and kiosks.

Berlin has fallen.

The British are at the Danish border.

The Germans are about to surrender.

Rumors? Or fact?

They left their bicycles a block away and slowly sauntered toward the building occupied by the Gestapo. There was a constant flow of grim, tight-faced Germans, civilians and military personnel alike, in and out of the place.

Sven frowned. They would have to find a spot from which to watch. It would not be easy. A large sign had been erected prominently in front of the building:

> ### ADVARSEL
> Al Sammenstimlen og
> Stillestaaen er forbudt
> og bliver ikke taalt!
>
> ### [WARNING
> All assemblage and
> standing is forbidden
> and will not be tolerated!]

They knew all too well the warning was being strictly enforced. The SS troops standing guard attested to it.

They were across the street, a couple of houses away from Gestapo Headquarters, when with sudden shock a gigantic explosion literally shook the ground. Columns of black smoke licked by the flames of fire shot from a row of windows in the Gestapo building like a salvo from a dreadnaught. A raw blast of boiling sound slammed across their ears. Instinctively they hit the ground.

Shattered windows rained splintered glass into the street to swell the hail of debris that erupted from the building.

Tom and Sven struggled to their feet. *"Det var som Fanden!"* Sven exclaimed in awe. "I'll be damned! He did it!"

Tom looked at him. "Did what? Who?"

"A friend," Sven answered. "He repaired their typewriters." He stared at the havoc. "Look at that! Jesus!" He shook his head. "He *said* someday he'd blow the damned place up!"

"Hell of a time he picked," Tom said bitterly.

They stared at the demolished building. Smoke and dust still billowed from the gaping soot-blackened windows.

The brief stunned hush that followed the thunderous explosion had given way to a growing piercing cacophony of hellish sounds. The pain-wracked screams of the injured and maimed mingled with cries of panic and terror; the fiery crackling of flames was punctuated by the sharp sounds of falling debris and shattered glass; the shouts of would-be rescuers cut through the bedlam roar of confusion as wounded Germans streamed from the building, bleeding, blackened and dazed. Others rushed toward the entrance with the SS guards to render what aid they could.

"This is our chance!" Tom said quickly. He turned to Klaus. "Stay here!" he called. "Keep your eyes open. Sven! Come on!"

Together they ran for the bomb-blasted Gestapo Headquarters building. They raced to the floor where the blast had taken place. The area was a nightmare scene of destruction. The acrid stink of cordite from the explosives hung in the dust- and smoke-filled air. Water from broken pipes gushed and gurgled over the rubble. Mangled, badly injured Gestapo men lay everywhere, some screaming in agony, others moaning in mindless shock.

The body of one officer lay hurled, decapitated, across a shrapnel-scarred desk. With part of his whirling mind Tom observed at least a half dozen mutilated dead.

Those who were able to and had not fled from the gore and carnage were milling about in aimless confusion.

Tom realized it would be impossible to spot Rudi, were he indeed there. But there was Dettling.

He grabbed an SS man who was staggering down the corridor clutching his bleeding, bone-slashed right arm to him. "Dettling!" he shouted at the benumbed man. "*Wo ist* Sturmbannführer Dettling?"

The man stared at him in uncomprehending shock. He whimpered, tears running from his eyes.

Tom let him go. He stopped a Scharführer who came running with an armful of scorched records, his face sooted and blood-streaked. "Sturmbannführer Dettling?" he demanded with curt authority.

The sergeant shook his head. "Don't know," he said. "Perhaps in his office." He nodded down the corridor. "Down there." He ran on.

Tom and Sven made their way through the rubble and litter. The door to one of the offices had been blown half off its hinges. They glanced inside. The place was a total shambles. Part of one wall had imploded, blasting broken masonry through the room.

On the floor, leaning against a splintered desk, sat an SS officer, holding his right leg with both hands, staring at it in stupefied horror. It had been sheared off below the knee. The blood spurted from the stump in rhythmic crimson jets.

Tom instantly recognized his rank insignia: Sturmbannführer.

The two men rushed into the demolished office. Tom knelt by the crippled officer. "Dettling?" he asked hoarsely.

The man nodded. *"Zu Befehl*—At your orders," he mumbled automatically, never taking his dazed eyes from his bloody leg stump.

Tom at once tore at the black SS tie around the man's neck. He freed it. Quickly he made a tight heavy knot in the middle of it. He brushed the SS officer's hands away from his leg and tied the necktie around his thigh above the knee. He looked around. He grabbed a jagged piece of wood from the splintered desk, inserted it under the tie, and turned.

The tourniquet tightened. The blood spurts from the mangled leg stump slowed and stopped.

The officer looked up at Tom. "Get me . . . away from here," he said hoarsely.

Tom glared at him, his eyes burning. "First," he snapped, "you answer a few questions!"

Dettling stared at him, his agonized, drawn face uncomprehending.

"Rudolf Kessler," Tom barked at him. "Have you seen him?"

Dettling's face turned deathly white. He began to tremble. He said nothing.

"You are dying, Dettling!" Tom said savagely. "You want to live?"

The man nodded, terror-stricken.

"Then talk, dammit! Now!"

Dettling's mouth worked. He shivered violently. From pain . . . and fear. He was rapidly going into shock.

"Where is he, Dettling?" Tom demanded. "*Where?*"

Panic-stricken, Dettling shook his head.

Suddenly Sven pushed Tom aside. He grabbed the wood splinter in the tourniquet and roughly tore it away. Instantly the blood began to spurt from the maimed stump. Sven put his face close to the SS officer, a face of cold fury. "Now you listen to me, you German son of a bitch!" he snarled. "If you want to bleed to death all over the goddamned floor, go ahead! If not, you had better talk! You had better make it good! And *I* will decide if it is!" His voice was low, controlled but vicious. "And just so we understand one another, Sturmbannführer Dettling, I don't give a shit whether you live or die!"

The German frantically tried to stay the flow of blood from his leg. He stared in horrified supplication at Sven. "For God's sake! Please!" he begged. "Please! Don't let me die."

"*Rudolf Kessler!*" Sven snapped inexorably. He reinserted the wood splinter in the tourniquet and stanched the spurting blood.

Dettling watched, mesmerized. He nodded. "He . . . he was here."

"When?"

"This . . . morning."

"Where is he now?"

"I do not know." The SS officer looked terrified. "Believe me! I do not know!" He looked wildly from one of his interrogators to the other.

"Did he get any instructions from you?" Sven asked.

Dettling hesitated.

"Make it quick," Sven spat. "You have not much time!"

Dettling nodded. "I . . . I gave him the list," he whispered.

"What list?"

"The . . . the final Sleeper list," the man murmured. "For the operation in America."

Sven shot a grim glance at Tom. "What else?" he asked tautly.

"I . . . I informed him that his cover had been compromised. All exfiltration plans . . . canceled. I . . . instructed him he must activate . . . alternate plan."

"What plan?"

Dettling looked petrified. His terrified eyes flitted from one to the other. "I do not know," he whispered, beseeching them to believe him. "I only know there *is* an alternate plan."

Sven and Tom exchanged glances. Tom turned to Dettling. "Did Kessler know the alternate plan?" he asked.

"No."

"If you did not give it to him, where would he go to find out?"

Dettling's face was chalky white. He stared empty-eyed straight ahead of him. "Tosca," he breathed.

"Tosca?"

Sven said quickly, "It's a German café. Restaurant. Here. In Frederiksberggade."

"Who, at Tosca?"

"Undercover . . . agent," Dettling said. His strength was ebbing away, spreading in a crimson pool oozing on the rubble-strewn floor. "A . . . waiter."

"His name?" Tom pressed urgently. *"His name?"*

For a moment Dettling remained silent. Then he breathed, "Wolff."

Tom stood up. He stopped a couple of SS medics hurrying by in the corridor. "In here!" he barked sharply. "Get this man out of here! *Schnell machen!*—On the double!"

The medics jumped to obey as Tom and Sven hurried from the devastated Gestapo building.

The name rang in Tom's mind. The name whispered by Dettling. And by Helga Rasmussen: *Wolff.*

Tom, Sven and Klaus were hurrying toward Frederiksberggade and the notorious German Café Tosca.

Tension on the city streets was stretched to the breaking point. The expectant pressure was building moment to moment. Everyone felt certain that the end of five long years of oppression and despotism was near. But how would it come? When? What would happen? Would there be fighting in the streets? Would Copenhagen in the last desperate moment be turned into a bloody battlefield? The whole town was like a giant boiler without a safety valve, ready to blow.

The three men were riding through a narrow street in the old quarter near the University. Small groups of excited young people were everywhere. Ahead of them a group of about a dozen students were cheering a speaker.

Suddenly a shot rang out from a rooftop above. And another. One of the young men fell. At once everyone scattered, two of the students dragging their wounded friend to safety. In a moment the street was empty.

Tom and the two Danes with him had come to a halt. "Snipers!" Sven said angrily.

"Trigger-happy bastards." Tom peered up toward the rooftops.

"*Hipos.*" Sven nodded. "They are nervous," he said grimly. "They have reason to be. They know what is in store for them." He got off his bike. "We'll leave the cycles here," he said. "Cut through the back yards. It's only a few blocks."

Within minutes they stood before Café Tosca. It was dark. Abandoned. Closed as tight as a Nazi hand salute.

Rudi smoldered with suppressed fury. He'd missed his rendezvous with Wolff. The Tosca had been dead and deserted when he arrived. He cursed silently. His next contact with Wolff was not possible until 1200 hours the following day. Saturday, May 5th. He glanced at his watch. Close to 2000 hours. Sixteen *verfluchte* hours wasted, at the worst possible time. But Wolff had gone underground. Hanging around the Tosca had become dangerous because of the mood of the people. There was no possible way for him to locate the man. Damn security and secrecy!

He finished dressing. The blue pants bunched at the waist when he tightened the belt. He knew the seat looked baggy.

When he'd found the Tosca closed, he'd needed time to think, time to take stock. He'd gone to a public bath only a couple of blocks away. In Studiostraede. What better place to be alone for a couple of hours? And safe. But he couldn't stay there forever. He had to get out.

The situation in the streets was fluid—unpredictable. Tense, restless crowds were surging through town, waiting. It could be dangerous to walk about with his compromised ID. An unnecessary risk. He needed new papers. Temporary papers.

He suddenly felt hunted. He set his face grimly. The hunted of necessity must be able to turn disadvantage into advantage. *Schon gut!*—Fine!

He would join the damned crowds in the streets. He'd mingle with the

Copenhageners. He'd even wave a Danish flag if he had to. The devil take it! And he'd keep his eyes open for someone of his own build, his own age. In the chaos of the developing conditions, a simple robbery should not be too difficult to carry out.

He had finished dressing. Resolutely he left his damp little private sanctuary. On the way out of the public bathhouse he nodded pleasantly to the fat middle-aged lady at the desk dispensing soap and towels. He was on his way. In search of a temporary identity. Good until 1200 hours, May 5th.

For the second time that day Sven and his "moles" were gathered in the undistinguished little apartment across the yard, second-floor-left.

Klaus had been left in Frederiksberggade to keep an eye on the Tosca in case the waiter named Wolff should show up. But Sven and Tove and most of the others had returned.

A plan of operation had to be formulated. They would have to canvass the neighborhood around the German café—question neighbors and shop-keepers in the area, anyone who might provide them with a lead to Wolff. Tom was deeply concerned. It was a time-consuming procedure. And time was running out.

The Freedom Fighters were restless. More than anyone they felt the anxious uncertainty shared by the whole town.

Holger interrupted the discussions. "It is time," he said.

At once everyone converged around the radio. In silent, taut suspense they watched Holger manipulate the dials. Reception was noisy with static, interference by German jamming transmitters. But through it the familiar Beethoven's Fifth signature of the BBC could be heard. London was on the air. It was 8:30 P.M., Friday, May 4th.

The Danes listened with every conscious fiber of their bodies.

An announcer spoke. In Danish. With measured delivery the words cut through the static. The British are close to the Danish border. No estimate when they will reach it.

"That's Johannes Sørensen," Tove whispered to Tom as she listened to the familiar voice.

There was more. Bits of news. Commentary on the fall of Berlin. Hamburg. Then suddenly there was a few seconds' pause.

When the announcer came back on the air his voice had a clarion ring to it: *"I dette Øjeblik meddeles det, at Feldmarskal Montgomery har oplyst, at de tyske Styrker i Holland, Nordtyskland og Danmark har overgivet sig!"* His voice broke with emotion. *"Danmark er atter frit!"*

For a moment there was a stunned hush in the room. Then a jubilant shout of victory went up from the little group of Freedom Fighters. It rose and swelled. Awesomely, it was like a primer for a gigantic explosion of joy, relief and deliverance that roared up from a million throats, building, gathering, rolling in triumph and rejoicing over the rooftops as the news like instant flash fire engulfed the entire city.

Tom did not have to understand Danish to realize what he had just heard.

At that moment Montgomery had announced the surrender of all German forces in Holland, North Germany and Denmark.

Denmark is free again!

Tove ran to the windows. With savage vehemence she tore the ugly, hated blackout curtains down and hurled them to the floor.

Sven held up his arms. "Break it down!" he shouted.

Instantly the young men were galvanized into action. Two of them manhandled a large worn sofa away from the wall at the far end of the room. Another pushed aside an end table, from which yet another snatched a lamp with a scorched paper shade.

Holger stood before the bare wall. Suddenly he aimed a violent kick at the drab wallpaper. His booted foot crashed through the wall. At once eager hands ripped and tore at the breach. It was a false partition. Behind it was a large walk-in closet, which had been concealed by the false wall panel. It was an arsenal.

Quickly the Freedom Fighters handed out the weapons and equipment stacked in the hiding place. Guns. Ammunition. Steel helmets. They helped one another fasten armbands around their upper left arms—blue, with red and white stripes and Denmark's coat of arms. The army of Freedom Fighters was mobilizing.

Sven came up to Tom. He was at once excited and sober. "You understand, my friend," he said. "We can no longer help you. The time we have been waiting for, training for, arming for—the time to do our duty—has come. At last!"

He swept the room with his eyes, proudly. "All of us here must now report at once to our predetermined positions. It is expected of us. We must follow the specific plan. It has been carefully laid. Others depend on us."

He looked earnestly at Tom. "One cannot know what now will happen in the streets, Tom," he said. "*We* may be the only true force ready to save our town from destructive fighting. *We* may be the only force to bring the guilty ones to justice—and prevent them from dragging down the people and the city with them in their defeat."

He placed his hand on Tom's arm. "You must understand," he said solemnly.

Tom nodded. "I do, Sven," he said gravely. "I do."

He did understand. The responsibilities confronting Sven and his group of Freedom Fighters now had to take precedence over anything else. And that included the hunt for Rudi A-27. He felt excited and happy for his Danish friends. Their ordeal had come to an end. It was time for action. He also knew that without their help he had no chance of successfully completing his own vital mission. He had lost.

Sven watched him with concern.

"What will you do?" he asked quietly.

Tom tightened his mouth. What the hell *would* he do? Shit! He refused to admit defeat. Dammit, you weren't licked until you admitted you were. "Keep trying," he said defiantly.

Tove had joined them. She looked at Tom with her big serious eyes. "You will need help," she said simply. "I will stay with you."

Tom turned to her quickly.

"You will need me," she said.

He looked at her. "Yes," he said. "Yes. I will."

Sven and his Freedom Fighters left.

Denmark is free again! With one brief sentence, spoken in a foreign country far away, the hunted had become the hunters.

The streets of the city were crowded with jubilant people. The very air was electric with excitement. Officially the formal surrender would not become effective until 0800 hours the next morning. It was no deterrent to the exulting celebrants sweeping the city, shouting, singing, embracing in boundless joy. It was over! Freedom had come!

Tom and Tove were making their way through the ecstatic throngs toward Frederiksberggade. One last check of the Café Tosca. The entire city was ablaze with color and light. Every neon sign, every billboard, every streetlight and every spotlight blazed in bright brilliance. Yet, most impressive of all were the candles. Magically, miraculously, a lighted candle had appeared in every window, casting a glow of joy and gladness over the hectic scene below.

Public loudspeakers blared forth national and patriotic songs, all but drowned out by the joyful roar of the crowds. The big yellow tramcars lumbered through the streets, clanging their bells, overflowing with young people hanging from the windows and clinging to the sides and crowded on the roofs, waving Danish flags, singing at the top of their youthful voices. It was an orgy of joy. It was deliverance.

Tom and Tove, infected by the all-embracing spirit of excitement and exuberance, pushed across the Town Hall Square, which was swarming with cheering celebrants. He took her hand. For a moment their eyes met. Her hand was vibrantly alive in his.

They reached Frederiksberggade. The Tosca was no longer closed tight. Every window, every door gaped wide open. In their flush of triumph, in an outburst of pent-up release the people had taken their revenge on the hated German café.

It had been totally razed. Gutted. Every window shattered. Every stick of furniture smashed. Every piece of equipment destroyed and hurled out to lie in heaps of trampled rubble in the street. Someone set fire to the mound of debris, and quickly the flames were shooting high up into the air.

The Tosca was dead. Wolff, the waiter, would never be needed again. Neither would Wolff, the undercover agent, ever return.

Rudi waved his little Danish flag wildly over his head. At the top of his lungs he shouted, *"Kongen laenge leve!*—Long live the King!" as he let himself be jostled through the street by the surging, agitated crowd. He was enraged. His contempt for the undisciplined mob of Danes was abysmal. He felt a deep outrage at their barbaric behavior.

He had passed by the offices of the Ufa motion picture corporation in Nygade only a few blocks away. The building of the great company, producers of some of Germany's—and the world's—finest films, had been viciously ransacked and demolished by the unruly rabble. Furniture was pitched from the windows, papers and documents scattered to the winds to be trampled beneath the vandal feet of the lawless mob.

He looked around him, scanning the milling crowd, as he moved along, cheering and singing enthusiastically with the rest. He was searching for himself. Someone who could provide him with a new identity. But no one looked the least like him. Or did they? Did he really know what he looked like? Does anyone?

He felt exposed. His compromised papers seemed to sear his pocket every time he passed a patrol of Freedom Fighters, their distinctive armbands prominent and portentous on their sleeves. He *had* to find someone. Soon.

Whoever it would be did not actually have to look like him. Only be the same build, the same height, the same age and the same coloring. There seemed to be something wrong with every candidate he scrutinized.

The crowd was streaming toward Amalienborg, the royal residence, to cheer the King. Close to the King's Newmarket, in Østergade, a bottleneck had formed.

When Rudi came near, he saw the cause of it. A large German bookstore had been broken into, looted and laid waste. Piles of books and pamphlets lay strewn in the street. Laughing, joking hoodlums were milling and jostling around the devastated shop, wantonly destroying the German works, flinging them by the armful into the street and onto blazing bonfires.

A young Dane came running from the shop. He held a couple of books in each hand high above his head in wild triumph, screaming his excitement to the cheering throng. *"Mein Kampf!"* he shouted. *"Mein Kampf! Mein Kampf!"* He hurled the books on the flaming fire.

Rudi watched him closely. Could be his own age. Same approximate height and build. Hair only slightly lighter. He was the man.

The young Dane ran back into the shop. Rudi followed. Inside, the bookstore was a shambles. Torn and ripped books littered the floor. Everything had been mercilessly smashed and wrecked. In the back a door stood ajar. Rudi pushed it open. He peered inside. It was a small storeroom. It was empty. Quickly he looked around for his man.

There—busily tearing a series of colorful German posters from the wall.

Rudi ran up to him. "Hey!" he said, excitement in his voice. "Come see what I found! Give me a hand!" Without waiting for an answer, he ran to the storeroom door and disappeared inside.

The young Dane followed. He came hurrying through the door into the darkened room.

Rudi was waiting for him. He stepped up behind him and slammed a violent blow with the hard edges of both his hands to the unsuspecting young man's neck. He dropped without a sound.

At once Rudi went through his pockets. His wallet. Quickly he looked inside. Not much money. But identification. Work papers. DSB. *De Danske Statsbaner*—the Danish State Railway. And a fishing license. Enough. "Christian Madsen. Railroad worker."

He turned to leave. He stopped. He bent over the unconscious man. He grabbed hold of his watch and tore it savagely from the wrist, breaking the skin. His motive had to be unquestioned.

He quickly replaced his own compromised papers with the new Madsen ID. He picked up an armful of books and ran to the street. To the cheering applause of the onlookers he tossed the books on one of the bonfires.

Quickly they caught, blackened leaves curling up and dying. Books. Words. Being burned to ashes. But not the beliefs they had brought!

He hurled the last book into the blaze—and with it his old papers. "Rudolf Rasmussen" went up in flames. "Christian Madsen" melted into the crowd. He had fourteen hours to wait.

There was a surging crush of happy, joyful people flowing and eddying around the beautiful old church on the canal. "Holmens Kirke," Tove had called out.

They were on their way to Christiansborg Castle, the seat of the government. They might get aid there, Tove thought. Information. Members of the Freedom Council would be there.

The crowd of jubilant people before the church were singing the freedom song.

Tove stopped. Her eyes shone with the bright unshed tears of happy emotion. She joined in the singing: *"En Vinter, lang og mørk og haard . . ."*

She held on to Tom's hand, squeezing it tightly. She dug her fingers into him in exhilaration. Her young voice soared with her compatriots':

"A winter, long and dark with fears,
Through five eternal, cursèd years,

> Has crushed the nation in its hold,
> With hardships, hunger, grief untold. . . ."

Tom gazed at her. He felt like taking her in his arms and crushing her to him. She was like a young, golden Viking goddess.

> "Rise up! Resist! All Danes as one,
> And make our Denmark free!"

He loved her.

They were crossing the bridge over the canal. Ahead of them rose the verdigris copper-dragon spire of the Stock Exchange. Next to it the majestic edifice of Christiansborg dominated the district.

Suddenly a volley of shots rang out. Instantly Tom hit the ground, pulling Tove down with him. A group of fanatic *Hipo* traitors, lying in ambush, had opened fire on a detail of Freedom Fighters crossing the castle square on the far side of the bridge. Several of the men were down. Dead or wounded.

The Freedom Fighters at once spread out, took cover and began to return the fire. Savage staccato bursts from semi-automatic weapons drilled holes of slaughter in the sound of celebration that blanketed the city, like the punching out of a macabre dance of death on a player-piano roll.

Throughout the area people quickly darted for safety. Not everyone made it.

Tom pressed close to the stone parapet edging the bridge, shielding Tove with his body. Part of him was wholly alert and conscious of the violence that had erupted before them. Another part was fully as conscious of the warm, vibrant closeness of the girl.

The fire died down. The screams of the injured could suddenly be heard. The firing resumed.

Tom turned his face toward the girl. "It's no good, Tove," he said grimly. "The whole city has gone crazy. The situation is too damned unpredictable."

He glanced toward the square across the canal. "We won't get anywhere tonight. Tomorrow perhaps." He looked at Tove. "I want to get you off the streets."

She returned his look gravely. "I have a room," she said. "A small room. It is not too far from here." She pointed back the way they'd come. "That way. We can go there."

It *was* a small room. One room with a tiny kitchen, on the top floor of an old building. But it had a warmth and a feeling of cozy comfort which at once made Tom feel safe and at home. The muscles in his back suddenly ached. He had not been aware of the rigid tenseness that had gripped him in the streets.

"I can make you a cup of coffee," Tove said. "Not real, of course. I'm sorry."

"Anything hot'll be fine," he said.

He watched her walk to the little kitchen. Her movements had a lithe grace. She busied herself. Through the open door he could see her move about. He did not take his eyes from her. She was making up a little tray with two cups and two little plates with biscuits. He thought it beautiful to watch.

She brought the tray to him. She looked up at him, her eyes huge. She stood breathlessly still.

Tom's heart raced. He was stirred to the core. A feeling of overpowering tenderness flooded him. He did not try to stop it. He felt it possess him in a warm flush of longing, of desire. An overwhelming need to throw off the tension, the anxiety, the horrors of the years of war and violence. To lose himself wholly in the beauty, the softness and the womanness of the golden girl before him.

He said not a word. Neither did she. He took the tray from her hands, and put it down on a chair. He stepped close to her. Slowly, tenderly, prolonging and savoring every soft moment intensely, he put his arms around the slender body. She shivered. He drew her to him. He felt her melt into his very being. He buried his face in the silken hollow of her neck, fragrant with excitement.

And suddenly it was as if a leaden burden was ripped from him and his entire pent-up flood of love and desire poured out. He kissed her. Hard. She clung to him. Urgently he pressed his mouth upon hers. Upon her eyes. Her lovely, radiant eyes. Her neck. He caressed her supple, yielding body. She dug her fingers into him.

He tore at her clothes. At his own. He did not know how, but they were free of them. Just he and she. He held the warm, soft, eager girl body tight. So tight he thought he might be hurting her. But she strained against him.

They sank down to the floor, desperately needing to be part of each other. And they made love. It was a violent, fierce release from all the outrages and all the malignity of years of stress and torment for both of them, lashing out . . . It was savage, fiery, unbridled—a clawing, straining possessing one of the other. It was a total abandonment to joy. . . . And it was tender and loving, soft and wholly satisfying.

They lay in a close embrace, both young bodies glistening with the sweat of spent passion. He looked into her face. Her eyes were closed. There was a small serene smile on her soft lips. She was beautiful. He did not want to leave the nearness of her. Ever.

He reached over and pulled the cover off a studio couch nearby. Carefully, tenderly he wrapped it around them both. Slowly, their entire beings at ease, they went to sleep, safe in their cocoon of love.

The dark night streets of the German harbor town of Flensburg, hard on the Danish border, rumbled and teemed with urgent life despite the late hour.

Although the twelfth-century seaport itself was relatively undamaged by the war, the important shipyards and submarine pens of the naval base showed the jagged scars of heavy British bombing raids.

A short, stocky man, hunched in a large SS greatcoat, turned-up collar effectively concealing his face beneath the peaked gray cap, bare of insignia, strode heavily and hurriedly toward the wharves. Around him swirled the hustle of desperate last measures, the death spasms of the vaunted Thousand Year German Third Reich. On the pier he paused briefly. He cast a quick glance back. There was nothing for him to look at. Nothing.

Abruptly he tore himself away and marched across the gangplank of a U-boat, Type XXI, ocean-going, *Schnorchel*-equipped. He disappeared into its bloated metal womb.

Reichsleiter Martin Bormann had taken the first fateful step along the road of KOKON. The grim metamorphosis had begun. The fierce new entity, latent with might, would be ready to emerge irresistibly in all its power and mastery when the stimulus of one Rudi A-27 would transform it from its cocoon into a ruthless, unconquerable imago—the Fourth German Reich.

12

Bells. His universe was filled with bells. Chiming. Pealing. Clanging. Filling his every pore with sonorous sound.

He struggled up through the resounding clangor, up from the depths of the sleep of deep exhaustion. He opened his eyes.

The bells were still there. Church bells. Spreading a swelling, ringing cover of joyous thanksgiving over the entire country of Denmark.

Tom glanced at his watch. It was 0800 hours, Saturday, May 5th. It was Denmark's hour of liberation.

The streets of the delirious city, reborn from oppression, were already swarming with excited people when Tom and Tove left the little flat. Tom had only one tenuous lead to the Sleeper Agent left—Wolff, the missing waiter from the Tosca. It was obviously useless to look for him at the gutted café, but Tove knew of another restaurant that catered to the Germans, *Rydbergs Kaeller*—Rydberg's Cellar. It was barely possible that Wolff might have gone there, or that someone from the place knew of him and where to find him. It was worth a try.

The inner city was still crowded with exultant, joyful people. A red and white sea of flags—the white cross on the red field of the Danish flag, *Dannebrog*—waved and billowed triumphantly over their heads. But the mood was subtly different. The jubilant celebration was starkly punctuated with moments of panic and fear as snipers opened up from their hiding places and firefights broke out between the Freedom Fighters and the Danish *Hipo* traitors and their Nazi masters.

The Freedom Fighters were inexorably rounding up the hated informers and collaborators. Cars and trucks filled with grim armed and helmeted men roared through the streets, the names of underground groups proudly painted on their sides: *BOPA. Korps Aagesen. Holger Danske. Ringen.*

Suspects were being cornered everywhere and checked against lists prepared in advance for this day of reckoning. The subjects stood shaking, hands high, facing the wall, while being examined.

Open flat-bed trucks crammed with white-faced *Hipo* men and other traitors and informers, arms held stiffly above their heads, guarded by patriots armed with machine pistols, lumbered toward prisoner collection points throughout the city, followed by the derisive howls and shouts of the onlookers.

Girls with swastikas crudely smeared across their chests were marched away—the despised and accursed "field mattresses," the mistresses of the Nazis.

As Tom made his way with Tove toward Rydberg's he realized bleakly that he was searching for the proverbial needle. Only this needle was different. It was deadly.

They were hurrying past a complex of German military barracks. The crowd was less dense here. In the broad square in front of the barracks several octagonal brick barricades had been constructed to afford protection for the guard posts. They looked exactly like squat Teutonic *pissoires.* Each was manned by two apprehensive German soldiers. Only their steel-helmeted heads and their field-gray shoulders were visible above the concealing breastwork.

Suddenly a shot rang out. And another. They were instantly answered by a quick volley. Sniper! At once the German sentries brought their guns to bear on the sound of the firing.

Tom pulled Tove into a doorway. Directly before them, out in the square, was a German brick barricade. The heads and shoulders of the uneasy Nazi soldiers barely showed above the shielding.

Suddenly Tove laughed. She pointed at the barricade. "Look!" she said. "Look what someone has written on it."

Tom looked. In white paint, under the barely protruding heads of the German guards, a crude swastika had been painted on the wall of the barricade, and under it the words NAZISTERNE HAR TABT BUKSERNE!

Tove giggled. "It means the Nazis have lost their pants!" she said.

Tom grinned. Danish humor was irrepressible. A few minutes later he found himself utterly devoid of any humor whatsoever.

Rydbergs Kaeller lay before him, devastated, ransacked, burned to a scorched and blackened empty cavern. His last lead had been obliterated.

Rudi felt uneasy. He did not like to be in the area around the demolished Café Tosca.

He'd spent the evening before in the Tivoli amusement park in the center of Copenhagen, losing himself effectively in the jubilant crowd celebrating the opening night of the garden with blazing lights. With music. Dancing. Singing. The thousands upon thousands of colored light bulbs strung overhead in garlands across the walks had made him feel as if he were diving in a sea of light and noise and sweating human flesh.

He had been there when the open air concert was abruptly interrupted and the message of the German surrender had been read over the loud-speakers. The throng had gone wild.

He had never in his life felt so depressed and bleak as he shouted and cheered with the rest and let himself be jostled through the park by the crush of frenzied people. But he solemnly resolved that *he*, Rudi A-27, would never surrender. *His* mission would be carried out!

When Tivoli finally closed, he'd gone to an all-night bar and spent the time drinking and carousing with new-found friends. As soon as the streets began to fill with people once again, he'd joined the crowds milling through town waving their stupid little flags and howling their stupid songs. Now he was only a few blocks from the Café Tosca.

The Freedom Fighters seemed to be more active in that section of town than anywhere else. Their trucks constantly roared through the streets. Patrols roamed the area searching for their victims. It was not an area he would have chosen to be in. But he had no choice. The time for his rendezvous with Wolff was drawing near. It was his last chance. He could not afford to lose it.

He shrugged off his feeling of foreboding. It was probably just his imagination. Being forced to be at a certain spot at a certain time robbed him of his own initiative. He did not like it at all.

He had seen the Freedom Fighters round up their suspects. Once caught, there was little chance of getting away, at least not without a thorough examination and a long delay. For him, both prospects would be disastrous.

He was walking quickly along one of the narrow streets in the old part of the city. There were not many people abroad. Not the crowds still rampant in the more open parts of town. That was another thing that bothered him. He felt too exposed without his cover of revelers. Ahead of him a group of half a dozen young men were hurrying down the street toward him.

Suddenly a small truck roared into the street behind Rudi. He whirled toward it. Several armed Freedom Fighters leaped from the truck. The pedestrians stopped dead in alarm.

In the same instant another truck came screeching to a halt in front of him, disgorging more grim-looking Freedom Fighters, guns trained on Rudi and the little group.

He and the others were effectively boxed. The young men instinctively huddled together, backing up against the wall of a building.

The Freedom Fighters shouted at them, "Up! Up! Up with the hands!" They gestured menacingly with their guns. *"Up!"*

The men raised their hands high above their heads. Rudi followed suit.

The gun stuck in his belt in back under the blue jacket suddenly felt like a cannon.

Verflucht! he thought bitterly. Caught in a *verschissene*—stinking— dragnet! His thoughts raced. He *had* to get away. *How?*

His eyes flew over his fellow captives as the Freedom Fighters ran toward them. They all looked apprehensive. Unsure. His trained mind took in each one of them. In detail.

Two of the young men stood quite close to him. One was barely into his teens. The other— Suddenly Rudi flew into action. He threw himself on the man next to him. He grabbed him in a painful armlock.

The startled man sank to his knees with a groan of pain.

"Here!" bellowed Rudi excitedly. "Over here! I got him!"

Several of the Freedom Fighters ran toward him.

"I got him!" he shrieked. "The *Hipo* swine! Look at his boots! His boots! The bastard is trying to hide them with his pants. But they are boots! Look! *German boots!"*

The Freedom Fighters grabbed the shaken man and slammed him

roughly against the wall. "Papers!" one of them demanded brusquely.
The man began to fumble with his coat. He was petrified.

Rudi leaped at him. "Swine!" he shrieked furiously. "Traitor! *Hipo*
bastard!" He began to hit the man viciously with his fists. "Bastard! Bastard! Bastard!"

Two of the Freedom Fighters pulled him off. "Hey, hey, hey, easy!" one
of them said with a cold grin. "Easy. Leave him to us. He'll get what's
coming to him!"

Rudi backed off.

The Freedom Fighters turned toward the battered, shaken young man,
fumbling in his coat pocket. "Get those papers out, damn you!" one of
them growled. "And make it fast!"

Rudi backed slowly away. He watched the Freedom Fighters. They were
all absorbed in examining their victim. The victim *he* had given them.
They did not notice as he quickly ducked into an alley and silently slipped
away.

The bleak feeling of frustrated impotence lodged like a tight lump in
Tom's chest. Somewhere in this city of frenzy and turmoil was a man
infected with a deadly disease that he would spread throughout the world
if he were not stopped. Now.

Here. So close. And yet beyond reach.

He clenched his jaws. There *had* to be a way. There *had* to be another
lead to Rudi A-27! He strained every cell of his brain. He fought to conjure
up the key. He could think of nothing.

Rudi was able to masquerade as a native Dane. Even if he, Tom, knew
his cover identity, which he did not, it would be impossible to ferret him
out in the tumultuous chaos of the liberated city. His only possible lead
remained Wolff.

To find *him*, he'd have to be too damned lucky. He did believe in luck.
But only the kind you made yourself. He had always believed that *luck* was
a tag given by the non-doers to account for the accomplishments of the
doers. But there was nothing he could do. Nothing.

He suddenly tensed. He turned to Tove. "Who exactly are the men the
Freedom Fighters are rounding up?" he asked. There was a new urgency
in his voice.

She gave him a quick look. *"Hipos.* Traitors. Informers," she said. "Collaborators. They have lists—"

"Who else?"

Tove frowned. "No one," she said. "The girls . . ."

He shook his head impatiently. "What about Germans?" he asked.

"No," she said. "No Germans."

"What if a man—a German—was *thought* to be a Dane. A collaborator. Would he be on the lists?"

"Yes."

"What happens to the men the Freedom Fighters pick up?"

"They . . . they will be investigated," she said.

"Where?"

"At collection points. Throughout the city. That is where they are taken on the trucks."

Tom frowned in concentration. "Is there . . . is there one point, one central place, where information about the captives would be coordinated?"

She nodded. "Yes," she said. "Arrestgaarden, near Domhuset—the court house. That is the main collection and detention point."

"Take me there!" he said.

The area around Arrestgaarden teemed with curious people, watching and jeering the truckload after truckload of ashen-faced, fearful prisoners brought to the detention center.

All the shops and offices in the neighborhood had been closed up tight. One had a hastily scrawled sign prominently displayed on the door: LUKKET PAA GRUND AF GLAEDE!—CLOSED ON ACCOUNT OF JOY!

Inside, the center was a madhouse of controlled confusion. Tom and Tove were making their way through the flow of men and women when Tove spotted Klaus marching a pinch-faced young man toward a holding tank. The dark streaks from a bloody nose were still caked on the prisoner's chin.

"Klaus!" she called.

The man stopped. They hurried to him. "Who do we see about the arrest lists?" Tove asked.

Klaus shook his head. "No idea." He nodded down the corridor. "Sven is here. In the main office. He may know. If you hurry, you might catch him before he is off again."

They were already on their way.

Sven was pleased—and surprised—to see them. "Any luck?" he asked at once.

"We need your help," Tove said urgently. "We need to look at some sort of master arrest list. Do you know if there *is* such a thing? And where?"

Sven frowned. "I know of no master list," he said. He looked at Tom. "You think your man may be on it? He will not. He just arrived here, did he not?"

Tom nodded. "I know the Sleeper won't be on any list. Under any name. I'm not concerned with him. I want Wolff!"

Sven and Tove glanced at each other. Sven nodded. "There is a chance. He was a waiter. A Dane. Working in a pro-German place. Yes. It is quite possible."

He walked quickly to a desk. "I shall put out an alert. To notify me if the waiter Wolff is caught and brought in. Especially the patrols in the Tosca neighborhood must know. If Wolff is not on their list now, he will be."

He scribbled something on a piece of paper. He gave it to Tom. "Take this, my friend. It is the telephone number of this office. If you are picked up, tell them to call here. You will be cleared."

Tom took the paper. "Thanks," he said.

"I cannot know where I will be," Sven continued. "If you will go to the apartment, our meeting place, at"—he looked at his watch—"six o'clock tonight, I will call you there if I have any news."

He started to leave. He turned, soberly. "Be careful," he said. "There is much fighting. SS troops and *Hipos*. Some parts of town are very dangerous. Stay away from them. The Guards Barracks. The Nyboder School. The gasworks. Lyngby Road. There are fire battles going on there."

"I need a gun, Sven," Tom said. "How about it?"

Sven pointed to a pile of confiscated guns lying in a corner of the room. "Help yourself," he said. He gave them a last look. "Take care." He left.

Tom quickly searched through the stack of weapons. He selected a black-handled pistol. A Walther P-38 9-mm automatic. He was familiar with it. He checked the magazine. It was full. Eight rounds. He stuck it in his belt. He felt whole again.

Rudi felt keyed up, wholly alert, as he hurried down the street toward Frihavnen, the city's Free Harbor.

The meeting with Wolff had been brief. The undercover agent had been visibly on edge, nervous and resentful at having to be out in the open near the hated Café Tosca and forced to stay operative during this most dangerous period only for Rudi's sake. He had been eager to return to the safety of the German barracks.

But he had given Rudi new instructions. He was ordered back to Flensburg at once. Alternate exfiltration plans were being activated. He was to report immediately to the German cruiser *Nürnberg* lying in Copenhagen's Free Harbor. The captain had orders to wait for him. The cruiser would take him to Flensburg, where the ship would join the remaining German fleet under Admiral Doenitz. He was to use the password *Siegerfähre*—Ferry of Victors.

He grinned coldly. Whoever the idiot was who thought up passwords was either hopelessly out of touch or full of gallows humor.

Wolff had addressed Rudi with his cover name, Rudolf Rasmussen. He had not told the undercover agent about his new ID papers.

"Trust no one," Bormann had said. He would remember.

Now that his evacuation was imminent, he realized how tense he had been. And he realized it was of paramount importance to get out of Denmark before he was caught in the maelstrom of total surrender, the wholesale roundup of anyone even remotely cross-eyed.

He had already had one close call. It was enough. He was crossing Østergade. He was almost there. He'd make it. The first sudden shots shocked him out of his reveries with a cruel jolt. A volley of small arms fire abruptly rang out from the waterfront ahead.

Rudi hit the ground. Almost at once the rifle fire was answered by savage machine gun fire. Heavies. Rudi rose to one knee, hugging the wall. He peered ahead. The firing intensified. Crouched low, he ran to the corner.

The *Nürnberg* was under attack! A large group of determined Freedom Fighters were attempting to take over the cruiser by force! Their positions on the quay were being raked by heavy machine gun fire from the warship.

Suddenly the deep-throated bark of heavier guns hammered through the clattering staccato machine gun bursts and the sporadic crackle of small arms fire. The cruiser was employing its 20-mm guns. Geysers of broken pavement and shattered brickwork shot into the air from the position of the Danes.

Suddenly, from behind Rudi, came the sharp reports of high-power rifles. Snipers. Shooting from vantage points in buildings on Østergade.

The massive barrels of the *Nürnberg*'s 27-mm guns pivoted ponderously in search of the sniper nests. They roared their wrath, belching fire and smoke. In the dust-billowing explosions of masonry and shattered glass from the blasted buildings the snipers fell silent.

Rudi withdrew. He was shaken. With the *Nürnberg* under attack, under siege, his last avenue of escape from the city had been effectively cut off. Things were happening too damned fast!

Hugging the walls, he ran away from the field of battle. He could not afford to become involved. A few streets away he stopped. The firing could still be heard in the distance. Whatever the outcome of the foolhardy attack, the *Nürnberg* could not possibly be of any use to him now. He had to find a way to get to Flensburg by himself. He was on his own.

Quickly he walked away from the harbor area. He looked grim. But he had no doubts he would make it.

Tom looked at his watch. He had performed the identical gesture countless times in the last few minutes. He knew it. It was an obsession. He stared at the telephone. Ring, dammit! Again he glanced at his watch. 1817 hours. Where the hell was Sven?

Tove sat quietly on the big worn sofa, hugging her knees. She was watching Tom with grave concern.

He suddenly jumped as the shrill ring of the telephone knifed through the silence. He snatched up the receiver. "Yes?" he barked.

It was Sven. "We have him," he said.

Tom felt a wild surge of excitement shoot through him. "Where?" he shouted. "I'm on my way!"

"Hold it," Sven said quickly. "First listen."

Tom stood impatiently, coiled for action, the telephone receiver pressed to his ear. "Make it fast!"

"Here it is. Wolff had his meeting with your man Rudi," Sven said crisply. "He relayed orders to him to report in Flensburg. At once." He stopped.

"What else?" Tom asked.

"That is all we got," Sven said. He sounded drained.

"That's a piece of shit!" Tom flared. "Where is he? I'll get that bastard to open up!"

"I think not, my friend." Sven sighed.

"Don't bet your ass!" Tom retorted fiercely.

"He is dead, Tom."

Tom took the telephone receiver from his ear. He stared at it. Accusingly. As if the black instrument itself were to blame. He sank down on a chair. Slowly he put the receiver back to his ear. "What the hell happened?" he asked, his voice flat and dull.

"Some BOPA men cornered two *Hipo* snipers," Sven said. "In the inner city. One was liquidated on the spot. The other took refuge in a doorway. There was a man already hiding there. In the shoot-out he was badly wounded. It was Wolff."

"Dammit, you could have called me!" Tom said bitterly.

"Understand, my friend," Sven said quietly, his voice tired and spent. "Wolff knew how badly he was injured. He claimed, he insisted he was an SS major. That 'Wolff' was only a cover name. A cover identity. He was German. . . . The BOPA man in charge of the group had had a sister tortured by the Gestapo. She died. He counted over seventy cigarette burns crushed into her breasts. She was nineteen. He was in no hurry to summon help for the man who claimed to be SS. You must understand. Wolff screamed at him about his rights under the Geneva Convention, and the BOPA man gave him back the callous sophism *he* had been given when he'd tried to help his sister: To hell with the Geneva Convention! The Third Reich is too great to be hamstrung by a mere piece of paper. By the time they realized that Wolff was the man I was looking for, by the time I got there, Tom, he was half dead. It is a wonder he could say anything at all." He fell silent.

For a moment Tom sat quietly. He felt utterly defeated. "Okay, Sven," he said finally. "Did he say anything else? Think! Where is the Sleeper?"

"A few hours ago he was still in the city."

"Under what name? What cover?"

"Wolff referred to him as Rasmussen."

"Anything else? Papers?"

"No. Nothing. Only routine papers in the name of Wolff."

For a few seconds Tom sat in silence, his thoughts bleak. Rudi A-27 was probably still in town. He had known that. Rudi A-27 was probably still using the Rasmussen cover. It was utterly immaterial. Rudi A-27 had been ordered to Flensburg. That was new information. But how in hell did it help?

"Sven," he said, "thanks. I know you did what you could."

"We have his address, Tom," Sven said dispiritedly. "Wolff's address. We can make a search. Perhaps—"

"Give it to me," Tom said. He listened. He jotted the address down. "Go through the place, Sven," he said. "Unless I come up with something else, I'll meet you there." He hung up. He stared at the silent telephone, not seeing it.

It was useless. A man like Wolff would not keep incriminating information in his rooms. Certainly nothing that could possibly lead to the capture of Rudi A-27, with whom his involvement had only been very recent and very limited. The odds of finding anything of value at Wolff's place were simply nonexistent. Sven had known that, too.

He stared glumly into space. Into a dead end.

Tove uncoiled herself from the sofa. She came over to stand by him. "Sven did not find out anything, did he?" she asked softly.

He shrugged. "Rudi has been ordered to Flensburg," he said. "At once. That's all."

She frowned. "Tom," she asked, "how will he get there?"

He looked up at her sharply, suddenly shocked into keen alertness. "Yeah!" he said. "That's one hell of a question. *How?*" He stood up. He began to pace the room. "He sure as hell can't wait and be evacuated with the regular German troops," he thought aloud. "That might be days. Weeks. His orders said, At once. There'd be screenings. Checks. He could not afford that."

"Korsør," Tove said suddenly.

He gave her a quick questioning look.

"Korsør! It is the town from which the ferry leaves, Tom. The ferry that connects with the trains to Flensburg."

"Why would he go by train? Why not by car?"

"Too risky, Tom. Most cars are commandeered by the resistance. The

Freedom Fighters. You have seen them in the streets."

"You're right!" he said. "You are goddamned right! He *can't* take that risk. He *can't* let himself be checked out!" He took her by the shoulders. "The trains, Tove? They still run?"

"Yes. From Hovedbanegaarden—the main railroad station."

The huge central portico of the main railroad station was somewhat less crowded than other public places in Copenhagen.

Tove went straight to one of the ticket windows. For a few moments she spoke earnestly with the ticket seller, a rotund man with a ruddy plump face and sparse, carefully husbanded hair.

Presently she hurried over to the waiting Tom. "The trains are still running," she said quickly. "But the schedules have been badly disrupted. Because of the shooting. There has been heavy fighting at the engineers' barracks near Svanemøllen and other places."

"What about trains to that ferry town you mentioned?"

"Korsør. Nothing has left since just after two o'clock."

Tom frowned. "Right on the damned borderline," he said. "He *could* have made it. Or he could still be in town. Waiting. *If* he decided to go by train."

Automatically he looked around, searching the faces in the station. The face on the little photograph in Mrs. Rasmussen's locket was indelibly stamped on his mind. He was certain he would recognize Rudi A-27. If he showed up.

"When is the next train to Korsør?" he asked.

"No one knows," she said. "They are posting new timetables at the gates."

"Let's take a look," he said. "Lead the way."

Before the revised timetables tacked up on a makeshift bulletin board next to the closed and locked Korsør gate, half a dozen travelers stood studying the notices. Other passengers were hurrying by, carrying suitcases and packages.

As Tom and Tove drew near, a large heavy-set man in a rumpled tan raincoat standing at the outer edge of the group at the bulletin board turned away with a gesture of angry disgust.

Tom stopped dead in his tracks. The man in the raincoat had revealed someone else standing in front of him. A smaller man in a blue suit. The pants seemed to bag in the rear. The loose jacket was too big in the shoulders. As the raincoated man stalked off, the stranger in the blue suit quickly glanced after him, a cautious gesture of awareness, before returning his attention to the bulletin board.

To Tom, his brief glimpse of the man's face, like a bolt of lightning burned in afterimage on the retina, seemed etched everlastingly on the fabric of time itself.

It was the face from the locket. *It was Rudi A-27.*

"Stay here!" he whispered hoarsely to Tove.

"But—"

"Do it!" he snarled savagely. He put his hand under his coat, grasped the gun and eased it from his belt, holding it under his jacket.

He began to walk toward the Korsør gate with just the right amount of purpose—not too fast, not too slow.

Two of the people before the bulletin board walked away. Another joined the group. An elderly lady.

Dammit! Tom thought. He wanted as few bystanders as possible. He knew what he had to do. He walked up behind the man in the blue suit. He stopped two feet from him. He could feel the man in front of him become aware of his presence, waiting a couple of beats before turning to check him out.

He took his gun from under his jacket, locked it tightly against his abdomen, and pointed it straight at the man's back, his finger firm on the trigger. He spoke in a low, sharp voice. "Rudi," he said. "Don't move!"

The man was good. Damned good. There was only the slightest twitch of the hairline. An almost imperceptible tensing of the shoulder muscles under the ill-fitting blue jacket. He did not turn around. Instead he unconcernedly brought up his hand to scratch his nose pensively, seemingly engrossed in studying the timetables.

For a chilling instant Tom had a sinking feeling. Had he made a mistake? No. Had he spoken too softly? Had he not been heard?

He took one more step toward the man in front of him, his locked gun arm relaxing as he moved. He opened his mouth to speak.

Suddenly, explosively, without the slightest warning, the man before him whirled and twisted around. In the same split instant his right hand swung back in a vicious chop, striking Tom's gun-hand wrist a numbing blow.

Tom's reaction was instantaneous. A shot rang out, reverberating thunderously through the huge portico. The bullet ripped through the loose blue jacket and crashed into the emergency timetables at the exact moment the gun was knocked from his grip. It clattered to the floor, skittered across to slide under the locked gate—out of reach.

For the flash of a split second the eyes of the two men locked. Tom stared into the face of his foe. It was the cold, flat face of controlled violence. Of fanatical ruthlessness and invincible determination. It was the face of Rudi A-27. The face of KOKON.

In the same twisting motion, Rudi shot his knee viciously into Tom's groin. It was an instinctive action—instinctively anticipated and parried. Tom caught the brunt of the kick on his hip. The force brought him to his knees.

A savage kick to his solar plexus, only partly blocked, shot a searing, blinding pain through his very being and sent him sprawling in gasping, nauseous dizziness. He doubled up in agony.

Tove was at his side.

Torturously he struggled to his feet, fighting to keep down the bitter vomit gurgling in his burning throat. In one blurred glance he registered the gun lying out of reach on the other side of the locked gate. He saw Rudi racing toward the big doors at the near end of the station hall.

Nothing. No one stood in his way. The travelers in the railroad terminal, conditioned to the sudden eruptions of violence, had scattered and taken cover immediately after the shot rang out.

Tom straightened up. Every cell in his body shrieked in pain-ridden protest. "Stay here!" he shouted hoarsely to Tove. He ran after the fleeing Rudi.

Tove followed.

Rudi ran from the station. He was coldly angry. He had nearly allowed himself to get caught. At best, his safest escape route from the city had been sealed off. He would have to devise another way to get out. Fast.

He dismissed it. For now. His primary concern was to get away from his immediate pursuer. The *Ami* agent. He had no doubt that it was he who had tracked him down. He had to lose himself. Fast. How? Where? He ran along the street.

Across from him was a stone portal. A gatehouse. Lights. Turnstiles. A metal accordion gate. Tivoli! It was a side entrance to the amusement park. In there he could lose himself in the crowds. Slip away undetected.

He at once crossed the street. There was no one in sight at the entrance, but the accordion gate stood partially open. He vaulted the turnstile and slipped through the gate opening. He stopped short.

Before him lay the amusement park. Quiet. Dimly lit. No crowds. No one at all. Where yesterday the jubilant Copenhageners had thronged, cheering and celebrating, the garden was silent and deserted. The protection of the crowds was gone. Tivoli was closed.

He turned back. Quickly he glanced toward the railroad terminal. He saw the American and someone else come hurrying from the building.

At that moment an elderly uniformed guard came out from the little gatehouse. He saw Rudi in the open gate. *"Hov, hov,"* he said amiably. *"Vi har lukket i Aften!*—We are closed tonight!"

Rudi ignored him. He threw a last glance toward his pursuers running down the street toward the park gate. He was committed. At once he turned and raced into the dark, deserted amusement park.

Tom came running toward the Tivoli gate. Rudi was nowhere to be seen. He saw the guard at the gate and headed toward him.

The gatekeeper planted himself resolutely in front of the turnstiles. As Tom came up to him he said firmly, *"Tivoli er lukket!"*

Tove came running up. Tom gave her an angry look. "I thought I . . ." he began.

"Wait a little, Tom," she interrupted him quietly. "I do not wish to be left behind like that. And you need me."

He glared at her. She was right. "Ask this fellow if he has seen anyone," he said, nodding toward the protective gatekeeper.

The man's face lit up. "Oh, you are an Englishman!" he exclaimed delightedly. "I talk good English. Can I help? It is unhappy that Tivoli is closed this night," he said sadly. "Last night we had open. Tomorrow again. Only tonight closed. It is because all is so dangerous. One never knows—"

Tom interrupted him. "Did anyone enter the park?" he asked urgently. "Now? Anyone at all?"

The guard nodded with obvious disapproval. "One young man," he said. "Very rude."

"How long ago?"

"Only a small piece of time." He held up his right index finger. "One minute." He held up his left index finger, crossing it with the right. "One half minute. No more."

"Which way did he go?"

The guard pointed. "That way. Along to Koncertsalen—the concert hall. The one the Nazis blew up and burned in revenge upon the people of Copenhagen for the sabotage." He shook his head with great sadness. He clapped his hands in front of him once. "All the music," he said. "The instruments . . ."

"Thanks," Tom said. He started for the gate.

The guard blocked his way. "Tivoli is closed!" he said sternly.

"Look!" Tom snapped. "The man you saw run in there is a damned Nazi informer. A terrorist. Very dangerous. We *must* catch him. Understand?"

Wide-eyed, the gatekeeper stared at him. *"Naa saadan,"* he said. "Like that." He stood aside. "I let you go in!"

Tom at once started away. He stopped. He turned back to the guard. "Do you have a gun?" he asked.

The man looked startled. "Gun!" he exclaimed.

"Yes. A pistol. A gun."

The gatekeeper looked indignant. "No Tivoli *Kontrollør* need to have a gun, *Her,*" he said. "No, no." He shook his head, looking embarrassed.

Tom eyed him closely. "Do *you* have one?" he asked pointedly.

The man did not meet his eyes.

"It is important," Tom said.

The man sighed. He ducked into the gatehouse. Almost at once he returned. He handed a gun to Tom. "I shall have it back," he said. "It belongs to my brother. He was in America."

Tom looked at the gun. It was an old single-action Colt .45 Cavalry Peacemaker, model 1889. A real six-shooter. He flipped it open. He spun the cylinder. It was full.

The gatekeeper watched him. "You understand," he said apologetically. "It is . . . the times."

Tom fished the piece of paper Sven had given him from his pocket. "You have a telephone?" he asked.

The guard nodded. "In there." He pointed at the gatehouse.

Tom looked at Tove. Firmly she shook her head. He turned back to the guard. He held the paper out to him. "Call that number," he said. "Talk to anyone. Tell them . . . tell them that Tove and the Moles need help. At once. In Tivoli. At the bombed-out concert hall."

Automatically the man took the paper. Open-mouthed, he looked up to protest, but Tom and Tove were already hurrying toward the dark, dimly seen ruins of the Tivoli concert hall.

Rudi ran silently, easily along the paved walk in the dark amusement garden. Every nerve end, every fiber in his body was keyed up. The adrenalin surging through his system made everything exquisitely clear to him. His thoughts churned.

The man pursuing him was the *Ami* agent who had discovered his dossier. Somehow he had tracked him down. It was not important how. Not now. One man. One American. In Denmark. He could not possibly have the necessary support to mount a thorough manhunt. Not here. Not now. He *had* to rely upon himself. Even as he, Rudi, did. The two of them. One against the other. That was it. The *Ami* agent was the only real threat to him and to his mission.

It was no longer enough to avoid him—escape from him for the moment. The man was too good. Too tenacious. He would catch up to him again, the devil take it. He had to be eliminated. Destroyed. Now!

He felt wildly stimulated. Wholly capable, wholly alert, invincible, as he ran along. He had been trained. Honed to an epitome of efficiency. He would put his training to use. He would do it now. He felt totally confident. His decision was made. He felt free. He had long since learned that making a decision, good or bad, brings relief. Until it is made, you live in both hells. He would kill the *Ami* agent. Annihilate the threat to himself and KO-KON.

Quickly he glanced around the darkened park as he ran. Ahead of him loomed the dark nightmare shapes of twisted beams and crumbled fire-sooted walls. The ruins of a large building.

He altered his direction slightly. He ran toward the exposed misshapen skeleton of the ravaged structure. He was suddenly conscious of the crunching sounds his footsteps made as he left the paved walk and ran across a stretch of gravel.

He dismissed the thought. It did not matter. He knew what he had to do. *He knew how.* He disappeared into the forbidding ruins.

It had once been a chase. Suddenly that was millennia ago. Now it had become a chilling contest to the death.

Tom and Tove ran cautiously along the shadow-streaked Tivoli path. Suddenly Tom stopped. He listened intently. In the distance, from the direction of the contorted ruins of a large structure, came the faint sound of footsteps running on loose gravel. Then silence.

He glanced at Tove. "The wrecked concert hall?" he whispered.

She nodded.

He looked into the girl's upturned face. His thoughts whirled through his mind. Rudi appeared to be headed for the ruins. Should he wait for help to arrive?

No. Rudi undoubtedly would be long gone before that happened. He had to keep the pressure on.

Tove? He could not let her go along. He could not place her in danger. There was another way she could be useful.

"Look, Tove," he said, his voice low, urgent. "Will you help?"

"Of course," she said unhesitatingly.

"It looks as if Rudi's making for the concert hall. I'm going in after him."

She started to speak. He stopped her short. "I want *you* to circle around. Quickly. Approach the place from the opposite side. Then make a little noise. Let him hear you."

Her eyes grew bright. "I understand. It will be like a . . . a game drive."

"Exactly. But don't overdo it. Don't get too close. Don't be obvious. Just worry him. Get his attention."

"I will."

"Go!" he whispered tightly.

Quickly, silently she ran off, disappearing into the gloom of the deserted park.

Tom took the gatekeeper's gun from his belt. It was heavy, unwieldy in his hand. Ludicrous. He stared at it. He felt ridiculous. Wyatt Earp stalking the badman? Still, it was a weapon.

He glanced around. On his left was a large open space. Benches. Flowerbeds. Trees. Barely made out in the dim reflected light from the city outside. On his right stood a row of shoulder-to-shoulder darkened buildings. Booths. Little restaurants. Souvenir shops. All closed. Dead.

He moved close, into the deeper shadows along the buildings, and noiselessly made his way toward the bomb-blasted concert hall ahead. He stopped.

The ruins loomed before him directly across the walk. A long single wall still standing, hollow sockets of empty round-arched windows above great onion-topped archways, staring hauntingly down on a ghostly sea of twisted, tortured steel girders and beams and charred wooden rafters and logs. An abominable monument to wanton, malicious destruction.

A barrier surrounded the area, cutting it off from the rest of the park, isolating its ugly affront from the beauty, the serenity and fairyland spell around it.

Crouched low, he silently crossed the walk and took cover at the barrier. A black-lettered sign read, ADGANG FORBUDT. He guessed it meant "Entrance Forbidden." He had a quick impulse to obey the warning.

He vaulted the barrier. He froze, standing next to a cluster of twisted pipes. He listened tensely. He stood motionless in a bubble of silence. There was nothing to be heard except the steady faint, jumbled roar of the surrounding city.

He stared into the shadowy shapes of the forbidding ruins. The diffused reddish light from the battery of gaudy neon signs and street illumination in the business section of the city ringing the amusement park seeped sluggishly through the jungle of monstrously twisted and buckled steel girders, pipes and beams, the charred and scorched timbers and the jumble of hulking bomb-scarred masonry peopling the ruins with weird and ominous shadow creatures. The eerie indistinctness of the reflected light lent a disturbing aura of impending menace to the scene.

Tom felt it enter his body, penetrating to the very marrow of his bones. Cautiously, silently he took a few steps deeper into the unearthly maze. He stopped. Slowly his eyes swept the labyrinthian confusion of tortured debris rising above him.

He listened. There was no motion. No sound. He took another step— and stopped short.

From the distance, across the darkened ruins, came the faint sound of metal scraping metal, a soft plop—and silence.

Tove.

His blood rushed faster, pounding in his ears. Quickly, noiselessly, he moved farther into the entanglement of warped metal, blackened wood and shattered masonry.

Again he stopped. Nothing. Before him yawned a large black pit. A gutted basement. Jagged, pointed steel spikes reached up toward him from the murky depth, like the spears and lances from a giant deadfall trap.

A couple of massive steel beams, toppled in the long-ago holocaust, had fallen across the gaping hole, forming a rusty bridge across the inky pit a foot or two from a towering wall.

For a moment he stood motionless, listening. Once again he heard a distant muffled noise. Cautiously, his senses fully alert, he started across.

Suddenly he froze. The skin on his back crawled icily. He did not know if he had heard a barely audible sound very near, or if he had been touched by the cold finger of pure instinct. But he knew he was not alone.

And then he heard it. A sharp, chilling whispered command from the blackness before him: *"Stillgestanden!*—Don't move!"

Rudi felt elated.

It had been easy. Almost too easy. He had not let himself be distracted by the decoy sounds in the distance. He had been certain the *Ami* would follow him. He had to. He had picked his ambush spot carefully. The damned *Ami* was pitifully exposed. He could kill him at once. Be free. Safe. He and KOKON. But, dammit, he wanted the enemy to *know*. Know that he had lost. Know that he, Rudi A-27, was taking his beshitted life!

He stepped from the shadow cover. He raised his gun. *"Du hast verloren!"* he said. "You lose!"

The fraction of a second between Rudi's taunt and Tom's reaction was broken up into myriad small eternities.

Only dimly could Tom make out the figure that had suddenly appeared on the beams before him. Only the gun pointed unwaveringly at his guts stood out clearly. But he knew who it was.

He was dead.

The German Sleeper would not hesitate another heartbeat before he fired.

He wondered why the man had found it necessary to call out to him.

Did he want him to know he was about to die? Was it that important for him to . . . to gloat? The trait of a true Nazi?

In a rush he was suddenly flooded with the meaning of *death*. Never again to fill his lungs with crisp air on a forest walk, never to feel the cool surf breaking over his body, never to listen to the Moonlight Sonata, never to fall exhausted into bed, never to read a good book, watch a fine movie, never to enjoy a juicy steak heaped with smothered onions, never to laugh or hear laughter, never to cry, to weep, never to shake the hand of a friend, never to pet a dog, never to sit quietly and think, never to know sorrow or joy, pleasure or pain, never to hold a woman, to love—

Tove.

He felt infinite sadness. Not to live . . .

With the ultimate speed only thought can achieve, it all raced through his mind before he acted. He knew he had only a dismally small chance. He knew he could not possibly whisk his own unwieldy relic of a gun halfway into position before the slugs from the Sleeper's gun would tear into him.

He did not try. He let the gun fall from his hand—and in the same instant he hurled himself down on the beams. The sudden motion slightly shifted the steel girders, one grating against the other with a metallic screech.

Rudi's finger was already tightening on the trigger when the screeching sound struck his ears. It penetrated to the very essence of his being—*the hideous scream of a mangled beast shrieking from hell.* For a split instant his finger froze on the trigger. It was enough.

Tom had gripped the beam with both his arms and was dangling beneath it. He swung toward the wall. He planted both his feet against the massive stones and kicked with all his power. He felt the beam jar violently, and dimly felt the piercing pain of the sharp metal edge biting into his arms.

He heard the shot explode in the black stillness and felt the bullet sear across his left forearm. He heard a dull thud. And silence.

He tried to pull himself back up on the beam. He did not have the strength. The pain in his left arm was a knife of fire. He looked down into the black void trying to make out what was below him. It was too dark.

He let go. He plunged down into the shadowy pit. Consciously he relaxed his entire body. Jarringly he struck a pile of broken bricks and other rubble. The sharp and jagged corners bit into his knees and arms.

He rolled away from his point of impact and crouched tensely in the darkness, deliberately ignoring the throbbing, burning pain in his arm.

Rudi was there. Rudi was with him. In the black basement pit. He waited. Listening. Nothing. . . .

Gradually his eyes made the final adjustment to the deeper gloom in the cellar depth. Any instant he expected to see the red muzzle flash of a gun and feel the slug slam into him.

Nothing. . . .

Slowly he stood up. And he saw his enemy. Rudi A-27. A contorted form sprawled against a bizarre jumble of steel. Motionless.

Slowly, cautiously he worked his way closer. He stopped, eyes wide with shock.

Rudi had fallen on a spiked steel fragment. It had entered his back, impaling him as on a spit. The sharp, moist steel point protruded through his guts, glistening red.

For a moment Tom stared at the mangled apparition that was Rudi A-27. His mind sought escape from the sickening sight, hiding from the horror in ironic thought. The ruins. The concert hall, created by the Danish people for beauty, pleasure and enjoyment, had been turned by the vengeful Nazi terrorists into an instrument of execution for one of their own.

He stared at the Sleeper Agent, the twisted nightmare shapes of destruction looming over him like ghoulish guards of steel. Guarding death.

He felt a sudden chill. Not so. Rudi was not dead.

He was watching his *Ami* enemy with burning eyes, black holes of unspeakable agony. Rudi had trouble focusing his eyes. He seemed to exist, unable to move, in a sea of livid red pain washing over him in torturous waves. He knew he was dying. He looked uncomprehendingly at the crimson-tipped steel spit protruding from his stomach. He had failed.

His eyes roamed the dark, distorted ruins around him. For a moment he thought he saw a gray cat sitting in the shadows, its tail curled around its paws. Waiting. Patiently.

He was aware of a figure beside him. The *Ami.* He stared up into the face of his enemy. His mouth worked. "Kill . . . me," he whispered, his face a taut mask of pain.

Tom's mind whirled in abysmal darkness. He could not kill the German Sleeper. He knew he would find the final list of Sleeper Agents destined for the States given Rudi by his Gestapo contact. He knew the network would be destroyed. He also knew that Rudi had to live. Sooner or later he would give up everything he knew.

"Rudi," he said quietly. "What is KOKON?" He stared into the young German's eyes. It was like plunging down into hell itself.

Slowly, fitfully, a mocking smile stretched the Sleeper's pallid lips.

Suddenly Tom grew aware of movement among the twisted beams above on the rim of the cellar pit. He saw a figure appear. Another. And another. Silently, ominously, converging on the edge. He saw someone hurriedly climbing down into the hole.

Tove. The Freedom Fighters had arrived. Tove ran to him.

For a moment they stood close to each other, no words spoken. He felt a small soft hand steal into his. He knew he would want to keep it there forever.

Rudi was drifting on his sea of agony. He suddenly became conscious of a leaden weight pulling at him, weighting down his right arm hanging limply at his side, dipping into the blackness below him.

Abruptly, with startling lucidity, he knew what it was. His gun! Miraculously, as if each separate muscle in his body had been individually trained to perform its own specific duty and had obeyed, he had held on to his gun, even through his fatal plunge into the pit. *His . . . gun.*

He watched the two shadowy figures before him swimming indistinctly in the gloom. With superhuman spasmodic effort he moved. He brought up the hand clutching the gun.

Closer . . . closer . . .

Suddenly a flashlight blazed to life from the rim of the black hole. It quickly found and speared the German Sleeper Agent with a beam of light. At once another joined, and another, imprisoning Rudi in the center of a web of light.

Quickly Tom turned. Mesmerized, he saw Rudi bring up his gun. Suddenly the Sleeper barked a short, coughing laugh. His gun was at his ashen face. Lovingly he placed his bloodless lips around the blue-black muzzle. His blazing, mocking eyes never left Tom.

KOKON . . . would . . . die.

He pulled the trigger.

POSTSCRIPT

The Sleeper Agent project is fact. Sleeper Agents went into operation in the United States prior to and during World War II, planted here long before by both Japan and Germany.

There *were*—and *are*—more than one far-flung escape organization in existence to aid high-ranking Nazis and war criminals. During the latter part of the war, Sleeper Agents were trained in Nazi espionage schools such as Schloss Ehrenstein, and many hundreds of them were graduated.

Where are they today?

Who are they?

And to whom do they owe their allegiance?

ESCAPE ROUTES

Of the escape route organizations that successfully assisted thousands of high-ranking Nazis, war criminals and Sleeper Agents in exfiltrating Germany and finding concealment and refuge abroad, the best known are the following three: *Die Schleuse* (The Sluice), *Die Spinne* (The Spider), and *ODESSA.*

These organizations, which all had their beginnings during the last months of the war, were aided through the years by numerous other societies and agencies that sprang into being throughout Germany and the rest of the world, organizations such as General von Manteuffel's *Brüderschaft* (Brotherhood); *HIAG—Hilfe und Interessengemeinschaft der Ehemalige Angehörigen der Waffen SS* (Aid and Mutual Interest Society of Ex-Waffen SS Members); *Der Rudel Klub,* originally founded by the Nazi ace Hans Ulrich Rudel in Argentina; *Stille Hilfe* (Silent Aid); *Die Vatikanische Hilfslinie* (The Vatican Aid Line, also known as The Monastery Route); *Der Salzburger Zirkel* (The Salzburg Circle); *HINAC* in Holland; *St. Martin Fonds* in Belgium; *Dansk Frontkämpfer Forbundet* in Denmark; *Kameradschaft IV* in Austria; *Hjelporganisasjonen for Krigskadede* in Norway; and many others.

All the secret escape routes operated along similar lines. With organizational headquarters in a major German town and branch offices located wherever needed, they were financed by the numerous hidden Nazi accounts and funds, as well as large caches of money and looted valuables within Germany itself or secretly transferred to neutral foreign countries well in advance of the contemplated escape operations.

The organizations set up a series of "stops" every thirty or forty miles along the escape route—*Anlaufstellen*—staffed by one or two loyal members who knew only the next point on the route. They provided the members "traveling" the escape route with money, transportation, safety and new identification papers made out in false names.

Die Schleuse (The Sluice or Lock-Gate) was one of the first major escape routes to be organized. Already in the fall of 1944, selected high Nazi officials received their false papers—passport, identity *Kennkarte*, birth certificate, marriage license, and work permit—prepared by the special bureau of the Gestapo set up for the purpose, or by such operations as *Aktion Birkenbaum* (Operation Birch Tree), which was created to manufacture such false documents for use by the future escape route travelers.

The main routes of *Die Schleuse* were the Northern Route: Hamburg, Kiel, Schleswig, Flensburg into Denmark, and on to the Americas; and the Southern Route: Austria to Italy and Spain as the gateways to the Middle East and South America.

Die Spinne (The Spider), the organization that planned to cover Europe like a giant spider's web, was at war's end undoubtedly the main secret underground escape route, its network spanning Germany, Austria and Italy.

Known in Spain as *La Araña* and in France as *L'Araignée*, the organization for a while was headed by General Paul Hausser, a co-founder of the Waffen SS. With headquarters in Augsburg or Stuttgart, *Die Spinne* operated the successful *B-B Achse* (B-B Axis), a north–south route using the B's from Bremen in northern Germany and Bari on the southern tip of Italy in its code name identification.

Apparently discontinued shortly after the war, it formed the foundation for the largest and most efficient of the escape networks, *ODESSA*.

ODESSA—Organisation der Ehemalige SS Angehörigen (Organization of Ex-SS Members) had, and possibly still has, its headquarters—*Verteilungskopf* (Allocation Center)—in Munich, after being controlled from Augsburg and Stuttgart in its earlier period of operation, with branches all over Germany and Austria as well as in South America.

ODESSA operated two main southern routes—from Bremen to Rome, and from Bremen to Genoa—and a northern route through the Flensburg escape hatch into Denmark.

One of the most notorious travelers along the *ODESSA* escape route was Adolf Eichmann.

BIBLIOGRAPHY

The following books and publications in English are among those that, together with the author's own observations, investigations and documentation, have furnished authentication and facts for *Sleeper Agent.*

Allen, Robert S. *Lucky Forward: The History of General George Patton's Third U.S. Army.* New York: Vanguard.

Bar-Zohar, Michael. *The Avengers.* London: Arthur Barker Ltd.

Bezymenski, Lev. *The Death of Adolf Hitler.* New York: Harcourt, Brace & World.

Brossard, Chandler. *The Insane World of Adolf Hitler.* New York: Fawcett.

Carlson, John Roy. *Under Cover.* New York: E. P. Dutton.

Cookridge, E. H. *Gehlen, Spy of the Century.* New York: Random House.

Delarue, Jacques. *The Gestapo.* London: Macdonald.

Dollinger, Hans. *The Decline and Fall of Nazi Germany and Imperial Japan.* New York: Bonanza Books.

Dulles, Allen W., ed. *Great True Spy Stories.* New York: Harper & Row.

Dyer, Georges. *XII Corps, Spearhead of Patton's Third Army.* XII Corps History Association.

Eisenhower, Dwight D. *Crusade in Europe.* New York: Doubleday.

Farago, Ladislas. *Burn After Reading.* New York: Pinnacle Books.

————. *The Game of Foxes.* New York: David McKay.

Flender, Harold. *Rescue in Denmark.* New York: Simon & Schuster.

Gehlen, Reinhard. *The Service.* New York: Popular Library

Goldston, Robert. *The Life and Death of Nazi Germany.* Greenwich, Conn.: Fawcett.

Harbottle, Thomas B. *Dictionary of Battles.* Briarcliff Manor: Stein & Day.

Hymoff, Edward. *The OSS in World War II.* New York: Ballantine Books.

Koch, H. W. *Hitler Youth: The Duped Generation.* New York: Ballantine Books.

Lampe, David. *The Danish Resistance.* New York: Ballantine Books.

Langer, Walter C. *The Mind of Adolf Hitler.* New York: Basic Books.

Leckie, Robert. *The Story of World War II.* New York: Random House.

Lenton, H. T. *German Submarines.* New York: Doubleday.

Manvell, Roger. *The Gestapo.* New York: Ballantine Books.

———, and Fraenkel, Heinrich. *Himmler.* New York: G. P. Putnam.

Mentze, Ernst. *Five Years: The Occupation of Denmark in Pictures.* Malmö: A. B. Allhem.

Military Intelligence Services. *Order of Battle of the German Army.* Restricted.

The Military Service Publishing Company. *The Officer's Guide.*

National Archives, Records, U.S. Army Historical Division.

Neumann, Robert. *The Pictorial History of the Third Reich.* New York: Bantam.

Payne, Robert. *The Life and Death of Adolf Hitler.* New York: Praeger.

Pia, Jack. *Nazi Regalia.* New York: Ballantine Books.

———. *SS Regalia.* New York: Ballantine Books.

Roussel, Aage. *The Museum of the Danish Resistance Movement.* Copenhagen: The National Museum.

Ryan, Cornelius. *The Last Battle.* New York: Simon & Schuster.

Schellenberg, Walter. *Hitler's Secret Service.* New York: Pyramid Books.

Shirer, William L. *The Rise and Fall of the Third Reich.* New York: Simon & Schuster.

Smith, Harris. *OSS.* London: UCLA.

Speer, Albert. *Inside the Third Reich.* New York: Macmillan.

Stevenson, William. *The Bormann Brotherhood.* New York: Bantam.

Sulzberger, C. L. *Picture History of World War II.* New York: American Heritage.

Toland, John. *The Last 100 Days.* New York: Random House.

Trevor-Roper, H. R. *The Last Days of Hitler.* New York: Macmillan.

Tully, Andrew. *Berlin: Story of a Battle.* New York: Simon & Schuster.

U.S. War Department. *The German Campaign in Poland, September 1 to October 5, 1939.*

Whiting, Charles. *Gehlen: Germany's Master Spy.* New York: Ballantine Books.

———. *The Hunt for Martin Bormann.* New York: Ballantine Books.

Wiesenthal, Simon. *The Murderers Among Us.* New York: McGraw-Hill.

Wighton C., with Guenther Peis. *Hitler's Spies and Saboteurs. New York: Universal-Award House.*